SACRIFICE

DAUGHTERS OF LILITH:
BOOK 3

Jennifer Quintenz

SECRET TREE PRESS

Cover design by Jennifer Quintenz

Printed in the United States of America

First Printing, January 31, 2014

ISBN-13: 978-0991522200
ISBN-10: 0991522206

Secret Tree Press
www.JenniferQuintenz.com

To Mom, my trusted beta-reader,
cheerleader, and friend.

CONTENTS

ACKNOWLEDGMENTS	i
CHAPTER 1	1
CHAPTER 2	11
CHAPTER 3	27
CHAPTER 4	41
CHAPTER 5	53
CHAPTER 6	65
CHAPTER 7	77
CHAPTER 8	95
CHAPTER 9	111
CHAPTER 10	129
CHAPTER 11	151
CHAPTER 12	161
CHAPTER 13	171
CHAPTER 14	185
CHAPTER 15	205
CHAPTER 16	213
CHAPTER 17	223
CHAPTER 18	237
CHAPTER 19	245
CHAPTER 20	255
CHAPTER 21	261
EPILOGUE	269
A NOTE FROM THE AUTHOR	277
ABOUT THE AUTHOR	279

ACKNOWLEDGMENTS

This is book three, so if you've read my previous acknowledgements, you already know the usual suspects.

I am, as ever, indebted to my parents for first encouraging my creative endeavors. My sister, Amanda, lets me talk her ear off about my plans for Braedyn and her crew (even though she hates spoilers). My husband, James, continues to give me the irreplaceable gift of time to write. And Asher keeps me laughing, even when I'm bogged down in story woes.

I'm also continually amazed and astounded by the talent and devotion of some incredible friends. They have offered notes and feedback on all stages of this project from outline to final draft. Marc, Bethany, David, Barbara, thank you all for sharing your insights. I learned a long time ago that if someone gives you a good idea, you should take it and run with it. You have all contributed to this world and this particular story, and it's better because of you.

The earth quakes before them;
the heavens tremble.
The sun and the moon are darkened,
and the stars withdraw their shining.

- Joel 2:10

1

Color bled out of the sky, casting everything in the indigo glow of twilight. It was a tranquil moment, perfectly balanced between day and night—a moment full of promise. Lucas shifted toward me, and the world around us seemed to drop away, fading into the shadows at the edge of my perception.

His fingers brushed the hair back from my face. I bit my lip. Lucas pulled back to study my face.

"What's wrong?" His eyes shone, shifting from gold to green as he held me.

My heart beat a wild staccato rhythm against my ribcage. "Are you sure about this?"

In answer, his lips brushed against my ear, sending another shiver across the surface of my skin. His fingers traced the line of my jaw, catching my chin lightly, tilting my face up. Even knowing this was what we had planned, what we both wanted, I hesitated. Lucas stopped, waiting for me to decide.

Then I moved, and our lips brushed.

Sensation roiled through me like molten gold, shooting white-hot licks of fire into my veins… only it didn't hurt. The flame it kindled was intoxicating in its warmth. I let it burn. An involuntary reflex, my fingers tightened around him.

Lucas let out a soft moan. He shifted his weight, pulling me down onto the soft grass beside him. I encircled his neck with my arms, pulling him closer. He shifted again, and I moved with him. The warmth of him—the weight of him—it felt right. Natural. Like this moment was meant to be.

We broke the kiss, breathless. I smiled up into his eyes, feeling weirdly bashful. Lucas gave me an equally shy smile.

Wordlessly, I tugged at the fabric of his t-shirt. Lucas shifted, helping me pull his shirt off. My eyes dropped to his chest. I felt a slow blush burning in my cheeks. Look, I knew Lucas was fit. We trained hard enough with Hale and the others that we were both lean and strong. But knowing it, and seeing it in the flesh…? Two very different things.

Lucas smiled. Amusement played around the corners of his mouth. "Do you need a minute?"

I punched Lucas in the shoulder. He laughed out loud. I sprang, rolling him over, straddling him, pinning his wrists to the ground. My hair hung down around us in a silky curtain. Lucas's eyes twinkled. He didn't resist.

I smiled down into his face. "I think you overestimate your effect on the ladies, mister."

Lucas gave me an infuriating grin in response. "All evidence to the contrary."

I released his wrists and started to withdraw. Lucas caught me around the waist and kept me from escaping. He sat up, meeting my eyes. In his gaze, I saw a smoky intensity that stole my breath. His smile faded.

His gaze dropped to the buttons of my shirt. Gingerly, he lifted his hands and undid the first button. When he had worked it free, he glanced up with a question in his eyes. I reached for the second button, pulling it free. We worked together, until my blouse hung open.

A muscle jumped along Lucas's jaw. Slowly, and ever so gently, Lucas lifted a hand to slide the blouse off my shoulders. I felt the cool evening air wash across my skin. Lucas traced his finger along one satin bra strap.

He pulled me close, pressing me to his chest. I melted into his embrace, relishing the feel of his skin against mine. Lucas lay back down on the grass. I curled myself against his side, running my fingers lightly down the firmness of his stomach. My hand hesitated at the button of his jeans.

Lucas watched me, waiting. "We don't have to do anything you're not comfortable—"

I covered his mouth in another kiss, drowning out his words. Another swell of fire rose inside of me. Lucas responded, curling one hand in the soft tangle of my hair. Without breaking our kiss, I slid my hand back down his stomach, seeking the top of his jeans. My fingers strained to work his top button free—

"Wake up." Gretchen's voice cut through the haze of my desire.

I pulled back, suddenly cold. The world around us flared into bright daylight.

"What's wrong?" Lucas looked at me, startled. He rose to his elbows, squinting against the sudden brightness.

"Braedyn. Wake up!"

Lucas studied me, concerned. He couldn't hear her voice.

"Gretchen needs me." I felt a sudden urge to smooth my hair and straighten my clothes, which—of course—was completely unnecessary.

Lucas sat up, alarmed. "Be careful, Braedyn."

I leaned forward and gave him one more kiss. "We'll have to pick this up la—"

I lurched awake with a ragged gasp of surprise. Fingers of icy liquid clawed through my hair and down the neck of my shirt. It wouldn't have been a great feeling anywhere, but it was especially unpleasant in the frigid night air of the stone mission. "Gretchen?!"

"The Seal." Gretchen eyed me grimly, holding an empty-and-dripping soda cup in one hand. She turned. I forced my anger aside and followed her gaze.

We were sitting against one of the large stone columns ringing the sanctuary of the old mission of Puerto Escondido. Beyond us, blending almost seamlessly into the stone floor, was the gateway between this world and the realm of the Lilitu. For thousands of years, the Seal had kept the beautiful demons out of our world. Now, it stood open.

It had been three weeks since the Seal had been breached. The Guard stationed soldiers and spotters here around the clock to watch for escaping Lilitu. But in those three weeks, we hadn't seen so much as a shadow cross the Seal's perimeter.

Until now.

I stood. Gretchen was at my side in a moment.

"What is that?" I strained, trying to force my eyes to focus on a smear of shadow marring the air above the Seal.

"I was hoping you could tell me." Gretchen kept her voice low. I could sense her shifting her weight, and out of the corner of my eye I caught the gleam of her Guardsmen's daggers.

Following suit, I drew my daggers out of the sheath I'd strapped to my jeans earlier in the evening. They came free in a soft *ssshhing*. I pressed the daggers' hidden release and the two blades sprang free of one another, revealing two cruel, serpentine edges. One dagger in each hand, I stepped closer to the Seal, hoping to get a clearer view.

It was like trying to make out the image in a blurry photograph. No matter how my eyes tried to adjust, the smear of shadow wouldn't come into sharp focus.

And yet—

"Something's in there." I glanced at Gretchen and saw the grim set of her lips. She saw it, too. Movement at the edges of the mission's dim sanctuary caught my eye. Three Guardsmen had seen us approach the Seal. They straightened, drawing their own daggers. Three. *Only three.* I glanced at Gretchen, keeping my voice low. "Where are the rest of the soldiers?"

"Rounds."

I nodded, frowning. Every hour, Guardsmen would walk the perimeter, leaving three of their fellows behind to guard the Seal alongside the spotters. They mostly chased away high school kids and college kids looking for a private place to hang out or drink. It only took about five minutes, but it was worth it to keep clueless civilians away.

Gretchen motioned for the Guardsmen to keep their distance from the Seal.

Misgiving shifted in my stomach. "Maybe we should hold back until the others get back from patrolling—"

It leapt through the smear of shadow. Adrenaline shot through my system as my brain struggled to process fragments of the scene before me. Long brown hair streamed back from her face. Silvery claws extended from her fingers, glinting even in this dim light. And her eyes—black and soulless as a shark's—were fixed squarely on me.

I stumbled back a step before planting my feet. Hale's training kicked in; even as panic raged through my head, my muscles moved, performing motions as exact as a clock's.

I felt the Lilitu connect, but before her claws could slice through my skin, time seemed to slow. I'd managed this once before—the night the Seal was opened. Memories flooded through my head—

Crashing through the stained glass. Racing toward the stone floor 30 feet below. And then time slowed, as though I—and everything around me—was caught in molasses. With effort, I had shifted my weight, managed to turn in the air and land with my feet on the ground before everything slipped back into normal time.

Like that night, I felt the air pressing in on me. I focused all my attention on shifting my wrist, redirecting the Lilitu's force away from vital organs and arteries. While our bodies were twisting in achingly slow motion, I marked the placement of the other Guardsmen in the room. Gretchen was turning toward the Lilitu; she'd just started to raise her blades in response to the attack.

The three soldiers hadn't yet moved. Their expressions ranged from shock to fear. Less than a second had elapsed.

As the Lilitu's expression started to shift, I concentrated on bringing my other hand around, dagger poised to slice across her ribs—noticing too late that she'd swept her foot behind my ankle to break my stance.

I lost my focus. Time slammed back into full-speed.

My wrist shot out, blocking the Lilitu's claws from ripping through my skin. But her kick, already in motion, succeeded in sweeping my foot out from under me. A sharp, stabbing pain shot through my left wrist. One of my daggers slid across the floor, but I couldn't spare the time to chase after it. I hit the ground hard, rolling away from the Lilitu, meaning to give Gretchen a clear shot at the demon.

But the Lilitu was focused on me. She ignored Gretchen, instead throwing herself after me. We tangled in a sprawling mass on the floor before I could kick free. I scrambled awkwardly backwards, still clutching one dagger in my good hand, until I collided with the sanctuary wall. My left wrist throbbed—best case scenario it was sprained. There was no way I'd be able to fight with it.

The Lilitu clawed her way toward me, her long brown hair gleaming in the mission's candlelight.

I shifted the dagger in my good hand, but before I had a good grip on it, the Lilitu knocked my wrist aside, sending the blade skittering into the darkness behind a line of pews. She circled one clawed hand around my neck. A wash of terror flooded through me, almost instantly muted by the thought drifting across my mind; *she could rip out my throat. She could kill me right now.*

I looked into her eyes. The pure hatred I saw there stabbed straight into my heart. It felt—*personal.*

"I'll admit, I expected… more." Her beautiful mouth twisted in disgust.

"Who are you?" I searched her faces—both the perfect human mask and the deeper, demonic visage hidden beneath it. I wracked my brain for any memory—no matter how faint—of having seen her before. Her human face would be considered beautiful by any standard. Long brown hair swirled luxuriously around her shoulders. Her fair skin was marred by no visible imperfection. Her human eyes gleamed a startlingly vibrant blue. The demon beneath? As all corrupt Lilitu, her skin pulled tightly over angular bones, white save for where it melted to black at her lips and down toward her fingertips. But neither face called up even the smallest flicker of recognition. She was a perfect stranger.

Gretchen gestured to me wildly over the Lilitu's shoulder. I shifted my gaze to her face. When our eyes connected, Gretchen held one of my dropped daggers up, then set it on the ground and kicked it over to me. The Lilitu turned as the dagger skated across the floor. I moved, slamming my fist into her throat. She dropped back, gagging. I lunged for the weapon, but just as my hands were about to close on the dagger's hilt, the Lilitu grabbed my ankle and pulled me sharply back. The dagger overshot my reach. Almost lazily, the Lilitu stopped its wild slide and picked it up.

Gretchen and the soldiers raced forward.

"Braedyn!" Gretchen flung her hand out, gesturing for me to move. I didn't need the prompt. I was already clawing my way forward, struggling to get to my feet.

The Lilitu tackled me from behind, slamming me chest-down onto the cold stone floor. She grabbed a fistful of my hair and wrenched my head up, exposing my neck. She placed the dagger tip against my carotid artery.

"Stop!" Gretchen threw a hand up and the soldiers froze in place.

For a moment, the only sound was the heavy breathing of the six of us. I was hyper conscious of the dagger at my throat, afraid of making any movement. Even small scratches from these daggers could do serious damage to a Lilitu; it wasn't something I wanted to experience firsthand.

Gretchen watched the Lilitu on my back with the same caution you'd show a rattlesnake. "Ball's in your court, demon."

"You fight to protect her, spotter?" I could hear the bemusement in the Lilitu's voice.

"I won't lie, it took a little getting used to." Gretchen didn't relax her grip on her dagger. Gretchen's eyes dropped to mine. I willed her to keep talking. Somehow, Gretchen seemed to sense my plea. "And it hasn't been smooth sailing the whole time. But she's earned my trust."

"She is Lilitu."

"That hasn't escaped my notice." Gretchen's even voice belied the tension visible in her slight frame.

"And you do not mind that she shares dreams with your ward?" The Lilitu's voice was light, taunting.

I felt my breath catch. Clearly this Lilitu had been watching me for a while. But why? I eyed the doors. The rest of the Guardsmen should return at any minute.

Gretchen winced slightly but forced a smile. "My ward, wow. That's so… Batman and Robin."

"Dreams wherein they share intimate knowledge of each other's—"

"I don't need the details," Gretchen snapped. I saw her cheeks flush with anger. "Look, that's the deal. They can have their dreams. Just as long as they keep their hands to themselves in the waking world."

"Do you honestly believe you can contain a Lilitu's desire in a simple dream?"

Gretchen's eyes shifted to my face once more. For a fraction of a second, I saw her doubt.

The mission's main doors opened as the patrolling Guardsmen returned. I felt the Lilitu above me shift, giving a low hiss of frustration.

In one motion, I caught hold of the hand wielding the dagger and threw my head back into the Lilitu's face. I heard a satisfying crunch at the contact, followed by an air-rending shriek. The Lilitu recoiled, releasing her grip on my hair and dropping the dagger.

I clutched the dagger tightly and rolled out from under her, kicking out. My feet connected. The Lilitu went skidding back into the sanctuary wall.

I was vaguely aware of the Guardsmen racing to join the fight, but I kept my eyes locked on the Lilitu facing me. Slowly, I stood and edged away from her. If she attacked again, I'd be ready for her.

The Lilitu clamped a hand over her nose. Dark blood seeped through her fingers, spotting a few oily-metallic drops on the ground at her feet. But then she straightened. She lowered her hand, staring me down haughtily, completely ignoring the fact that her nose was streaming blood.

"I had envisioned great power. Instead?" She shrugged. Again, I saw disgust flicker over her face. "I find a simpering fool, eagerly wearing the Guard's collar. You are no Daughter of Lilith. You are weak. Pitiful. You will be destroyed."

Anger swelled in my chest. "You're one to talk. Maybe you haven't noticed, but you're kind of surrounded."

"Them?" The Lilitu, glancing around at the half-dozen Guardsmen ringing her, looked like she might actually laugh. "They are like ants; they are no threat." Two smoky, bat-like wings unfolded in the air behind her.

"She's cloaking," Gretchen shouted.

The smoky wings snapped closed around the Lilitu. She blew me a kiss, then barreled toward the closest Guardsman.

"Chris!" Gretchen raised her daggers. The Guardsmen ringed Chris, trusting their training to protect them against the demon they could no longer see. They moved through the ancient Mesopotamian fighting form at the root of all Guard training. Their blades, slicing through the air in perfect synchronicity, narrowly missed the Lilitu. She dropped to her knees and slid through an opening on the far side of the line of Guardsmen.

"Braedyn?!" Gretchen, trapped on the other side of the fray, gave me a desperate look.

"I'm on it!" I raced forward, chasing the Lilitu back toward the Seal. She'd lost some time, scrambling to her feet. I closed the distance between us before she reached the Seal. As her foot crossed the edge of the Seal, I grabbed her arm, spinning her around.

"I don't care how many of you try to convert me," I hissed. "I've made my choice."

The Lilitu smiled, but the effect was chilling. "You mistake my purpose. There is no place for you among our number, traitor."

"Then—?" I glanced over my shoulder. The Guardsmen were edging closer, still uncomfortable with a cloaked Lilitu in the room. "Why come here? Why attack me?"

"I owe you no explanations." The Lilitu took a step backwards, toward the heart of the Seal. I gripped her arm tighter, but she pulled me onto the Seal with her.

When my foot connected with ancient round stone, I felt a wash of power. It circled through the Seal like a vortex, drawn into the heart of the stone. Standing there, I felt it pulling on me—but it wasn't until my foot actually slid forward that I realized the sensation wasn't simply in my mind. There was something else—something drawing the power inwards. Something deep within the Seal.

Alarmed, I let the Lilitu go, stumbling off the Seal. As soon as I'd stepped off the ancient stone, the draw of the power released me. It was like someone had flipped a switch, turning off a powerful magnet. I stumbled, unbalanced.

"What the hell—?" I looked up, meeting the Lilitu's gaze. Her cold smile deepened at my confusion. My eyes dropped back to the ancient stone at our feet. I'd never felt anything like that before. The Seal—somehow it was *changing,* almost as though it were taking on a life of its own. But that wasn't possible, was it? I sought out the Lilitu's face once more, but if she had answers, she wasn't likely to share them with me. Her amusement shifted to disdain.

"As I said. Pitiful." The Lilitu slipped back through the shimmering veil over the heart of the Seal, and in the blink of an eye, she was gone.

"Braedyn!" Gretchen rushed forward and steadied me. "What did she do to you?"

"It—it wasn't her. It was the Seal. It tried to pull me in."

Gretchen's eyes slid from my face to the stone at our feet. I felt her hand tighten on my arm. "What?"

"Something's happing to the Seal." I shook my head, at a loss to put the feeling into words.

"Okay. Okay." Gretchen bit the side of her lip, thinking. "Maybe we should get you out of here for the time being, just to be on the safe—"

"Gretchen." I covered her hand with my own, as much for comfort as to draw her attention back to the Seal. "Do you see them?"

Gretchen's breath came out in a hoarse curse. As one, we stumbled several paces back from the Seal.

"We have to tell Ian and Thane." Gretchen's eyes found my face. She looked haunted, sick. "You go. I'll finish the shift."

I turned and ran for the mission's doors. But I couldn't stop myself from steeling another look back. There, in the center of the Seal, the shimmering veil between our world and the Lilitu plane was crisp and clear now. And through the veil of shadow, Gretchen and I had seen dozens of gleaming eyes in the darkness. Watching. Waiting.

The question was, what were they waiting for?

2

The Guard had no answers by the time the first day of spring semester rolled around.

Despite waking early, I felt sluggish that morning. There was something off about going back to school, knowing the door between our worlds was sitting ajar—that the stage was set for the final battle. All of a sudden I was expected to focus on things like uniforms and schoolbooks and grades. How? The world as we knew it could come crashing down around our ears at any time.

And yet, the routine was also a strange balm to my nerves. Going through the motions of normalcy, even if everything else was standing on its head, felt comforting. Absentmindedly, I pulled a fresh shirt out of my closet and donned it. The New Mexico winter was still bitterly cold, so I skipped the plaid skirt in favor of grey pants, topping the whole ensemble off with a cozy burgundy school sweater. I glanced at myself in the mirror. Sometimes it still surprised me—seeing the girl in the reflection. Growing up, I'd always felt like a bit of a wallflower, perfectly happy to go unnoticed in the background of high school life.

Until my Lilitu powers began to develop.

Now, even if I wanted to blend in, I couldn't. I'd never need to wear eyeliner or mascara to highlight the drama of my eyes. No foundation could match the natural perfection of my skin. My brown hair, once so listless and mousey, shone like brushed silk. My lips—meant to draw attention like the vibrant flower draws in bees—curved in a perfectly enticing pout that no lipstick could amplify.

These were my weapons, whether or not I wanted them. This deadly beauty was my Lilitu heritage.

"Your dad's almost done banging around in the kitchen." Karayan stood at the door to my room. Her eyes strayed over my uniform almost wistfully. When she noticed me watching her, she glanced away. "He sent me to tell you, 'breakfast is served in T-minus five minutes.'"

I picked up my brush and ran it through my hair. "Welcome to the ritual first-day-of-school pancake extravaganza."

Karayan's lips quirked up in a small smile. "You're going back after three weeks off. You're telling me that rates a first-day-of-school pancake extravaganza?"

"Oh yes." I flashed Karayan a smile. "And be forewarned; Dad takes this stuff pretty seriously. There are also birthday pancake extravaganzas, holiday pancake extravaganzas, and hey-that-new-movie-I-want-to-see-comes-out-tonight pancake extravaganzas. The differences are subtle, but they are real."

Karayan leaned against my doorjamb, grinning. "Should I be worried?"

"Only that you're going to be ruined when it comes to other breakfast foods."

"That good, huh?"

I shrugged in answer, as if to say, *don't take my word for it… you'll find out soon enough.*

Karayan shook her head. "Okay, whatever. He's setting three places. I'll see you downstairs."

Karayan slipped back down the hall. I turned away from the mirror, feeling a pang. I set my brush down and picked up the cameo Dad had given me for my sixteenth birthday; a beautiful carved angel, suspended from a velvet cord. It was his way of telling me that no matter my ancestry, he knew which side I was on. Sure, I might have been born a Lilitu, but I had a family who loved me. Friends who trusted me. I had a place to belong.

Karayan—well, she was still getting used to her return to the Guard. And the Guard was still getting used to her.

I fastened the cameo around my neck. It rested comfortably against my collarbone, peeking out from the top of my shirt. Time to get the second half of junior year started.

I walked down the hallway, passing Dad's room on the left. I could smell the spicy scent of his soap wafting along the hall. He must have gotten up and showered before I'd even woken up. So maybe I wasn't the only one having trouble sleeping.

Downstairs, I spotted Karayan hovering in the doorway to her room—formerly our guest room. Though, honestly, she hadn't done much to make it hers yet. Aside from a few scattered clothes, the room had all the personality of a motel. I hesitated, then bypassed the entrance to the kitchen, heading instead for Karayan.

"Is something wrong?"

She looked at me, feigning nonchalance. "Nope."

"Okay. Well, I'm going to grab something to eat." I started to turn away, but Karayan cleared her throat.

I stopped. Karayan caught her bottom lip in her teeth. She looked *unsure.* The gesture was so uncharacteristic that I stared. "Karayan, you're not thinking of leaving us again?"

"'Leaving us?' That implies there's an 'us' to leave." Karayan shrugged. "The Guard hasn't exactly rolled out the welcome mat."

"You know you're welcome here," I started.

"Sure. Murphy's great. But he's not exactly a typical Guardsman. Most of them treat me like a time bomb."

"What about Thane? Have you two had a chance to—?"

"Thane?" Karayan snorted derisively. "He's the worst of them all."

"He'll come around. It's just going to take time."

"I get that this optimistic thing is one of your endearing qualities, but Thane is never going to come around. Trust me. We've got the kind of history that—" Karayan spread her hands. "Some mistakes can't be forgiven. And when those mistakes are made by Lilitu? Let's just say, the Guard has a long memory."

Her words burned in my ears. I dropped my eyes, at a loss for words. It hadn't been a month since Senoy, one of the three Guardian Angels tasked with fighting the Lilitu, had died in my arms. Because of a mistake I had made. Because I'd trusted the wrong person. Because I hadn't listened to the Guard.

Karayan must have realized she'd struck a nerve. "But what the hell do I know? Come on. Let's eat." Karayan looped an arm over my shoulders and guided me toward the kitchen.

Dad had set three plates on the kitchen island. He was transferring a nice stack of golden pancakes to the last plate as we entered.

"Morning, sunshine." Dad gave me a warm smile and gestured to the fridge with his chin. "Mind grabbing the maple syrup?"

"Sure." I headed to the kitchen, breathing in the rich aroma of pancakes fresh off the griddle. The buttery scent had my mouth watering in two seconds flat. I grabbed the syrup out of the fridge and set it on the island, taking a seat on the middle stool.

Karayan took the seat to my left. Dad set the last plate of steaming pancakes in front of her.

"What do you like on your pancakes? We've got it all."

Karayan looked at my dad, her eyebrow arched. "All? You intrigue me."

I groaned happily, drowning my pancakes in maple syrup.

Dad rubbed his hands together, ready for the challenge. "Butter, peanut butter, syrup, chocolate chips, blueberries, strawberries, bananas, whipped cream, cream cheese—"

"Easy, tiger." Karayan grinned. "Hook me up with some blueberries and whipped cream."

"Coming right up." Dad strode to the fridge.

I took a bite of my pancakes and glanced at Karayan, catching her in an unguarded moment. She watched my dad with a vulnerable gratitude I'd never have expected to see from the snarky and self-confident Lilitu. For the second time that morning, I felt a pang in my chest. No matter how coolly she played it off, I knew Karayan had longed to be part of a family like this since she was a little girl. But while I'd grown up with Murphy, Karayan hadn't been so lucky. Thane had raised Karayan as a soldier, a weapon. And when she'd finally exploded in retaliation, he'd used her desertion as justification that no Lilitu could be trusted, ever. Murphy, on the other hand, had raised me as his daughter. And while it had taken me time to forgive him for hiding the truth of my lineage for so long, the truth was—I was incredibly grateful to have Murphy as my dad.

Dad returned with a bowl of blueberries and a canister of whipped cream. He waited for Karayan to scoop out all the berries she wanted, then shook the canister with a flourish.

"Say when." He sprayed piles of gorgeous whipped cream over Karayan's pancakes.

Her eyes widened at the bounty. "When."

Dad stepped back, folding his arms over his chest and waiting.

Karayan took a bite of her pancakes. A half a second later, her eyes closed and she smiled blissfully. "Braedyn, you do not exaggerate."

"Told you." I gave my dad a thumbs-up. He beamed.

"Okay, scoot over, kiddo. All this cooking's fired up my appetite." Dad took the stool to my right. For a few heavenly minutes, we ate together in companionable silence.

When the front door opened, Karayan stiffened next to me. We both knew the only people who'd just walk into our home unannounced were Guardsmen. I glanced at Karayan, but she was keeping her eyes fixed on her plate, her expression neutral.

Hale walked into the kitchen with his usual focus.

"Murphy. Girls." Hale offered his hand to Dad, who stood to meet him. The men shook hands briskly.

"What is it?" All levity had left Dad's voice.

Hale hesitated, eying Karayan uncomfortably. He glanced back at Dad. Dad's eyes flicked over to Karayan with just the tiniest flash of worry.

"We're almost done here," he started.

Karayan, who'd caught all the unspoken wariness of the Guardsmen, stood. "Thanks for the pancakes, Murph." She daubed at the corners of her mouth with a napkin and gave Hale a pointed glance. "I'm going for a walk. It's a little stuffy in here." Karayan abandoned her half-eaten pancakes and walked out of the kitchen. She headed straight for the front door, closing it behind her a bit harder than necessary.

I glared at Hale, torn between giving him a piece of my mind and going after Karayan.

"How's it working out?" Hale asked, before I had a chance to speak. He studied Dad's face carefully, clearly concerned.

Dad sighed. "You should give her some tasks. I think she's feeling a little… adrift. She needs to know her place in the organization. Until she feels like part of the team, I don't think she's going to fully trust us."

"Trust is a two-way street." Hale frowned. "As for giving her some tasks… I'll work on finding something for her to do."

"So, what brought you here?" Dad gestured to the empty stool Karayan had just vacated. Hale took it.

"Thane and Ian are concerned."

Dad shook his head ruefully. "When are they not concerned?"

"They're worried about the timing of this attack." Hale's eyes flicked to my face briefly. He gave me a small smile. "And as happy as we are that you weren't seriously injured, it brings up all sorts of uncomfortable questions."

"Tell me about it." I pushed the last of my pancakes away. Suddenly they didn't seem as appealing.

"What questions, specifically?" Dad leaned closer, giving Hale his full attention.

"Why now? The Seal's been open for weeks, why haven't they tried to breach it before? Are they testing us?" Hale's eyes shifted to mine again. "Or was it because Braedyn was there? Are they targeting her?"

I heard Dad shift behind me, and it didn't take much imagination to picture the expression on his face. I kept my eyes riveted on Hale, though, hoping for more.

"Uh-oh." Dad pushed back from the island and stood. "Look at the time, kiddo. You're going to be late."

"What?" I stared at Dad. It took a moment for what he was saying to register.

"For school. Not the way you want to start the last semester of your second-to-last year at Coronado Prep, is it?"

I stared at Dad. He gave me a neutral smile, and clapped a hand on my shoulder. I sighed, recognizing the look. No use arguing. He wasn't going to budge.

Lucas slid into the passenger side of my car, looking as harried as I felt. He ran a hand through his dark hair, sweeping glossy, dark bangs back from his face.

"Another exercise in pointlessness," he grumbled.

"That's the winning attitude I love to see on the first day of school." Gretchen reached through the window and tousled his hair affectionately.

Lucas grimaced. "Gretchen, seriously? I'm almost eighteen years old."

Gretchen ignored him and gave me a smile. "Drive safe."

"If you insist." I tried to catch a glimpse of something in Gretchen's face, but if she knew anything more than I'd managed to glean before Dad shooed me out of the kitchen, she wasn't giving it away.

"Cute." Gretchen stepped back from the car and waved. "Have fun at school, kids."

I pulled into the street. In my rear view mirror, I saw Gretchen heading into my house, presumably to join the conversation with Hale and Murphy. Whatever they were keeping secret, I vowed not to pry. The last time I'd tried to work behind the Guard's back, I'd ended up helping the incubus Seth open the Seal between our worlds. I couldn't afford to make another mistake of that magnitude, not ever again.

Lucas was watching me closely from the passenger side. "Did Hale tell you what's got Ian and Thane in such a tizzy?"

"Not really. Just that they're wondering if I'm somehow connected to why the Lilitu finally decided to try crossing through the Seal."

Lucas stared at me, unsettled. "Connected, like, how?"

"Well, that would be the question, wouldn't it?"

We drove the rest of the way to school in contemplative silence. I knew it was a new semester, but we'd only been off for three weeks and it didn't feel that much different.

At least, it didn't feel any different until I parked and got out of my car.

As I straightened with my book bag, the first person I caught sight of was Cassie. Her eyes met mine and she froze. She and I hadn't spoken since the night Seth had tricked me into helping him open the Seal. The night Royal had been attacked. The night we'd witnessed the angel Senoy's death. A sick sense of dread balled heavy in my stomach as the images played through my mind again. I'd made many mistakes that day, but this was one I could fix. I wasn't ready to lose Cassie as a friend.

While she stood there, frozen in place, Parker approached her. I felt my blood start to boil. I'd ordered him to stay away from Cassie before. I'd used *the call* on him, utilizing my Lilitu power in an effort to make him back off. Somehow, he'd resisted my powers. And now, he was bugging her again, in the very first moments of the semester. Cassie said something that made Parker step back. He looked devastated, but Cassie—turning away from him—didn't see the expression on his face. Her eyes had flicked back toward me once more.

Feeling a surge of hope—maybe this meant she was finally ready to talk with me?—I took a step toward Cassie. She turned on her heel and practically dashed into the nearest building.

"She's not talking about it." Royal joined us at my car. I glanced at him. He was looking in the direction Cassie had just fled. "Whatever happened in the mission that night? She's not talking about it."

I stared at Royal. His usually twinkling eyes seemed somehow flat and tired. His skin was a strangely pale hue. He looked sick. He was sick, I suppose. But not in any way a doctor could help. Seth had attacked Royal, playing on Royal's feelings for him. And when they'd shared their intimate encounter, Seth had pulled on Royal's life energy, draining him as only a Lilitu could. Royal's injuries ran deeper than skin and bone, blood and tissue. His were injuries of the spirit—injuries of the soul.

Given time, Royal could recover—provided he was never attacked by a Lilitu again. But in the meantime, while he healed, he was just a shadow of his former self.

I felt Lucas squeezing my hand and turned. He was watching me, worried. I gave him a half-smile, and turned back to Royal.

"But she's talking to you?"

Royal shrugged with a wry smile. "If you can call it that. We have conversations, but neither of us says anything real." Royal stopped talking then. He shoved his hands deep into his pockets and looked away at the mountains, purple and soaring in the distance.

I felt another swell of fury. These were my friends, broken because of me. I couldn't help but picture Seth preying on Royal's affections, attacking him—*seriously damaging* him—for no other reason than to keep me distracted. And Cassie… I couldn't fathom what private hell she must be living through, unable to talk about what she'd seen with anyone.

"Enough." I gripped my books tighter to my chest. "This can't continue."

Royal gave me a look with something approaching his old snark. "And you will change things how?"

"It's time for an intervention." I eyed Royal and Lucas, daring them to argue. "We have to get Cassie to talk about that night. About what she saw. What she's feeling. It's the only way she'll get through this. And I can't lose her."

"So this is all about you?" Royal's lips twitched in bitter

amusement.

"This is about us," I snapped. "It's about not letting the Lilitu destroy what we have. This is war, and it's time to fight back." Royal's smirk faded. He nodded.

"Okay. I'm on board."

The day's classes squeaked by with agonizing lethargy. Teachers welcomed students to the second term of the year, people reoriented themselves to the day's schedule, and life at school slowly ratcheted back to normal. Cassie was nowhere to be found at lunch, which hardened my resolve to sit her down and break through this wall of silence between us.

By the time the final bell rang, I was twitching with anxiety to see my friend again. Royal and I had hatched a plan at lunch. It meant I'd go and wait in one of the private study rooms in the library while Royal convinced Cassie to come talk to me. Lucas, who felt it might be best if he wasn't involved, offered to walk me down to the library to wait.

I took his hand, grateful for the warmth in the stinging cold January afternoon.

"She'll come around," he said.

"How can you be so sure?"

"Because she's Cassie. You're Braedyn. He's Royal. You're like the Coronado Prep triumvirate—nothing is going to keep you guys apart for long."

I squeezed Lucas's hand in answer, longing for the same confidence.

When we reached the library, Lucas brushed his lips against my cheek. "Good luck."

"Wait." I caught his hand as he started to turn away. "What should I say to her?"

"Just *listen.* She'll tell you what she needs." Lucas gave me an encouraging smile. "I'll meet you at the car when you're done." I let his hand go, and watched him leave the library.

I walked into the private study room that Royal had reserved for us this afternoon. I sat down at the table. And I waited. I had no idea how long it would take, or what would happen if Royal failed to convince Cassie to join me here. Surely he'd let me know? But as the minutes ticked by, I grew less sure. I was starting to wonder if Royal had, in fact, forgotten we'd planned to do this today, when I heard the doorknob start to turn.

I stood, another wave of anxiety crashing over me.

Royal opened the door and Cassie walked through. When she saw me she froze again—but only for a moment. She turned, seeking escape. Royal blocked her.

"Cassie."

"No. Royal, let me out."

"Just talk to her."

"There's nothing to say!" Cassie tried to push past Royal. Weak as he was, he blocked her again.

"You saw something at the mission." I tried to keep my voice calm, but it trembled nonetheless. "You must have questions."

Cassie stopped struggling against Royal. She turned back to face me, her eyes alive with anger. "Questions?"

"Talk to me, Cassie. Please."

"What do you want me to say?" Cassie crossed her arms, her body as stiff as her voice. I glanced at Royal. He nodded in understanding and left, closing the door behind him. Cassie looked over her shoulder at the sound. Then she glared at me again.

"Whatever you want to say." I sat back down at the table, hoping she'd follow my lead.

"What I want to say—that's pretty funny."

I just waited, trying to keep my face neutral, despite the feelings coursing through my veins.

"What I want to say is *crazy*." Cassie paced behind the table, gripping her sides tightly.

"Because of what you saw?"

Cassie stopped and shot me a piercing look. "I—I don't know what I saw."

"Don't you?"

She shook her head, but her anger was fading. In its place, fear blossomed. And suddenly I understood.

"You're not crazy, Cassie. What you saw was real."

"That's impossible." Cassie's voice was barely more than a whisper. "I saw—you killed a woman. She had—her eyes—" Cassie shook her head again.

"She was a demon," I said softly. "That's why her eyes were pitch black. Why she had claws."

Cassie's eyes locked onto my face. "That's—no. No." But she

looked unsure.

"I know." I bit my lip. "It sounds insane. It *is* insane. When I first learned they were real—" I shook my head at the memory. "It didn't matter what anyone told me. I wouldn't believe it until I saw one with my own eyes." I met her gaze and held it, keeping my voice steady. "You've seen one too, Cass."

Cassie licked her lips. "It can't be real," she whispered. "It's some kind of mass hallucination thing. I mean, shouldn't we be talking to a shrink or something?"

"Cassie, if you'll just talk to me—"

Cassie shook her head. "There are too many things—too many things that don't make sense."

I softened my voice. "Sit down. Ask me anything. I won't keep secrets from you anymore." I waited, and after a moment, Cassie pulled out a chair and sat. She watched me warily, but she was listening.

"What do you mean by 'demon?'" she finally asked.

"A Lilitu, specifically. A demon that preys on humans. They're powerful. They can make themselves invisible. They can mess with people's minds. And they can disguise themselves as humans, usually very beautiful women. But they're not women. They're like vampires, only instead of feeding off blood, they feed off of the spirit of their victims."

Cassie's eyes sharpened. "Royal—?"

"Yes. Seth got to him."

"Seth? Seth is a demon—and you let him get to Royal?!"

"I didn't know." I fought to keep my voice even. "Male Lilitu are incredibly rare. Seth was the first we've ever seen in the flesh."

Cassie watched me, her expression growing more difficult to read.

"Do you remember what Seth told you that night?" I asked. "We left you with him at my house. You were supposed to stay with him, but instead you followed me to the mission. What did Seth tell you?"

Cassie's gaze turned inward. Her brow furrowed. "He—just suggested I tell you how angry I was with you. But once he'd said it, it was all I could think about."

"He enthralled you." I felt myself grimace at the thought. "It's one of their powers. He put a thought into your head and made you believe it was your own."

"But why?"

"To keep me busy, I'm guessing. So I couldn't stop his larger plan."

"At the mission."

I looked at Cassie sharply. "Yes. Seth wanted to open the door between our worlds, so more Lilitu could come here. When we figured out what he was doing, we tried to stop him." I bit my lip. "We failed."

"So, the door is open?"

"Yes."

"Who is 'we?' You keep saying 'we.'"

"I mean the Guard. They fight to protect human kind from the Lilitu. Lucas is a Guardsman. So is my dad."

"And when you say fight—?"

"We're in a war. The Earth is at stake. If we lose, the Lilitu will claim this world for themselves. Human kind will become nothing more than their cattle."

Cassie fell into silence for a moment. "Let's pretend for a second that I believe you. You said these Lilitu things can make themselves invisible."

I felt a lump in my throat, but I forced it down. "Yes."

"I saw you disappear." Cassie looked up, straight into my eyes.

"Yes," I whispered. "I'm Lilitu, too."

Cassie's face seemed to go still. I waited while she turned this over in her mind. "So. You can disappear. You can 'prey on men'—and for now I think I'll pass on the explanation of exactly what that means. But when you say 'mess with minds—?'" She eyed me uneasily.

"I'm still learning the ins and outs," I whispered.

"But you've done it?"

I nodded.

"To who?"

I lowered my eyes. "To Lucas, for one," I said quietly. "Do you remember the car accident we were in the night of Winter Ball?"

"Yeah. Lucas was in a cast for months."

"It wasn't a car accident. Lucas was attacked by a very powerful, very old Lilitu. She kidnapped him. We thought we'd lost him. But I was able to locate his mind. It was like I could see out of his eyes, hear with his ears. I was able to figure out where she'd taken him."

Cassie looked surprised. "So, you helped him."

"That time," I said, keeping my voice measured. Cassie's eyes narrowed; she could tell there was more. "But I've also hurt him. He had a secret—" My voice caught. Memories flooded my head, and that sick feeling of guilt welled up in my gut all over again. "I thought it could help me win the battle with the Lilitu. So I went into his mind and I took it. He didn't want to give it up. I—I pulled the memory out of his head." I felt my body trembling at the memory. "I will *never* do that again."

Silence fell between us.

After a long moment, Cassie swallowed. "Royal knows?"

"Yes."

"How long?"

I couldn't look at Cassie. "A little over a year."

"I see." Cassie's voice was cold. "Is that everything, then? Or are there any other big secrets you need to tell me?"

"Just one." I lowered my hands to my lap, clasping them tightly together outside of Cassie's line of sight. "Parker."

Cassie's eyes snapped up. "What about him?" If her voice had been cold before, it was like ice now.

"After he—did what he did to you, I wanted to punish him." But at that, I found I couldn't go on.

Cassie's stare bored into me. "You're the reason he tried to kill himself, aren't you?"

Feeling sick, it was all I could do to nod.

"I didn't ask you to do that," Cassie said.

"I know."

Cassie lurched to her feet, agitated. "I don't want this on my conscience."

I looked up, surprised. "It's on me, Cassie," I said. "You had nothing to do with it."

"Really? If I hadn't been your friend, would you still have gone after Parker?"

I stared at Cassie, flabbergasted.

"Well?" Cassie glared at me. I shook my head, no. Cassie turned away from me. "I—I need time to think about this." She faced me, and in her expression I saw distrust and confusion. "You'll have to give me some space."

"Of course." My voice sounded wooden. I stood, feeling

completely useless. "Whatever you need."

Cassie turned and walked to the door. She put her hand on the doorknob then glanced back at me once more. Whatever she was feeling, I couldn't decipher it.

Then Cassie opened the door. Royal was waiting on the other side.

"How did it go?" But the hope in his eyes died as he read our expressions. "Oh."

"I need a ride home," Cassie said, pushing past Royal.

"Right." His eyes lingered on mine for a moment, before he turned and followed Cassie out of the library. As he left, he pulled the door closed. He knew me well enough to know I needed to be alone.

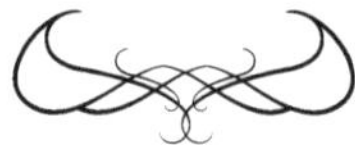

Once I'd collected myself enough to leave the study room, I took my time wandering back up to the parking lot. I knew Lucas was waiting for me. It was time to head back home. But as I passed the administration building, I heard a sharp argument.

I paused, at the edge of the administration building's courtyard. Inside, I could see Amber and a pretty older woman—her mother?—having a tense conversation.

"And I'm telling you we can't afford to keep sending you here," the woman snapped.

"What about college?" Amber's voice was rising in panic.

"Please, Amber, save the histrionics. We're sending you to Puerto Escondido High, not the salt mines. I got into a perfectly fine college and I graduated from public high school, you can do the same."

"Have you even talked to Dad about this?"

The woman spun on Amber, her fury visible even from across the courtyard. "Your father and I agree about this. I'd appreciate it if you'd stop fighting with me." The woman straightened her coat and turned away from Amber. Amber grabbed her arm.

"Wait. I'll get a job," Amber said. "I can pay my own way."

"Don't be ridiculous. You have responsibilities at the house."

"Responsibilities? You mean babysitting your son?"

"He's your little brother, Amber, and I'll thank you not to use that tone with me."

"Fine. I'll watch Charlie, just pay me a fair wage. That can be one of my part-time jobs."

"I simply cannot believe how self-absorbed you are sometimes." The woman pulled her arm free from Amber's grasp. "This discussion is over."

Before Amber could respond, the woman had marched past her and back into the administration building.

Amber threw her arms up in frustration—and then she saw me. I felt my cheeks flush with embarrassment. I turned and stumbled toward the parking lot.

I heard Amber's steps behind me, but I wasn't expecting her to grab my arm. I turned to face her reluctantly.

"I bet you're just loving this." Amber's face was blotchy with shame and anger.

"No, Amber, I'm not." I sighed, suddenly tired. What would it take to end this feud?

"You'd better forget what you heard. Because if you tell anyone—"

The threat, so familiar, suddenly kindled a white-hot spark in my chest. "You'll what?" I stepped closer to Amber. Startled, she stumbled backwards a pace. "Hurt more of my friends? Maybe actually kill one of them this time?"

Amber faced me down, but instead of her usual sadistic calm, I saw real pain in her eyes. "Just keep this to yourself." She turned and stalked off, scraping together what was left of her dignity.

I watched her go, feeling sick. Amber was a spotter, something the Guard was in sore need of right now. I knew it, and Lucas knew it, but neither of us wanted Amber anywhere near the Guard. So we'd agreed not to tell anyone about her. Now, if only my conscience would get on board. Because as it stood, every time I saw Amber, I felt another little stab of guilt for keeping her a secret from the Guard.

3

I picked myself up off the practice mat, winded. Hale, concerned, hurried forward, offering me a hand. I took it gratefully.

"Good one." I managed a smile as Hale helped me to my feet. "Guess I let my attention wander for a second." It was partly true; I'd spent the prior evening convincing Karayan to start training with us in the basement. She'd agreed to come and check it out, but was way beyond lukewarm about the idea of sparring with Hale or any other Guardsman. A small part of me wanted to show off for her, to make sparring more appealing. So it was while I was sneaking a look at Karayan to gauge her reaction that Hale struck. I hadn't seen the punch coming fast enough to block it. Hale's fist connected solidly, tagged me hard in the shoulder.

"Maybe you should sit down for a moment." Hale studied my face, his brows drawing together.

"Probably not a bad idea." I glanced back to the wall, where Karayan stood watching us, arms crossed. I walked over to her, grabbing my water bottle off the table. "So," I started, forcing a bit too much cheerful enthusiasm into my voice. "What do you think?"

"I think you're lucky Hale didn't take your head off." Karayan's eyebrow quirked up. "I've found, when you're in a fight, it's usually a good idea to keep your eyes on your opponent."

"Right." I took a long drink of water, blushing.

Hale joined us, blotting at his face with a small towel. "So, Karayan. Interested in starting some training with us?" His voice was measured. Not too friendly, but not too cold, either. He hadn't made up his mind about her. I glanced at Karayan, and saw an equally reserved expression on her face.

The basement door opened above us as several newcomers started down the stairs. I heard them talking with each other long before they came into view. I felt a tightening in my chest and battled the urge to cloak myself. Not that it would do any good. The new spotters—the spotters that Hale and Dad had tried so hard to keep me away from—would see through my cloak in an instant. I didn't want to give them another reason to mistrust me. Being Lilitu was more than enough to put me on their hit list.

After the Seal had opened and Karayan had joined our side, Hale decided the time had come to introduce us to the spotters. It was a very tense meeting. Gretchen had managed to talk them out of attacking me, but only after they'd verified that none of the Guardsmen were currently in Thrall to me. Not that I'd expected the meeting to be easy, but I'd hoped that once they'd realized I was on their side, they'd warm up to me. They hadn't. In fact, since that first meeting, none of the new spotters had said word one to me.

Rhea saw us first. The temperature in the room seemed to drop several degrees. Short and stocky, with pinched eyes and a thin smile, Rhea was the one spotter I had no interest in getting to know better. She was maybe 40 years old, and she carried herself like she believed the world was out to get her. There was something about her, something mean and spiteful. Frizzy, dirty blond hair framed her pale face, while a smattering of freckles dusted her cheeks. In another lifetime, she might have been cute. But whatever was wrong with her inside eclipsed any potential beauty outside. She was the spotter for one of the last units that arrived in Puerto Escondido before the Seal was opened. I hadn't had too much interaction with her. That being said—what little interaction we'd had was more than enough for one lifetime. She froze, hands automatically moving to the daggers at her side. The other spotters tensed in response.

Karayan stepped up beside me, offering a united front. The spotters eyed us with open hostility.

"Nice afternoon for a practice session." Hale moved forward to greet them, subtly putting himself between the spotters and Karayan and me.

Rhea's eyes slid from Hale to me. "We didn't realize the basement was occupied."

"Actually, I usually train Braedyn and Lucas every day after school around this time," Hale said, keeping his voice warm and open, "but I don't see any reason why we can't all train together. There's more than enough room. If you need more practice mats, you'll find them over there." Hale gestured at a line of mats stacked up against the far wall of the basement.

Rhea hesitated, giving me another beady glare. "Fine." She turned on her heel, heading for the mats. The other spotters followed suit, more than one taking a moment to gawk at Karayan or me before helping set the mats out.

Hale turned back to me and I saw his shoulders ease. So he'd been more worried than he'd let on.

"How's the shoulder?" Hale moved forward and touched my shoulder. I hissed as his fingers made contact.

"Sorry. Still a bit sore." I knew the bruise—if it even formed—would fade quickly. That was one—on a very short list—of the advantages of being a Lilitu. But the initial pain of the injury was just as intense for me as it would be for a regular human girl. I edged the collar of my shirt aside. Sure enough, an angry red welt was blooming across my shoulder.

"Should we call it for today?" Hale asked.

I glanced at Karayan and sighed. It had been hard enough to get her to come down here with me. "No, I want to keep going." Before Hale could argue, I smiled lamely. "I promise to pay more attention this time."

Hale shrugged. "If you're sure." He walked out onto the mat.

Before I joined him, I turned to Karayan and dropped my voice. "I know you're not sure about this, but training is about more than just learning how to fight."

"Oh?" Karayan sniffed. "Enlighten me."

"It's about showing *them*," I didn't have to point to the spotters behind me; Karayan's eyes sought them out, "that you're one of the good guys. It's about building trust with the Guard, and earning their trust in return. It's about becoming part of the family." I saw my words strike home.

"Family, huh?" Karayan's eyes hardened. "Then you might want to turn around. Your bitchy older sister is headed this way."

I turned. Rhea walked straight toward me, a neutral little smile on her lips. "So. Brenda, right?"

"Braedyn." I said, forcing myself to smile.

"Braedyn, sure. We've got odd numbers, and I noticed you guys have odd numbers, too. So how about you spar with me?"

I felt a little shock of surprise. "Sure."

"Great." Rhea turned and walked back to an open mat. I followed her, unsettled. From any of the others, I might have taken this as an overture of friendship.

Rhea planted herself at one end of the mat. I took my place at the other end. Before I'd settled into my stance, Rhea lunged. I swung for her, startled at the attack. Rhea dodged under my swing and stepped into my personal space, smashing a fist into my stomach. I dropped to one knee, breathless. Dimly, I was aware of the other spotters snickering behind me.

"Easy!" Hale rushed forward. "What the hell was that?" He spun on Rhea, who eyed him levelly.

"Sorry." Rhea shrugged, but she didn't look sorry. "We were taught not to pull our punches when we train."

"I'm not asking you to pull your punches." Hale's fists were balled tight with fury. "She wasn't ready for—"

"You want to fight, spotter? Fight me." Karayan strode forward, something almost feral in her grin. Alarms blared in my mind. The last thing we needed was open war between the spotters and Karayan.

"It's okay." I pushed myself to my feet, refusing to let the pain of Rhea's blow register on my face. "She barely got me." I eyed Hale, urging him to deal with Karayan before things got out of hand.

"Why don't you spar with me, Karayan?" Hale asked. Either he'd picked up on my silent plea, or he could see where this was headed the same as I could.

Karayan looked at me, a question in her eyes. I nodded in encouragement. "Fine," Karayan sighed. "Show me what you've got." Karayan followed Hale back to his practice mat. I watched them, curious.

"Well?" Rhea stepped into my line of vision. "Are we doing this or not?"

"I'm not sure what you're doing, Rhea." I met her gaze, keeping my voice level. "I'm getting a drink of water." I pushed past Rhea and headed back to the safety of the wall. I heard more snickers behind me, and did my best to ignore them. I picked up my water bottle again and sat on the ground, trying not to strain my tender body any more.

Rhea turned her back on me, returning to her group. I put her out of my mind, focusing instead on Hale and Karayan.

Hale was showing Karayan a few basic moves. She looked irritated, and gestured for him to get to it already. Hale shrugged and stepped back. Karayan took a defensive stance. Hale attacked, a simple but powerful charge.

Karayan twisted to the side, slicing her arm down to block his blow. Hale overshot her but recovered quickly. He spun back to face her, his face a mask of concentration. Karayan watched him with a bland expression. Hale attacked again, this time swinging out with the full force of his arm. Karayan slid past the punch and dropped to the mat, sweeping Hale's foot out from under him. Startled, Hale dropped to the mat. I couldn't help but let out a *whooo!*

The spotters turned in time to see Karayan offer Hale a hand. He took it and let her help him up.

Hale eyed her, grinning ruefully. "Nicely done."

Karayan crossed her arms, but I could tell she was pleased. "You do realize Thane started me training in hand-to-hand combat around the time I could stand, right?"

"And look how well that turned out." Rhea's voice, though directed to the other spotters, was loud enough to carry.

It wiped the small gleam of satisfaction out of Karayan's eyes. Hale turned, irritated.

"Rhea?"

"Hmm?" She gave him a flat look, daring him to call her out.

"Is there a problem here?"

"Is there a problem?" Rhea gave him a look of pity. "The fact that you can't see it makes it all the more serious."

"If you have something to say, please, go ahead." Hale was keeping his anger on a tight leash, but I could see the muscle in his jaw jumping. I glanced at Karayan, worried.

"Look. We've been watching that Seal for almost a month, right? And nothing. Then you put her on duty—" without taking her eyes off of Hale, Rhea pointed her finger directly at me, "and a Lilitu comes through. It doesn't take a rocket scientist to see what's going on here."

I was on my feet in an instant. "What are you—Are you accusing me of *helping* them?"

Rhea shrugged. "I just think it's interesting timing, that's all."

I charged Rhea, fury drowning out caution. Hale caught me around the chest, keeping me from reaching the smirking spotter. "I'm loyal to the Guard," I hissed.

"Right. So, answer a question for us—'cause we weren't there, and no one seems willing to tell us—how exactly was the Seal opened? I mean, you were there, right? So what happened that night?"

An icy splash of fear drove out my anger. Hale, sensing my change, released me. He caught my eye, worried.

Karayan's laugh filled the room like the peal of bells.

Rhea glanced at her, irritated. "Something funny, demon?"

"You are." Karayan's laugh faded, and her eyes glinted. "Braedyn, don't let them get under your skin. They're clearly threatened. Not only can we do their job, but we're faster than they are, stronger than they are, and—" Karayan tossed her glorious hair, playing up every one of her remarkable advantages. Hale had to tear his eyes away from her. "Well. Maybe I should leave it at that. No need to get catty."

Rhea's eyes strained with outrage. "Really? You just saw me drop your little friend with one punch."

"Oh, sweetie, no." Karayan's voice dropped to a dangerous tone. "She'd take you apart in a fair fight."

"Okay, I think that's enough training for one afternoon." Hale ushered Karayan and me out of the basement.

But as I followed them up the stairs, I risked one look back. Rhea's pinched eyes were still fixed to me, radiating cold hatred. I sighed. Looks like we weren't going to be planning a girl's night out any time soon.

With Rhea and the spotters starting to hang out at Hale's house, school became more of a haven for me during the week. Sure, there was still Amber and her posse to dodge, but campus was a lot bigger than Hale's basement, and I had my friends to keep me company.

At the start of the third week of the semester, I pulled into the parking lot, running late.

"Hey, look." Lucas, sitting in the passenger side, pointed. I followed his gesture and saw Royal and Cassie getting out of Royal's car. Cassie heard our car approaching. She turned, saw me, and gave a small wave before heading into the north hall for first period.

I traded a glance with Lucas. Cassie had kept her distance since our talk, and—respecting her wishes—I hadn't approached her. But I missed her, and seeing that little wave sent a surge of hope washing through me.

"Progress," Lucas said.

"Let's hope this means things will get back to normal soon."

"Normal?" Lucas looked at me with a lopsided smile. "You don't think that ship has sailed?"

"You know what I mean." I parked in an empty space and killed the engine. Royal waited as I closed and locked my door. "How is she?"

"Seems to be doing better," Royal said. He tried for a smile, but it didn't reach his eyes. I hesitated, searching his face.

"Royal, you don't look so good."

"Compliments, compliments. You're going to make me blush." Royal tried to brush me off, but I caught his hand.

"Seriously. Maybe you should take a sick day."

Royal's face paled to an almost ashen hue. "No."

"Are you sure? You look like you could use some rest."

"I don't want to be alone." His eyes, usually alive with mischief or amusement, seemed hollow, listless. I felt my heart twisting in my chest. This was Seth's doing. How could I have been so blind?

"Come on, we're going to be late for first period." Royal turned and headed toward the north hall. I caught Lucas's glance. He looked worried, too. There was a darkness hovering over Royal that hadn't been there before Seth got to him.

Morning classes passed, one by one, and when the bell for lunch rang I was one of the first out of my seat in Physics class. Royal and Cassie were still packing up their notes. I hesitated, unsure if I should approach or give Cassie more space.

"Don't forget, test on Thursday," Mr. Harris called after his fleeing students.

I decided to play it safe. I left, hugging my physics books to my chest. Lucas was waiting by my locker. We walked into the cafeteria together, making our way to our usual table.

I volunteered to grab the tray of food from the cafeteria. We ate family-style at Coronado Prep, and today it was chicken fajitas with Spanish rice. I loaded my tray up with tortillas, sour cream, diced tomatoes and onions, guacamole, a bowl of steaming chicken and grilled peppers, and a bowl of Spanish rice. It smelled incredible, and I felt my stomach grumble in anticipation of the meal.

I returned to our table with the tray. Royal took the plate of tortillas, serving himself and passing them to Lucas. We shared the food around until our plates were full. I assembled my fajita, spooning the meat, tomatoes, onions, and guacamole into a warm tortilla, then adding a dollop of sour cream on top. As I was lifting the first fajita to my lips, someone joined our table.

"Did you save any for me?" Cassie took the empty chair beside Royal.

"She returns!" Royal grinned at Cassie, and something like his old fire gleamed in his eyes for a moment.

"Well, fajitas," Cassie said, as if this explained everything.

I grinned and pushed the tortillas toward Cassie. "There's more than enough."

Cassie smiled shyly as Royal and Lucas crowded her with the other bowls. As soon as she'd served herself, she sat back.

"Okay. I'm in." Cassie caught my gaze and held it. "I'm sorry it took so long for me to work it out, but there was a lot to process."

"Yeah." I felt a lump forming in my throat, and caught Lucas's hand, giving it a squeeze.

"So. Tell me everything." Cassie took a big bite of fajita, watching me with undivided attention.

"I will," I promised. I glanced around. Tables were full of kids eating, goofing off, and generally blowing off steam before afternoon classes began. "But not here."

"Sophie's?" Lucas asked.

"Just like old times." Cassie looked pleased.

I smiled at my friend. It was a nice thought. But this was nothing like old times.

The lunch crowd was long gone, and the dinner crowd wouldn't be here for hours yet, so Sophie's was quiet when we arrived. We made our way through the dim restaurant toward the back, finding an empty booth near the wide adobe hearth. A large fire crackled happily, and I felt some of the tension ease out of my shoulders in its glow. As we slid into the booth, I couldn't help but picture the last time we'd all been here together. It had been my seventeenth birthday. Seth had joined us, and we'd trusted him, thinking he was a friend. Royal eyed the place, and I realized he must be thinking the same thing.

"Royal?"

Royal looked at me. Then he glanced around the table. We were all watching him, concerned. "I know," he said, finally. "I know he was an incubus and I was nothing more than prey to him. But—for me it wasn't just some fling." Royal looked down at his hands, struggling for the words. "I thought—I mean, I *was*—I was in love with him."

Cassie reached across the table and took Royal's hand. He let her squeeze it in silence for a long moment.

"Do you think Seth will go after Royal again?" Cassie looked at me.

"*No*." They looked up at the vehemence in my voice. Lucas eyed me, concerned. I cleared my throat and continued. "No. We'll protect him from Seth."

"Like you protected Derek?" Royal shifted his eyes to look at me. His words sliced through my heart. The truth was, ever since Seth had escaped through the Seal, a fear had taken hold of my heart. As long as Seth was out there, Royal was vulnerable. I felt goose bumps scattering across my shoulders at the thought, then clenched my fists. Vulnerable just meant we'd have to be extra vigilant.

Cassie watched us, eyes full of questions. I knew we'd get to answering all of them in the next few hours, but right now, I needed Royal to understand something.

"Royal. I promise, I will do everything in my power to keep you safe."

Royal met my gaze and nodded slowly. We fell into a momentary silence. Then Lucas leaned across the table to catch Royal's eye.

"And I'll do everything in my power to make sure she keeps that promise," said Lucas, his tone every bit as serious as mine had just been.

Royal glanced at Lucas. His lips twitched. Then he laughed. The sound did more to warm me than the hearth behind us. "See that you do." After his laughter subsided, Royal actually looked a little cheered.

The waitress dropped by and we ordered a few quesadillas and sopapillas to share.

While we waited for our food, Lucas and I filled Cassie—and Royal, as far as the bits he'd never heard before—in on the history of the Guard. We told them about Lilith, and her flight from Eden. About how God had sent three angels—two of whom were now dead—after Lilith to bring her back. And how the war between the Sons of Adam and the Daughters of Lilith had begun when Lilith refused to return to Adam. We told them about the hierarchy of the Guard. How each unit had been operating independently for hundreds of years, but now they were all collecting in our town, ready to defend Earth against the forces of Lilitu who could erupt from the Seal at any moment. We talked until our throats were sore.

Finally, nearly three hours later, Cassie sat back, satisfied. "Okay. So, what can we do? To help?"

Of all the questions I'd expected, that wasn't one of them. Royal and Cassie—seeing my confusion—traded a look.

"There must be something we can do. I mean, I know we're not soldiers or super-bad-ass-demon-girls, but seriously." Cassie looked at me again, getting a little flustered. "You can't just drop a bomb like that and expect us to go on about our normal lives as if nothing's changed."

"I think that is exactly what they expect," Royal said, giving me a miffed frown.

"Royal, you of all people know how dangerous it is to get mixed up in this stuff." I turned to him, hoping for an ally.

"I think, knowing what I know now, I'd rather be able to fight than sit back and hope I don't get caught in the crossfire. You know—again."

I cringed, feeling the accusation more acutely than I think Royal intended.

Royal shifted in his seat. "I don't think Cassie's asking you to give her a sword and send her out to face a demon head on." He glanced at Cassie for confirmation. She nodded. "But we know what's going on. And we don't *look* like the kind of people who'd know what's going on. So maybe that could be useful. That's all I'm saying."

"Yeah." Cassie met my eyes, waiting for my response.

I glanced at Lucas, unsure what to say. Lucas shrugged, equally at a loss.

I sighed. "Okay. We'll figure out something for you to help with."

"Awesome sauce!" Cassie beamed.

"Something very safe," I added, frowning. Cassie shrugged, pleased, and picked up the last bit of quesadilla off the plate.

Now, all I had to do was figure out something for her to do that made her feel like a part of the fight, without actually putting her in harm's way. Because if there was one lesson I'd learned since joining the Guard it was this: Lilitu don't care who they hurt. And all of Cassie's sweet optimism would count for nothing if she ever had to face a Lilitu in a fight.

The sun had set by the time we left the restaurant. I pulled my jacket closer against the icy gusts of wind. Despite the cold and dark, the Plaza was alive with activity. A few buskers played guitars and sang for passersby. The coffee shop had patio heaters set out, so patrons could sip their coffees or hot chocolates and enjoy the lights of the Plaza. Long strands of small round bulbs were suspended over the street, bathing the cobblestone in a warm glow.

"What is that?" Lucas squinted his eyes, straining for a better view.

At the edge of the Plaza, a group of young women were handing out flyers to people as they passed. As we drew closer, I recognized a girl with a cute strawberry-blond bob. It was Carrie, Missy's older sister. She'd been a senior when I was a freshman. Our school paired seniors with groups of freshman that first year as sort of unofficial mentors, and Carrie had been mine.

I was surprised to see her. I'd thought she'd gone out of state for college.

Carrie looked up and spotted me. Recognition flashed in her eyes, and she waved us over.

"Braedyn Murphy, right? Oh my gosh, it's been so long!" Carrie threw her arm around my shoulders and squeezed.

"Hi, Carrie. How are you doing?" I smiled, disentangling myself from her grip.

"So good," she beamed. Her coat was loosely belted over a shirt—I recognized the logo. It was the shirt baristas wore at the Plaza coffee shop. "You have amazing timing. Here. Check this out." She shoved a flyer in my hand. "We're meeting tonight after the rally, actually—"

"Good evening!" Behind Carrie, a charismatic older woman climbed the steps of the gazebo, raising her hands for the crowd's attention. She was tall and slender, but age and experienced had etched themselves into her skin. Her face, surely once quite beautiful, still shone with a handsome strength. Her hands, though veined, gestured with power and eloquence. "We welcome all who seek empowerment."

"Oh, hold on a sec." Carrie turned to listen to the woman, almost enraptured.

"For too long, we and our sisters across the world have struggled against the injustice of inequality. Inequality in education. Inequality in the workplace. Inequality in our relationships. And while we have languished as second-class citizens, men have plundered our mother earth, leaving destruction and corruption in their wake."

"Should we be here?" Lucas whispered to Royal. I shot him a small smile.

"It is time for womankind to take back our rights. It is time for us to stand up for our mother earth. It is time for us to reconnect with the first mother. Join us, and embrace the strength of womankind. For we are all her daughters in spirit. Join us on a journey to rediscover the power of Lilith!"

I felt my jaw drop.

"Isn't she awesome?" Carrie turned back to me, beaming. "Hey, I've got to hand more of these out. If you want to come tonight and hear more, just let me know." Carrie hurried off, passing out another handful of flyers to pedestrians who'd stopped to take in the gathering.

"What the—?" Lucas looked at me, his eyes bulging in shock. Cassie and Royal watched the crowd, disbelief painted across their faces.

I looked down at the flyer in my hand. Written across the top, in clear, bold letters, it read, *Help Us Rebuild Her Temple.* It depicted a beautiful woman, with gracefully curved wings arching up behind her. She had a benevolent expression on her face. Beneath the image, was a small caption.

Lilith, mother of storms, fierce protector of planet Earth.

I looked up again. All around me, young women, their faces alight with excitement and enthusiasm, passed out flyers to passing women. And at the heart of it, the charismatic old woman watched it all, eyes full of tender concern.

One thing was for sure; whoever these people were, not one of them had ever met a Daughter of Lilith in the flesh.

4

Lucas, Cassie, Royal, and I crowded onto the couch in the Guard's living room. It sighed in resigned protest. Hale had just left to find Thane and Gretchen.

"Is this a joke?" Dad stared at the flyer in his hands, a dark look gathering on his face.

"I don't think so." I turned to my friends; their eyes mirrored the growing unease I'd felt since we'd fled the gathering in the Plaza.

"I don't think they know what they're saying," Lucas offered.

"While I appreciate you wanting to give them the benefit of the doubt, we must investigate this further before we can dismiss it as simple asinine foolishness," Thane said, sweeping into the room. He plucked the flyer out of Dad's hands. Dad grimaced, but crossed his arms and made no comment.

Ian, Gretchen, Matt, and Hale entered steps behind Thane. Ian joined Thane by the big bay window at the front of the room. They studied the flyer together, muttering observations to one another too quietly for me to make out.

Gretchen glanced at the four of us sitting on the couch, her eyebrows hiking up. "Hey, Cassie. Royal. It might be time for you guys to head on home."

"They know," I said. Gretchen turned to look at me, but it was Hale who spoke first.

"When you say 'they know,' I assume you mean—?"

"You said keeping them in the dark would protect them." Emotion welled inside me, filling my mouth with a bitter taste. "It didn't. Royal was attacked by the incubus. Cassie was at the mission when the Seal was opened. If Karayan hadn't shown up to help me fight, we could have all been killed. I never wanted them to get mixed up in all of this, but the truth is—yes, they know. There's no going back now."

Gretchen tensed. Matt, standing beside her, draped an arm over her shoulder, diffusing her anger. Neither of them looked happy about this.

Hale looked like he wanted to argue, but one glance at Royal silenced him. He fixed me with a look that said, *we'll discuss this later,* then turned toward Ian and Thane. "All right. What are we dealing with here?"

"Having nothing but this flyer to go on?" Ian shrugged. "It appears someone is founding some kind of group in Puerto Escondido based on some pro-feminist myth of Lilith."

"Is this a new thing?" Dad eyed the archivists. "Is there historical precedence for this sort of... group?"

Thane and Ian exchanged a troubled glance.

"There were rumors of Lilith worshippers in ancient times," Ian said, "but there has been no mention of a group celebrating Lilith in modern times, as far as I know." He turned to Thane, who shook his head in agreement.

"What about this Temple," Dad asked. "Does that ring any bells?"

"Could be figurative. Could be literal. No way to tell without some context. We need more information." Thane flipped the flyer over, frustrated.

Dad ran a hand through his hair, a movement I knew all too well; he was deeply troubled. "The Seal was just opened a few weeks ago. This cannot be a coincidence."

"I agree." Hale reached for the flyer and Thane handed it over.

Matt glanced at Hale. "So, why do you think they're here? What do they want?"

"Exactly," Hale muttered. "Exactly what we need to find out."

"Well—" Cassie raised her hand tentatively. The Guard turned to look at her and she licked her lips. "Um, sorry to interrupt, but there is a meeting tonight."

"Okay." Hale pointed at Dad. "Murphy. You and I will go to this meeting and get a lay for the land."

"Right." Dad reached for his coat, ready to leave.

"Point of interest?" Royal raised his hand, too.

"This isn't a classroom," Gretchen snapped. "You don't have to raise your hands. Just spit it out."

"Well, that group passing out flyers was kind of exclusively women." Royal eyed Dad and Hale pointedly. "A couple of big burly guys? I'm just thinking you might stand out."

"He's right." I stood, facing Hale. "I can go."

"I'll go with you," Cassie said, standing beside me. Her eyes gleamed with an eager anticipation.

"You know, actually, I think it might make more sense for Gretchen to back me up," I said. Cassie's face fell. "Just because we've trained together," I added lamely.

"Right." Cassie sat down, staring at her hands in her lap.

"Where is this thing?" Gretchen asked.

Hale glanced back at the flyer. His brows drew together. He flipped the flyer over again, looking for something that wasn't there. "It doesn't say."

"Typical cult behavior," Thane muttered.

"Cult? Really? We're jumping straight to cult?" Dad frowned. Thane shot him a cold glance.

Ian glanced between the two men, and gave Dad a conciliatory smile. "I think what Thane means is simply that this group is operating from a non-traditional—"

"What I mean is this group is acting like a cult," Thane snapped. "They were recruiting members in the Plaza, weren't they? So why pass out flyers without any useful information? Why target the young if not because they're seeking malleable minds?"

"I think he just called you a sucker," Royal murmured to me. That earned a smile from Ian, who did his best to hide the reaction by covering his mouth and giving a fake cough.

Thane's eyebrows twitched, betraying his irritation. "If it looks like a cult, and it acts like a cult..." Thane flicked his gaze back to Dad. "They seem particularly interested in shrouding their meetings in secrecy. I'd be willing to wager only initiates will know where the location is. And since none of us are initiates—"

"Missy's sister," I blurted out. "Carrie. She's the one who gave us the flyer. She said something like, if I wanted to go to the meeting, to let her know."

"So give her a call," Gretchen said.

"I don't have her number." I glanced at Cassie, who was only half listening to the conversation. "Cass? Could you call Missy?"

Cassie startled out of her reverie and stood up, pulling a cell phone out of her pocket. "Yeah. Just a sec." Cassie snatched up a pen and an envelope off the living room coffee table. She walked into the foyer, dialing her phone. The Guard waited in silence as Cassie had a quick conversation with Missy. In less than two minutes she returned with a number written on the back of the envelope.

"Thank you." I dialed the number on my cell. The line rang once, then went directly to voice mail. "Um, Carrie, it's Braedyn. Murphy. I was interested in going to that meeting you talked about, but I don't know where it's going to be. Could you give me a call back when you get this?" I hung up.

Thane grimaced. "If the meeting is tonight, we don't have much time."

"Short of waiting for Carrie to call us back, I'm not sure exactly what we can do," said Dad.

"Get back to the Plaza," Thane growled. "Try to catch her before the end of their little rally."

"Wait." I straightened, remembering Carrie's shirt. "I think she works at the Plaza coffee shop. If the rally's over, we might be able to catch her there before the meeting tonight."

Hale nodded. "Okay. Go. Keep us updated."

"You got it, boss." Gretchen grabbed her jacket from where she'd tossed it over the back of a chair. Matt caught her hand and she turned toward him.

"Be careful."

"It's me," Gretchen said with a winning smile. She turned and strode for the foyer.

"Braedyn." Dad caught my shoulder as I turned to follow Gretchen out. "Reconnaissance only. Keep your head down."

I gave Dad a quick kiss, then hurried after Gretchen.

Gretchen drove us down to Old Town in her ancient little car. It didn't have anywhere near the power my Firebird did, and I found myself twitching with impatience. I had to clasp my hands together to keep my fingers from drumming on the passenger door.

She parked a block away from the Plaza, unwilling to fight for a spot closer to the popular shops. We sprinted into the Plaza, but as soon as we hit the edge of the cobblestone walk I could see the rally had ended.

"The coffee shop," I said, pulling Gretchen along with me. "Maybe Carrie's still at work." Gretchen followed me through the Plaza to the coffee shop. Most of the tables outside were empty now. Even with the patio heaters it was too cold to sit out here comfortably.

But inside, the coffee shop was warm and cozy. We closed the door behind us before the icy evening air could follow us in. The rich aroma of coffee and hot chocolate was as comforting as a blanket. I scanned the shop, looking for Carrie's distinctive strawberry-blond bob.

"Do you see her?" Gretchen—who'd never seen Carrie before—watched me closely.

"No." I turned, making another pass over the faces in the coffee shop. Carrie wasn't behind the coffee bar, not that I could see. And she wasn't sitting at one of the crowded tables, or—

I grabbed Gretchen's arm. "There. Those girls." I indicated a table as discretely as I could. Gretchen glanced over at it. Three college-aged girls were drinking coffee, sitting at a table. "I'm pretty sure they were at the rally, passing out flyers," I whispered.

"Okay. If your friend doesn't show up, we can follow them."

"No need." I spotted Carrie exiting from the back of the coffee shop. She'd changed out of her barista uniform, and was pulling her winter coat on over a cute indigo-blue shirt. She stopped by the table, and one of the other girls stood, embracing her. Carrie held up a finger, gesturing for a second. She pulled a small gadget out of her coat pocket and touched it to the tip of her finger, wincing slightly. *Testing her blood sugar,* I realized. Carrie had been born with diabetes; it was a part of her life but she didn't let it define her. Satisfied with the results, Carrie slipped the gadget back into her pocket and clapped her hands with excitement.

The other girls downed the last of their coffees and gathered their things. I pulled my phone out and sent a quick text to Dad and Hale; *we found them.*

"They're on the move," Gretchen said. "Do your thing."

My phone buzzed. I thumbed it on and read Dad's response: *Be careful.*

I walked after Carrie and her friends as they headed toward the exit. But before they stepped outside, Carrie pulled her phone out of her pocket, frowning. "Hold up, guys," she said. Her friends waited while she retrieved her messages. As she started listening, her eyes landed on my face and lit up. "Hey, Braedyn! Just in time." She held up her phone. "Got your message. Sorry, we're supposed to keep them off while we're working."

"No problem," I said, putting on a smile. "So, can I still come with you?" I looked at the other girls, watching me with a range of expressions from curious to bored to impatient. "I mean, is there going to be room in your car?"

"No car required. We're meeting at a local place. Come on. You can walk with us." Carrie looped her elbow through mine. Her friends took this as the signal to move. We followed them out of the coffee shop into the cold night air. I didn't have to glance over my shoulder to know Gretchen was close behind. "So," Carrie leaned closer to me. "My sister tells me you helped her organize the most successful charity dance in Coronado Prep's history."

"Oh?" I blushed, remembering the Winter Ball I'd "helped" Missy organize. We'd originally planned to host it at the Raven club, but an ancient Lilitu and her army of Thrall had forced a change of plans. "Well, she did most of the work."

"That's not the way Missy tells it." Carrie grinned at me. "So, are you excited?"

"Excited?" I looked at Carrie blankly.

"About the meeting."

"Right, yeah. Yes. Totally excited." I felt myself blushing. "I mean, I didn't hear much in the Plaza, but that lady seemed pretty intense."

"She is." Carrie closed her eyes rapturously. "I first heard Idris speak at college. She was amazing. She's all about helping people define their own roles, never mind what other people think you should be doing. Listening to her talk—it's so liberating."

We crossed the Plaza and headed down one of the cobblestone avenues of Old Town. The girls walked toward a shop. I recognized the place, it was the herbalist's shop where Seth had found some of the harder-to-get-a-hold-of ingredients for the fateful ritual. The owner of the shop stood outside, smiling and waving the girls closer. I ducked my head, hoping she wouldn't recognize me. When we'd shown up to collect the tinctures for the ritual, she'd told us she couldn't sell alcohol to minors. I'd snuck back in, cloaked, and taken them. Whether or not Seth had left the money behind as he'd promised, I was the one who had robbed this lady.

"Upstairs, girls. Enjoy the service." The herbalist waved us past. I shouldn't have worried; she didn't give any of us more than a passing glance.

A small metal staircase climbed the side of the building, leading up to a rooftop patio. Carrie and I followed her friends up the stairs. The patio, though old and in need of some repairs, was gorgeous. Bowls of floating candles edged the patio. Narrow, vine-covered pergolas lined the space, creating the illusion of walls but leaving the center of the patio open. The floor was covered with white- and cream-colored wool blankets, muting the sound of the crowd's footsteps to a whisper. Stars dusted the sky above, crisp and twinkling against the black New Mexico night. The almost-new moon wouldn't rise for hours yet, so there was nothing to compete with the light of the stars.

Young women mingled across the patio, embracing friends and making new acquaintances. But the overall feeling was one of anticipation. Everyone here was waiting.

Carrie gave my hand one last squeeze. "I'm so excited for you. Nothing is going to feel the same after tonight." She waved at some friends and gave me a quick smile. "I've got to sit up front with the others, but I'll catch up with you after the service?"

"Sure." I bit my lip as Carrie headed into the crowd.

"So. This is the super secret Lilith Cult meeting?" Gretchen slid up next to me, frowning. "It feels more like a DIY wedding."

"I'm going to tell Dad we're here." I pulled my cell phone out and started a text, when a wizened hand covered my screen. "Hey—" I looked up, irritated.

Idris smiled at me. "Leave the trappings of this physical world behind you tonight, daughter. They deafen us to the truth of our nature. To hear that truth, you must listen with your full mind and heart."

The assembled young women fell silent, watching Idris with adoration. Blushing hotly, I pocketed my phone. Idris rewarded me with a beautiful smile, and then turned toward the crowd. I felt myself smiling back—until I saw Gretchen eyeing me with disgust.

"They don't call it a cult for nothing," Gretchen murmured in my ear. "Stay sharp, Braedyn. I don't have time to add getting you deprogrammed to my list of things to do this week."

I blushed again, then scowled when Gretchen's lips twitched in amusement.

Idris glided through the gathering. People moved out of her way, reorienting themselves to face her as she took her place at the head of the gathering.

"Good evening," she said, raising her hands. "Open your hearts and feel the power of the first mother rising up through you." Idris raised her arms, lifting her face to the night sky and closing her eyes. The assembled young women mimicked her, lifting their faces and closing their eyes.

Gretchen made a small sound of irritation in the back of her throat. I was the only one close enough to hear. "Well, this was a waste of time. I only see human idiots. No Lilitu present. You?"

I glanced around, searching for the telltale hints of shadow that marked a Lilitu in hiding. Nothing. I shook my head.

"Great. Just a bunch of flower-children playing a delusional game and dragging Lilith's name into it to make it themselves feel mysterious and powerful." Gretchen glanced at her watch. "I'm missing my favorite show for this crap."

"Welcome, daughters." Idris lowered her hands and opened her eyes. As one, the assembled young women sat, cross-legged on the patio. Gretchen and I were forced to stand out or follow suit. Reluctantly, we walked forward to an available spot on the wool blankets and sat.

Before us, Idris stood, surveying the eager faces of the women waiting for her words. The service was about to begin.

The wool blanket was surprisingly warm. It kept the chill from the patio floor at bay, taking my body heat and reflecting it back. It was actually pretty comfortable, sitting like this. I looked up at Idris. Behind her, I had a beautiful view of the night sky. The glow of the candles rose up around us, bathing the patio in a soft glow. The overall effect was peaceful, almost reverential.

"I am Idris, a humble servant of the First Woman, Lilith." Idris bowed her head, looking genuinely deferential. "You are here, because you seek the truth. I am here, to share that truth with you. But we have a greater purpose, and that is to rekindle the spirit of Lilith in our lives, and in the world."

I leaned in, suddenly alert. Beside me, Gretchen's gaze sharpened, too.

"In the beginning, God created Adam and Lilith, giving them equal dominion over this earth. Adam, unsatisfied with his share, took Lilith's also. And for millennia, the Sons of Adam have used and abused this world, mining it for profit, stripping it of its vitality, spoiling its natural beauty. It is time for us to take the world back in her name, to fight the destruction of the established order. This is a mission for young, strong women. Women like you. And if you take up this cause, you will have the strength of Lilith behind you. We will rebuild her Temple together." Idris raised her face to the night sky and breathed in deeply. "This land is sacred," she said. "It has been touched by her hand."

I reached out and gripped Gretchen's hand. Gretchen and I exchanged a tense look. Could Idris be talking about the Seal?

"There is a story, a myth, a legend—it has been told and retold in a thousand varieties, but the heart of the story remains the same. Long ago, the First Woman, banished from her world, struggled day and night until she had fashioned a door that could lead her home."

"I don't believe it," Gretchen whispered. "We have to tell the others."

"And even though she was considered lower than a beggar, lower than a thief in her homeland, the First Woman treasured the time she could spend walking this earth, feeling the sun on her skin, tending the vines." Idris smiled again, and more than one of the young women in her audience sighed wistfully. "So grateful was she, she built a Temple that—according to myth—endures to this day. It became the center of her power—"

A commotion stirred in the heart of the gathering. Idris paused, surprised.

I sought out the source of the disturbance, and my heart leapt into my throat.

"I'm sorry, but no." Amber shrugged off another young woman, trying to silence her.

"What troubles you, daughter?"

"Look, I'm all for saving the trees and crap, but then you had to go and throw Lilith into the mix."

"Lilith is the mother of storms, who—" Idris started.

"Lilith is *evil*." Amber stood, glaring at the gathering. "I get that you want some strong female role model to look up to, but trust me, Lilith is not it."

Idris tilted her head to the side, regarding Amber with sympathy. "You are parroting propaganda spread by established Judeo-Christian hierarchy to frighten—"

"We shouldn't need propaganda to be frightened of Lilith and her daughters," Amber snapped.

Idris didn't look flustered in the least. "You are misinformed, child. I have felt the love of mother Lilith, enfolding me like a blanket of warmth. I know it to be true."

"Well, I've *seen* one of her daughters in the flesh, and I've seen the damage they can do to real people. I think that trumps a hot flash."

Idris's eyes sharpened on Amber. But there was no flash of surprise or shock; instead, Idris seemed… angry. The expression was gone almost as quickly as it had appeared on her face—but once I'd seen it, I suddenly knew. This *priestess,* whatever she might say, knew Lilitu were real. So what was the deal with this charade? Idris smiled, her face once more composed with tender concern.

Gretchen, sitting next to me, was still fixated on Amber. "Who is this girl?" she whispered, leaning closer to me. "I think I love her."

I let out a soft groan. So much for keeping Amber secret from the Guard.

"Given your feelings, perhaps this isn't the right place for you, dear." Idris gestured. I heard a stir of movement at the edges of the room. I turned my head and froze. The hairs along the back of my neck prickled painfully. I grabbed Gretchen's hand. She looked at me sharply then, seeing the look on my face, followed my gaze.

Three forms walked forward from the shadows. To human eyes, they would appear as beautiful young women, not unlike the women assembled here. But Gretchen and I could see beneath their masks, to the black eyes and glittering metallic teeth beneath.

Lilitu.

Gretchen and I watched, helpless, as the Lilitu walked toward Amber.

"You can't seriously believe this stuff?" Amber glanced around at the crowd, irritated. But when she saw the first Lilitu, she stumbled back, falling into the seated crowd. Women lurched to their feet angrily. Amber rose to her feet again, pointing at the Lilitu.

"That's one of them!" Her eyes rolled to the side and she saw another Lilitu. And then she saw me. "You!" Amber's lips peeled back from her teeth in a grimace of pure hatred. "I should have known you'd be here."

"Oh crap." Gretchen grabbed me and pulled me to my feet.

The other Lilitu were already turning toward us. As the closest one turned to face me, I froze. The Lilitu with the long brown hair—the one who'd attacked me at the mission—she was here.

The beautiful demon's face twisted with a growl of rage.

"Meeting's over," Gretchen hissed into my ear. "Run!"

5

The brown-haired Lilitu sliced through the gathering with a dancer's precision, angling her body into a powerful attack. Gretchen and I split, racing for opposite ends of the rooftop patio. Gretchen's dash took her straight for the stairs. She was halfway there before she realized I wasn't close on her heels.

"Braedyn!" Gretchen's voice, thin and high with panic, cut across the murmurs of the crowd. I whipped my head around, taking a mental snapshot. Two of the Lilitu were closing in on Amber. The brown-haired Lilitu was just steps behind me. I grabbed one of the pergola supports as I passed it, running full speed. My momentum spun me around the post but I held on, careening to a stop. The brown-haired Lilitu overshot me, colliding with the roof's railing before she could regain her footing. I had two seconds to decide; escape with Gretchen, or keep the Lilitu from gutting Amber. My eyes sought her out. Amber had given me plenty of reasons to turn my back on her. But Dad had spent his life teaching me compassion and empathy; I couldn't just switch them off when it was inconvenient.

"Damn it, Amber." I pushed off the pergola and darted forward.

The gathering was in chaos. Nearly everyone was on their feet now, pooling into tight groups, unsure what was happening or what they were supposed to do. I dodged through the crowd, reaching Amber as the first Lilitu grabbed hold of her arm.

I tackled Amber, wrenching her free of the Lilitu's grasp. We hit the floor and rolled to the edge of the patio, knocking over two bowls of candles in the process. One of the candles came to rest at the base of a pergola support post. The flame teased the dry stem of a vine that had grown up around it like vertical kindling. Fire licked up the vine, spreading faster than I would have thought possible. Someone screamed, and the crowd scattered, buying us a few moments before the Lilitu could disentangle themselves from the panic.

"Get up!" I rolled to my feet. Amber glared at me, refusing to budge. "Amber, this isn't a game. Get up!" I hauled Amber to her feet beside me. Before the chaos could subside, I willed my shadowy wings to manifest. They snapped around us both, cloaking us from human vision—not that it would do much to protect us from the Lilitu. We were trapped together, tightly bound beneath my wings, like two caterpillars in a cocoon.

"Let me out," Amber hissed, fighting me with all her strength.

"We have to get away from here." I tightened my grip on her arm. The two Lilitu who'd been closing in on Amber broke free from the crowd. Their eyes latched onto us. "Crap." Our path forward was blocked—several women had jumped toward the fire and were trying to beat it out with some of the smaller wool rugs. I cast a quick glance over the side of the building. The drop wasn't welcoming, but it was our best bet.

Amber's eyes bulged. "What are you doing? Braedyn?!"

I looked up at Amber. Whatever she read in my expression freaked her out. She turned, trying to push through my wings to escape.

The Lilitu surged forward, cloaking themselves with their own dark wings.

"Hold on." I grabbed Amber in a bear hug from the back. She sank her teeth into my arm. Shooting pain lanced across my skin, but I didn't release her.

With all the strength I could muster, I kicked us backwards, over the edge of the building. I hit the sturdy awning beneath us back first, feeling a flash of relief when the thick canvas fabric held. Amber crashed down on top of me. My grip weakened, and we rolled apart. Amber grabbed the edge of the awning as she slid over, managing to control her drop the last ten feet to the ground. I wasn't so lucky—still recovering from breaking Amber's fall, I wasn't fast enough to grab the edge of the awning. I slipped off and fell ten feet to the ground, landing on my side on the pavement below. Amber dropped to her feet beside me, eyes blazing with fury and adrenaline. I glanced around. We were alone in the little side street between buildings.

"What the hell is wrong with you?!" She glanced up the side of the building. "I could have died!"

I pushed myself up to my hands and knees, groaning. It didn't feel like anything was broken, but I'd be pretty sore in the morning. I planted one foot on the ground and stood, feeling more than a little wobbly.

Amber scrambled back away from me, alarmed. "Stay away from me."

"Sure. Next time I'll just let the Lilitu kill you."

Amber's eyes narrowed. "I don't know what you're—"

I heard a dull impact on the awning above. The sound sent spikes of fear shooting through me. Amber's gaze lifted. Horror washed the color out of her cheeks. I didn't have time to think things through. I grabbed Amber's arm, propelling her forward.

"Don't look back!" I raced for the main street, hauling Amber with me. At least she wasn't fighting me anymore. We reached the edge of the building and burst out onto the main street. There wasn't much foot traffic at this hour; the streets seemed eerily quiet, save the pounding of our feet as we ran.

One of the other Lilitu rounded the far edge of the herbalist's shop. Her eyes latched onto us and she sprinted forward.

"Move!" I yanked Amber around, changing our trajectory. It cost us too much time. Another Lilitu caught up to us. They were hemming us in. There was only one way to go. I dragged Amber forward, realizing too late that the demons had corralled us into a blind alley.

Amber and I skidded to a stop in the alley.

"What did you do?!" Amber stared at our prison, then ran for the steel door embedded in one wall. She hauled on it, but it didn't budge. She pounded her fists against the metal, desperate for any way out of the trap.

The three Lilitu reached the edge of the alley, walking now. They had all the time in the world, and they knew it.

I shoved Amber behind me and faced the Lilitu, fumbling to pull my daggers out of my deep coat pocket. I felt steadier with the hilts in my hands. The blades gleamed wickedly in the streetlights. Amber made a low growl of fear behind me, but I didn't turn around.

The brown-haired Lilitu walked into the alley, eyeing my daggers with disdain.

"How did you get past the Guard?" I asked, clenching the daggers tighter.

"Is that her?" One of the other Lilitu tilted her head, examining me curiously.

The brown-haired Lilitu glanced back, silencing her comrade with a look.

"How?" I asked again. "We never leave the Seal unguarded. How did you escape?"

Her beautiful lips curved up in a cruel smile. "Stand aside, and I'll tell you." Her eyes slid over my shoulder, fixing on Amber behind me.

"Elyia," one of the other Lilitu said, her voice sharp. The brown-haired Lilitu turned, irritated. "The spotter comes. Be quick."

"Elyia, is it?" I adjusted my stance, ready for a fight. "You and your friends might want to take off before Gretchen gets here. She's having a bad night. She's already missed her favorite TV show. If you're still here when she arrives, she's going to take it out on you."

Elyia's eyes darkened. "I've got a job to do."

I saw her center of balance shift, so I was ready when she rocketed forward. I stabbed out with the first dagger, catching the edge of her shirt. She twisted aside, and the blade tore open a long gash along the side of her shirt, parting the simple cotton with no effort at all. Elyia kicked out, catching my thigh and shoving me back.

I wheeled around, regaining my balance and facing Elyia—but she'd managed to slip behind me, placing me between her and the other two Lilitu.

Amber pressed herself up against the alley wall, sliding back as far as she could from the fight. Her eyes whipped to the mouth of the alley behind me. I saw the urge to run in her face, but she'd never make it past the Lilitu.

"Braedyn, behind you!" Gretchen's voice rang through the alley, half a second before one of the Lilitu gave a horrible shriek. I risked a glance back. Gretchen had sliced a long gash across one Lilitu's arm. The second Lilitu was just steps away from me, her claws extended. Gretchen whipped her arm and I saw something flash in the streetlights. The dull thud of impact stopped the Lilitu cold. She fell, face forward, one of Gretchen's daggers buried to the hilt in the base of her neck.

I spun back for Elyia. She stared at her fallen peer, and when she dragged her gaze up I saw hatred burning in her eyes.

Before I could reach her, Elyia had sprung. She caught Amber by the hair, dragging her away from the wall.

Amber gave a full-throated scream. Elyia backhanded her, sending Amber whimpering to her knees.

"Enough!" I charged. Elyia spun to face me, her human aspect falling away. Dark eyes seemed to draw light in. Her sneer revealed a mouth full of pointed teeth, gleaming weirdly with an almost metallic sheen.

We connected. Elyia's clawed hands fastened around my wrists. I dropped one of my daggers, grabbing Elyia by the collar and trying to pull her closer, trying to leverage my other hand out of her grip.

Another horrible shriek sounded behind us. Elyia's eyes darted over my shoulder. Whatever she saw seemed to stop her cold.

"Another time, sister," she whispered into my ear. And then she kicked me off of her. As I slid into the alley wall, I saw Gretchen racing toward us. The last of the Lilitu had turned tail and fled.

Behind me, Elyia grabbed Amber by the scruff of her jacket and shoved her at Gretchen. Gretchen reached out to catch Amber before she slammed into the alley wall. I rolled to my feet, scrambling to collect my daggers, but by the time I stood, Elyia was gone.

Gretchen examined the shaking Amber quickly. "Are you hurt? Did she claw you anywhere?"

"She's fine," I said, sheathing my daggers.

Amber turned at the sound of my voice. "Why?" Her voice trembled. "You're one of them. Why did they attack you?"

I grimaced. "Because I'm their enemy, Amber."

Amber's eyes were round pools of fear. "What's the Guard?" she asked, her voice barely above a whisper.

I glanced at Gretchen, but any hope I'd had of Gretchen's keeping the Guard's secret faded when I saw her face. Gretchen was eyeing Amber with that same protective attention I'd seen her show Lucas when he was hurt or troubled.

"Don't worry." Gretchen bent to retrieve her dagger from the back of the dead Lilitu's neck. "You're about to find out."

A small fire crackled in the fireplace of the Guard's living room. I huddled next to it, perched glumly on the stone hearth, watching the Guard surround Amber. She sat on the couch, clutching her sweater around herself. Gretchen regarded her, excitement virtually bubbling out of her. Matt hadn't been more than a step away from Gretchen since we'd returned. He watched her closely, smiling at her evident joy.

"She's a spotter." Gretchen's words sent another wave of dread through me. "Can you believe it? Another spotter right here in town and we didn't even know it." Matt gave her shoulder a squeeze. She beamed at him.

Hale and Dad eyed Amber with interest. Recognition flickered across Dad's face. "You go to Coronado Prep."

Amber looked up at him, still shell-shocked from our encounter with the Lilitu. "What?"

"Give her some space, Murphy. We had a rough night." Gretchen sat on the couch beside Amber.

"What happened at the meeting?" Hale lowered himself into one of the armchairs on either side of the couch.

"We might have a bigger problem than we—" but Gretchen stopped as the back door opened.

Lucas and Cassie entered, carrying armfuls of freshly chopped wood for the fire. Lucas froze when he saw Amber, then his eyes sought me out.

"You told them?"

"What?" Gretchen turned to face Lucas, but an instant later she spun on me. Spots of rosy anger colored her cheeks. "You knew? You knew she was a spotter and you didn't tell us?"

"She tried to have Lucas killed," I said.

Gretchen's anger cooled. She turned on Amber, her eyes sharpening. "The car accident?"

Amber's eyes found mine.

"She was trying to send me a message." I kept my voice level, afraid of letting my anger through.

The Guard froze, studying Amber. A sudden chill descended over the room. Matt, still standing beside the couch, eyed Gretchen warily. But Gretchen didn't strike, as I might have anticipated. Instead, she clenched her fists in her lap and took a deep breath.

"You sent those boys after my little brother?" Gretchen stared

Amber down, waiting for a response. I felt a surge of jealousy. Gretchen hadn't known anything about me when we'd met, but she'd assumed I was evil because I had a Lilitu for a mother. Now, faced with the truth of Amber's sociopathic nature, she was still willing to hear Amber's side of the story?

"She's a demon," was all Amber said. "And he was helping her."

Gretchen sat back, troubled.

"Wait, hold on." Lucas dropped the wood he was carrying next to the fireplace. "She as good as admitted to attempted murder, and you're going to let it *slide?*"

Gretchen met Lucas's anger calmly. "She didn't know you were Guard. She didn't know Braedyn was on our side. If I'd been in her shoes—" She let the thought trail off. Lucas and I exchanged a stunned look.

"Spotters," Matt offered, seeing our dismay. "They share more than the ability to see cloaked demons."

His words sent a shock through my system. Of course. Gretchen would know that Amber had lost someone to a demon—it was how spotters gained their abilities in the first place. How could she turn on another who'd experienced the same kind of agony she had when she'd lost Eric to that Lilitu? As painful as it was for me to admit it, spotters shared a bond that wouldn't be easily broken.

Cassie glanced at me, clearly uneasy. I knew she hated conflict; she must be wishing she could melt through the walls right about now. I gestured for her to join me at the hearth. She sat beside me gratefully, stacking her logs next to the fireplace.

"Still," Thane said, glancing toward Lucas and me. "You should have told us what she was as soon as you learned of her abilities."

"You don't want her help," Lucas growled. "Trust me. She's a scorpion."

"Alright. Let's table this for now." Gretchen stood abruptly. She glanced at Amber, clearly conflicted. "Like I said, we had a rough night—"

Out of the corner of my eye, I saw someone entering the living room from the foyer. Karayan, wearing a light grey hoodie for warmth against the cool evening air, eyed Amber with suspicious curiosity.

"*Demon!*" Amber sprang off the couch, pointing straight at Karayan.

Amber's panic flashed through the room like wildfire. The Guard sprang into action, instinct and adrenaline driving them before they had time to think. Karayan's hoodie covered her distinctive honey-blond hair—in the panic of the moment, all the Guard saw was an intruder. Gretchen pulled Amber behind her and drew her daggers in one fluid motion. Hale leapt to his feet, spinning to face the threat with a dagger in each hand—

"Stop!" I was on my feet, but too far away to reach Hale as he stabbed his daggers forward.

Karayan recoiled back into the wall, her wings half-extended in fear. But the look on her face—it was a sort of recognition, like she'd been expecting this for a long time.

Hale recognized her just in time. He adjusted, stabbing his daggers harmlessly into the wall on either side of her—there was no way he could have stopped his own momentum. He stood there, face to face with the breathless Karayan for a long moment, then strained to pull the daggers out of the wall.

"Karayan." Hale lowered his daggers, breathing hard. "I'm sorry. I didn't know it was you."

Karayan, struggling to recover, didn't move for a moment. Her eyes sought me out, and I felt a stab of empathy for her. In that instant, I understood. For one agonizing second, she believed the Guard had turned on her again. After she'd helped me fight Seth, she'd as good as declared her allegiance to the Guard. The Lilitu would never welcome her back. For Karayan, the Guard was her last option. I glanced around the room. No one else seemed to understand her predicament.

Karayan straightened. She forced a smile, shifting her gaze back to Hale. "'Cause all us demons look alike, right?"

Hale gave her a half-smile in return. "I really am sorry."

Karayan shrugged. "If it happens again, don't be surprised if I kick you in the tender bits."

Hale sheathed his daggers with a rueful chuckle. "Fair enough."

"She's one of you, too?" Amber's voice was strained. She eyed the Guardsmen with disdain. "How many demons are you keeping around here?"

"Just these two," Hale said, trying to hide an amused smile.

"That's funny to you?" Amber's eyes narrowed. "One of those *things* killed my boyfriend. And she—" Amber stabbed her finger at me, "she tried to get my friend to kill himself."

Thane stepped forward, raising a hand in a calming gesture. "No one thinks this is funny, child."

"Why are you hanging out with them? You should be fighting them." Amber glanced at Gretchen, looking for an ally. "You saw. There were Lilitu all over that meeting tonight. What are you doing to stop them?"

"Lilitu?" Hale glanced at Gretchen sharply. "Lilitu at the meeting?"

"Three of them," I said. The Guard turned toward me. "One was the Lilitu who attacked me at the mission."

"What?!" Dad stared, stricken. "How did she get past the spotters?" He glanced at Gretchen, who blushed hotly.

"We're spread thin as it is, and with the increased shifts—" Gretchen threw her hands up in the air. "I don't know. Someone must have lost focus."

"Or, we have a bigger problem on our hands," Thane said quietly. "A traitor in our midst." The group turned to look at Thane, unsettled. "Someone who'd choose to look the other way, should a Lilitu attempt to slip out of the mission undetected."

"A spotter?" Gretchen stiffened, pissed. "You're saying you think a spotter—?"

"Or two," Thane said, shrugging. "Spotters aren't supposed to leave their posts. So unless both spotters fell asleep, logic dictates that one or both of the spotters on duty when this Lilitu escaped allowed her to pass without alerting the Guard."

"Logic?" Gretchen's fists balled tightly at her sides. "You can take that logic and shove it up your—"

"We have to consider all scenarios," Hale said, moving toward Gretchen with a conciliatory gesture. "But I agree with you, Gretchen. It's extremely unlikely that a spotter would knowingly allow a Lilitu to escape."

"I find the prospect of an accidental lapse in attention equally troubling," Thane said. "It means that we are vulnerable in ways we have not planned for."

"No," growled Gretchen. "Like I said, it means we are spread too thin." She turned to Amber. "Which is why we need more spotters on the team."

Amber glanced up. "What?"

"You've got a very special talent—" Gretchen started.

"No. No way." Amber's eyes narrowed.

"Sorry?" Gretchen studied Amber's face, confused.

"No way am I joining your little circus. I've got more extracurricular activities than I can handle as it is." Amber pulled a cell phone out of her pocket. "I should be getting home."

"Extracurricular—?" Gretchen's eyes narrowed. "You've seen what kind of damage they can do, and you're willing to just turn a blind eye?"

"I'm seventeen years old," Amber sniffed. "What exactly do you think I can do?"

"You can see them!"

Amber took a step back, startled by the power behind Gretchen's outburst.

"We need spotters." Gretchen grew quiet, but the intensity of her voice sent a shiver across my back. "We can train soldiers. We can teach people how to fight. But only a tiny fraction of humans ever develop the ability to see through a Lilitu's disguise. And without the ability to see the Lilitu, our soldiers are helpless to fight them." Gretchen's voice grew hoarse with emotion. "We need you, Amber."

"I'm sorry." Amber retreated toward the foyer. Hale blocked her path. She glared at him, but her fear was evident in her voice. "I want to go home."

After a moment, Hale moved aside. Amber fled, slamming the front door behind her.

"You let her go?" Gretchen clenched her jaw.

"You heard her, Gretchen. She doesn't want to help." Hale sighed. "And if I'm not mistaken, holding her here against her will is a felony. So until we can change her mind, we have to respect her wishes."

Gretchen let out a growl of frustration. "So this whole night was a disaster!" She threw herself onto the couch.

"How do you figure?" Dad asked.

"Well, our covert surveillance plan is blown," Gretchen muttered. "I think it's safe to say neither Braedyn nor I will be welcome at another one of their meetings."

"We'll have to get another spotter to go," I said.

"Yeah." Gretchen sighed. "Maybe Rhea and June?"

"If we dedicate more spotters to the cult, we'll have to increase shifts for the rest of you," Hale said.

Gretchen glowered at him. "This is just perfect."

"I could go." Cassie stood slowly. "I mean, if most of the people at these meetings are girls anyway, no one would suspect me, right? It sounds like you need all the help you can get."

"No." I caught Cassie's hand. "It's way too dangerous, Cassie. Leave this to the Guard."

"Sorry, kiddo," Dad said, seeing Cassie's disappointment, "but Braedyn's right."

Cassie sat back down, blushing. I tried to catch her eye, but she kept her gaze fixed on her lap.

"I wouldn't turn down anything at this point," Karayan said. "You're going to have to figure out something, and fast. This Cult of Lilith isn't some misguided girl-power fad. Lilitu are involved, and that makes it a serious threat. You still don't know what they're hoping to achieve, and if you can't get a mole into those meetings, you're never going to find out."

Cassie looked up at Karayan with a small smile of gratitude.

"Besides," Karayan added. "Cassie's right. You're going to need all the help you can get."

6

What I wouldn't give for a night of human dreams. To wander once more through the surreal landscapes of my subconscious mind, lost in some random narrative whose logic—upon waking—dissolves in the light of a new day. To be spared, even for a few hours, the anxiety of my waking life, the knowledge of this war.

When I was a little girl, I used to dream of flying. Those dreams were gifts; even if they started out as nightmares where I'd be running from some unseen enemy, they ended up full of joy. Nothing matched the sensation of pure freedom those dreams of flying gave me.

It had been over a year since my Lilitu powers had awakened. One of the side effects? I no longer had dreams, not in the way I used to. Now, I had conscious command of my dreams—whether or not I wanted it. Yes, I could fly in my mind, but it wasn't the same. I knew it was a dream, and that alone killed most of the pleasure of the sensation. My mind couldn't deceive me into believing I had discovered this amazing ability to glide through the skies. I was aware it was simply a trick of my imagination. If I chose not to dream, I could pass the night in empty darkness. Or I could slip into Lucas's dreaming mind and give over control to him, riding the dream almost like a human dream. Almost. Because, again, I was aware of the nature of the dream, even if I wasn't in the driver's seat of my own experience.

Those blissful dreams of flight were lost to me now, and might be forever. How much farther could I stray down the Lilitu path before I'd gone too far to turn back?

I rolled over in bed and looked at my alarm clock. I let out a soft groan when I saw the gleaming green read out: 4:55 AM. Too early to get up for school. And yet I couldn't stand to lay here any longer. I pushed my comforter back, shivering against the February chill in the air. Our automatic thermostat wouldn't adjust the temperature of the house to 68 degrees for another hour. At night, it let the temperature drop to 50 to save energy, which was great—unless you needed to get up. I dressed quickly, pulling on a fleece jacket over my school sweater to battle the crisp morning air.

Heading down the staircase, I saw warm light spilling out of the entrance to the dining room and kitchen. When I reached the foyer, I stepped into the dining room and had a clear view of the kitchen. Dad was sitting at the island, hands cradling a mug of coffee. He looked up as I entered. His eyes, tight with concern, eased when he spotted me. He smiled and patted the stool next to him.

"Couldn't sleep?"

I shook my head and took the stool next to him. "You neither?"

Dad looked back at his mug. "The Lilitu who attacked you, did she give any indication what she wanted? Why she went after you specifically?"

I bit my lip. "I've been thinking about that." I'd had more than enough time since the meeting last week to mull it over. It was almost the only thing I could think about. It was like she *knew* me, but how? "She—it's like she's got something personal against me. But I never saw her before she attacked me at the mission."

"Describe her to me."

"She's got long brown hair. Blue eyes. Slight build, but tall." I looked up, hearing my words. "She looks kind of like me, I guess."

Dad studied me. I could feel his unease.

"Did Hale figure out how she slipped past the Guard?"

"No." Dad's brows drew together, and his hands tightened on the mug. "Thane and Ian are investigating the mission, trying to find an explanation. It's possible the spotters simply missed her." Dad's voice trailed off.

"But you think there's something else going on?"

He nodded slowly. "There've been too many coincidences lately."

"The cult." I felt a sour lump rising in my throat.

"We just don't have enough information about them." Dad took a drink of his coffee.

I caught his hand and gave it a warm squeeze. "We'll get some of the other spotters to infiltrate the next meeting."

"Provided we can find out when and where the next meeting takes place." Dad covered my hand with his, giving me a kind smile, but it was tinged with a deeper concern.

"Dad?" I tried to catch his eye, but he avoided my gaze. "What's wrong?"

"This talk of the Temple. I can't get it out of my head. Whatever this woman, Idris, knows—" Dad sighed. "Well, one thing we can be sure of; she knows we're onto her now. If I had to guess?" He shrugged. "She'll take her meetings underground. I doubt we'll catch her followers passing out flyers around town again. It'll be personal invitation only from now on."

"We still know Carrie."

"But she doesn't know our spotters. It'll take them time to forge a relationship with her, and they'll risk showing their hand if they ask about the Cult directly."

I frowned, unsettled. "So we follow Carrie around the clock. She'll lead us to the next meeting, right?"

"Let's hope so." Dad's gaze turned inward. "The trick will be getting inside the meeting. But Rhea's resourceful. I'm sure she'll figure something out."

"Yeah. Resourceful. Among other things." I heard my voice harden. Dad glanced at me sharply.

"Hale told me about your sparring session with Rhea. Is she still giving you grief?"

"Whatever." I forced a smile, shrugging it off. "It's not like I have to see her very often. And it's not like I have to like her. Let's just hope she can worm her way into the cult."

Dad looped an arm around my shoulders and gave me a warm squeeze. "Right. What do you say I make something interesting for breakfast. Goat cheese and roasted red pepper omelet?"

I leaned into his hug, feeling some of my tension ease. "Sounds awesome."

Dad started puttering around the kitchen, collecting the necessary tools for his culinary creation. As I watched him, I tried to shrug off this feeling of helplessness. Until Ian and Thane figured out how the Lilitu had escaped the mission, until Rhea got an inside line on the Cult, there wasn't much I could do but keep my eyes open and wait.

The sun had done little to warm the day by the time Lucas and I arrived on campus.

"Another Monday," Lucas sighed. I leaned into him. Surprised, Lucas wrapped his arms around me. "What's this for?"

I closed my eyes, drinking in the sensation of his embrace. I felt a stirring through my core; the Lilitu storm was waking. I held it at bay, trying to savor this moment. As the storm twisted inside me, I sighed and pulled back, meeting Lucas's eyes. They looked almost green against the cloudy sky. "Thank you."

Lucas gave me one of his little half-smiles, and I felt my heart flutter in my chest. "You're no end of mystery, Braedyn Murphy."

"We never did finish that dream," I murmured.

Lucas's eyes sharpened on mine. "Does that mean you want to?"

I swallowed. "What I want is for us to be together without fear. Right now—unfortunately—a dream is our best option."

"If you say so."

I looked up at him, surprised by the note of doubt in his voice.

"Missy!" Cassie's clear voice cut across the morning.

I turned and Lucas followed my gaze. We watched as Cassie caught up to Missy on the quad. I couldn't hear their conversation, but Missy looked at Cassie with genuine surprise, then shrugged and wrote something down on a paper for Cassie.

"What do you think she's doing?" I asked.

"I don't know." Lucas frowned, studying Cassie with a speculative look on his face.

Missy gave Cassie a hug and walked off toward North building. Cassie studied the scrap of paper in her hand, lost in thought—until Parker approached.

Even from where we stood, we could hear Cassie's voice, harsh with anger. "Leave me alone, Parker. I told you, I don't want to talk. I don't want to see you. Just leave me alone!"

Parker made a soothing gesture, saying something too quietly for me to make out. Cassie shoved Parker back, growing even angrier.

"That son of a—" I growled, taking a step forward.

First bell rang out, summoning students for the start of the school day. Cassie tucked the paper into her pocket and dashed into North Hall, leaving Parker staring after her.

"What do you think he wanted?" Lucas asked.

Watching her go, I couldn't shake a sinking feeling. "I'll ask her in first period." Lucas and I parted ways, each heading off to class. Cassie and I shared Mr. Landon's history class for first period. I made my way to class, taking my usual seat. Cassie entered a few minutes later, talking on her cell phone.

"Great, thanks so much. I'm really looking forward to it." She hung up, turned her phone off, and took her seat, flushed and smiling.

When she'd gotten settled, I leaned over and caught her eye. "What's going on, Cassie?"

Cassie shot me a sharp look. "It's nothing. Missy was just helping me out with a project I'm thinking about proposing for an independent study," Cassie mumbled.

"No," I said, "I meant with Parker. What did he—" But then I read the guilt in Cassie's eyes. "Independent study?"

"Oh, Parker?" Cassie blushed. "Whatever. It's been the same thing with him for a year now. Like I'm ever going to give him another chance. What does he think I am, an idiot?"

"Cassie?" I leaned closer to her, alarm rising in my chest. "What independent study? What are you talking about?"

"A psychology study," Cassie said, not meeting my eyes.

"Really." I kept my voice level, battling down another swell of anxiety. "I didn't realize you were into psychology. Let me guess; you want to study the dynamics of group behavior within the context of a cult?"

Cassie's eyes cut to my face, as good as admitting her guilt.

"*Cassie.*" I leaned forward, gripping Cassie's arm harder than I meant to. Cassie winced, but I didn't let go. "I told you to leave this alone."

"You also told me we're fighting a war that most people aren't even aware of. That the fate of the world rests in our hands."

"Not *your* hands," I hissed.

"No?" Cassie's eyes flashed. "Are you forgetting what I *saw?* I watched an angel die, Braedyn. And the demon that killed him escaped into another world right in front of my eyes. Through a door—by the way—that could let who knows how many of them back into our world. I know I'm new to this whole thing, but from where I stand it looks like you're *losing* this war. So let me help."

I stared at her, at a loss for words.

"All right, class, let's get started." Mr. Landon entered, heading straight for the whiteboard. "The Battles of Lexington and Concord, April 19, 1775." He started writing on the board. Around us, students bent over their spirals, taking notes.

Cassie stared pointedly at my hand, still clutching her arm.

"You have no idea what you're getting yourself into," I whispered, releasing her arm.

"Guess I'll have to figure it out as I go along." But after a moment, Cassie's anger melted into something new. She glanced at the head of the class. Mr. Landon was still writing names and dates on the whiteboard. Cassie turned back to me, lowering her voice. "Look. It's not like I want to go chasing danger. But put yourself in my shoes. Could you ignore the truth once you'd learned it? Just sit back while your best friend puts her life on the line to save yours over and over again?" Cassie studied me so intensely that I had to look away. Her voice softened. "There's so little I can do to help. I'm not a fighter. I'm not a spotter. But going to a meeting and listening? That's something I *can* do. Please. Let me help."

"Ladies?" Mr. Landon fixed us with a stern look. "If I'm interrupting your conversation, just let me know."

"Sorry, sir." I sat up straighter, blushing.

"Perhaps you can answer a question for me, Ms. Murphy. Who was Thomas Gage?"

"Um…" I struggled to remember the passages I'd read over the weekend. "He headed the British forces garrisoned in Boston."

Mr. Landon nodded, satisfied. "Correct, Ms. Murphy." He turned back to the whiteboard, drawing a quick sketch of New England on the board. I slid down in my chair, still unsettled by my conversation with Cassie. Amber caught my eye. She was glaring at me from her seat across the classroom. I sighed. Cassie was willing to throw herself into this war without any training or skill, but Amber—with her exceptionally rare ability to spot demons through their cloaks—wouldn't lift a finger to help us. I bent over my notes, putting Amber out of my thoughts. I had to figure out a way to keep Cassie safe, and she wasn't making it easy on me.

By lunchtime, I was sick with anxiety. Lucas and Royal met me outside the dining hall. Lucas's eyes narrowed with concern as soon as he spotted me.

"What happened?"

"Cassie got herself invited to a cult meeting."

"What?!" Royal stared, stricken. "When did this happen?"

"This morning." I realized I was chewing my nails to the quick, and lowered my hand.

Lucas's expression darkened. "Okay, so she comes down with a cold and can't make it."

"You too?" Cassie joined us, giving Lucas a pained look.

"Cassie, Braedyn's right." Lucas turned on Cassie. "This is a terrible idea."

"Really?" Cassie crossed her arms. "Because, unless you've read my mind," and here she glared at me, "none of you even knows what my idea is yet."

I glanced at the others. Royal kept his lips firmly sealed. Lucas's expression was grim.

"Why don't you tell us your idea, which just might be a brilliant one, Cassie?" Cassie asked in a lilting voice. "Oh, sure, guys, glad you asked," she answered herself. "Let's grab some lunch and I'll fill you in." Without waiting for a response, Cassie walked into the dining room. Lucas, Royal, and I had no choice but to follow her.

Ten minutes later, we'd collected our food, settled around our usual table, and served ourselves. No one paid much attention to the food; all our eyes were fixed on Cassie.

"So let's hear it." I stabbed a piece of broccoli with my fork. Cassie shifted in her seat, glancing around to make sure no one else was listening.

"Okay," Cassie said quietly. "I talked to Missy, and she says Carrie's clammed up about the meetings."

"Missy's interested in this stuff?" Royal looked surprised. "Seems kind of airy-fairy for her."

"No, Missy thinks the whole thing is stupid," Cassie said. "She attributes Carrie's involvement to some college-girl woman-power kick. Apparently Carrie took some kind of women's studies class last semester and Idris came and spoke. Whatever she said was strong enough to get Carrie to take a semester off from college." Cassie shrugged. "Like I said, Missy thinks she's insane."

"What's the plan, Cassie?" Lucas asked.

"I'm getting to it. Patience." Cassie shot Lucas an irritated glance. "The plan is I go to the meetings, and Braedyn listens in."

Royal shook his head, confused. "If these guys are as paranoid as you think they are, won't they search newcomers for listening devices?"

"Not with a listening device," Cassie said, glancing at me. "She's going to listen *through* me."

I stared at Cassie, surprised.

"Huh." Lucas glanced at me thoughtfully.

Royal looked from Lucas to me. "What am I missing here?"

"Braedyn might be able to make contact with Cassie's mind to see and hear what Cassie sees and hears," Lucas said slowly. "She's done it before."

"But—" I shook my head, trying to process everything. "That was a crisis. I don't know if I can just pop into someone else's mind like that." I snapped my fingers.

"Then we should practice before I go to the meeting," Cassie said.

"Hold on." Royal pushed his plate away. "You can mind-spy on people and I'm just hearing about this now?"

"It's not a skill I've been cultivating," I said sourly. I turned to Cassie. "You're ignoring the very reason I didn't want you involved in this in the first place. You're putting yourself in harm's way."

"Yes, there's some risk," Cassie said, "but there'd be risk for anyone attempting to spy on the Cult, wouldn't there be?"

"The spotters are trained to fight," Lucas reminded her.

"And I'm nothing but a high school junior?"

"I didn't mean it like that," Lucas said.

"Don't you get it? I'm the perfect mole," Cassie insisted. "I don't look like a fighter. I won't ruffle any feathers. I'm just going to listen." Cassie glanced at me. "And if you sense any real danger, you'll know where I am. You can swoop in and save me."

I didn't answer her. Cassie sat back. They all turned toward me, waiting.

"There's one problem with that logic," I said. "If you run up against *real* danger, I might not be fast enough to save you."

"Then let's hope we get what we need quickly." Cassie met my gaze with an intractable gleam in her eyes. I glanced back down at my plate. Cassie was resolved to do this; that much was clear. Which meant, if anything did happen to her at one of those meetings, I'd have a front-row seat to watch my best friend's death.

I stumbled through the rest of the afternoon, feeling off kilter and out of focus. After school, I found myself dragging my feet as I walked to my locker. The halls cleared out around me as students took off to enjoy what was left of their afternoons before heading home for dinner and homework. I pulled a few books out of my locker and loaded them into my school bag before I realized I'd left my English book behind. I headed back to Mr. Avila's classroom. He was already gone. The lights were off, but I spotted my book still sitting on the desk where I'd left it a few minutes before.

I tucked it into my school bag and headed back for the hallway. The sounds of an argument stopped me in my tracks.

"You've got to be freaking kidding me!" Ally's high-pitched voice was strained with anger.

"What am I supposed to do, Ally? I have to get a job." Amber's voice rang through the halls, full of frustration.

"So schedule your burger-flipping for *after* practice!"

"I can't." Amber's tone shifted into bitterness. "My step-mom wants me home every day by six to help with her kid. I have to figure out how to fit the job in between school and—"

"Seriously, Amber? You made a commitment to us."

"If I don't do this, I can't stay at Coronado Prep!"

"Bull crap. We're this close to qualifying for State," Ally snapped. "You're the captain!"

"You'll do just fine without me," Amber said quietly. "You're the one with the gymnastic medals under her belt."

"What is up with you?"

"I told you, it's my step-mom—"

"No. You've been totally weirding out lately. Like, for months."

I glanced out the door.

Amber stared at Ally, looking caught. "It's—I've been dealing with some stuff lately, is all."

Amber looked so lost, I felt an alien twinge of sympathy for her. Before I had time to think it through, I walked into the hall.

Amber and Ally saw me coming and clamped their mouths shut. Ally eyed me with distaste.

"You do realize it's just cheerleading," I said, giving Ally my most disdainful look. "I mean, technically your job entails jumping up and down and hollering for the football team which, correct me if I'm wrong, is what pretty much every spectator is doing, too."

"Excuse me?" Ally's eyes bulged, giving her horse-like face a strained look. "Like you would know anything about the discipline it takes to do what we do." Ally turned her back on me and gave her ponytail a haughty flick. She stabbed Amber in the chest with her index finger. "You know, fine. Deal with your stuff alone. The team and I have way too much to prep for to take on your drama, too. Just don't come crawling back to me in a month, hoping to rejoin the team. You leave now, you're out for good."

Ally stalked off down the hallway.

I turned toward Amber. Her face was a naked mask of pain. "Amber," I started.

She spun on me, eyes flashing. "What the hell are you doing?" she hissed.

I took a step back. "Uh, I was trying to help you."

"Don't. I don't want your help." Amber glared at me for another second. Then she turned and fled down the hall.

Serves me right for trying, I thought. But it wasn't as easy to dismiss the misery on Amber's face. I knew—too well—how fast someone's life could change when Lilitu were involved.

Lucas was waiting for me near my car, concerned. The parking lot had nearly cleared out, but Lucas took one look at my face and sensed I didn't want to talk. We drove home in near-silence. When we parked, I caught his hand and held it for a long moment.

"Thanks for not prying," I said.

Lucas gave my hand a squeeze. "Just let me know if you want to talk. Or study for that Spanish test together."

"That's not a bad idea." I gave him a watery smile. After another moment, I released his hand. We exited my car and walked together toward the Guard's house.

Lucas held the door open for me. We settled down to study at the Guard's large round dining table. It was a vocabulary test, so we spent the first half hour writing words and their definitions on the opposite sides of index cards. As we finished making the cards, I heard the door to the basement open behind us. Sitting where we were, we were hidden from the hallway; they didn't know we were here.

Rhea's voice sent a shock through my body. "I want an answer, Gretchen!"

"Oh, you don't say?" Gretchen's voice was heavily laced with sarcasm. "Would that be why you're hounding my every step?"

"They're all exhausted," Rhea hissed. "You know it as well as I do. How long do you think we can keep this up?"

"As long as we have to," Gretchen answered, her voice hard as nails. "It's what we signed up for. No one promised it'd be easy."

"And when we burn ourselves out? What use will we be to the cause then?"

"Look, what do you want from me?"

"I want the truth. Is there another spotter in town?"

I glanced at Lucas, tension knotting through my back. He looked as disturbed as I felt.

"Yes," Gretchen said, "but she's not interested in joining the Guard."

"Are you kidding me with this shit?" Rhea laughed bitterly. "I don't care if she's not interested. We need her."

"Well, good luck recruiting her."

"Where are you going? We're not finished here!"

We heard a heavy thud, followed by Gretchen's growl of outrage. "Get your hands off of me!"

Lucas and I heard a pounding as someone charged down the stairs from the second story above. "Whoa, whoa! What the hell is going on here?" Hale's voice cut through the scuffle.

"Nothing," Gretchen said, breathing heavily. "Internal spotter disagreement."

"Rhea?" Hale's voice was cold.

"I don't know what's going on here, *sir,*" she practically spit the title out, "but you need to get your people organized. If there's another spotter in town, we need her onboard. I don't care what it takes. We are spread too thin. We're starting to make mistakes—"

I stood, pushing my chair back with a scraping sound. The group in the hall fell silent. I walked to meet them. Rhea's expression darkened when she spotted me.

"Karayan and I can take more shifts," I offered. "We've taken shifts to cover sick spotters before."

"Yes." Hale actually looked relieved. "That's a great idea, Braedyn."

Rhea glared at me, but turned her outrage on Hale. "Seriously? You know of another *human* spotter in town, and you'd rather assign the responsibility to a demon?"

"Rhea, whatever your problem with Braedyn is, get over it." Hale's tone as good as said this discussion was over.

Red splotches of anger bloomed on Rhea's cheeks. "If something goes wrong, it's on you, Hale." Rhea raked her eyes over my body before she snorted her disgust and walked away.

Gretchen's shoulders sagged slightly. She glanced at me, concerned. "Sorry about that. She'll come around."

"Do you really believe that?" I asked.

Gretchen glanced at Hale, conspicuously not answering my question.

"Don't worry about Rhea," Hale said, clapping a hand on my shoulder. "I'll keep her in line. And thanks." He gave me a gentle smile. "For stepping up. Rhea's not wrong. The spotters are stretched too thin right now. Any relief we can give them will go a long way to keeping our forces strong and ready to fight."

"Amen to that," Gretchen said, stretching her shoulders. "And on that note, I need to grab a few Zs. I'm on shift tonight."

Gretchen headed up stairs, giving me a friendly wave goodbye. I smiled back at her, but my thoughts circled around Amber. I didn't want her to have any part of the Guard… but was that really my call?

7

Waiting. I hated waiting, stranded on the sidelines without a sense of which way to turn. A week passed with no news. Cassie heard nothing from Carrie about the meeting. Ian and Thane discovered nothing that would indicate how the Lilitu had slipped past our safety net at the mission. Whatever our enemy was doing, we were blind to it.

To make matters even more awesome, Rhea and the other spotters had started making it clear just exactly how much they didn't want me around. If I showed up for a sparring session in the basement while they were training, they'd clear out wordlessly. If I passed them coming in or going out of the Guard's house, they'd find some way to shoulder me aside "accidentally." And if they spotted me with Lucas, they'd follow us, staring at me with open hostility, doing nothing to disguise the fact that they thought it was insane that Hale allowed me to fraternize with him.

After an excruciatingly long weekend dodging the spotters at the Guard's house, I was more than ready to head back to school. Just the thought of having a day to hang out with Cassie and Royal and Lucas—and no spotters—was enough to lift my spirits.

But when I saw Royal exiting his flashy sports car on Monday morning, all those good feelings evaporated in a flash of panic. He'd been looking tired and sick for weeks now, but something had changed for the worse. His skin was sallow, almost sunken. Dark circles rimmed his bloodshot eyes. His normally artfully tousled brown hair hung limp and dull. *He looks like a corpse,* I thought, immediately chilled by the image.

"Holy crap," Lucas breathed, spotting Royal moments after I had.

"Something's wrong." I grabbed Lucas's hand. We walked together to meet Royal. Cassie was getting out of the passenger side. She looked as worried as I felt, her eyes riveted to Royal as he shouldered his school bag.

Royal saw us coming and forced a smile. It didn't reach his eyes, and after a moment he let it fade. "You look like you've seen a ghost," he said. Even his voice was listless. But the spark of Royal was still there, somewhere deep inside. His eyebrows quirked and he said, pointedly, "come on. You're going to give a guy a complex."

"You feeling okay, man?" Lucas asked gently. "You look like you could use a good night's sleep."

Royal shivered, and a shadow of terror crossed his face. "Pass. I've had more than enough sleep. I just wake up feeling worse than when I went to bed."

The icy prickle of recognition crept over my shoulders. "Royal?" I caught his arm and turned him to face me, trying to keep my voice from exposing the panic that just sent my heart racing. "Have you been dreaming about Seth?"

Royal's face registered shocked surprise. "How did you know that?" he whispered.

"Oh no," Lucas breathed.

I turned abruptly away, afraid of letting the others see the sudden rage blazing inside.

Cassie spoke behind me, suddenly catching on. "You think—you think Seth is visiting his dreams?"

"It would explain why he's so tired after a full night's sleep." Lucas's voice was measured, but I could tell he was shaken, too.

"How?" Fear tinged Royal's voice. "How does that explain anything?"

"Because he's feeding off of your energy while you sleep," I said, turning back around.

"So… exactly how bad is this?" Royal's face drained of the last of his color. "I mean, is he—he can't turn me into a Thrall?"

"Not unless he attacks you again in the physical world," Lucas said.

"These dreams, they—they're really vivid," Royal said, running a shaking hand through his hair.

"But—I have vivid dreams all the time," Cassie said. She glanced from Royal to Lucas and me, her eyes pleading. "How do we know Seth's involved?"

"There's one way to find out." Lucas glanced at me. "Braedyn can search for any sign of Seth, any evidence that he's been messing with Royal's thoughts."

Royal eyed me, uneasy. "And how would she go about doing that?"

"By visiting your dreaming mind." I met Royal's gaze. He licked his lips, his eyes darting to Lucas and Cassie. The bell rang, and the last of the stragglers started heading inside for first period. I caught Royal's hand then. "I promised to keep you safe, Royal. And right now, that means defending your dreams from that psycho creep."

Royal nodded slowly. "Do what you have to do." He gave me a lopsided smile. "Just try not to break anything while you're in there, okay?"

I smiled in return, but as soon as Royal turned away, I let my smile fade. Royal meant nothing to Seth. If he was tormenting my friend, it was about something bigger than exploiting a schoolboy crush for a midnight snack. I'd thought Seth was in our rearview mirror. I'd thought wrong.

When I got home that afternoon, Thane, Ian, and Hale were waiting with Dad in the dining room. Ian and Dad stood as I entered.

"What's this?" I set my book bag down and shrugged out of my overcoat.

"Thane and Ian have a theory. They want to talk with you. Why don't you join us." Dad pulled out an empty chair next to him, making room for me at the dining room table—and ensuring he'd placed himself between the archivists and me. I joined them, eyeing Thane uneasily. He remained seated, eyes tracking my every movement. Beside me, Dad's shoulders were knotted with tension. As closely as Thane watched me, Dad watched Thane.

"What do they think I've done?" I couldn't mask the defensive note in my voice.

"Guilty conscience?" Thane's eyes glittered with malicious amusement.

Since the night of Senoy's death, it was hard for me to be in the same room as Thane. The memory of him raising a sword to strike me down was too fresh. If not for Sansenoy, Thane would have executed me that night. Something Dad wasn't about to forget, either. I felt a swell of gratitude to him for shielding me.

"Braedyn, it's okay," Hale said quickly. "You're not in trouble."

"We've come to ask a favor, child," Ian said, smiling kindly. Thane gave him a sidelong glance. If I had to bet, I'd say this theory was Ian's, not Thane's. "From you and Karayan, actually. Is she here?"

Dad didn't take his eyes off Thane. "Karayan? Could you join us for a moment?"

I heard the door to the guest room open down the hall. In a moment, Karayan emerged. She perched against the entryway to the dining room. She was wearing a pair of snug jeans and a tank top, despite the cool February day. Her hair hung loosely over her shoulders with the same casual elegance that stylists work for hours to achieve for their clients.

Her eyes flicked over the assembled. "You rang?"

"Yes, thank you. Neither we nor the spotters have been able to detect how the Lilitu got past our soldiers," Ian explained. "So Thane and I got to theorizing. Perhaps there are subtleties to the Seal that a Lilitu might pick up on, something not even the spotters can see."

I glanced at Karayan. She met my eyes and shrugged. "Maybe."

"We would like you to return to the mission and do a thorough examination of the Seal and the surrounding area." Ian leaned forward. "Anything you might see could be significant."

"Sure." I glanced at Dad.

He nodded slowly. "I'll come with you."

"I'll come, too," Hale added. "Murphy, can you drive?"

"Let me grab my coat." Dad stood.

"If you find anything, no matter how trivial it seems, please report it," Ian said.

Twenty minutes later, we were heading out of town toward the mission poised in the foothills of the mountains surrounding Puerto Escondido. Karayan and I sat in the back of Dad's SUV while Hale rode shotgun.

Hale glanced back at Karayan. "I appreciate your help."

"I've been waiting for the Guard to give me something useful to do." Karayan gave Hale a winning smile. "I'm not just a pretty face, you know."

Hale's eyes caught on Karayan for a moment. Then he gave her a smile and turned back to face the road. "I suppose it is time you started earning your keep."

"Aye, aye, Captain."

"Technically, it's sergeant." But Hale sounded pleased.

"Hang on, everyone. It's going to get a little bumpy." Dad turned off the main road, slowing as the SUV made the transition from paved to gravel road. The road to the mission cut back and forth in a serpentine path up the side of the mountain, finally opening onto a small plateau.

The mission overlooked the town of Puerto Escondido, and the view was breathtaking. From here, the town looked like the kind of picture you'd see on a Christmas card. Thin trails of wispy smoke rose from a few fireplaces. Snow edged the mountains all around us, frosting the land in a sparkling white. The snow also acted as a natural sound-dampener. Even our breath sounded distinct against the quiet of the landscape. It was overwhelmingly peaceful. But that sense of peace faded as I turned to face the mission. Inside, a door stood open between our world and the world of the Lilitu. That made this ground zero in our war.

We made our way into the stone mission. Somehow it felt even colder inside, although candles lit the space, offering their meager warmth for our comfort. A dozen or so Guardsmen were standing watch, along with two spotters—I think their names were Taryn and Ellie–who gripped their dagger hilts as they eyed us.

"So, how do we do this?" Karayan crossed her arms, turning her back on the spotters nonchalantly.

"Let's split up." Dad scanned the sanctuary. "Braedyn and I will search inside. You and Hale can check the perimeter of the mission. It's possible the Lilitu slipped our net by finding a way outside that we missed."

Karayan and Hale exchanged glances. "Okay by me," Karayan said.

Hale turned and gestured back at the large oak doors. "After you." They walked back out into the cold afternoon.

Dad and I approached the Seal cautiously. We didn't need to bother; the Seal was as active as a lump of dirt on the side of the road. I could sense the shimmering veil separating this side from the Lilitu side, but there were no eyes watching us this time. I put a foot on the

Seal.

"Whoa—" I started. Dad grabbed my hand and pulled me back. I leapt off the Seal, clinging to his arm, scared. "What? What did you see?!"

The Guardsmen were by our side in two seconds, weapons drawn.

"Sorry." Dad released me, turning to face the Guardsmen. "Sorry, my mistake. Stand down. False alarm."

The Guardsmen withdrew slowly, eyeing us with concern. I turned to face Dad, lowering my voice. "False alarm?"

"You sounded alarmed. I overreacted." He eyed the Seal. "I don't love the idea of you touching that thing."

"Okay, I'll choose my words more carefully from now on." I turned back to the Seal. "I was going to say the last time I stepped on the Seal, there was this draw, like the Seal was trying to pull me in."

"Really?" Dad's jaw tightened. "And you were going to tell me this when, exactly?"

I felt my cheeks growing warm. "Sorry."

Dad sighed. It looked like he wanted to say more, but he turned back to the Seal. "And this time?"

"This time I didn't feel anything."

"Still. Don't let your guard down." Dad's hand strayed to the hilts of his daggers. "It could be a trap."

We edged closer to the Seal, and started our examination. It was a long process. By the time I'd made it around the large, circular stone, the sun had long since set in the west. Karayan and Hale returned from their sweep of the perimeter, and together we combed over every last inch of the sanctuary. All to no avail.

"Well, Sarge, I think you're going to have to find some other way for me to prove my worth." Karayan stretched, arching her back in a graceful curve. "This appears to be a dead end, and while I don't need my beauty sleep, I'm afraid the same can't be said for you."

"Flattery will get you nowhere." Hale clapped a hand on Karayan's back. "And don't worry, this is just the first in a long list of fruitless tasks I've got planned for you."

Karayan grinned in response. It was such a genuine look of happiness I felt my breath catch. No one else seemed to notice the change in Karayan.

Hale turned to Dad. "We should call it for tonight."

Dad shrugged, then gave Hale a half-smile. "You *could* use some beauty sleep."

"No lip from you," Hale said. "I'm still your superior officer."

Dad chuckled, and we headed back to the SUV. The drive home was strangely light-hearted, considering the complete failure of our mission. Hale and Dad ribbed each other, and Karayan got in a few sizzling quips—at Hale's expense—that made Dad laugh out loud.

When we pulled up outside our house, everyone piled out of the SUV, still chuckling. Thane was waiting on our front porch. Hale helped Karayan down from the back seat.

"Careful, soldier boy," Karayan said, grinning. "Your chivalry is showing."

"What did you find?" Thane's stern voice cut through our cheer as effectively as a knife. He glared his suspicion at Karayan.

Dad, sensing the tension, cleared his throat. "Nothing, Thane. We searched inside and out. No trace of anything usual."

Thane's eyes returned to Hale. Under his glare, Hale frowned. Thane's eyes narrowed even farther. "I wonder," he mused quietly, "if your full attention was on the task at hand?"

Hale stiffened. I saw a muscle in his jaw jump, betraying his anger.

"We did what you asked, Thane," Dad said. "Now if you don't mind, I think we all could use some rest." Dad gestured for Karayan and me to join him. I hurried to his side, giving Thane a wide berth. Karayan hesitated, glancing at Hale as though she wanted to say something, but then she dropped her head and followed us onto the porch.

Thane strode away from the house. "Hale. A word, if you don't mind."

Hale's eyes burned, but he turned his back on us and followed Thane into the Guard's house without complaint.

Dad opened the door behind us. Karayan fled inside, disappearing into her bedroom before either Dad or I could talk to her. Dad gave me a searching look. I shrugged my shoulders.

"Okay, kiddo." Dad gave me a kiss on the forehead. "Get some rest. Things will look brighter in the morning."

I nodded and headed upstairs. I might be going to bed, but I wasn't counting on getting too much rest.

The vast field of crimson roses shivered in the breeze. I took a deep breath, willing my thoughts to settle. As I gained control over my fear, the wind—spawned by my own unease—died down.

My dream garden. It used to be a place for me to center myself. My own private bubble in the infinite, universal dream world that all living creatures shared. No longer. The roses—once a gleaming white, now that fiery red—were a reminder of the harm I had done to others—a reminder of the stain on my soul.

What scared me most about them was the newest change; the line of black that edged the top of each soft petal. They had changed from white to red the same way, starting with a small stain that spread over the face of each petal, until it devoured every last glimmer of white.

If this was some kind of warning, some kind of visual measure of how far I'd strayed down the Lilitu path, then this is how I would know when I'd passed the point of no return—when the black had consumed the last dregs of red.

I turned my thoughts away from the roses. Folding myself into a cross-legged position, I placed one hand onto the dirt before me. As I touched this illusion of earth, my senses expanded. I could feel the bubble of this dream floating in the vastness. What I needed now was to find Royal's sleeping mind.

A pool of silvery liquid grew before me; a window into the larger dream world beyond the walls of my sanctuary. I concentrated on Royal—not the sickly boy from the past few weeks, but the Royal I'd know since we were in elementary school, the snarky, witty, loyal friend I was determined to protect.

A glimmering spark ascended from the silvery pool, rising to greet me. I closed my hand around it, and felt Royal's presence. With the slightest shift, I was inside his dream.

Royal was wandering through what appeared to be an abandoned mansion, looking for something. The tension was almost palpable. A nightmare, then. Well. I could do something about that.

"Royal." I put my hand on his shoulder.

He spun, eyes rolling with terror. "Braedyn?! What are you doing here? Did you see him?"

I felt my breath catch in my throat. "Who, Royal? Who are you looking for?"

Royal glanced around, as if unsure himself. "I thought I saw—someone was here." He looked at me, pleading with his eyes. "Don't leave me?"

"Royal. It's okay." I faced him directly, catching his face in my hands. His eyes locked onto my face. "This is a dream."

Confusion rolled over his features. But then the first flicker of recognition struck him. "Braedyn?" Royal glanced around. The world around us flickered—and then Royal himself started to fade.

"Stay with me, Royal," I said. Without the skills of a lucid dreamer, like Lucas, most people wake up as soon as they realize they're dreaming. But in order for me to search Royal's dream, he needed to be here. I caught his hand, willing him to fight the urge to wake up.

Royal's form solidified, even as the last traces of his dream-mansion vanished. We stood in a uniformly grey space, like a theater stage without a set.

Royal let out a sharp breath. "You did it. I can't believe it. You're actually in my dream." Royal looked around, more curious than afraid. "So, what's with the grey?"

"You tell me." I released Royal's hand. "This is your dream."

Royal shivered at my words, and something moved in the darkness at the edge of our space. I turned, creeped out. It was like another dream was trying to take shape, but he was fighting it.

"Royal, if I'm going to help you, you have to show me these dreams you've been having."

"You want a guided tour of my nightmares?" Royal's lips were pressed tightly together. "That's nice and horrible."

"I'm here with you," I said, making my voice as soothing as I could. "I won't let anything bad happen to you."

Royal closed his eyes and took a deep breath. "Fine. Welcome to Royal's House Of Horrors."

Royal opened his eyes. The world of his dream shifted, snapping into focus. I looked around. It could have been one of the hiking trails that laced the hills behind Royal's house, except everything here was leeched of color. I was reminded of a charcoal drawing—a nightmarish one. Skeletal trees stood out against a pale grey sky. It was surreally quiet.

"This is where he meets you?" I asked, whispering in spite of myself.

Royal nodded. "Is he here?"

"I don't think so." I tried to muster some strength in my voice. I gave Royal a smile. He glanced at me, but didn't return it.

"That's not exactly encouraging."

"Let me look around." I turned my feet down the path and started walking. Royal shadowed me closely, so closely I could feel his dream aspect breathing down my neck. We walked for close to an hour. The path kept winding through the landscape, like it was on an infinite loop. More than once I thought we'd crossed the same tree, but they all looked so similar I couldn't tell.

As I was getting ready to stop the search, frustrated at our lack of progress, I stopped.

Something small and white was hanging from one of the grey trees. It looked almost like a bone, but as I drew closer I recognized it.

My blood froze in my veins. I pulled the scroll off the tree. Like the scroll I'd once found in my own dream, this one was tied with a satiny ribbon that fell away as I touched it. I unrolled the scroll and found the message he'd left for me.

Careful, Braedyn. I know your soft spots.

Seth had been here.

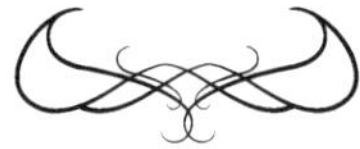

I bolted awake, covered in a thin sheen of sweat. My suspicions were correct. Seth was back.

"No. No!" Grief, anger, and—worst of all—guilt crashed through me. Seth was targeting Royal. He'd been torturing Royal in his dreams for weeks and I'd done nothing to stop it. I suddenly felt the depth and breadth of my helplessness. I could talk as big as I wanted; that didn't mean I was prepared to go head to head with the incubus who'd wormed his way into the lives of my friends. I'd promised Royal I could protect him. But how? After the intimate night they'd shared, Seth had a very real grip on Royal. I couldn't break that connection—short of finding and killing Seth.

I heard a thump down the hall, then Dad threw my bedroom door open. He flipped the switch on my wall. We both recoiled from the sudden blaze of light.

"Braedyn?!" His eyes were bleary but wide with panic.

"Dad. *Dad.*" But the words stuck in my throat.

Dad rushed forward and enfolded me in his arms. At his touch, the dam within me broke. Hot tears flooded my eyes. I clung to him, my body shaking with grief and shame.

"Shh." He ran a hand over my hair, the same way he'd done when I'd skinned my knee or gotten into a fight with a friend as a little girl. After many long moments, I managed to quell my tears.

I pulled back from his embrace. Dad handed me a Kleenex. That's when I saw Karayan, standing in the doorway to my room, unsure what to do. She saw me looking at her. "What happened?" Her voice resonated with concern.

I had to take another shaky breath before I could speak. "It's Seth."

Dad sat back, his eyes suddenly hard. "What did he do to you?"

"Nothing." A surge of nausea rose in my throat. "It's Royal he's been hurting."

"Oh, Braedyn." Dad clasped my hand. Mirrored in his eyes, I saw the same helplessness I felt.

"He's back, huh?" Karayan leaned against my doorjamb, lost in thought. "So what's that little weasel planning?"

"I don't know," I whispered.

"Too many coincidences." Dad looked haunted.

"You think he could be involved with the cult?" I stared at Dad, trying to see how the pieces fit together.

"I'd be willing to bet the answer to that question is 'yes'," said Karayan.

Dad stood abruptly, pacing out his frustration. "We have to get someone inside that cult. Maybe we can recruit this Carrie." He looked at me. "You know her. What would she need to hear to convince her to help us?"

I shook my head slowly. "She left college to follow Idris," I said. "I think she's pretty committed to whatever it is she thinks they're doing."

"We have to try." Dad ran a hand through his hair.

I bit my lip. Karayan, watching from across the room, saw the gesture. She stared at me, as if she knew I was hiding something. I sighed.

"There might be another way," I said.

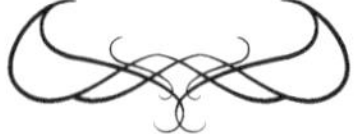

It was settled at a meeting of the Guard leadership the next morning. Cassie—until we found a better alternative—would be our mole. Hale told me to bring her around after school. If she was going to be spying for us, he wanted to make sure she had at least some basic self-defense training.

"Yes!" Cassie cheered when I told her Hale's plan. "So awesome."

"This does not make me think you're taking the whole life-threatening-situation thing seriously." I crossed my arms, frowning.

Cassie tilted her head to one side and gave me a smile. "I'm just excited you're letting me help, that's all."

While Cassie was eager to begin her new duties for the Guard, I was less than enthusiastic about starting mine.

Hale had finally put Karayan and me on the rotation for guard duty at the mission. Friday night was my first shift. Dad had argued that if I were going to take a night shift, it had to be at the beginning of the weekend so I'd have time to recover before school on Monday. So, when Friday rolled around, I found myself driving out of town, blasting the Firebird's radio in an effort to give myself the energy I'd need for the long night ahead.

Only, when I pulled up to the mission, Rhea was standing at the doors, arms crossed, fighting with Hale. Hale looked up as I got out of my car. I thought I saw him wince. Rhea glared at me, but turned back to Hale, defiant.

"No way, Hale. Find someone else."

"It's not up for discussion," growled Hale. "This is your shift. I am your commanding officer."

"What are you going to do? Place me under house arrest?" Rhea's eyes flashed. "You need me, Hale."

Hale grit his teeth. I got the distinct impression he was battling the urge to throttle her. "Yes. I need you. Just like I need Braedyn. And I need you to learn to work together."

Rhea cast her eyes my way again, her lips peeling back in a thin sneer. "I can't make this any clearer, Hale. I don't trust them. No matter what you or the others say. She is a demon. You want her help so bad? Let's see how she does guarding the Seal on her own."

Rhea pushed past Hale and stormed toward a little two-seater parked in front of the mission.

"Rhea!" Hale turned—which is when he spotted the Guardsmen, edging out of the mission to watch the fight.

The soldiers looked more than a little uneasy. More than one of them glanced at me with suspicion. Matt, standing among them, wore an expression of alarm. Hale saw it, and seemed to reevaluate the situation. Instead of fighting Rhea, he pulled out his cell phone and dialed.

"Murphy? No, she's fine, she just got here." Hale caught my eye and gave me a small smile. "I'm calling about Karayan. Could you send her over? I'm having… personnel issues with the spotters. I think it might make more sense to keep Karayan and Braedyn together on shifts, instead of trying to mix things up. At least for a little while." Hale nodded, then sighed. "Thanks, Murphy. We'll be waiting."

Rhea's car peeled out of the mission, kicking up a shower of gravel and dust. I threw up a hand to block my eyes, and in a few moments the sound of her engine gunning receded into the distance.

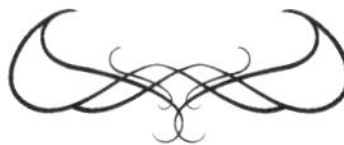

Hale turned back to the other Guardsmen. "We're fine. Replacement's on her way."

"Okay guys, let's get back to our posts," Matt said. As the Guardsmen turned back to the mission, Matt met my eyes and gave me a small nod—a gesture of solidarity. I smiled, warmed.

Though some of the Guardsmen looked like they wanted to argue—and still others threw me one last suspicious look—they all melted back into the Sanctuary.

Hale gestured me forward. "Sorry about that. I knew Rhea was hotheaded, but I didn't think she'd risk a mission over this."

"It's okay." I shrugged. What else could I say? It wasn't like we could fire her or kick her out of the club.

He studied me closely, then dropped a hand onto my shoulder. "Don't let her into your head, Braedyn. You just keep being you. No one can serve beside you for long without seeing the goodness in your heart. You're one of us. No question."

"Thanks." I gave him a genuine smile, touched. Hale clapped me on the shoulder once more, then gestured to the mission.

"We should get in there. Can't leave the gate to hell unguarded."

"Right." I hurried inside the mission.

The evening was about as thrilling as you might imagine sitting and staring at a big rock would be.

Karayan joined us about 30 minutes after I'd arrived. She and I took up our posts, facing the Seal. It was quiet, tedious work. Hale came by a few hours later to join us while the majority of the other Guardsmen left to do a quick patrol of the surrounding area.

"Thane just called. He's suggesting we station one of you in the balcony to keep a bird's eye view on the Seal." Hale shrugged. "Not a bad idea. Any takers?"

"I'll do it," I said. I liked it up there. Lucas and I had stumbled onto the secret balcony this past fall. It was cramped, but kind of cozy. Anyway, it'd be a nice change after the last few hours of sitting and staring at the Seal from ground level.

When the others returned, I headed up to the balcony. From here, I had a perfect view of the Seal. Of course. The monks who'd built this sanctuary on top of the Seal must have planned a variety of ways to watch and defend against Lilitu attempting to cross over. I let my mind wander, picturing what it must have been like all those long centuries ago. Who were the monks who'd stood guard where I am right now? Would they ever have guessed a Lilitu would one day take up their fight?

The hours stretched slowly out. I found myself starting to nod and jerked to my feet. No way was I going to fall asleep on the job.

I heard something below, a soft sound, almost like a giggle. I looked down. Hale and Karayan stood directly below, leaning against a column—the column that concealed the staircase to get up here, actually—and staring at the Seal.

I couldn't see much more than the tops of their heads, but I could hear them very clearly.

"Tell me more," Karayan whispered, her voice warm with amusement. "I'm picturing you line dancing in some bar in Texas."

"Don't knock the line dancing," Hale murmured in response. "I charmed many a lady with those fancy boots."

Karayan giggled softly again. I stared, feeling a prickle of alarm trickling down my arms.

"I don't suppose *you* ever had to take any jobs you're too ashamed to mention in the light of day?" Hale asked.

Karayan cocked her head to one side. "Well, there was this one thing. My first job, actually, after I left—" but then her voice faltered. She cleared her throat and continued. "I got this gig serving drinks for a high-end caterer. They did all these crazy themed parties, stuck us in costumes, sent us out with trays of booze to get drunk old men even drunker. So gross."

"No way."

"Oh yeah. I drew the line when they wanted to stuff me in a micro-mini baby doll costume for some corporate Christmas party. Like I was some fantasy toy. No thanks. I didn't want to risk getting unwrapped."

Hale glanced at Karayan. "You didn't…?"

"What, prey on those drunk bankers? Eww." Karayan laughed, but this time it was tinged with that old bitterness. "Believe it or not, I actually tried the avoid-temptation school of thought for years after I left the Guard. Guess Thane beat that lesson into my subconscious pretty good. Whatever. I never even kissed a guy until I was 23 years old. Once I had a taste, though—" Karayan shrugged. "It seemed a whole lot easier to just charm and disarm the guys when I needed something to eat or a place to stay."

"Oh." Hale's voice hardened and he turned back to the Seal.

Karayan glanced at him quickly, then her shoulders seemed to slump. "I had a code you know," she said. From where I sat, she sounded almost wistful. "Never sleep with a guy more than once. I knew it'd hurt them, but I also knew they'd recover."

Hale turned back to Karayan. "But you broke your code."

"Once."

I stared, stunned. Derek? Derek was the only Thrall she'd ever turned? Doubt rolled through my thoughts. It seemed so incredibly unlikely. Was this just some angle she was playing?

Hale seemed to share my doubts. "So you're just a little bad, is that what you're saying?" he asked, almost gently.

Karayan shook her head, meeting Hale's gaze. "No. What I did to

Derek, that was awful. But it's not the worst thing I've done. Just the worst *Lilitu* thing I've done."

"I don't understand."

Karayan sighed. "I know."

Before Hale could ask what she meant, another Guardsman approached him. "Hale. Time for rounds."

"Right." Hale turned and looked up toward the balcony. I jerked back, trying to hide the fact that I'd totally been eavesdropping on them. "Braedyn, why don't you come down, watch the Seal with Karayan while we do rounds."

I hurried down the hidden staircase, taking care with my steps. It'd be a nasty fall if I tripped over my feet in the tight spiral. When I reached the bottom of the staircase, Hale and the others were already leaving the mission.

I spotted Karayan, who was staring at the Seal with a faraway look in her eyes.

"What are you doing?" I asked, when I was sure none of the remaining Guardsmen were close enough to hear us.

"What do you mean?"

"You and Hale. What was that, a date?"

Karayan's cheeks flushed. "Don't be ridiculous."

"Come on," I said. "You're going to tell me you two weren't flirting with each other?"

"What? No." Karayan shrugged, blowing this off. "We were just talking."

"Really? 'Cause from where I was sitting, it sounded more like a Class A over share."

Karayan faced me, suddenly defensive. "Okay, Little Miss Bit, what exactly are you saying?"

"I just want you to be careful," I said, trying to soften my tone. "I'm worried. It's been a long time since you've had any real connection with a guy and Hale—" I looked over my shoulder, double checking that we were alone. "I don't want you to get carried away and hurt him."

"Wow." Karayan shook her head, turning back to watch the Seal. "I find it particularly choice that *you're* lecturing *me,* given you're the one with the boyfriend."

"Karayan—" I started.

"Seriously? You've made your point."

"No, Karayan, look!" I pointed at the Seal. Something was happening. The twining ribbons of shadow I'd seen the night the Seal opened seemed to shimmer over the Seal, rotating around one another with greater power than before.

"Do you feel that?" Karayan took two steps closer to the Seal.

"Careful!" I grabbed Karayan's arm as her foot contacted with the Seal. The power of the invisible vortex pulled Karayan's foot out from under her. If she hadn't been holding my hand, she might have been swept into the heart of the Seal.

As it was, she clawed onto my arm and screamed bloody murder. Guardsmen came running, weapons at the ready.

Hale and the others burst through the mission's doors as I dragged Karayan back from the Seal. We stared at the stone, but the twining shadows were already subsiding.

"What the hell was that?!" Karayan stood shakily, eyes glued to the Seal.

"I don't know. But whatever it was, it looks like it's over." I glanced at Karayan. She met my gaze with an expression of fear that was all too familiar.

"Okay." Hale gestured to groups of Guardsmen. "I want a tighter perimeter around the Seal for the duration of our shift. Weapons at the ready." The Guardsmen hurried to obey, taking their positions with daggers in hand. Hale glanced at us. "We need our bird's eye spotter."

"I'll go," Karayan said.

"Oh." Hale blinked, surprised. "Right. Just, let us know if you see anything."

"Yeah. This shift can't end soon enough." Karayan eyed me coolly and turned for the hidden staircase leading up to the balcony above.

I took her place, drawing my own daggers. Hale risked one more glance after Karayan, not quite managing to hide his disappointment.

I clenched my teeth together. *What do you know,* I told myself bitterly. *Rhea is right. We do need more spotters.*

Because leaving Karayan and Hale alone together on another shift would be a recipe for disaster.

8

Finally, as March rolled over the town with its rainstorms and temperature swings, we got some news.

"This is it!" Cassie bounded over to my locker, leaning in close. She dropped her voice, grinning. "Missy just told me there's a cult meeting tonight. I'm going to James Bond the heck out of this thing."

In an instant, I forgot all about the books I was collecting for first period. "Cass."

"Oh come on. What's that look for?" Cassie leaned back against the adjacent locker door, crossing her arms. "I know the rules. I'm going to listen, keep my head down, and if I sense any trouble, I'm going to slip away. Easy peasy."

I shook my head, frustrated.

"You're the one who convinced the Guard to let me try it," Cassie said, exasperated.

"Doesn't mean I can't still hate the idea." I pulled a textbook and my history spiral out of my locker, closing and locking the door.

"You're a complicated girl. Believe me, I get it." Cassie gave me a smile, trying to win one in response. "Come on. Don't you trust me, even just a little bit?"

"You're not the one I'm worried about." But, whether or not I liked this idea, Cassie was the best chance we had of getting eyes on the cult. "I just wish you weren't so excited about walking into the lion's den, that's all."

"Wow. You're like another mom lately. Come on. We're going to be late for class." Cassie looped her elbow through mine. But as we approached the door to first period, I spotted Amber. She was staring into a compact, slicking some lip balm on before class.

I felt for the letter in my pocket—it was still there. Hale had drafted it in five minutes this morning, almost as soon as I'd proposed my plan to him. I'd known the Guard was desperate, but I hadn't realized the resources they had to work with until I'd asked. And yet, even though I'd set this whole thing in motion, I hesitated. Once I made the offer, there'd be no taking it back. I sighed.

"I'll meet you inside," I said. Cassie followed my gaze and saw Amber. She eyed me with uncertainty. "Go on. I just need a minute."

Cassie shrugged. "Okay. But if she attacks, take off the earrings." Cassie ducked into class at the same time Amber snapped her compact shut.

I took a deep breath and approached her. Amber looked up, her expression hardening as she saw me.

"What do you want?"

"I want to offer you a job, Amber." I pulled the letter out of my pocket and handed it to her.

Amber eyed me suspiciously. "What's that?"

"Just read it." Hearing the edge to my voice, I tried again. "Please."

Amber took the letter, searching my face for a long moment before she opened it and started to read. Her expression changed from hostile to surprised. When she finished reading she looked up. "Is this for real?"

"Yes."

"You're telling me the Guard will cover my tuition. All of it."

"Until the day you graduate," I said.

"*If* I work for them."

"That is typically how the whole job thing works," I said. "Compensation for services rendered."

"And what exactly would those services be?" Amber's eyes narrowed, suspicion bleeding through her features once more.

"Train with the spotters. Hone your abilities. Learn how to fight."

"You mean, learn how to fight demons like you?"

I felt my shoulders stiffen, but I didn't take her bait. "I told them about your schedule limitations. Hale would like you to train for two hours every day after school. That should give you time for cheerleading, and still get you home before your step-mom blows a gasket."

"You did this?" Amber examined the letter in her hands again.

After a long moment, she looked up. "But… you hate me."

I shrugged, giving her a small smile. "You're not my favorite person, no."

"Then why help me?"

"I'm helping the *Guard*." I crossed my arms. "So that's the job. Are you interested or not?"

The bell rang, announcing the official start of school.

Amber glanced at the classroom door behind me. After a moment she met my eyes. "I'll consider it."

Amber brushed past me, but before she entered the class she shot me one last, considering look. I let out the breath I'd been holding. Whatever happened now, at least I'd done my part.

Cassie's excitement grew over the course of the day. At lunch, we filled Lucas and Royal in about the cult meeting scheduled for that night.

Royal glanced at me, uneasy. "And you're sure you can monitor her thoughts?"

"Well, we haven't exactly tried it yet," I bit my lip, "but I think so."

"Maybe you should do a dry run," Lucas said.

"Good idea." Cassie gave me an encouraging smile. "Library? After last period?"

I nodded. Sensing my unease, Lucas caught my hand and gave it a squeeze.

"It's going to be okay," he said. "We'll be as close to the meeting as we can get without being spotted."

Royal nodded his agreement.

Afternoon classes passed more quickly than usual. Minutes seemed to vanish as if by magic. By the time last bell rang, I was frazzled and on edge. I dumped my books in my locker and hurried to meet the others in the library.

"So what should I do?" Cassie asked, when we'd settled into one of the private study rooms. Royal and Lucas turned to look at me, waiting for my answer.

"Um…" I glanced out the small window in the study room's door.

"Maybe wander around the library. I just want to make sure I can find your mind if I can't see you."

"Sure thing." Cassie popped up and headed out the door. It closed behind her with a click. I took a deep breath, trying to center my thoughts.

Royal glanced at Lucas. "Should we be here for this?" he whispered.

"I don't know," Lucas whispered back. "I don't know what she needs."

"She needs quiet," I said, giving them a sharp look.

Royal and Lucas clammed up.

I closed my eyes. As I focused on it, I could sense the dream world in the background of my conscious thought, permeating everything around us. I let my mind venture out, aware of my body still sitting in the quiet study room. My consciousness passed through the door, out onto the library's main floor. I stared, surprised. Everywhere around me, books shimmered with a buzzing energy. Other objects—the chairs, the tables, the shelves—they had no inner life. But the books… each one seemed to vibrate with its own distinct energy.

I moved closer to a shelf—when a student walked through the space my consciousness was occupying. I caught a swirl of thoughts, something about a girl he liked, and then he was gone. I gave myself a mental shake. *Explore later. We don't have time to waste.*

Centering my thoughts once more, I focused on Cassie. I held the picture of her in my mind, embracing all that made Cassie *Cassie;* her quirky sense of style, her optimism, her genuine spirit. It was as if a beacon lit in my peripheral vision. I felt myself turn toward it and the room started to rush past me—

And I was suddenly in Cassie's mind, watching her hand as it trailed over a row of books. Through Cassie's eyes, the books were just books; they'd lost their strange energy. Abruptly, Cassie froze.

"Braedyn? I think I can feel you," she whispered. She pulled a book off the shelf at random. "Let's try an experiment." Cassie lowered her eyes to the book and read a passage. It was a biology textbook, and she'd picked a page about cell division. She read the paragraph twice, and then put the book away.

I rode like a passenger in her mind as Cassie bounded back to the private study room. She opened the door and I saw Lucas and Royal turn. Beyond them, I saw myself—

With a startled gasp, I opened my eyes.

Cassie grinned. "Well?"

"Cell division," I said. Cassie gave a whoop and pumped her fist in the air. Royal and Lucas looked at us, mystified.

"It totally worked," Cassie said, answering their unasked questions. "Alright, crazy cultists. Ready or not, here we come!"

We packed up our things and headed for the parking lot. I drove Lucas home in my Firebird, and Royal gave Cassie a lift behind us. I led the way into the Guard's living room.

Hale was talking to someone as we entered. She turned. Amber.

Hale saw me. His face lit up. "She's in." He turned back to Amber and offered his hand. Hesitantly, Amber took it. "You have no idea how much this means to us, Amber."

"I guess it's good to be wanted." Amber shook Hale's hand, then shot a quick glance in my direction before turning back to him. "So. Next week?"

"I'll notify the other spotters. They're extremely eager to meet you."

Amber nodded, casting her eyes over Hale one last time before walking past us and out the front door.

Hale shook his head, beaming. "You were right, Braedyn. I'll admit, I didn't think we'd ever convince her to help, but you did it." Hale clapped a hand on my shoulder. "This calls for a celebration."

Lucas, Royal, and Cassie gaped at me, disbelief plain on their faces.

"Yeah, well," I said, uncomfortable. "You can thank me later. The cult is meeting tonight."

Hale's expression changed in an instant. He turned to Cassie. "You're still up for this?"

"Ready as I'll ever be," she said, but she couldn't dim the twinkle of anticipation in her eyes.

Hale was all business. "Where's the meeting?"

"I don't know," Cassie said. "I'm catching up with Carrie at the coffee shop and she's going to drive us there."

"We'll let you know as soon as we have a location," I murmured.

Hale nodded, considering this for a moment. "Alright. I'll gather the others." Hale turned to Cassie. "You won't see us, but we'll be right around the corner. If you need anything, we'll come running."

Cassie nodded. "Okay."

"Be careful, Cassie." Hale caught Cassie's gaze and held it. "Trust your instincts. If you sense any danger, don't wait. Get out of there." She nodded again. Hale turned to the rest of us, his eyes lingering on mine last. "And if *anyone* sees Seth, this mission is over."

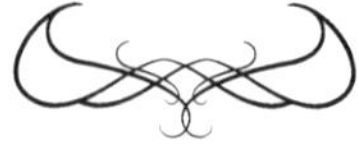

It's a strange feeling, watching the world through someone else's eyes.

After Cassie had met up with Carrie, she'd bundled herself into Carrie's car, and the two girls set off for their meeting. Carrie fluffed out her cute strawberry-blond bob as she drove.

"Why all the secrecy?" Cassie asked, glancing out as the road flashed past. "It feels so cloak-and-dagger." I gave her a mental kick, urging caution. If she felt the warning, Cassie didn't acknowledge it.

"I know, right?" Carrie shook her head, irritated. "But you weren't at the last meeting. This little snot, Amber Jenkins—" Carrie turned to study Cassie. "She's a friend of Missy's. Do you know her?"

"I know of her," Cassie said. "We're not exactly compatible, her being a self-absorbed, vain, cheerleader—and me having an actual, you know, soul."

"Hm." Carrie smiled grimly and turned back to the road. "My feelings exactly. Anyhow, she crashes our meeting, interrupts Idris just as she's welcoming everyone, and then starts talking *crazy*. Seriously, seriously wacko. Like, demons and crap." Carrie grimaced sourly. "And then everything went totally nuts. I think she scared off at least two potential new members." Carrie glanced at Cassie again. "Actually, Braedyn was one of them. I thought you two were tight. Didn't she tell you about that night?"

"Oh." Cassie cleared her throat, stalling for time. "Yeah, we're not as close as we used to be. She didn't even tell me she was going to that meeting." Cassie bit her lip, uncomfortable with the lie.

"No?" Carrie's eyebrows hiked up. "Haven't you guys been besties for like, forever?"

"We had a falling out."

"Over?" Carrie glanced at Cassie, curious.

"Uh—over a guy, actually." I could sense a heat rising in Cassie's cheeks.

"What guy? Does he go to Coronado Prep?"

"Parker?" Cassie's voice jumped unnaturally high at the mention of Parker.

Carrie mistook Cassie's expression. "That sucks, Cassie. Boys—yeah, they can do a number on friendship."

"Yeah." Cassie relaxed back into her chair, reeling from the cross-examination. I felt her grasping for a change of subject. "What exactly happened at the last meeting?"

Carrie sighed, but kept her eyes on the road. "There was this fire and I had to help put it out. When that was taken care of, I looked around but Braedyn had already vanished. I so wanted to talk to her, explain that it's not always like that. But she never called me back." Carrie sighed. "She seemed really interested, too."

"Yikes. I guess it's a good thing I wasn't there."

"Yes." Carrie shot Cassie a quick smile. "Tonight's going to be amazing. No more crazies, I promise." After another minute of silence, Carrie turned down a side street. "Here we are." She pulled over and parked. Cassie glanced around, finally spotting a street sign. It read, *Cresta Luna.* I could feel Cassie urging me to pay attention, and I tried to give her a mental nudge that I'd seen the sign.

The girls got out of their car and headed down a street.

Back in Royal's car, I spoke, keeping my eyes closed. "They're walking toward a building on Cresta Luna, just off of Main." I focused my mind's eye. Cassie spotted a street address for me. "The 400 block."

"Got it," Lucas said. I could hear him dialing his phone. After a moment, someone picked up. "They're on the 400 block of Cresta Luna. Yeah, we'll let you know." Lucas leaned forward, lowering his voice as though he were afraid of waking me up. "They want the address of the building where the meeting's being held."

"Just a minute." I let my consciousness drift more fully back into Cassie's mind. Carrie caught her hand and pulled her off the sidewalk, up some stone steps leading to an old wooden door. Cassie scanned the building's facade, but there was no visible address. Instead, there was a tattered, red awning opening up over the front door. Good enough.

"Look for a red awning," I said. As Lucas relayed the message to the waiting guard, Royal turned his key in the ignition. I tuned them out, keeping my thoughts with Cassie.

The inside of the building was stark. It looked as though it had been abandoned for some time. Once again, wool rugs covered the floor and candles edged the space with their flickering gleam.

Idris walked among the assembled girls, touching a hand here, a shoulder there. Everywhere she walked, she left smiling young women in her wake. Idris turned and spotted Carrie.

"You've brought another friend?" Idris turned to Cassie. "Welcome, dear."

"Um, hi," Cassie said. I could feel her unease, but she played it off as bashfulness.

"You have a gentle spirit, I can tell." Idris tilted her head to one side. "And something of a wild creative streak as well. Are you an artist?"

"She sews amazing clothes," Carrie said. When Cassie turned to her, surprised, Carrie elbowed her gently in the ribs. "My sister gets the lead in a musical, you don't think I'll fly home for the weekend to see it? She told me all about your golden fingers." Carrie turned to Idris. "She's very talented."

"Then I hope to see some of your work someday." Idris gave Cassie a warm squeeze on her shoulder and moved on.

"You didn't have to say that." I could feel Cassie smiling sheepishly at Carrie.

"Please. You've got a gift. Idris would be the first to tell you to celebrate it." Carrie spotted a friend across the room and waved. "Come on, we should grab a seat. It's going to start soon."

Carrie and Cassie joined the other girls settling themselves down on the rugs.

Idris walked to the front of the gathering, carrying a small, bronze bowl and a wooden mallet. She struck the bowl with the mallet, and a sweet gong-like tone rang out through the room. The girls grew still, lifting their faces and closing their eyes.

Cassie cast her eyes around the room. Out of the corner of her eye, I saw something that sent me crashing back into my own body.

"Oh!" I lurched forward, momentarily fighting against the seatbelt holding me in my seat.

"Braedyn?!" Lucas still had the phone to his ear. "Hale, something's wrong."

"Elyia," I gasped. The brown-haired Lilitu. She was sitting just three girls away from Cassie, eyes closed, face upturned. I almost hadn't recognized her. Through Cassie's eyes, I couldn't see any of her Lilitu aspect.

"What happened? Did they figure Cassie out?" Lucas grabbed my arm, pleading for direction. "Should we send in the Guard?"

"I—I don't know." I forced myself to breathe.

"Is she in danger?!" Royal asked, pulling his eyes off the road to study my face.

"I don't know!" I said again.

"Find out!" Royal gripped the steering wheel tightly.

I closed my eyes and sought out Cassie's mind again. I was so rattled, it took me several minutes to make the connection. By the time I'd located her, Royal had parked just off of Cresta Luna. He and Lucas were half-ready to bolt out of the car.

"Wait," I said. "She's okay."

Beyond being okay, Cassie was still excited. She evidently hadn't sensed my panic upon spotting Elyia. I clamped down on my emotions, afraid of what might happen if Cassie realized she was sitting so close to a Lilitu. Right now, her best protection was ignorance.

Idris was addressing the assembled, using the same kind of flowery, girl-power rhetoric she'd used at the last meeting. Cassie was paying strict attention to everything the white-haired woman said, which meant she wasn't exactly looking around the room. I couldn't tell what Elyia was up to, but I didn't want to urge Cassie to look for her, afraid of tipping my hand. So I listened to another impassioned speech about the power of the first mother and how modern women should embrace it. I sensed myself drumming my fingers against the door handle of the car, impatient—

Until Idris mentioned the Temple of Lilith. Something about the way she said those words sent a bolt of electric fear through me, and Cassie seemed to pick up on that. She sat up a little straighter, listening even more intently.

"This is my sacred duty," Idris was saying. "Mankind has his rituals. It is time for womankind to rediscover her own rites. It's time for us to embrace our feminine power. For this journey, I must withdraw from you for a time." There was a rustle of concern in the crowd. Idris raised her hands, calming the unease. "Be at peace. When I return to you, I will share whatever wisdom I have gleaned. Together we will all grow stronger."

Another wave of disappointment, bordering on grief, flooded through the crowd. Cassie turned to Carrie and saw tears gathering in the corners of her eyes.

"Listen closely, my daughters. I cannot make this journey of discovery alone. I require three acolytes to aid me in my work. Search within yourselves. The acolytes I seek will have courage, conviction, and a lightness of spirit akin to that of a child. Who among you will join me in this quest?"

All around Cassie, hands slowly rose into the air. Gingerly, Cassie raised her hand, despite my voice in her mind, screaming for her to sit still.

Idris walked through the crowd. She took a young woman's hand and helped her stand. "Emily. You've been with me since my first meeting in Puerto Escondido. It seems fitting that you should also be my first acolyte."

Emily clutched her hands over her mouth, eyes bright with unshed tears. She hugged Idris fiercely. The beautiful old woman laughed, delighted.

"Thank you," Emily whispered.

Idris made a fluid gesture, sending Emily to stand at the front of the room. When Idris glanced back at the crowd, several of the hands strained higher into the air. Idris studied the assembled. Her eyes snagged on Cassie. She walked toward her, reaching out a hand to clasp Cassie's hand. The others turned as one, studying Cassie with a jealous curiosity. I felt a sharp pang of fear as Idris drew Cassie to her feet.

"And you, my newest daughter," Idris said. "You remind me of a fawn. Timid, yet eager. Wide-eyed with innocence, yet thirsty for new experiences."

"I do?" Cassie blushed, shrinking from the spotlight Idris had just shined on her.

Idris chuckled gently. "Tell me, child. You must have many questions, and yet you volunteer for this important work. Why?"

I felt a surge of panic roiling through Cassie. She was going to give herself away. In desperation, I flooded her with all the confidence and strength I could summon. Cassie straightened, and looked Idris straight in the eye. "What you said about embracing our feminine power—" Cassie glanced down at Carrie. "I've always hidden my talents from others. I don't know why." She met Idris's eyes once more. "I'm tired of hiding. I'm ready to grow stronger."

Idris examined Cassie for several long moments. "I think you are," she murmured at last. "Remind me of your name, daughter?"

"Cassie. Ang." Cassie swallowed, her nerves breaking through the confidence I'd just showered her with.

Idris turned to the gathering. "Cassie. Newly come to our fold, but with the spirit of innocence I am seeking. She will be my second acolyte."

The group eyed Cassie, expressions ranging from wistful speculation to naked anger. Clearly, some of these women didn't feel Cassie had earned this honor. Through Cassie's ears, I heard Carrie give a soft sigh of longing.

Idris smiled another beatific smile. "Do not despair, my dear." Idris held a hand out to Carrie, helping her to her feet. "Carrie. You have been one of my most devoted followers. It gives me great pleasure to select you as my last acolyte."

Idris walked with Carrie and Cassie in tow, back to the front of the gathering. She directed the girls to join Emily, then turned back to face the miserable crowd. "I will call you together again, daughters. Until I do, be strong for one another. Remember, you walk in the footsteps of the first mother, Lilith, the mother of storms, fierce protector of our natural world. Her strength is yours to embrace."

It must have been the traditional end to the service, for the assembled slowly got to their feet and mingled. More than one shot veiled glances at the chosen three. Idris turned to her acolytes, spreading her hands.

"You have become part of a great work," she said. "Together, we will restore the Temple of Lilith."

"What do you need from us?" Carrie asked, anticipation shining through her face.

Idris met her eyes, and shook her head slowly. She took a moment to meet each of the girls' eyes. "Patience, daughters. All will be revealed to the faithful in time."

By the time Cassie made her way back to the Guard's house, the rest of the team was waiting, eager to debrief her personally. Thane and Ian were talking to one another animatedly—clearly they saw this as a victory. Hale and Dad had cornered Lucas, trying to wring out every bit of information they could about the meeting. I was sitting, frozen on the couch—until Cassie walked in.

"What the hell were you thinking?" I sprang to my feet and charged at Cassie.

Lucas lunged at me, catching me by the arms and keeping me from reaching Cassie. "Whoa, easy!"

"Braedyn?" Dad was at my side in two quick steps. He tried to catch my eye, but I was focused on Cassie.

"You promised me you'd keep your head down!" I heard my voice, strangled with emotion. "Didn't you feel me in your head?"

Cassie's triumphant grin faded. "I did what I had to do. You heard her. She was closing up shop. If I hadn't volunteered we'd have totally lost contact with her."

"It was a judgment call," Hale said. He gave me a stern look. "And I can't say it was a bad one."

"It doesn't change the fact that she's just jumped from some random high school girl to one of three hand-picked acolytes for Mother Crazybrain," I hissed. Dad put a hand on my shoulder but I shrugged it off. "No. This is way too dangerous."

"To state the obvious," Thane said, standing slowly. "Your young friend is now uniquely suited to the task of covert surveillance. As you say, she was handpicked by this woman. We do not know her designs on the girls, but she clearly plans to keep them close. Cassie has done us a great favor. We are indebted to her."

"So… you're fine with just sacrificing her for the cause?" I stared around the room. Hale and Dad traded a grim look.

"Thane isn't wrong, Braedyn—" Hale started.

"You're taking his side?" I turned to Dad, desperate for an ally. "Dad, this is *Cassie* we're talking about."

Before Dad could speak, Cassie caught my arm. "Let me do this."

I spun on her, but she didn't flinch. "Braedyn, you have no idea how horrible it was to feel so powerless, so *clueless* at the mission. I have the power to do something now. Let me help. You'll be with me for every meeting. You can keep an eye on me."

"I don't see any alternative," Thane said. "We cannot turn down this gift of an opportunity. Not when we know so little about this Temple of Lilith—"

"No." I shook my head, glaring at Hale. "I gave myself wholeheartedly to the Guard to help protect my friends. Don't do this. Don't put her on the front lines."

Hale lowered his eyes, considering my words for a long moment. "Braedyn. This could be the end of days." Hale looked up, and the depth of pain in his eyes struck me to the core. "There's no telling which soldier might make the difference in this war." Hale placed a hand on Cassie's shoulder. "Cassie has committed herself to this cause. None of us has the right to refuse her help."

I stared at Hale, at a loss for words. One by one, everyone turned from me to Cassie.

Cassie watched me, her eyes tight with concern. My mind unspooled a flood of memories from our past together, from sharing crayons in elementary school to the first time we'd gone to the fabric district together to buy material for our Halloween costumes as spindly 13-year-olds. Cassie had been a part of my life ten times longer than the Guard had. It felt like my worlds were colliding. No. Worse. It felt like this new reality I'd been exposed to since learning of the existence of the Lilitu was devouring my old reality, one loved one at a time.

I dropped my eyes, unable to face Cassie. "What do we do now?" I asked quietly.

"What we've been doing," Hale said. "Guard the Seal. Wait for the cult's next move. Watch for Lilitu."

"And us?" I glanced at Cassie and Royal.

No one spoke for a moment.

Then Dad pulled an envelope out of his coat pocket. "Well, if you're looking for something to keep yourselves occupied, there's always this." He handed me the envelope. "It came in yesterday's mail. The school's organizing a practice SAT for the entire Junior class after finals."

"You can't be serious?" I looked up.

"A practice SAT, huh?" Gretchen looked at Lucas. "I don't recall getting that letter."

Lucas shifted his feet unhappily. "I figured, with everything else that was going on—"

"You figured wrong," Gretchen said.

Lucas groaned, but Royal and Cassie traded a small smile. School was familiar. School was safe.

"Sounds like a plan," Dad said. He threw an arm around my shoulders and pulled me into a hug. I let him hold me for a long moment. I knew what he was thinking. Dad had to believe I'd have a future beyond this war. And that meant, willing or no, I'd be taking that test. To refuse would be admitting the possibility that we might fail. And there was no way I was going to do that to my dad.

I woke up early again the next morning. Rather than lay in bed, I got up and got dressed. I headed downstairs, hoping I might catch Dad up, but as I passed his bedroom I heard the faint sound of his snores. I sighed. At least one of us had managed to beat insomnia tonight.

I made my way into the dark kitchen, opting to turn on the under-counter lights. They illuminated the space with a gentle glow, much more suited to my current mood than overhead lights would have been. I put some water on to boil, meaning to make some tea.

I heard the bolt turn at the front door. Karayan had filled in for another sick spotter, partnering with Gretchen—who was the only spotter willing to work with either of us. She must be returning from the late shift. I was walking through the dining room to offer her a cup of tea when I saw her turn back to face someone on the porch. I pressed myself against the wall in the dining room, suddenly unsure what to do.

"I'd invite you in, but I think that'd send the wrong message," Karayan was saying.

"Strange that two adults have to worry so much what other people think." It was Hale. I held my breath, frozen against the wall. "Like we'd ever do anything stupid."

There was a long silence, and then Karayan sighed. "I had fun tonight."

"Me too," Hale said. "You know, 'fun' within the context of guarding a supernatural portal to another realm filled with malicious demons waiting to destroy the world."

"Right." Karayan laughed quietly. "Within *that* context, I had a blast."

"It does make one wonder in what other contexts we might have fun."

"It does indeed." Karayan's voice was rich with amused affection. "Well."

"Yeah." Hale cleared his throat. "I should probably get some sleep."

"That whole 'beauty' problem," Karayan agreed.

"Exactly. Good night, Karayan." I heard Hale turn and walk off our front porch, heading back to the Guard's house next door.

"Sleep tight," Karayan whispered, her voice filled with regret. After another long moment, she closed the door.

I stepped out from my hiding place. Karayan saw me and froze. Then her eyes shifted to the kitchen, where the dim under-counter lights offered the only illumination.

"Couldn't sleep?" she asked, a little too brightly.

"Karayan—"

"If you're making tea, I could use a cup." Karayan walked past me and into the kitchen. I followed her inside. Karayan busied herself at the counter, pulling two mugs out of a cupboard. "Do we have any chamomile left?"

I wanted to confront her. To ask what was going on with Hale. To advise her—if they were going to try to form any kind of relationship—to be open about it. To warn her how dangerous it would be to keep this secret from the rest of the Guard.

But then she glanced at me. In her face I saw a mixture of pain, longing, shame, fear.

"You're falling for him," I said simply.

Karayan shook her head. But she couldn't bring herself to voice the denial. A rosy blush stained her cheeks, and she turned back to the cupboard. "Found it. You probably want something with caffeine, though. How about Earl Grey?"

Karayan glanced back at me. She'd managed to get her expression under control, but I could still see the urgency in her eyes, begging me not to push.

I hesitated. There was nothing simple, nothing harmless about this crush. But I couldn't make myself voice my fears. I shrugged. "Earl Grey sounds great."

Karayan rewarded me with a tremulous smile and reached for the kettle on the stove. I sighed. Maybe she and Hale were right. They were two adults. They knew the risks. If Karayan needed me to pretend I didn't see the truth, who was I to challenge her? As long as she didn't act on her feelings, the only one Karayan could hurt was herself.

9

Amber was as good as her word. That next Monday, she arrived at Hale's after school, ready to begin her "job."

Lucas and I were sitting at the Guard's old round dining table, hunched over our homework, when she walked in. We had opened a window, taking advantage of one of the first warm days of Spring to let in a breeze. We heard her car pulling up outside. When Amber approached up the stairs, Lucas stared at her out the window in surprise. She looked ready for Spring, too, wearing deep purple yoga pants and a tank top over a sports bra. She carried a backpack casually over one shoulder, and her hair was pulled back into an artful ponytail. She knocked, the opened the front door, peering into the house. Her eyes landed on us and she walked inside without ceremony.

"So, I'm here," she said, closing the door behind her. She eyed the house with distaste, and I was suddenly conscious of how worn and threadbare the Guard's furnishings must look to Amber, who—up until very recently, apparently—had lived a charmed life in one of Puerto Escondido's most exclusive neighborhoods. "What now?"

Lucas glanced at me with thinly veiled curiosity. Still wondering why I recruited her, I'd bet. "I'll get Hale." Lucas pushed back from the table and walked into the foyer, passing Amber without a second glance. He ascended the stairs, leaving us alone on the first floor.

Amber's eyes settled on me. She shifted her weight. I returned the look, unsure what to say. We shared an awkward silence until Lucas reappeared at the head of the stairs with Hale in tow.

"Amber. Excellent." Hale bounded down the steps, grinning broadly. "Let's get straight to it." Hale led Amber down the narrow hall beside the staircase, stopping at the door to the basement.

I had just settled back over my history book when Hale called my name. I looked up, startled. "Yeah?"

"You too. Let's go." He jerked his head toward the basement stairs. "Amber's going to need a sparring partner."

I glanced at Lucas, as if he could free me from this obligation. Hale wanted us to train *together?* With a sinking feeling in the pit of my stomach, I closed the heavy book and stood. My feet suddenly felt like lead weights. This was not how I'd wanted to spend my afternoon.

Amber seemed equally thrilled about the prospect of us training together. She pursed her lips and flicked her eyes toward Hale. If he saw the irritated expression on her face, he ignored it. Hale started down the stairs and Amber followed. I was the last one into the basement.

"You two should go ahead and warm up." Hale turned to Amber. "Do you know some good stretches to get started—?"

Amber dropped into a front split, right leg forward. She reached forward, lowering her body nearly flat against her thigh. Hale's eyes bulged slightly.

"Well, great." Hale turned to me. "You should warm up, too, Braedyn."

I joined Amber on the mat and started my own stretches—which were nowhere near as limber as Amber's. A spark of irrational competition flared in the back of my mind and I squashed it. After we'd warmed up sufficiently, Hale clapped his hands together.

"Okay. So, Amber, have you ever done any kind of self-defense training."

"No." Amber crossed her arms, giving Hale a flat look.

"She's a cheerleader," I offered brightly.

Amber shot a dark glance at me. "I've studied dance and cheer since I was six."

"Fantastic." Hale gestured Amber and me closer. As he positioned us facing one another, he gave Amber an encouraging smile. "You're clearly very familiar with your body and what you're capable of. I'm betting much of what you've learned in your other pursuits will translate very well to what we're going to be doing."

"Does this mean I get to hit her now?" Amber gave me a cold smile.

"You can try." I shrugged lightly, daring her to make a move.

Hale glanced between the two of us, and for the first time a flicker of uncertainty passed over his face. But then he shook his head and met my gaze.

"Braedyn, defensive position, please."

I got into the basic stance, hands raised, elbows close to my body, relaxed but ready to move.

Hale turned back to Amber. "Go ahead, Amber."

She eyed him, startled. "Go ahead and what?"

"Try to hit me, cheerleader," I muttered.

Amber's eyes flashed. She brought her fists up awkwardly, hands balled too tightly. And then she struck. Or tried to. She launched a fist at me, putting almost none of her body behind it. It was a simple matter to knock her fist aside. My muscle memory took over then, following up the block with an attack of my own, suddenly eager to drive my fist into her stomach—

Hale caught my wrist and twisted it to the side, forcing me up onto my toes. I gave a furious shriek of surprise. Amber's eyes glinted in surprise.

"I expect you to control your feelings," Hale murmured into my ear. "Is that clear?"

I swallowed and nodded, feeling my cheeks go red. Hale released me, but he put a hand on my shoulder in a conciliatory gesture. I rubbed my sore wrist and avoided Amber's gloating smirk.

"You want to land a punch?" Hale turned on Amber, keeping his voice light. "Then apply yourself to our training with as much dedication as you do to your dance. Actually, the only real difference between fighting and dancing is that fighting might save your life."

Amber's smirk faded. She eyed me with a new understanding. "Fine."

"Let's start from the top, then, shall we?" Hale walked up behind Amber and began with the first lesson he'd ever taught me. For nearly two hours, she drilled the same basic punch over and over again. I blocked every one of them, but at the end of our session I was breathing hard and my arms were noodley with fatigue.

Amber was… surprisingly good at this for a beginner. Hale knew it, too. He grinned as Amber and I downed our bottles of water after practice.

"This was an excellent start to your training, Amber. I hope we didn't tire you out too much."

Amber shrugged. "It was a good workout, I'll give you that. It'll be interesting to see what's next." She eyed me, with a calculating look that made my skin crawl. "How long before I get good at this stuff?"

"Let's just take it one session at a time." Hale glanced at his watch and stretched. "I'm on duty tonight, so I need to grab some sleep before my shift starts. Same time tomorrow, girls?"

We nodded agreement with varying degrees of enthusiasm.

"Seriously. Nice work today." Hale gave us another proud smile and walked out of the basement, leaving me alone with Amber.

"Well." I flashed a brief smile at Amber and eyed the stairs. "I should probably get back to history." I headed toward the stairs.

"You and Lucas spend a lot of time together," Amber mused out loud.

I stopped and glanced back at her. "And?"

Amber shrugged. "Your Lilitu powers. I mean, are you sure you can control them?"

"Yes." I felt a hot rush of anger flooding my cheeks, and knew I must be blushing crimson. I gripped the banister tightly in one hand.

Amber studied me shrewdly, tilting her head to one side. "Really? I mean, you're *sure* sure?"

"I wouldn't do anything to hurt Lucas," I said. But even as the words passed my lips I hesitated. Memories of all the times I had already—if inadvertently—hurt him poured through my mind.

"Wow." Amber read my expression again. "You really do care about him. It must be awful for you, knowing you're the one thing in the world that poses the biggest threat to his life."

A fist of lead clutched tightly around my heart. This was not a conversation I wanted to have with Amber. Not now. Not ever. "You know where the front door is," I hissed. "You can let yourself out."

I turned and hurried up the staircase, pausing in the hallway outside to get a grip on my emotions before anyone saw the open rage on my face. I listened closely, but didn't hear Amber heading up the stairs behind me. I let my shoulders sag for a moment, then shook my head. *Stop it!* A voice in my head shouted. *You might have to train with her, but you don't have to let her mess with your head.*

I took a deep breath and straightened. Let Amber try to screw with me, like she had all through middle school. I was a different person now—a stronger person. Standing in that narrow hallway, I made a silent promise to myself; Amber would never see me that vulnerable again.

Every day that week, Amber showed up after school, ready to train. She mastered the basic punches quickly, and Hale had started her on simple combinations by the end of the week. Each day, while Amber practiced her sparring techniques, I practiced concealing my feelings. She'd make little off-hand digs at me when Hale wasn't paying attention, but after that first session, I didn't show her even a crack in my facade.

It was harder to brush her words off as I lay down to sleep, though. The things she implied about my relationship with Lucas—and how selfish it was of me to continue hanging out with him—burrowed deep into my subconscious. On more than one occasion, her words kept me from visiting Lucas in his dreams. While I longed for his comforting presence, I didn't want the doubts she'd instilled in me to taint any of the dreams I shared with Lucas. Until I got control of my own fears, I decided to spend my dreams alone.

At the beginning of practice on Friday, Amber slid into a straddle splits. She glanced at Hale, who was holding a pair of wooden practice daggers in his hands.

"So when do I meet the other spotters?"

Hale looked up, her question snapping him out of his thoughts. "Hmm? Oh. They've been checking in on us."

I eyed Hale, unsettled. "What do you mean? They're watching us train?"

"One or two of them watch from the top of the stairs for a couple of minutes most days." He glanced at me, surprised. "You haven't noticed them?"

I shook my head. Hale frowned. "Well. They're very interested in Amber's progress." He gave Amber a confident smile. "And they're very encouraged to see you holding your own against—" But Hale didn't finish the thought.

"Against a Lilitu?" I felt a rush of goose bumps over my skin. Why keep their observation secret, unless they were also gauging how well I fought? Preparing against the day we might find ourselves on opposite sides?

Hale shrugged, trying to put me at ease. "I wouldn't take it personally."

I glanced at him, but his words did nothing to soothe my fears.

Hale clapped his hands. "Okay. Let's get started. I've got a new combo for you today, Amber." While Hale drilled Amber on a new combination of punches, I glanced up the stairs, suddenly feeling unseen eyes on me. How had they watched us without my ever sensing their presence?

"Okay, Braedyn. Ready to defend yourself?" Hale gestured for me to face Amber. I settled into my stance, but my mind wandered up the stairs, trying to sense whether or not we had intruders.

Amber attacked. I blocked the first two punches, but the third connected with startling force into my left side. I staggered backwards, winded. Amber's face barely reflected surprise. She simply stopped moving and watched me as Hale ran forward. Her expression was bland, but I saw the faintest glimmer of triumph in her eyes.

"That one looked like it stung. You need a minute?" He tried to meet my eyes, but I avoided his gaze.

I shook my head, forcing myself to straighten. "Just let myself get distracted."

"It's okay if you need to grab a seat." Hale eyed me, concerned. "I can run through another combo with Amber for a few minutes."

"I'm fine." My voice came out sharper than I'd intended. Hale shrugged, stepping back.

Amber faced me again, letting the smallest of smiles play across her lips. "Lots of people underestimate me. Once."

"You got lucky," I said, forcing myself to sound bored. "I wouldn't let it go to your head."

"Alright, ladies. Let's take it from the top." Hale stepped back, but I could tell by the way he kept his eyes fastened to us that he could sense the animosity sparking between Amber and me. It was a grueling session. Amber was—though it pains me to admit it—getting kind of good at this stuff.

After our session, Hale turned to praise Amber on her progress. I left, eager to put as much distance between Amber and myself as I could. Lucas looked up from his place at the dining room table and smiled at me.

"I'm going to study at home," I mumbled. Lucas glanced at the basement behind me. I knew he sensed something had happened at practice, but I was too desperate to leave Amber behind to stop and explain. We'd catch up later at dinner.

I hurried through the Guard's lawn and up to my front porch. Dad was inside, listening to the news on the radio and cleaning his daggers.

"How was practice today?" He looked up from the gleaming dagger he was polishing.

"Fine." I stalked past him and into the kitchen. I pulled the fridge open and rummaged for a snack, bypassing carrot sticks in favor of something salty.

Karayan entered the kitchen. "You're home early. Rough training session?"

"Not now." I glared at her and pulled a stick of cheese out of the fridge.

Karayan studied me. "Let me guess. Situation Amber's getting a little messy?"

"I know the Guard needs her, but—" I shrugged, unwilling to finish the thought.

"It would feel *so good* to push her off the top of a tall building," Karayan finished wistfully.

I smiled grimly, taking a bite of the cheese. "Something like that."

I heard the front door open and Karayan turned, smoothing a hand through her hair quickly.

"Are you looking for Braedyn?" Dad looked up from his work at the dining table.

"No, Karayan, actually." It was Hale.

"They're both in the kitchen," Dad said, jerking his head toward us.

Hale walked through the dining room and into view. He nodded when he saw me. "How's the side? Still tender?"

Karayan's eyes widened. "Oh, man. You let her *hit* you? No wonder you're in such a pissy mood."

I glared at Karayan. Hale bit back a smile. I pointed the remainder of my cheese at him. "I saw that."

"Sorry," Hale shook his head ruefully, "but it was a good reminder to keep your guard up."

I let out a disgusted breath and leaned against the counter to finish my cheese in peace.

Hale turned to Karayan. "Are we still on for tonight?"

"I'm up for it if you are," said Karayan.

"I'll tell Gretchen." Hale gave Karayan a small smile. "Pick you up at eight?"

"Actually," Karayan glanced at me. "Braedyn, why don't you join us tonight. It is a Friday night, and that'll give Gretchen some time to rest and hang out with Lucas." Karayan's eyes held mine, full of an unvoiced plea.

Hale looked at me, surprised. "Would you be up for that, Braedyn?"

"How do you know we don't have plans?" Dad asked from the dining room behind Hale.

"Do we have plans?" I asked back.

Dad sighed. "I guess not."

"Sure." I gave Karayan a smile of understanding.

"Okay, then. I'll pick you both up at eight." Hale gave us another quick smile and left, walking back out the front door.

Karayan caught my hand and gave it a small squeeze. "Thank you," she murmured.

"Sure." I smiled back, warmed. Maybe this meant Karayan was taking my warning to heart, that she wanted someone around who could keep an eye on her and Hale, help her manage her attraction to him.

"I don't want anyone else suspecting us." Karayan turned and skipped out of the kitchen, anticipation gleaming in her eyes.

I felt my smile drain away. I wasn't helping Karayan fight her feelings for Hale. I was helping her keep them secret from the rest of the Guard.

That night, all my attention was focused on Hale and Karayan. A parade of Lilitu could burst out of the Seal but—unless they stopped to chat with the lovebirds—odds were slim that I'd even see them. It wasn't a conscious choice. I tried to force myself to zone in on the Seal. But every sound that travelled up from Hale and Karayan's station set my ears straining, my skin tingling.

For the first part of the night, they shared separate posts. But after the Guard's first rounds, Hale sent me up to the balcony and he and

Karayan took the center position together again.

Which gave me the perfect position to eavesdrop. Even if I hadn't intended to—and believe me, that was not the case—I would have had a hard time *not* listening to their conversation. The acoustics of the mission bounced sound from where they were standing straight up into my balcony perch.

At first, they kept the conversation light, and I felt my muscles unknotting as some of my anxiety slipped away.

But then I heard Karayan sigh. "You just don't seem like the other Guardsmen. How in the world did you get mixed up in all of this?"

There was a long pause. I found myself leaning closer as it dawned on me, I didn't know much about Hale's past, either. Hale finally cleared his throat. "My wife, actually," he said.

"You were married?" Karayan couldn't hide her surprise.

"Briefly. She was—well, she was everything." Hale's voice took on a far-away quality that sent a shiver across my back.

"What happened?" Karayan's voice dropped to a husky whisper, as though she wasn't sure she wanted to know the answer.

"One night she—" Hale fell silent for a long moment. "She walked in and found a Lilitu—with me. She interrupted things before—" Hale's voice grew softer. "She saved me. Maybe even saved my life. But the Lilitu was furious. It—it killed her. Opened her carotid artery with its claws, then fled. She died in my arms."

I stared down at them, stricken.

"Hale," Karayan breathed. The empathy in her voice was genuine, powerful.

Hale glanced down at his hands. I heard him take a long, shaky breath. "The cop who came to the scene took my statement. I—stupidly—told him everything. I just wasn't in the right frame of mind to consider how insane my story sounded. All I wanted was for them to catch the demon who'd taken Sarah—" Hale shook his head. "If it had been any other officer on duty that night, I'd have ended up in a psych ward or worse—on death row. But this cop, his brother was in the Guard. He knew enough about what I'd just seen that he believed me. He made a call, and an hour later I met my first Guardsman." Hale let out a long breath. "That's the long and the short of it."

"There are no happy stories here, are there?" Karayan's voice sounded soft after Hale's harsh confession.

"No happy beginnings." Hale turned his attention back to the Seal. "But I'm not ready to give up hope for a happy ending."

Karayan looked at him sharply, but Hale didn't take his eyes off the Seal.

It was a long shift. When our relief showed up an hour before the dawn, I was more than ready to leave the cold stone mission behind. Hale drove us home, and I dozed in the back seat of his truck. When we got home, I stumbled past Dad and up the stairs, thinking only of my bed and the sleep that awaited me.

I climbed under my covers and shifted into my dream garden with as little effort as flipping a light switch. It was early enough in the morning that Lucas might still be sleeping. I knelt and placed my hand on the earth of my garden. As always, connecting with the larger dream filled me with a sharp awareness of the billions of minds adrift in the darkness—most unaware of the universal dream we all shared. As a pool grew before me, full of the shimmering glimmers of those dreams, I let my thoughts drift back over the night's shift, and what I'd learned from Hale.

My thoughts inadvertently drew Hale's dream to the surface of the pool. As the glimmering spark of Hale's mind—sleeping already?—rose to greet me, I lifted a hand meaning to wave it away so I could locate Lucas's dream instead. But then I noticed a strange bluish-tint to Hale's dream.

And I knew.

Heart pounding in my chest, I closed my hand around Hale's dream. I felt the focused determination of Hale's presence as his dream unfolded before me.

Hale sat on the porch of a small house I'd never seen before. It showed some signs of disrepair, but it was nestled in a lush garden and surrounded by copses of trees.

Hale sat on an old wicker chair, near the edge of his seat, waiting for something—or someone.

I sensed movement and ducked deeper into the copse of trees I'd found myself hiding in.

Karayan appeared at the side of the little house. She took a moment to straighten her dress—a simple, floral print dress Karayan would *never* wear in the waking world. She looked like she was playing dress up, but instead of accentuating her assets, the dress suggested an innocence that clashed terribly with Karayan's natural sensuality. Karayan herself seemed unfazed by the dissonance. Satisfied, she walked forward. When she rounded the edge of the house, Hale turned to face her. As soon as his eyes found her, Karayan's appearance *changed.*

In place of the statuesque, honey-blond bombshell, a petite woman with long, pale hair and dark eyes took a few hesitant steps forward. Suddenly the floral print dress made sense.

"Sarah?" Hale stood, as if he couldn't believe his eyes. A thrill of horror shot through my core. *No—she wouldn't—?*

Karayan, disguised as this pretty, petite woman, ran forward. Hale opened his arms, and when she reached him he enfolded her, sweeping her off her feet and swinging her around in a joyful circle. She laughed, her voice thinner and lighter than Karayan's natural tone.

"Sarah, oh God, how I've missed you." Hale clung to her.

"I've missed you, too," she murmured into his ear.

Hale pulled back and looked into her eyes. She reached up and touched his face, smiling as a tear slid down his cheek.

"None of that." She brushed the tear away gently. "We have this time together. Let's not waste it on grief."

Hale studied her, a smile breaking over his face with such love it sent another jolt of pain stabbing through my heart. He enfolded her in another embrace, this time tipping her face up toward his lips. He kissed her, a slow, passionate kiss that made me blush. I pulled back further into the trees, letting the leaves obscure the couple from view for a moment.

But then I heard a rustling as two bodies lowered themselves to the soft grass at their feet and I had to look—

Hale pulled Karayan down into the grass with him. She nestled in his arms, safe in her disguise… but as she lay her head against his chest, a meadow of bluebells sprang up around them. I stared. Bluebells. Where my garden had always been full of roses, Karayan's was awash in bluebells. I'd seen them each time I'd visited her in her dream. They were an unconscious manifestation of her sense of self. Now, happy and unguarded, she might not even realize she'd brought them into Hale's dream.

Hale took a deep breath, savoring the scent of his Sarah, not realizing who he really held in his arms. How could he know Karayan had slipped into his dream, armed with the knowledge of how to be with him without his understanding or consent? Why else would she disguise herself as his dead wife?

Hale's hand roamed down her body—and I turned abruptly away. I knew I needed to stop this, to interrupt their tryst. But as the sounds behind me grew more amorous, another instinct kicked in and I snapped out of Hale's dream, back into my own garden.

I reeled, my heart pounding loudly in my ears. What now? Was this my responsibility to report? Should I confront Karayan in private? Warn her that I knew what she was doing? Should I tell Hale? For many long moments, I spun with confusion.

And then, exhausted and overwhelmed, I made my decision. That night, I slept in dreamless peace. I'd figure out what to do later.

I slept straight through until Sunday morning. When I finally woke up, the sun was already high in the east. As soon as consciousness returned, it brought with it the panic and indecision of the previous day. This wasn't a problem I wanted to have. But it had landed in my lap, and now I had to decide what to do.

I got up and pulled on some jeans and a T-shirt. As March had drawn to a close, the days had grown alternately wetter and warmer. Now, with April having officially arrived, we were getting more of the pleasant days—today was expected to reach 76 degrees, and I was beyond ready for the warmth.

As I headed downstairs, I smelled something cooking in the kitchen. Maybe Dad was up. The thought cheered me. I could use a good breakfast. It had been close to 36 hours since my last real meal.

But when I walked into the kitchen, Karayan looked up from the island, eating a piece of toast.

"Morning." She grinned. "I was wondering when you'd decide to wake up."

I squared my shoulders. It was the perfect moment to confront

Karayan. We were alone, she was in a good mood—but my confidence failed. "I—I thought I smelled breakfast." I glanced around the kitchen. A pile of dirty dishes filled the sink.

"You missed Murphy's frittata," Karayan said. "We meant to save you some, but then Hale came over and we got to talking and—" Karayan glanced at the clock. "Hey, aren't you supposed to be training with Hale and Amber this morning?"

I followed her gaze to the clock: 10:17 AM. "Crap!" I turned around and ran back up the stairs, tearing through my dresser for a clean pair of yoga pants and an old T-shirt I wouldn't mind sweating through.

I rushed across the yards separating our house from the Guard's house. Once I reached the front step of their porch, I paused to get control of my breathing. After successfully slowing my heartbeat down, I walked into the Guard's house. The foyer, living room, and dining room—what I could see of them—were full of off-duty Guardsmen, ribbing on one another, checking the news on their phones, or just enjoying a cup of morning coffee. No sign of Hale, which meant he and Amber were probably already downstairs.

I walked to the basement. The door was standing open, and as I stepped through I heard Hale and Amber talking. I meant to announce myself—apologize for being late—but as I set my foot on the top stair, I heard something that made me freeze.

"But how are you sure you can trust her? She's a demon." Amber's voice held a note of genuine concern that I'd never heard from her before.

"She's proven herself to us on more than one occasion," Hale said.

"But she's hurt people." Amber's voice took on a harsh tone.

"She's made mistakes," Hale acknowledged, "but she's learned from them. And she's done a lot to make up for those mistakes."

"Tell that to Parker."

"Trust me, Amber. We are not blind to the situation."

"No? You give her a pretty free rein." Amber made a disgusted sound. "I mean, what about her and Lucas?"

"You don't know the whole situation."

"You do realize, I've known Braedyn longer than you have." Amber's tone shifted again. I held my breath, straining to hear every word. "Up until last year, she was—nothing. Like, we pitied her.

There's no way that girl would have ever gotten a guy like Lucas."

My blood started to boil in my veins, but I kept my mouth tightly shut.

"Lucas and Braedyn met before her Lilitu powers started to present—" Hale started.

"Well, sure—they live right next door to each other. But when did he fall for her? Do you know?"

"What's your point, Amber?" Hale's voice was clipped, impatient.

"My point is, you think you know her. What if you don't?" Amber let her voice drop ominously. "She's a *demon.* Something no one around here can seem to remember."

"I have faith in her," Hale said.

"That's really sweet of you," Amber said quietly, "but what if your faith is misguided? What if she betrays you?"

"That won't happen," Hale said. I could tell he was reaching his wit's end.

"You're willing to bet your life—all our lives—on that?"

"Yes," Hale growled.

"Really?" Amber sounded genuinely shocked.

"I'll put a dagger through her heart before I let her betray the Guard."

It was as though someone had unleashed a flood of ice into my veins. My head felt strangely light. I could barely hear the rest of their conversation.

"Well, that's more like it," Amber said.

"Let's get back to work." Hale's tone was brusque, almost harsh. "Show me what you remember of that last combo."

I edged back into the hallway, then turned and ran directly into Lucas. His face was grim. He'd heard everything.

"Braedyn," he whispered. "He doesn't mean—it would never come to—"

I shook my head. "Don't."

I tried to walk past him, but Lucas caught my arm and pulled me to him. I fought to pull away, but he locked his arms around me, holding me to him. After a moment, I gave in, letting him hold me. His arms were strong and warm.

"We shouldn't," I murmured, even though all I wanted was to stay here, with his arms wrapped around me. Lucas pulled back, then led me down the hall, through the foyer, and out onto the front porch, away from the prying eyes of the Guardsmen. When we were safely out of sight, Lucas reached for me again.

I put a hand on his chest, keeping him from pulling me too close. "What if she's right?" Lucas shook his head, but I wouldn't be dissuaded that easily. "How do we know you aren't just under my spell?"

"That's stupid." Lucas grinned at me.

"Is it?"

Lucas's smile faded. "Yes." He took both of my shoulders in his hands and faced me straight on. "What we have? This is real, Braedyn. It's what I want. And beyond that?" Lucas's brows drew together, his handsome face growing fierce with anger. "It's none of Amber's business."

Lucas said all the right things, but I couldn't banish Amber's words from my thoughts. I'd managed to pull myself together and showed up for sparring practice about 30 minutes late. I preferred that to the scenario where Amber realized I'd overheard her and Hale and couldn't bring myself to face them.

It was a grueling sparring session, mostly because I was fighting to keep my emotions in check while defending against Amber's increasingly skilled attacks.

At the end of our session, I left before Hale had finished praising our efforts. I didn't want to hear it from him, not today.

I retreated to my bedroom, and spent most of the afternoon staring blankly at textbooks. I can't say I got any real studying done. Dad swung by when it was time for dinner. I joined him and Karayan downstairs for the meal, but left as soon as I'd finished doing the dishes.

When the time came to get ready for bed, I found I didn't have the energy to change out of my clothes. I lay on my bed and stared up at the ceiling, playing the overheard conversation back in my mind for the millionth time. Of all the Guardsmen, Hale had seemed the one most open to the possibility that I could be a force for good. To hear him so calmly declare his willingness to end me—?

I shivered and rolled over onto my side.

I heard a rustling outside and dismissed it as wind. But a few moments later, someone tapped lightly on my windowpane. I turned back to the window, needing no light to make out the figure clinging tightly to the trellis outside. Lucas. I rolled out of bed and hurried to the window, unlocking it and sliding the lower pane up.

"What are you doing?" I hissed.

"I know you had a rough day." He met my eyes, and I melted a little. The moonlight edged his dark hair in silver. I felt a longing to reach out and run my fingers through the silky black strands.

"Come inside before you fall," I said. I helped Lucas climb inside, then closed the window and pulled the drapes shut against prying eyes.

He was standing so close that when I turned to face him I brushed against his chest. I heard his quick intake of breath, and lifted my eyes to his face.

"What are you doing?" I asked again, but this time my voice trembled.

In answer, Lucas lifted a hand to my cheek. He drew his fingers down along my jaw, then tilted my head up. I felt my lips part, and my eyes half-lidded of their own volition.

"Lucas," I breathed.

"Let this be our night," he whispered.

I felt a surge of longing, and swayed into him. Lucas bent forward and captured my lips in a sweet kiss. A powerful swell of energy shot up from my core—a tornado of hunger, hell-bent on fastening onto Lucas, draining him of his spirit and vitality.

I pushed the storm back, fighting to keep it at bay. Lucas felt me withdraw.

"It's okay, Braedyn," he breathed.

"No." I looked up at him.

"I thought—I thought you wanted this, too." He looked at me, a crushing disappointment gleaming in his eyes.

"Why tonight?" I met his gaze, but Lucas couldn't hold it. "It's because of Amber, isn't it? Because of what she said? You want to comfort me."

Surprise flickered through Lucas's expression.

"When we have our night, I want it to be for us," I whispered gently. "Not in response to a bad day. Not because we're sad, or broken, or lost. I want it to be perfect. I want it to be a celebration. I want it to be an act of love."

Lucas studied me for a long moment. Then he smiled. He leaned forward and gave me a soft kiss on the forehead. "You can be scary wise sometimes, you know?"

I let out a long breath, half-relief, half-regret.

"Does this mean I have to go home?" He brushed a loose strand of hair back from my cheek and tucked it behind my ear.

"No." I took his hand and led him to my bed. We climbed onto the comforter and lay down together. I nestled against Lucas's side. He wrapped an arm around me. In time, Lucas's breathing changed to the deep, even sounds of sleep. I curled closer to him and felt his arm tighten around me in response.

It was everything I needed.

10

When dreams are all you have, you find a way to make the most of them. The sensations are muted. Objects are never quite as substantial as they are in the physical world. It just doesn't feel 100% *right.* But in that meadow, feeling the warmth of an imagined breeze blowing over my skin, staring into Lucas's eyes, I willed myself to believe it anyway. Lucas drew me to him for another kiss. Our lips met, and I felt a thrill moving through my center—

"Braedyn."

I heard her voice, but the dream was so sweet I didn't want to leave. I turned back to Lucas, letting my fingers trail through his hair. His eyes creased with concern.

"Did you hear something?" he asked.

"Braedyn, *wake up.*"

Now she was shaking me.

I opened my eyes. Karayan stood over my bed, biting her lip. I moved, and felt Lucas's solid form next to me. I sat bolt upright, alarm slamming the last foggy tendrils of sleep from my mind.

"Lucas." I shook him awake. He blinked in the light of the new day then—like me—jerked into a sitting position.

"I fell asleep." He looked around, groggy.

"Oh, you think?" Karayan eyed him with dark amusement.

"Did Dad…?" I met Karayan's eyes, feeling a knot of anxiety working itself tighter into my stomach.

"Don't you think you'd know if your father found you asleep in bed with your boyfriend?" Karayan crossed her arms and gave Lucas a flat look. "Speaking of which, you might want to head on home before someone—and by someone I mean Gretchen, your lethal, demon-hunting sister-in-law—finds out that you're missing."

"Right." Lucas rolled off the bed and stood, running hands through his bed-head in an effort to disguise the fact he'd just woken up. "Is Murphy up?"

"He's stirring," Karayan glanced back into the hall, growing quiet for a moment, "but I think you'll be safe if you go now."

"Thanks." Lucas shot one quick smile at me, then slipped quietly into the hall.

I waited until I heard the front door close softly behind him before letting out a long breath of relief. I collapsed back on the bed. How could we have been so stupid? What if we'd been seen? That was one way to ensure we'd never have another moment alone together as long as any member of the Guard was left standing.

"I owe you one, Karayan."

"Whatever. If we don't watch each other's backs, who will, right?"

I propped myself back up on my elbows. Karayan walked to my bedroom door and closed it softly. She turned back to face me, wringing her hands.

I swung my feet over the edge of the bed and sat up again, curious. Karayan joined me, sitting at the foot of my bed.

"You called it." She bit her lip. "I am—falling in love with him." She brushed a strand of hair back from her face, and I saw her smile wistfully. "He's a good man, Braedyn."

"I know he is," I said, more sharply than I meant to.

She glanced at me, startled. "Are you angry?"

"Yeah, actually, I am."

Karayan looked genuinely surprised. "Why?"

"What do you think Hale would do if he knew you were visiting his dreams disguised as his dead wife?"

Karayan's cheeks flushed pink. "How did—you've been spying on me?"

"You're using his feelings for Sarah to manipulate him."

"I was trying to comfort him!" Karayan glared at me, her eyes bright with anger. "I can't even believe we're having his conversation. You spend almost every night in Lucas's dreams."

"With his *permission*."

"Hale *can't* give me permission, but he—he's as good as admitted his feelings for me, too. I thought a dream was the safest—" Karayan lurched to her feet, her face ashen. "You know, forget it. I'm not asking a minor for dating advice." She turned and stumbled toward the door, looking for all the world like a lost child.

I jumped after her, catching her arm. "Wait. Karayan. Look. I—I understand."

Karayan stopped at the door. "Do you? The Guard actually *supports* this thing you have with Lucas."

I couldn't stop a half-smile from twisting my lips. "I wouldn't go that far—"

"No? You've kissed Lucas. What do you think would happen if I ever kissed Hale in the waking world?" She glanced at me then, eyes full of hurt. I didn't have to say anything. We both knew the answer. "They make allowances for you that they'll never make for me. I get it. Fine. I'm just asking you to let us have these dreams."

"Us?" I shook my head, miserable. "Hale's not even aware of what you're doing."

"I'm not hurting him. I would never hurt him. You have to believe that."

"I know you'd never do anything to hurt him *intentionally*."

Karayan shrugged my hand off her arm. "And you? You think you're all that different than me?"

"Well, I still have the hope of becoming human one day," I snapped. I wish I had the words back as soon as I said them.

Karayan jerked as if I'd slapped her. All the fight seemed to drain out of her eyes. "Oh. Right."

"That—came out wrong."

"No. I think you said exactly what you meant to say." Karayan bit her lip, lost in unpleasant thoughts for a long moment. Then she centered those beautiful eyes on me. "So what happens now? Are you going to tell him?"

"Are you going to stop visiting his dreams?"

"No." Karayan met my gaze. She didn't flinch. "He looks at me and sees a woman—a friend. I've never had this with anyone before, Braedyn. I won't give it up."

I shook my head, miserable—but whether I was willing to admit it or not, I couldn't help but empathize with her. Karayan read my indecision and sighed.

"When you decide what you want to do, let me know. In the meantime, you should probably change your clothes. You're going to be late for school." And with that, Karayan turned and walked out of the room.

When I made my way down to the kitchen for breakfast, Karayan was nowhere to be found. Dad was pouring himself a cup of coffee.

"We're out of eggs, but there are some English muffins in the fridge if you're hungry." He passed me on the way to the dining room and planted a kiss on the top of my head.

"You're in a hurry," I called over my shoulder. "Is everything okay?"

"Yeah, just some administrative stuff Hale wants me to take care of for the Guard." Dad shrugged. "You wouldn't believe the resources it takes to keep 100 Guardsmen housed, fed, and hidden in plain sight."

I pulled the English muffins out of the fridge, mulling this over. I knew the majority of the world's remaining Guard forces were here in Puerto Escondido, but I never saw more than a dozen of them at any one time—either on duty at the mission or hanging out here in their downtime.

"So… how much money does the Guard have?" I asked.

Dad shot me a smile from the dining room where he was finishing his cup of coffee. "Enough."

"That's not much of an answer."

Dad considered me thoughtfully. "Most of the Guard's income is generated by real estate; lands the Guard has owned under various names for centuries. We've been living off one trust for decades, but that's one trust out of several hundred that I'm aware of."

"And that's how we're paying for Amber's tuition?" I asked.

"Amber's tuition, your tuition, this house, our food—" Dad took another swig of coffee. "Like I said. It's enough." Dad shrugged into his winter coat. "Okay. I'll see you after school. Have a good day, honey." Dad walked to the front door, but when he opened it, Cassie was standing on our front porch. "Cassie."

"Mr. Murphy." Cassie looked like she was ready to burst. She strained to look past him until she spotted me.

"What happened, Cass?" I joined them in the doorway, hugging my arms against the cold of the outside world.

"Idris called me this morning. They're meeting again tonight." Cassie glanced at Dad. "I figured the Guard would want to know as soon as possible."

"Yes." Dad glanced at the house next door. "You say the meeting is tonight?"

Cassie nodded. "I'm supposed to meet Carrie at the coffee shop again at six. She knows where we're going."

"Okay. Why don't you two head to school."

"School?" I glanced at Dad, stricken. "Shouldn't we be—I don't know, fitting Cassie with body armor or something?"

"We should be acting normal," Dad said. "We don't know who's watching Cassie, or what might tip them off." He put a hand on Cassie's shoulder. "The best thing is to continue with your normal routine. But I'll alert the Guard. We'll be on hand to back you up tonight."

Cassie nodded. She glanced over her shoulder at Royal, waiting in his car on the curb. Then she looked at me with a small smile. "So… I guess that means I'll see you at school?"

"Yeah."

Cassie bounded away from us, slipping back into Royal's waiting car. They drove off together.

Dad, watching Cassie go, frowned. "Keep an eye on her," he said.

I nodded. No matter how seriously the rest of us took this stuff, Cassie still seemed to be treating it as the best adventure she'd ever had.

We dropped Cassie off at the edge of the Plaza in Old Town at 5:30 that night. We'd taken my car, but as soon as we let Cassie out, I scooted over into the passenger side and Royal took the wheel. The plan was for him to drive while I kept a mental eye on Cassie. Lucas had his cell phone at the ready; we'd be in contact with the Guard as soon as Cassie and Carrie left the coffee shop for the meeting.

We parked across the Plaza, with a clear view of the coffee shop door. I kept my eyes focused on the exit, waiting for Cassie to reemerge. Though the early days of April had been unseasonably warm, tonight was actually pretty chilly.

"So when she says 'acolyte,' what are we thinking that means?" Royal glanced into the rearview mirror, addressing the question to Lucas in the backseat. "Like, lighting some candles? Singing some songs?"

"Hopefully we'll find out tonight." Lucas put a hand on my shoulder. "Is that them?"

Two figures emerged from the coffee shop, bundled up against the crisp Spring evening. One of them turned toward us quickly. Cassie.

"This is it." I caught Lucas's hand in mine and squeezed it briefly.

Royal started the car. "Where to?"

I closed my eyes, relying now on a different sense to track Cassie. I centered my thoughts on my friend, opening up my mind to the larger dream world. Cassie's consciousness bobbed at the edge of my vision. It was a simple matter to direct my thoughts to follow her.

And then I was nestled snugly in the back of Cassie's mind. I felt her smile; she knew I was with her. Carrie was walking briskly to a parked car in one of the lots on the far side of the Plaza. I recognized it from Cassie's last foray. The girls got into the car and Carrie started the engine.

"It'll warm up in a minute," she said, giving Cassie a small smile.

"No problem." Cassie buckled her seat belt and tucked her hands into the crooks of her arms. "So… where are we going?"

Carrie pulled a folded piece of paper out of her coat pocket. "I'm not totally sure. The directions are kind of weird. Do you mind navigating?"

Cassie took the page. The directions indicated they'd be driving out of Puerto Escondido. I felt a little thrill of fear move through Cassie, and for a moment, I thought she might bail on the mission. But she cleared her throat. "So you're going to start by taking the highway north out of town.

"Okay." Carrie pulled out of the parking lot.

"North," I murmured, dimly aware of my own body back in the Firebird. I felt the car start to move, but my attention was still with Cassie. As the girls took the north road out of town, I relayed their directions to Royal, and Lucas passed the information along to the Guard. In 15 minutes, we were leaving the lights of Puerto Escondido behind us, heading deeper into the surrounding foothills. The road carved a path through the mountains. Later, it would meet up with an interstate. But for the next 100 miles or so it was a fairly deserted rural highway.

And that made things complicated for us. We couldn't follow too closely, as our headlights, cutting through the darkness, would announce our presence on the lonely road. And so we hung back, giving Cassie and Carrie a good 15-minute lead.

About 30 minutes outside of town, Cassie spotted an old sign for a campground. She directed Carrie to turn off the main road. Through her eyes, I recognized the sign. Dad had brought me out here for backpacking as a little kid. We'd hiked up into the mountains, spending four days by a little stream, fishing, hiking, and eating s'mores over the fire every night. We hadn't seen another living soul the whole time we'd been up there. I guess—if you were planning a super-secret occult ya-ya session—you could pick a worse location.

Carrie steered her car down the access road, slowing considerably when the paved road gave way to gravel.

"You're sure this is right?" She sounded skeptical, but kept her eyes fastened to the road before them.

"According to this, it should be just ahead."

Carrie followed the bend in the road, and at the end of it she saw three other cars parked in the darkness. "I guess we're here?" Her voice sounded unsure, but she pulled up beside the closest car and killed the engine. Cassie and Carrie exchanged a nervous glance. Carrie caught Cassie's hand and gave it a squeeze. "I'm glad we're doing this together."

Cassie nodded, but I felt her growing unease as she and Carrie got out of the car. Ahead in the distance, they could just make out a figure in white, holding a gleaming lantern and beckoning them closer.

Back in the Firebird, Royal had just spotted the turn off.

"Pull over here," I said. "They'll hear us if we get any closer."

As Royal parked, I let my attention move fully to Cassie. The gravel crunched under her and Carrie's feet with each step, sounding unnaturally loud in the still night. Yet, despite being deep in the mountains, the path was well lit; a full moon shone high in the sky overhead, casting a silvery light onto the earth.

Cassie and Carrie followed the path to the edge of a clearing and stopped.

In the center of the clearing, four women stood, all in white, with their long hair streaming in the gentle breeze. I felt Cassie's awe; their white gowns caught the light of the moon and reflected it, giving them an almost mystical glow in the darkness.

Idris turned. Her long white hair flowed around her shoulders, blending so seamlessly with the white of her gown that she looked almost angelic.

"Welcome, daughters."

Cassie studied the others, recognizing Emily immediately. The slender blond stood, clutching the skirt of her white dress self-consciously. She gave Carrie a warm smile, then gave Cassie a tentative wave.

Idris's eyes softened as she beckoned Cassie and Carrie forward. "Tonight is your initiation. With this ceremony, we welcome you into the inner circle of our family." Idris gestured, and one of the two other women moved forward, a white gown folded over each arm. She handed one to Cassie and one to Carrie. Idris approached. "The white vestments symbolize a new beginning. If you would oblige me, the dress should be the only thing worn during the ritual."

Cassie glanced at the gown in her hands, stricken.

Emily gave her a look full of empathy. "My advice? Change quickly. It's warmer than it looks."

Carrie and Cassie gave each other a nervous glance. As if reassured by whatever they saw in the other's expression, they started removing their clothes. Through Cassie's senses, I felt the shock of the cold night air, conscious—as she was—of the full moon illuminating her nakedness. When she'd stripped to her underwear, Cassie hesitated.

Idris gave her an understanding smile. "Do not be ashamed of your body, child. It is man who has taught us to fear what nature has bestowed upon us. Let this be the first small step you take toward embracing the strength of your feminine power."

Cassie glanced at Carrie, blushing. But then, taking a deep breath, Cassie shed her under things and slipped the dress over her body as fast as she could.

Emily had been right; shortly after Cassie had shimmied the dress around her thin frame, she started to feel warmer. The texture of the dress was slightly scratchy against Cassie's skin, but the comfort of the warmth it provided more than made up for that.

Idris beamed as Cassie and Carrie—now barefoot—walked forward to join the others in the center of the clearing. Altogether, they were six. Idris's attendants placed the girls in a line. The ground was cold as ice, and in moments, the bottoms of Cassie's feet were throbbing in protest.

"We are undertaking an important mission." Idris faced each of the acolytes in turn. "I must be sure of your commitment before we go any further. Take this moment to look within yourselves one last time. You must ask yourself if you are truly willing to devote yourself to our work. As acolytes of Lilith, you will be as crucial to our cause as the highest priestess. It is a great honor, but it is also a serious responsibility. We must be sure of each of you."

The attendant who'd handed out their gowns brought a beautifully carved wooden box to Idris, holding it at the ready. Idris opened the lid. Inside, three small daggers gleamed in the moonlight.

Back in the Firebird I felt my body jerk in response.

"Braedyn? What is it?!" Royal grabbed my arm.

I shook my head, needing to focus on the clearing, afraid to leave Cassie's mind. I was dimly aware of Lucas, urging Royal to wait. But I couldn't waste any effort on them, not right now. I poured my full attention back into Cassie.

She was glancing from the daggers to Idris. The old woman's usually gentle features were stern, almost severe. Idris took the first dagger out of the box.

"Our blood is our life." Idris presented the first dagger to Emily, supporting the slender weapon across her open palms.

Emily took it gingerly in one hand.

"As we commit our blood to Lilith, so too, we commit our lives." Idris pulled the second dagger out and presented it to Carrie.

Carrie took the dagger, turning it in her hands with an almost reverent expression.

"Your blood, as your life, is yours to give as you choose." Idris presented the final dagger to Cassie. Cassie hesitated, meeting Idris's eyes. I could feel the conflicting thoughts warring within her mind. Idris watched her. The older woman's eyes were free of judgment or suspicion. She simply waited for Cassie to make her choice. I held my breath. But then Cassie took the dagger, her hand shaking slightly as it closed about the hilt. Idris gave her a warm smile, then stepped back to face all three acolytes. She held up her left hand. A vivid white scar travelled across her palm.

"We have all made this sacrifice." Her eyes softened. "The pain is a small price to pay for all we receive in return." Idris turned her face toward the moon, closing her eyes. Carrie and Emily followed suit. After a moment, feeling acutely self-conscious, Cassie joined them. Her heart was hammering loudly in her ears, but as the minutes stretched out, she found herself growing calmer. And something else happened—time seemed to fade to a dull hum in the background, muting all sensation with it. Even the ache in Cassie's feet subsided to almost nothing.

Suddenly, Idris was beside her, whispering in her ear. "Make your choice, daughter. Now, while Lilith shields you from the pain."

Cassie's eyes snapped open, and she stared at her hands before her. She held her left palm out over the ground, and she'd rested the blade of the dagger across it, hilt gripped tightly in her right hand. When had she moved her hands? Cassie stared at the sight, and I felt a chill raking over my scalp. Cassie made her choice. The dagger slid across her palm, and for a moment I thought she hadn't pushed hard enough to slice through the skin. But then blood welled up into her palm; the cut was deep.

Idris caught Cassie's hand and tipped her palm to one side, catching the stream of bright red blood in a small bronze chalice before it could fall to the ground.

"Well done, child." Idris's eyes gleamed with approval.

Cassie glanced to her side. Carrie held her left hand over another chalice, her face twisted in pain. Emily had sunk to the ground, a few spots of blood dotting the hem of her white dress, a chalice on the ground beside her, full to the brim of dark liquid.

And then whatever dam was holding back the pain burst, releasing a storm of sensation back into Cassie's body. Cassie dropped the dagger with a strangled scream of agony. Idris—ready for this—caught her arm to steady her. "It will pass."

The second attendant bent to retrieve Cassie's dagger. When she straightened, Cassie met her eyes.

Elyia.

For the second time, I wrenched my consciousness out of Cassie's mind before she could sense my fear.

Royal was peering into my face. "Cassie?"

"She… she's been initiated," I said, forcing a neutral tone into my voice.

Behind us, Lucas relayed this news to the Guard on the other end of his phone. Royal held my eyes, sensing there was something I wasn't telling him. I glanced quickly away.

"I think it's almost over. Give me a minute."

I slipped back into Cassie's mind, acutely aware of Royal's anxiety in the seat next to mine. When I reconnected with Cassie, all the acolytes were kneeling together before Idris.

"You are Lilith's acolytes now," Idris was saying. "Three young women—among all your peers—deemed worthy of this sacred duty."

Idris took up each chalice, one by one, and emptied the contents into a larger bronze vessel, full of another liquid I couldn't make out in the light of the moon. It gleamed with an oily sheen. Idris took the vessel in her hands. She walked a circle around the girls, trailing a thin stream of the blood-mixture into the earth until she reached her starting place.

"This ground is now consecrated with the power of our commitment. We will meet here every Friday night at dusk to meditate and prepare until the solstice dawns. Now rise, acolytes."

The girls stood, shaking with a combination of adrenaline, pain, and the bitter cold of the evening. Idris embraced them one by one, giving each girl a kiss on the forehead. When she took Cassie into her arms, Cassie let her embrace her, then caught her arm before she could pull back.

"Prepare for what?"

Idris must have mistaken Cassie's anxiety for anticipation, because she smiled. "For Lilith's return."

"Well, at least now we know what they're planning." Hale's face was tight, drawn with concern.

I sank back into the Guard's couch, exhausted. I'd just finished telling Hale, Dad, Gretchen, Matt, Thane, and Ian everything I'd witnessed, with Cassie filling in some of the sparser parts of my report. She'd wrapped a thick bandage tightly around her wounded palm, but already spots of red were starting to show through.

"That's not really possible, though, is it?" Cassie glanced around the room. "They can't—I mean, *The* Lilith?"

"Let's not wait to find out," said Thane.

"What do you suggest?" Ian eyed Thane uneasily.

"Clearly we must strike now."

"And whom do you suggest we attack?" Ian's eyebrows hiked up.

"Idris. The Lilitu working with her." Thane's expression was hard, merciless. "To stop Lilith from returning, we must stop those trying to aid her in her return."

"You assume the only Lilitu working with Idris are the ones we've seen at the meetings. What if there are more? Eliminating Idris and her attendants now would only put the others on alert." Ian gestured to Cassie. "And what about the acolytes? They've been initiated by a blood rite we do not yet understand. Moving on the cult could jeopardize these young women—who I assume we can all agree are merely victims in this?"

Cassie blanched; I don't think she'd fully accepted her own peril before this moment. Hale and Dad traded a worried look.

Thane's eyes narrowed. "You propose we do nothing?"

"I propose we move carefully, Thane." Ian glanced around the room. "Yes, we must act. But we must act *intelligently*. Keep in mind, we have some time until winter solstice arrives."

"Why is it always winter solstice?" Royal groaned.

"It's the longest night of the year." Lucas glanced at Ian, but the old archivist gestured for him to explain. "It's a night of power for the Lilitu."

"I thought every night was a night of power for the Lilitu," Cassie mumbled.

Gretchen gave her a wry smile, and then eyed the bandage wrapped tightly around Cassie's palm. "I think you're going to need stitches for that. Come on. I'll drive you to urgent care."

"I'll keep you company," Matt said, stepping back to give Cassie room to stand.

Cassie stood, cradling her hand gingerly. She glanced back at the archivists, deeply concerned. "Do we even know what Idris needs to do to prepare for Lilith's return?"

"Would it be some kind of ritual?" I glanced at Ian. He considered me thoughtfully. "Or maybe it relies on some kind of supernatural artifact, like the vessel Seth needed to open the Seal. Have you guys ever read about anything like that?"

Thane and Ian exchanged a look.

"I have not. Have you?" Ian asked.

"A how-to for waking up the mother of demons?" Thane's lips twisted, as though he'd just bitten into a lemon expecting something sweet. "No."

"Perhaps a lesser text includes some mention of the particulars." Ian stood. "We can start with the compendium."

Thane grimaced. "I do not like this, Hale. We are playing with fire. Inaction, however prudent it may seem, is still inaction. Can we afford to waste what little time we have before winter solstice?"

Hale's brows drew together as he contemplated Thane's words. After a long moment, he sighed. "Let's see what our research digs up. If we've found nothing by the end of August, we'll shift to offense."

Thane shook his head slowly. "Time is our enemy. Each day that passes without action is another opportunity for victory lost. We risk too much by waiting—"

"Wait." I sat up straighter on the couch, goaded into action by a sudden flash of inspiration. Everyone turned toward me. "I think I can save us some time."

Dad's eyes searched my face. He knew me well enough to be worried.

"Are you saying you might know something about this ritual after all?" Thane's voice was dangerously quiet. His eyes danced with suspicion.

"No." I gave Thane a defiant glare. "But I know someone who will."

Dad flipped the light switch off, then crossed to take a seat in the chair he'd pulled next to my bed. I was sitting, cross-legged, on the comforter, leaning back against my headboard. Dad eased into the chair and crossed his arms.

"Dad, trust me. I can do this." I hoped to cut him off at the pass before he could launch into another lecture on why this was a supremely bad idea.

"I do trust you, sweetheart." Dad's eyes creased with concern. I wanted to reach out and hug him, but I was afraid he'd take that as a sign of fear. "But we know almost nothing about her, and you're getting ready to jump into her mind."

"I know this doesn't mean anything to you, but I'm *strong.* Stronger than Karayan, even."

Dad glanced over his shoulder toward the door, uneasy. "Karayan isn't as strong as you might think," he said quietly. "Her mother came from a long line of Lilitu who have been hunting and breeding in our world, presumably since the last great war with the Lilitu, over 3,000 years ago."

I studied Dad, confused. "What does Karayan's mother have to do with anything?"

"A Lilitu's power is directly related to her lineage. The farther removed by birth she is from Lilith herself, the weaker the Lilitu's powers."

A memory sprang to my head. Something Seth had said to Karayan during our fight at the mission. "She's... low-born?"

Dad looked into my eyes, surprised. "Yes. Exactly."

"Seth said his mother was Lilith-born."

Dad's eyes narrowed. "Did he?"

"So that means Lilith was actually his grandmother?"

Dad nodded. "I suppose that explains how he was able to enthrall Angela so completely." Dad's thoughts turned inward for a long moment. "Seth must be very old. Older, even, than we thought. To the best of our knowledge, the last of Lilith's daughters was exterminated during the Crusades."

I was suddenly struck by another thought. "What about my mother? Doesn't that mean—" I swallowed, scared. "That means Seth—if his mother was Lilith's daughter, and my mother—best case scenario—was Lilith's granddaughter, that means he's inherently stronger than I am."

Dad met my gaze, but he didn't answer.

I pulled my knees up to my chest, hugging them tightly.

"If you don't want to do this, honey—" Dad started.

"No. No. It's okay." I forced myself to smile, then scooted down, curling onto my side. Dad watched me, eyes full of trepidation. "You'll be here?"

"I'm not going anywhere." Dad reached out and caught my hand. He gave it a brief squeeze, then leaned back to wait.

I closed my eyes, taking a few moments to gather my courage. And then I willed myself into the dream.

My roses swayed in another rough breeze. I clamped down on my fear, and the breeze died down.

"This is the only logical move," I told myself. I thought I believed it, so why did my voice sound so shaky?

I knelt and placed my hand to the ground. As the pool opened up before me, I concentrated on her face. Long brown hair, stunning blue eyes, perfect, fair skin—

A shimmering spark rose out of the pool at my feet, haloed in that strange blue-purple light that distinguished Lilitu dreams from those of humankind. I closed my hand around the spark.

Elyia had woven a shield around her dream. But, unlike the smooth shield that Seth had erected around Mr. Hart's sleeping mind, this shield was rough—more like a briar patch than a seamless barrier. I let my mind skim over the surface of the shield, until I found a chink. With as little effort as it took to untie my shoes, I pulled on the shield. It came apart under my hand.

I slipped smoothly into Elyia's dream.

Elyia looked up as I appeared before her, still reeling from my having wrenched a hole in the fabric of her dream. When she saw me, her eyes bulged. I felt a mild pressure. She was trying to push me out of her dream.

I smiled a feral smile, confident now that I was stronger than Elyia. *Much* stronger. "That won't work."

Elyia staggered back, and the pressure around me shredded. "What do you want?"

"Information."

Elyia's eyes widened. She glanced around, as if she could escape.

I took a step closer. "Tell me about Lilith. How are you going to wake her up?"

"Wake her up?" Elyia's mouth twisted in a bitter smile. It shot a spear of ice through my core.

"Are you saying—" My voice caught in my throat. "She's already awake?" Elyia's smug satisfaction was all the answer I needed. "How long?"

"Oh, for a while now." Elyia's eyes glittered; she looked pleased with herself.

"But—" I wracked my brain, recalling what Idris had told Cassie. "She needs help to return."

Elyia's smile faded. Her eyes flickered across my face, suddenly uncertain.

"What does Idris have to do?"

Elyia's jaw clenched tight; she wasn't giving it up that easily.

"*What does Idris have to do before Lilith can return?*" I punctuated each word, moving closer to Elyia. "I know you only have until the solstice."

"How—?" Her voice was thin and reedy with panic. But then a puzzle piece seemed to snap into place for her. "One of the acolytes? One of the acolytes has been reporting to the Guard."

Fear flooded my mind. For a moment, I was too stunned to think.

"Which one?" Elyia's lips pulled back in a snarl. "The blond? Or is it the little dark-haired girl?"

Driven by panic, I knelt and put a hand to the ground. I knew what I had to do. Just like the horrible night I'd stolen Lucas's memory, I focused my energy, willing Elyia's thoughts to take on a physical form within this dream. A flower sprang out of the earth at my fingertips—a memory—the memory of this conversation. I put my hand around it and pulled.

"*No!*" Elyia dropped to the ground, clutching her head in agony—just like Lucas had. But now, I felt no hesitation. I had to protect Cassie. Elyia couldn't be left with even the faintest hint of suspicion that could implicate Cassie.

The flower's roots ran deep, and as I pulled, more blossoms sprang up. But I worked quickly, and in less than a minute, all of Elyia's concerns about the acolytes had been—literally—pulled out of her mind.

"What have you done?" She crouched facing me. Her eyes were dull with confusion. She blinked, struggling to recall a memory that was no longer present within her mind. Around us, the flowers—the representation of that memory—withered and crumbled into dust.

I felt my hands shaking, adrenaline and panic still washing through my system. But I forced myself to face her with a steely glare. "You still haven't answered my question," I whispered. "What must Idris do to prepare for Lilith's return?"

Elyia's eyes refocused onto my face. She glared murder at me, refusing to speak.

I placed my hand to the ground again, this time seeking information unfamiliar to me. After a few moments, a new spray of flowers erupted around us. "Last chance," I said, placing my hand around the first flower's delicate stem.

Elyia stared at the blooms with a sick look of horror on her face. "Do this, little traitor, and you will regret it to the end of your days."

"Suit yourself." I pulled the flower out of the ground. Its roots trailed up, scattering bits of earth across the other flowers. Images flooded into my mind. Blood. A knife. A slender finger of sunlight—

Elyia clutched her head, shrieking. "Stop!"

I looked up as the images sorted themselves in my head, revealing this first bit of her memory. "A sacrifice?"

Elyia glared hatred at me, gritting her teeth.

I pulled harder. As the roots emerged from the soil of her mind, they tugged another flower up out of the ground in a rain of dirt. "A *human* sacrifice," I breathed. Elyia groveled on the ground before me, but I could barely see her. All the warmth drained out of my body. "The acolytes? Are you going to sacrifice those girls?"

Recovering slightly, Elyia lifted her head. She was actually smirking at the question. "The *sacrifice* must be male." Her eyes glinted with malicious curiosity. "How can a Lilitu know so little about her own kind?"

I gripped another flower stem. Elyia froze, eyes riveted on my hand.

"So the sacrifice, I'm guessing it has to be performed on the solstice?"

Elyia licked her lips, meeting my eyes. "Yes."

"Where?"

Elyia eyed the flower in my hands, fear growing behind her eyes. "The temple," she whispered.

"The Temple of Lilith?" When she didn't answer, I jerked the flower out of the ground. Elyia howled in agony, doubling over onto the ground. More images flooded through me. Stone walls, deeply carved patterns, a massive stone altar— Another piece of the puzzle snapped into place in my mind. "You've been there?" My gaze sharpened on Elyia. She was panting now, pressing her fists to her temples in obvious pain. "Where is it?"

Elyia lurched to her feet. I felt her trying to escape the dream—to force herself to wake.

No—I couldn't let her go. Without thinking, I plunged my hand into the dirt at my feet. In that instant, I could feel the entirety of this dream, another fragile bubble floating in the vast darkness of the collective unconscious of all living beings. I concentrated, shooting a shield around the edges of the dream, trapping Elyia inside, leaving only the tiniest hole open for my own silver thread of consciousness.

Elyia spun on me, her face ashen. "Please. He'll kill me."

"Where is the temple, Elyia?" I stood. Elyia staggered back, trying to flee. I gestured almost lazily toward the ground at her feet. It went from solid to soupy in the blink of an eye. Suddenly Elyia found herself scrabbling through quicksand, unable to escape. As I approached her, the ground solidified for me.

"How—?" Elyia fell silent as I reached her. Her eyes rolled, wide with fear.

I lay a finger on her forehead. "Where is the temple?" But this time, I listened to the thoughts coursing through Elyia's mind. An image rose in her thoughts and I seized on it.

The dream around us shifted. Elyia's eyes rolled in fear. We were standing in a chamber, a low, cramped room more like a cave than a church—with the exception of the massive stone altar dominating the space. The same altar I had seen in the memory I'd ripped from Elyia's mind moments before. It was covered with intricate carvings, deep grooves cut into the stone that ran over the face of the altar and down onto the floor beneath. I recognized a few of the symbols as ancient Mesopotamian glyphs. I left Elyia, still trapped in place, and examined the space. No windows. Only one door opened out of the space; beyond the opening I could see a long hall, sloping upwards from the chamber.

The realization struck me and I let out a sharp breath in surprise. "It's underground."

Elyia let out a soft moan of despair. I glanced back at her, suddenly alert.

"How do I find it?"

Elyia eyed me with pure, unadulterated hatred.

"Where is the entrance?" I dropped my eyes to the sand at her feet, stirring it with my mind. Elyia gasped as the sand tightened about her painfully.

"It's hidden—" But she clamped her mouth shut before finishing the thought.

"Hidden where?" When she didn't answer, I placed my forefinger on her forehead once more. An image of roiling water filled my head. Elyia's eyes tightened, but at that moment I felt a tug at my shield—and the control I'd exerted over this dream exploded into a billion tiny fragments.

Seth appeared from nothing. Goosebumps crawled over my skin. The desperate urge to flee crowded out all other thoughts—but his eyes latched onto Elyia, not me.

"I gave you one simple task." Seth stood over Elyia, now freed from the quicksand I'd imposed on the dream. She recoiled, trying desperately to scrabble away from him. Seth's eyes shifted to me. He raised one finger, wagging it as though scolding a toddler. "And I believe I told you to stay out of my way."

I glared at him, willing a strength I didn't feel into my voice, even as I sent my mind wandering over the surface of the dream, looking for a way out. Seth had somehow knotted the thread of my consciousness into the dream, trapping me here as effectively as I'd trapped Elyia. "I know about Lilith's return," I said, hoping to stall for time.

"Oh?" Seth crossed his arms, examining me with faint amusement.

"There's no way we're going to let you sacrifice a human."

"See, *actually,* I think you're going to forget all about this little dream." There was something so confident in his face that I could only stare. Seth's smile broadened. "Because otherwise, I'll have to destroy your boy, Royal. As I'm killing him—and, trust me, the process will take some time—I'll tell him all about this little conversation, and how easy it would have been for you to spare him an agonizing death, simply by doing nothing." His words—spoken so calmly—sent a wash of ice through my veins. "Nighty-night, Braedyn." Seth gestured.

The world around me popped like a bubble.

I woke screaming. The daylight streamed into my room but I barely saw it, still clutched tight in the grip of my fear.

Dad lurched out of his chair, exhaustion dropping away from him in an instant. "Braedyn?!" He was at my side in half a second, clutching my shoulders, trying to read my face. I let out a ragged breath, then clung to him, burying my face into his shoulder.

I heard Karayan crash through the door to my room moments later. "What?! What happened? Braedyn?!"

When I finally pulled back, both Karayan and Dad were watching me, sharp fear evident in their eyes.

"Seth—he knows we know their plan."

I felt Dad's hands tighten on my shoulders. He searched my face, desperate for a reassurance I couldn't give him.

Horror sizzled down my spine. "Cassie. We have to pull her out of this thing."

"Does he know she's one of the acolytes?" Karayan asked.

I shook my head. "No. No. Elyia suspected for a minute, but I ripped the memory out of her mind." As the words left my mouth I considered them. If Seth had known Cassie was involved, wouldn't he have said something to me? No. He would have attacked her already. If Seth suspected Cassie, she'd be dead. It was time to pull the plug and get her the hell out of this mess.

"She's been initiated," Dad said, concern giving his voice a husky quality. "Will they let her just walk away now?"

"I don't care," I hissed.

"You should." Karayan gave me an even stare, daring me to argue. "Cassie is your connection to the cult."

"So I'll hitchhike in Carrie's mind, or Emily's," I said.

"Uh huh." Karayan crossed her arms. "And how well do you know those girls?"

"Why does it matter?" I glared ice at Karayan. She shrugged.

"Okay. Try it. Try contacting one of them right now. It's past 10:00, they should both be up." Karayan studied me shrewdly. "Go on. We'll wait."

Dad glanced at Karayan, trying to suss out what she was doing. I shook my head, exasperated.

"We don't have time for this. I have to call Cassie." I swung my feet over the side of the bed. Karayan put a hand on my chest, keeping me from standing up.

"Just try it."

"What is your problem? You're supposed to be on our side now!"

"Why do you think I'm doing this, sweetie?" But Karayan's eyes flashed with anger. "If you can reach either Carrie or Emily's mind, I'll back off and you can un-enroll your little friend from Madame Whitelock's school for Lilith Wannabes. If not, you need to think hard about your next move. You might need Cassie on the inside."

I glared at her. "Fine." I closed my eyes and tried to center my thoughts. As I turned my thoughts inward, I sensed the fabric of the dream world close. I summoned Carrie's face into my head. Nothing happened. I pushed harder, trying to remember the sound of her voice, or the way she tossed her strawberry-blond bob. A faint light danced at the edge of my consciousness. I turned my thoughts toward it—and it flickered out.

Surprised, I opened my eyes. Karayan was watching me closely. She looked almost resigned. "That's what I thought."

"I just need to focus." I closed my eyes again, and summoned Carrie's image back to the forefront of my thoughts. I tried to recapture the sound of her voice again, or the feel of her hand on my arm. Again, I just caught the flicker of her mind at the edge of my perception. But again, as I turned toward it in my mind's eye, it vanished. I let out a growl of frustration.

Dad caught my hand, worried. "What's wrong?"

"I can't pin her down," I admitted. I gave Karayan a sour look.

"It's because you don't know her."

"Yes I do," I snapped. "We went to school together for a whole year before she graduated."

"Oh, my bad. She invited you to a lot of slumber parties? You painted each other's toenails? Braided each other's hair?"

I scowled at Karayan. "Your point?"

"My *point* is, this isn't like finding someone in a dream. Human minds, they're open books as long as they're asleep. Unless some Lilitu is shielding them, you can walk right in anytime you want. But when that human mind wakes up? It's a whole different ballgame, sweetie. To share a conscious mind, there has to be a connection. Like, you know, a real, genuine thing you two share. That's why you were able to reach Cassie's waking mind. You two share a bullet-proof friendship-bond."

"You're forgetting," I said through gritted teeth. "I managed to connect with *your* mind long before I would have called you a friend."

Karayan smiled bitterly. "Yes, well, Lilitu." She gestured to herself and shrugged. "The rules are a bit different for us. Also, before you and I were friends, we were enemies. That can be a strong connection, too." Karayan shrugged. "You ever want to contact Amber's mind, for example—"

I turned my head, unable to look at her any longer. Dad gave my hand a careful squeeze.

"Honey?" When I didn't respond, he continued. "Whether or not it's something you want to hear, Karayan makes a point we can't afford to ignore. If we're going to have any hope of keeping tabs on this cult—"

"She's my friend."

"I know. But until we find another way in—"

I pulled my hand free from his grip. "I know, okay!" I gritted my teeth, trying to tame the surge of anger rising up in my stomach. "I know." Lilith was awake. The plan for her return was already in motion. We couldn't afford to let our one connection to the cult go. It had to be Cassie. But I didn't have to like it.

"Winter solstice is almost eight months away," he said, keeping his voice low. "We have time. We'll find someone else, I don't know—maybe you can get to know Carrie or that other girl better. In the meantime, we let Cassie stay in. We monitor the situation. We'll be ready to swoop in if she ever needs us."

I shook my head. But the truth was, I didn't have any better ideas. Cassie was our link to the cult, and it looked like that wouldn't be changing any time soon.

11

May arrived with a late spring rain. The deluge left the desert refreshed, kicking up that earthy smell so distinctive of New Mexico storms. I used to love this time of year—balanced on the edge of a changing season, with school about to end and summer stretching ahead, full of promise. Now, the uncertainty of what our future held made the changing season an ominous reminder of how little we knew about our enemies, or what they planned. More than that, though, the change of seasons served to highlight our powerlessness in the face of time. Even though summer had yet to officially start, each day that passed brought us closer to winter solstice.

At school, everyone was ramping up for the end of the semester. Teachers announced study sessions to help prepare students for finals. Cassie, Royal, and most of the other juniors and seniors were cramming in preparation for AP tests. I tried to focus on reviewing for AP History, but it seemed so insignificant in comparison to everything else we were facing.

Of my friends, only Lucas seemed to share my increasing anxiety. We started meeting in the basement for a warm-up session every day after school before Amber arrived. The extra training honed our instincts, but more importantly, it lessened our fear of the unknown. It felt good to be doing *something* to prepare for—whatever might be coming.

The Guard, on the other hand, was on full alert. Ever since I'd discovered that the Temple of Lilith was somewhere beneath our feet, the Guard had set out to locate it. Ian's thinking was, if they could find the temple, they could keep Idris from doing whatever it was she had planned for the solstice—but until they located it, it was too risky to move on Idris or the Lilitu helping her. Thane, reluctantly, agreed. Ian and Thane had started collecting geological surveys for the region, which piled up in the Guard's living room practically over night. They spent their days identifying every local cave, and then sending teams of Guardsmen out to search for anything matching the description I'd provided of the temple with its large stone altar.

It was a massive amount of work to go through all that material—and that didn't even include the manpower and man-hours needed to search the caves once they'd been located. I'd never seen Thane look quite so harried. Ian, on the other hand, seemed confident that they were on the right track. He made it clear that he believed a thorough, methodical search of all geological features in the area couldn't fail to turn up success. His confidence put the rest of us more at ease—well, all of us except for Thane. But I'd long since given up looking for positivity from *that* grizzled archivist.

Beyond school and the Guard's manic search for the hidden temple, I had Cassie to keep me occupied. Every Friday night, Cassie would meet up with Carrie and the two of them would drive out to Idris's clearing. No one—not Idris, not the Lilitu attendants—seemed to suspect that Cassie attended each meeting with a telepathic hitchhiker. I kept my eyes and ears open—through Cassie's eyes and ears—but tried hard to shield my own feelings from Cassie herself.

Reluctant as I might have been to let her continue with the cult, Cassie was unflagging in her efforts to learn as much as she could about Idris's plans. She'd proved to be our lifeline. As hard and thoroughly as the Guard searched for clues about the temple or the cult, Cassie was the only one turning up any information. As the weeks passed, I grew more comfortable with the idea of Cassie worming her way into the heart of this clandestine organization. Her naïveté and eager optimism ended up being the perfect disguise. She had only to be herself; Idris misinterpreted all of Cassie's curiosity as the interest of a devoted young acolyte, hoping to do her best in the service of Lilith.

The meetings themselves became rote very quickly. Cassie and the others would arrive in the clearing, change under the light of the moon into their vestments, and then the rest of the night would be taken up chanting, meditating, or performing "rituals of purity" that involved one of the acolytes standing in the center of the clearing while the others walked a circle around her, each gently swinging a small, filigreed bronze ball full of smoking incense—I think Idris called them thuribles.

Occasionally, Idris would let slip another clue about Lilith's return. At one point, she mentioned anointing an altar. At another, she said something about preparing a vessel. Each time she let slip one of these tidbits, Cassie would straighten, focused on soaking up each and every detail Idris managed to spill. Once, Emily—caught up in the mystery—pressed Idris for more details. I could feel Cassie's fingernails pressing into her palms in her anticipation for more information.

But Idris simply gave Emily a fond smile and answered, "all in due time, child. Our most important task is to be ready when Lilith calls upon us."

Though I could feel her frustration building, Cassie would fall back in line with the other acolytes. Elyia, present at each of these meetings, never gave any indication to Cassie that she was more than a simple attendant for Idris. And so, week after week, Cassie would attend a meeting where we might glean another tiny fragment of the puzzle—without ever being able to fully see the bigger picture.

As May came to a close, we were no closer to uncovering the location of the temple despite Ian's careful mapping of each underground feature in the surrounding 100 miles. It felt like treading water while hoping to catch sight of land on the distant horizon—hopeless, and yet it was our only option. The alternative meant sinking into fatal despair.

I came home after practice one afternoon to find Dad wolfing down a sandwich at the dining room table. I gave him a wave and shrugged out of my jacket, hoping to decompress upstairs for a few minutes before starting my homework.

"Hey," he mumbled around a mouthful of food. "Hold up."

"Sure." I joined him in the dining room, waiting for him to swallow.

"I'm taking part of another Guardsman's shift at the mission tonight."

"You are?" I sighed. "So I guess this means you can't run

flashcards with me after dinner?"

"AP History test?"

I nodded, glum.

"Sorry, kiddo. Why don't you see if Karayan can help you out?" Dad pulled his wallet out of his pockets. "Also, I meant to hit the grocery store today. I'll spare you the gory details—the long and the short of it is unless you want a mayonnaise-and-peanut-butter sandwich, you'll have to fend for yourself come dinnertime." He handed over a few bills. "Maybe order a pizza?"

"Hm. I might be able to make that work." I took the money and shoved it into my pocket, cheered. Pizza would make studying go down a little easier.

Dad's eyes twinkled. "Glad to see you making the best of a bad situation."

"So how long is this shift supposed to be?" I asked.

"I'm not sure, but it could be a long one. Don't wait up for me." Dad shoved the last bite of sandwich into his mouth and stood. He washed the bite down with some water, then flashed me a smile. "I'm proud of you for studying, given everything else you've got on your plate." He planted a tender kiss on the top of my head.

As he started to withdraw, I grabbed hold of him in a tight bear hug. "Thanks, Dad."

Dad's arm curled around my shoulders and he gave me a squeeze. "I am sorry about the timing. I was kind of looking forward to the history refresher."

I pulled back and grinned up at him. "Don't worry, there's still three days before the test. Plenty of time to brush up on all things American Revolution."

"Well, thank heaven for small mercies." Dad pulled his jacket on and ran a hand through his hair. "Okay." He opened the door and headed into the evening, pausing at the edge of the porch to wave goodbye. "Don't study too hard."

I waved goodbye and watched as he got into his car and pulled away. I closed the door and sighed. It was after 5:00, and I was already feeling hungry.

"Hey, Karayan!" I walked down the hall toward her room. "I'm getting pizza for dinner, you want in? Karayan?"

Karayan opened the door to her room before I had a chance to knock. She glanced down the hall behind me, then smoothed the front of her shirt. "I'm good."

"Okay." I shrugged and then, sheepishly, asked, "I don't suppose you'd be interested in running through some flashcards with me?"

"Flashcards?" Karayan looked at me, but I could tell her attention was somewhere else.

"You know, key word on one side, list of facts on the other... I'm studying for a history test."

"Oh. Oh." Karayan shook her head, as if coming back to the present. "Actually, Braedyn, would it be possible for you to study upstairs tonight?"

"Uh, yeah, that's possible." I eyed Karayan, suddenly suspicious.

Karayan noticed my look and shrugged. "Today's been a rough day for Hale, I figured he could use some company."

"When you say 'rough'—?"

"It's the anniversary of his wife's death." Karayan gave me a level stare, but a hint of red rose in her cheeks.

"Uh huh." I crossed my arms.

Karayan's lips tightened. "Don't. This is not an international incident. I'm doing something nice for him. As a friend."

"And you think this is a good idea?"

"If you're worried I'll lose control and go all smoochy on him, relax." Karayan shrugged humorlessly. "You'll be right upstairs. That kind of puts a damper on the amorous stuff."

"Does Dad know about this?"

"You'd have to ask him."

"So, in other words, no."

The doorbell rang and Karayan's eyes lit up for a moment. Her expression was unguarded, and in that moment I saw a hope in her eyes, so strong it was painful. She noticed me watching and cleared her throat, trying for nonchalance. "That's him. You can either play chaperone, or give me the benefit of the doubt and take the academic road show upstairs."

I pulled the cash out of my pocket. "You'll call me when the pizza gets here?"

Karayan's expression eased. "I'll hand deliver it to you myself." She held out her hand and I pushed the cash into it. "Have fun."

"You do realize I'm studying for *history?*"

Karayan made a little "shoo" gesture at me. I headed for the staircase. Karayan opened the door as I reached the top step.

I turned, catching sight of something in Karayan's hand—a bottle of a rich amber-colored liquid. Hale entered, and even from the top of the stairs I could see the solemn look on his face.

"I got your note," he said. "You needed to see me?"

Karayan hefted the bottle. Hale's eyebrows rose in surprise. "Scotch?"

"Not just any scotch," Karayan said, smiling. Hale took the bottle out of her hands and let out a sharp breath.

"You're not kidding." He perused the bottle, murmuring in approval. "Single malt, 21 years old… this is—"

"Yours."

Hale looked up, startled. "What's the occasion?"

Karayan shrugged, looking caught. "You seem a little down. I figured, maybe you could use something to take the edge off."

Hale looked down at the bottle in his hands. After a moment, he looked up again. "Care to join me?"

Karayan beamed. "I'll grab some glasses." She turned to head back to the kitchen, glancing up to where I stood at the top of the stairs. Her eyes caught on me and she gave them a little roll, as if to say, *Seriously, Mom? We'll be fine.*

I glanced back at Hale. He was still examining the bottle in his hands, but he wore a distant expression of such deep sadness my heart wrenched in my chest. I slipped down the hall to my room, closing the door behind me softly. Maybe Karayan actually knew what she was doing after all.

I was reviewing the Intolerable Acts of 1774 when I heard a splintering crash downstairs.

Sprinting down the hallway, I froze on the top stair at what sounded like Hale… *giggling.*

I edged down the staircase, peering into the living room. Hale and Karayan were flat on their backs on the living room floor, next to the remains of what had been one of the side-tables flanking our couch.

"What happened?" I rushed into the room, horrified. Hale and Karayan traded a guilty look with one another, and then burst into another fit of giggles. "You—you're drunk?!"

"Drunk is a strong word." Hale pushed himself to his feet then swayed unsteadily. "Though not entirely inaccurate."

I glared at Karayan. "Seriously?!"

"Don't be mad at her," Hale said. "Karayan was just being a friend."

"A friend in need," Karayan said.

"Indeed," Hale replied. Karayan giggled again. He offered Karayan a hand. She took it and let Hale help her to her feet.

"I didn't want you to have to spend the evening alone with your grief."

Hale glanced at Karayan. She blushed prettily, caught. Then her eyes shifted to the floor. "Looks like we made a bit of a mess, Hale."

I stared at the living room. Most of the furniture had been pushed to the edges of the room, leaving a large empty space in the center. "What the hell were you even doing in here?"

"Hale wanted a rematch," Karayan shrugged, grinning.

"I will admit to having been taken a little bit by surprise the first time I sparred with Ms. Karayan. We decided to figure out whether that first time was a fluke." Hale gave me a serious look that was completely undermined when he hiccupped tipsily.

"It wasn't a fluke." Karayan grinned at Hale. He held up a finger.

"The jury's still out."

"You want another rematch, pretty boy?"

Hale smiled. "You think I'm pretty?"

Karayan giggled again.

I threw my hands up in the air, exasperated. "We have to get this mess cleaned up before my dad gets home."

Hale glanced around. "Hm. We're going to need some glue."

"Glue isn't going to solve this." I sighed. So much for the Intolerable Acts of 1774. It looked like the rest of my night would be devoted to the intolerable acts of Hale and Karayan. "Just go sit down." I pushed Hale toward the dining room. "And someone put some coffee on."

I had just started to collect the shattered bits of our ex-side-table when I heard Hale and Karayan snickering again. I looked up, and saw

Hale had Karayan in a headlock.

"Okay," she said, "but remember you asked for this."

She shifted her weight—and the front door opened.

Dad entered just as Karayan launched Hale over her shoulder and sent him sprawling across the foyer.

Dad crashed back into the wall in surprise as Hale skidded toward his feet. "What the hell—?"

"Oh!" Karayan rushed forward to help Hale up. "I thought you'd resist a little!"

Hale grinned sheepishly. "It's okay, Murphy. We were just doing a little sparring."

Dad's eyes moved from Hale to Karayan. His jaw clenched. Then his eyes shifted to the living room, and the devastation I had just barely started to clean up. He caught my eye. "Stand up."

Shakily, I got to my feet. Dad approached and leaned close, taking a deep breath. My eyes flew open in horror. "You think I was drinking, too?"

Dad stepped back quickly. "No. No, of course not, kiddo." There was a tension lining his eyes that put me on alert.

"Dad?"

"There was—an attack at the mission."

Hale and Karayan straightened, alarmed.

"What kind of attack?" Hale's tipsy demeanor changed instantly, the news doing more to sober him than a gallon of coffee would have.

"An explosion."

"Oh, God—was anyone hurt?" I grabbed Dad's arm, searching his face. "Are you okay?"

"We were incredibly fortunate," Dad said. "Though I can't say the same thing for the mission itself. Someone set charges up on the roof. Most of the sanctuary's ceiling is gone. Mercifully, the majority of Guardsmen were on rounds. Those in the sanctuary had taken up stations beneath the balcony. One of the spotters, Jane, was knocked out by the blast, but a Guardsman dragged her out of the mission and revived her."

"Who?" Hale's eyes were solemn.

"Your guess is as good as mine." Dad ran a hand through his hair. "The bigger question for me is why? Why the roof? If they'd meant to hurt us, why not toss the charges in through the windows?"

"Maybe whoever did this hoped the whole building would come down on our heads," Hale mused.

"Maybe you should start posting Guardsmen on the roof," Karayan said.

Dad gave her a tight smile. His gaze flicked between Hale and Karayan, then he squeezed my shoulder lightly. "Why don't you go on up to your room."

Sensing the tension in the room, I turned and fled up the stairs. Instead of retreating all the way to my room, I hesitated in the hallway, just out of sight of the people below, still able to hear the confrontation clearly.

"I should probably clean up in the kitchen," Karayan said quickly.

"Good idea." Dad's voice was hard and flat. I heard Karayan escape into the kitchen and peeked over the railing. Dad caught Hale by the arm and pulled him away from the dining room, closer to the stairwell. He lowered his voice, but I had no trouble making out the words. "What are you doing, Hale?"

"Nothing. What? Nothing."

"You must know she's nursing a crush on you." Dad's voice grated harshly. "You forget how *dangerous* she is, Hale."

His words stung me, more than I could have anticipated. We'd lived with Karayan for months now, Dad had stood up for her more than once. If he still felt this way about her, what must he think of me? He knew I was stronger than Karayan. Didn't that mean I was more dangerous than she was, too?

"I'd never cross the line, Murphy." Hale's voice rang with a defensive edge. "I know what she is."

"And yet you get drunk with her?"

"She—she gave me a bottle of scotch."

"This explains everything how?"

"I guess she knew I wasn't thrilled about being alone tonight." Hale's voice grew somber. Dad eyed him closely.

"Tonight? Oh. Oh, of course." Dad's voice softened. "It's the anniversary of Sarah's death."

"Okay. Maybe I shouldn't be here. But—in addition to everything else she is—Karayan is also becoming a good friend."

Dad got quiet for a long moment. I leaned forward, and saw him glancing back at the dining room. I could still hear the water in the sink running. "How did she know about Sarah?"

"What?" Hale looked up, surprised.

"The anniversary. Did you tell her?"

"I don't know if she even knows. Maybe she just sensed I was sad." But Hale didn't seem too sure. "Or maybe I mentioned it. We've talked about Sarah."

"But you don't remember telling her the date?"

"Maybe—maybe someone else told her." Hale shook his head, as if trying to clear the fog of drink from his mind.

"Who else knows, Hale? Aside from me? Because I'm sure as hell not in the habit of sharing sensitive personal details with a Lilitu."

"Okay, so I must have told her."

"Think back, Hale. Did you tell her? Or did she find out?"

Hale grimaced. "She wouldn't do that to me."

Dad leaned in closer, tightening his grip on Hale's arm. "You're willing to bet your soul on that?"

"I'm a trained Guardsman, Murphy." Hale pulled his arm free from Murphy's grasp. "Nothing's going on here. Leave it alone."

Dad stared at Hale, then nodded slowly. "Okay. If you say so." Dad walked away from Hale then, into the living room. I heard him sigh in frustration, but I was still watching Hale.

After Dad left, Hale turned toward the dining room. He listened to Karayan working in the kitchen for a long moment. When he turned back to the foyer, I could see his face clearly. His earlier playful mood had evaporated. In its place—a deep and growing suspicion.

12

How is it that a day can seem to last forever, while weeks slip past so quickly that the dawning of a new month takes you completely by surprise? Since the explosion at the mission, the city had been in shocked outrage. Police and reporters had descended on the mission, seeking answers to who could deliberately destroy our local historical treasure. The upside to this was Dad's "security firm" had been officially hired by the city to oversee the mission, granting the Guard official status to protect the mission. The downside? More kids showed up now than ever before—eager to see the destruction first hand. Guard patrols—in official security guard uniform now—were kept busy chasing curious civilians away.

On top of all the Guard excitement, I still had school to contend with. After all the studying for the AP History test, building a mouse-trap car for my final Physics project, and writing up a major paper on Jane Austen for English, the last days of May burned past.

The first week of June brought with it the last week of my junior year. And that meant finals. Murphy convinced Hale to give Lucas, Amber, and me the week off to focus on our studies. Instead of training after school, Lucas and I piled into my living room with Royal and Cassie to pore over the year's notes. Royal and Cassie had started prepping for finals weeks ago. Royal shared his homemade flash cards, and Cassie brought some practice quizzes she'd written up.

Even though it seemed strangely dissonant to be so focused on the end of a school year when the end of the *world* could be just around the corner, it was also indescribably comforting to be with my friends, nestled in the warmth of my home as Dad brought us study snacks every few hours.

At the end of our Sunday night session cramming for physics,

Cassie stretched, yawning. "I'm pooped. There's just not enough hours in the day for everything I need to do."

"I wish they'd hurry up and figure out how to just download information directly into our brains already." Royal closed his physics book and packed his notes back into his school bag.

I said goodbye to my friends, then spent another hour or so going over my notes. I was tempted to visit Lucas's dreams for an added boost of energy, but I didn't want to leave him drained for the next day's test. So I spent the night in dreamless sleep, waking far too soon to suit my exhausted body.

Cassie, Royal, Lucas, and I met up early before school the next day to run through a few more practice questions, and then it was time for the real thing.

"Good luck, kids," Mr. Harris said, passing out the exams along with the blue books we'd be using to show our work. When he indicated it was time to start, I flipped my test over and read the first question. A little over two hours later, after checking my work for a third time, I turned in my test.

Mr. Harris gave me a smile. "Have a great summer, Braedyn."

"Thanks. You too." I walked out of class and made my way to the cafeteria, feeling strangely light. That was it. No more physics—unless I decided to take some physics classes in college. Provided college was in my future. Provided we *had* a future.

Royal and Cassie found me in the cafeteria.

"How did it go?" Cassie asked.

"Um, actually? I think it went okay," I said.

"That's the power of the homemade flash cards, ladies." Royal leaned back in his chair, grinning.

"English prep tonight?" Lucas asked, joining us.

"You even have to ask?" Royal patted his backpack. "I've got the cards prepped and ready to go."

And that was our finals week. Every night we'd meet up at someone's house to study. English, then history, then Trigonometry—and even though Cassie was in an upper level Calculus class, she joined us for a few hours to help us prepare. By the time we'd finished our last exam, we were exhausted but triumphant.

We met up on the quad after our last final. Cassie sat beside me, picking at a blade of grass.

"It's so weird to think back to last year's finals," she said. "Back then, I had no idea Lilitu existed. My biggest problem was—" She stopped, dropping her eyes to the shredded grass in her hands. "Was dealing with Parker. So much has changed."

I looked at her, suddenly seeing her more clearly than I had in a long time. Cassie wasn't the same girl that Parker had used and tossed aside. She was strong, brave, and more stubborn than I'd ever have thought possible. "That's an understatement, Cass."

Cassie met my gaze and seemed to read my thoughts. She blushed and smiled back. I reached over and caught her in a fierce hug. When we parted, I saw a few happy tears lighting the corners of her eyes.

Royal and Lucas looked at one another. "You," Lucas said, as though Royal were about to make him cry.

"No, you," Royal echoed, sniffling dramatically. Lucas and Royal threw their arms around each other in an overwrought embrace.

"They mock us," I said.

"Foolish," Cassie answered.

As one, Cassie and I tackled the boys in retaliation, finding their ticklish spots and digging our fingers in mercilessly until the boys cried uncle. We sat back, winded and laughing. It was the perfect end to junior year.

There is no rest for the weary—not if the weary are a part of the Guard, at any rate.

By early June, Ian's list of potential sites for the underground temple had swelled to over 300. As soon as finals were over, Hale assigned Lucas and me to search duty. My first day out, Dad and I headed to the east of Puerto Escondido to check out a small natural cave.

We followed the road as far as we could. When the GPS indicated our destination lay east of the last road, Dad turned off onto a high desert prairie and we followed the signal to the coordinates Ian had given us. The prairie was dotted all over with tufts of native grasses, sagebrush, and Piñon trees. We pulled to a stop at the bottom of a mountain ridge rising out of the prairie. Dad killed the engine and we got out of the car. It was quiet, save the whispering of the wind and the distant *scree* of a hunting hawk. We shrugged into our backpacks, prepared for a long hike. I felt the water sloshing in the bottles I'd packed. Just being out here, so far from a readily available water source, made me feel thirsty. I pushed the sensation to the back of my mind. Better to save the water for later, when we really needed it.

"Pretty," I said, looking up into the mountains.

"Reminds me of when we used to go camping," Dad said. He reached out and tousled my hair.

"Dad." I gave him an irritated smile, running a hand through my hair to smooth it back down.

"You sure have grown since then." Dad gave me a wistful look.

"You okay?"

"We just haven't had a lot of time together lately."

"Tell me about it." I glanced at the GPS in my hand, then pointed eastward. "Okay. It looks like we need to head that way."

Dad put a hand on my shoulder, startling me. "I'm proud of you, kiddo."

"Thanks."

"Seriously, Braedyn." Dad's voice grew husky with emotion. "You've really grown up these last few months. I've noticed a big change in you since—" Dad hesitated, his eyes clouding with unhappy memory. "Since winter solstice."

"You have?" I felt a lump form at the base of my throat.

"I'm not the only one. Hale's noticed it, too. I mean, bringing Amber into the Guard? Dealing so graciously with all of Rhea's bullshit—"

"Dad, language." I gave him a level smile.

Dad smiled back. "You're—you've really become a team player."

I dropped my eyes. "Everything that happened with Seth—I shouldn't have second-guessed the Guard. It was stupid and dangerous, and I put us all in danger because I had this feeling that—that I could make a difference."

Dad's brows drew together. I studied him, surprised at the look of concern in his eyes.

"What's that look for?"

"I appreciate what you're saying, but—" Dad sighed. "You've got a good head on your shoulders. Just don't completely ignore your intuition."

"My intuition's what got me into trouble last time."

"No. Seth manipulated you in a way none of us anticipated." Dad gave my shoulder a squeeze. "Don't let him make you doubt yourself."

"Yeah, okay."

Dad caught me in a big bear hug. I tucked my head tight against his chest, letting him hold me for a moment. Then I pulled back.

"Not to put a damper on the father-daughter bonding thing, but shouldn't we get going?" I glanced at the mountain before us. "I mean, this is number one on a list of what, 300 more caves we have to check?"

"I suppose you're right." Dad smiled and gestured toward the ridge. "I mean, not about the list. That thing's got at least 400 caves on it now, and Ian keeps adding new ones. Good thing we've still got six and a half months before the solstice."

"Yay." I sighed, picturing a long summer of us poking our heads into one small cave after another. "Onwards and upwards." I led the way up into the mountains.

It was a wasted trip. The cave was small enough that we could see the entire thing from ten steps inside. No sloping hallways. No altar. This cave was not the Temple of Lilith. Neither was the next cave we checked, or the one after that. Three caves, all busts. We returned home close to sunset.

Lucas and Gretchen pulled up around the same time we did. They hadn't had any luck with their search, either.

"Five caves down," I muttered. "That only leaves 395 to go."

About a week after school let out, Lucas and I got a pass for the day from searching more caves. By this point, Dad and I had searched another 15 caves, while Lucas and Gretchen had searched close to 20. That would have made me feel pretty good—if Ian hadn't added another 38 caves to the list of need-to-be-searched.

Regardless, Lucas and I were so relieved to be spared another day of dusty hikes and cramped caverns that we didn't even care the reason was so we could take the practice SAT. We'd met up with Cassie and Royal the night before to run through some practice questions from a pile of books Royal's SAT tutor had given him, but there wasn't much more we could do to prepare. Spirits were high; even though we faced one more huge test, it was the last thing separating us from a long, uninterrupted summer before our senior year began.

When the day of the test arrived, Dad made Lucas and I some tomato-and-avocado omelets along with bacon, toast, and hash browns. "Brain food," he called it. We ate, and then I drove Lucas to school. I saw Royal getting out of his car as Lucas and I pulled into the parking lot. I beeped my horn and Royal looked up. Something was wrong—his face was ashen, with deep circles under his eyes again.

"Braedyn?" Lucas had spotted Royal, too. His eyes narrowed in concern.

"I see him."

We got out of the car and hurried to meet Royal at the edge of campus.

"What happened?" I searched Royal's eyes for the telltale sign of another Lilitu attack—but his pupils were responsive, constricting against the light of the morning.

"Just another nightmare," Royal said.

"Seth?" I gripped my school bag so tightly I could feel my fingernails digging into my palm.

"It—it felt like a warning," Royal said slowly.

Lucas glanced at me. Anger surged through my head, drowning out the sounds of the morning around me. For a moment, my sight grew clouded—rage dialing down my peripheral vision to almost nothing.

"Hey, guys. Ready to shred this thing?" Cassie bounded up to us. But as Royal turned to face her, her cheerful smile vanished. "What happened?"

"Don't worry about it." Royal forced a smile for Cassie's benefit. "Let's focus on the test, I'll tell you all the boring details after."

When Cassie hesitated, Royal made a little *shoo* gesture at her. "This is an important day in your academic career, young lady," he said. "Scholarships are on the line. So get a move on. Chop, chop!"

Cassie gave him a smile. "Okay, *sheesh.*"

As Cassie led the way to the dining hall, I met Royal's eyes. He knew, as well as I did, that Cassie would need some good scholarships to cover her education. He smiled faintly, but I could see his bravado fading.

We crowded into the cafeteria. It had been transformed, with large cardboard dividers set up on each dining table to screen each students' work from the others. It felt weird to be back at school this soon after finals. As we arrived, we were each escorted to one divided cubicle of a table and given a booklet and a test that we were forbidden to turn over until the start of the exam.

Waiting for the proctor to announce the start, I couldn't banish the look on Royal's face from my thoughts. Had we done something new to spark Seth's vengeance? Were we getting close to finding the temple? Had he somehow discovered Cassie was one of the three acolytes Idris was grooming? No—if that were the case, we'd know. Sitting there, I had to face the possibility that the only reason Seth had hurt Royal again was because he could. The thought sickened me.

"Alright, everyone. Good luck. You can begin now." The proctor hit a button, and a large digital clock started counting down. We'd have three hours to finish the test. Which meant three long hours sitting and waiting for the full story from Royal, while my imagination spooled out a variety of nightmare scenarios Seth might have subjected him to.

Enough. With cold resolve, I decided Seth would never have another chance to hurt Royal in a dream. I'd find a way to protect Royal. And I'd find it tonight.

The test was a blur. I was only half-paying attention as I stumbled through the questions. When the proctor called time, I leapt out of my seat and was one of the first to drop my test off in the official collection box.

I waited outside for my friends, pacing in the warm June sun.

Amber left the dining hall as I turned, bringing us face to face. She let her eyes flick over me, but brushed past without a word. I turned to watch her go, irritated. We'd spent most afternoons together training for the last four months. You'd think that would have counted for something. But Amber was just as prickly toward me as ever. I dismissed her from my mind as Cassie and Royal emerged from the dining hall.

Lucas joined us a few moments later, stretching his arms up and over his head. "So glad that is over," he mumbled.

"Listen," I said, steamrolling the post-test grumbles from my friends. "I think I've got an idea of how I can keep Seth out of your mind."

"Didn't you already try that?" Royal eyed me, worried. "I mean, not that I doubt you, but what if you try and it doesn't work—and it just ends up pissing him off even more?"

I shook my head, grim. "This will work. It has to."

Lucas glanced at Royal. "I'd let her do it, man. Worst-case scenario, Seth keeps messing with your head. Best-case scenario? You never hear from that little prick again."

Royal considered this for a moment. Finally, he nodded. "Okay. What do you need from me?"

"Just get to bed on time. I'll take it from there."

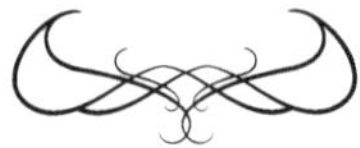

What I really needed was an example. A perfect shield. Something without any loose knots, or chinks, or weak spots. I knew it was possible. I'd come across a perfect shield around a human's dream last year.

Mr. Hart, the new drama teacher, had drawn my suspicions early in the semester. Seth, knowing I'd started to wonder if Hart was the incubus we were searching for, had shielded his dreams to make it impossible for me to identify him as human. Somehow, Seth had created a shield around Mr. Hart's dream—a shield so strong I hadn't been able to even sense Mr. Hart beyond it.

As I knelt in my dream garden that night, summoning the strength for what I needed to do, I let my thoughts draw Mr. Hart's dream to me. It rose to the surface of the silvery pool. I closed my hand around it, expecting to find the nothingness of the shield as I had before.

And yet… something had changed. It was as though the shield had started to degrade. It wasn't the perfect, impenetrable surface I'd last encountered. There was a stress around the edges of the shield. I followed the contours with my mind until I found a small tear. Ever so gently, I slipped into the dream.

Mr. Hart was there, absorbed in the weird logic of his dream. It looked like he was preparing for a role in some kind of elaborate production—but he didn't know his lines, he had no costume to wear, and he wasn't sure of his blocking. Anxiety swirled almost palpably around him, but I wasn't here for Mr. Hart.

I ignored him, keeping myself out of his way. He didn't even bat an eye in my direction, too absorbed with is own dilemma to notice me. I turned my thoughts to the shield around his dream, tracing it once more with my mind.

It was amazing.

From inside the dream, the shield was a complicated knot of energy. There were twists and turns I hadn't sensed from outside. I followed the pattern over and over again, until I started to see how it was constructed. And as I began to understand it, I also sensed how it might be repaired. I let my thoughts search out the frayed edges of the shield and—when I located them—I nudged them back into the pattern, in effect retying the parts of the knot that had worked themselves loose. I repaired the last knot and felt a tightening in the dream world around me.

As the knot slipped into place, I was expelled from the dream like a bullet fired from a pistol. The force of the expulsion left me shaken, and I reeled in the formless void of the universal dream for many long moments.

But—slowly—my shock transformed into triumph.

I didn't even bother returning to my dream to summon Royal. I focused my thoughts on him and pulled. Instead of drawing his dreaming mind toward me, I felt my consciousness rocketing across the dreamscape. Royal's dream rushed up to meet me, and before I could slow my momentum—

I was standing inside his dream.

He looked up at me as I entered, and once again the dream around us faded to a medium gray.

"So—?" He glanced at me, hope warring with fear on his face.

"I know what to do," I said.

Royal's face lit up. "You mean, you can keep him out of my head? For real?"

"It's called a shield. And yes, it'll keep him out of your head. It will keep *everyone* out of your head. I won't be able to visit your dreams again. Not for a long time."

Royal closed his eyes. His smile was so beautiful, so peaceful, I wanted to hug him. Then he opened his eyes, giving me an expectant look. "Well, what are you waiting for?"

"Right." I lowered my eyes, focusing on the dream around me. As I held it inside my mind, I could feel the edges of this dream, the boundary that separated Royal from the universal dream. Carefully, I began to form the shield knot. It was a long process, but as the knot grew in complexity, the pattern started to manage itself. I poured my attention and energy into it, feeding it the strength it needed to grow and contort back over itself, again and again. The knot spread along the borders of Royal's dream, growing in density until it was as hard and smooth as granite.

There was only one chink in the shield—the hole through which my consciousness had entered this dream. I turned my attention to it, doubling my efforts. The knot seemed to fall into this hole, as though sucked into a vortex. I concentrated, urging the knot to grow and contort faster. It worked—even though the vortex seemed bent on swallowing the knot, the knot was growing just fast enough to edge ahead. Finally, the knot twisted together into a plug strong enough to close the hole—

And I was expelled outside the dream once more.

It was disorienting, being this close to Royal's dream—unable to sense even the faintest glimmer of his personality. I swept over the surface of his dream, searching for any imperfection that might be leveraged into an opening. There was nothing. Triumph flared in my head. I'd done it. As the weight of this accomplishment sank in, I paused. A shield like this would be extremely valuable for the Guard. Dad, Hale, Lucas—I could protect their sleeping minds. But as I pictured Lucas's face, I felt a twinge. I could shield his sleeping mind, yes, but then he would be shielded from all Lilitu, myself included. We wouldn't be able to share any more dreams together. I felt guilt for even hesitating to protect him, but I wasn't ready to give up our nights together. I decided to save the moral questions for another day.

Exhausted, I let myself fall into a dreamless sleep. As my consciousness unspooled into the larger dream, one last thought floated through my mind.

At least no one will bother Royal's dreams again. He is safe. He is finally safe.

13

I floated back to consciousness late the next morning. Sensations returned piecemeal; the weight of sheets across my body, the warmth of the sun on my shoulder, the faint sound of birds singing their greeting to the new day. I stretched, luxuriating in the peace of the moment.

When I finally opened my eyes, my bedside clock read 10:15—Dad and I would be heading out for another day of pseudo-spelunking in an hour or so. I swung my feet off the side of the bed and rummaged through my dresser for something tough enough to weather climbing over boulders, but summery enough for the warmth of the day ahead.

Downstairs, I found Karayan humming to herself in the kitchen. She was scrambling some eggs in a skillet along with cubed potatoes, onions, and green chilies. My mouth started watering.

"Don't suppose there's more than one helping in there?" I pulled a stool out from the kitchen island and sat, eyeing the sizzling eggs on the stove.

Karayan turned. She flashed me a mischievous grin. "And she returns to the land of the living." Karayan hefted the skillet off the stove and gave it a jerk. The eggs flipped neatly over, sizzling as they reconnected with the hot surface. "Grab a plate."

I hopped off the stool to rummage through the cupboard. Karayan met me at the island and scooped a healthy portion of eggs onto my plate.

"Yum." I started to sit, preparing to dig in.

"Ah, ah, ah!" Karayan returned with a bowl of shredded cheddar cheese. "The finishing touch." She sprinkled my plate with the cheese. It started to melt as soon as it made contact with the steaming eggs.

"This is what happiness smells like." I closed my eyes and breathed in the aroma.

"Well, eat your happiness before it gets cold." Karayan sat beside me, sprinkling a second serving of her creation with cheese.

"Since when do you cook?" I shoved a spoonful of eggs into my mouth. So. Awesome. "Not that I'm complaining."

"Long day ahead. I need the energy." She shrugged, hiding a small smile with a bite of food.

"Yeah?" I glanced at Karayan, curious.

The doorbell rang, and Karayan's eyes shifted over my shoulder eagerly.

"Ooo. Gotta go." She bounced off her stool and made a beeline for the front door. She'd left her phone on the island. I shoveled another bite of eggs into my mouth, then picked it up.

"Hey, you forgot your phone—" I froze at the threshold between the dining room and the foyer.

Karayan had opened the door. Hale stood on the threshold, clutching a magnificent bouquet of bluebells in one hand. Dozens of slender stalks arched from his grip, each supporting a collection of vibrant, purple-blue blossoms.

Karayan gave a little squeal of delight. "For me?" But then she hesitated, her eyes snagging on the blossoms. Slowly, she lifted her gaze to Hale's face. He wasn't smiling. The color drained out of Karayan's face as realization struck her. *He knew.*

"So it's true?" Hale lowered the bouquet. It hung, forgotten, by his side. "You've been coming to my dreams? Pretending to be my *wife?*"

Karayan opened her mouth to answer, but no words came.

Hale studied her, his grief transforming slowly to anger. "I wondered about all the bluebells, showing up night after night. It's one of the things they train us to watch out for in the Guard, unusual repetition of objects or symbols."

"I can explain." Karayan lifted a hand toward him, but he jerked away from her touch, letting the bluebells drop to the ground beside him.

"Don't bother."

"Hale, I was just—"

"I know what you were doing." A muscle in his jaw jumped. I could see the tension gathering in his shoulders.

Karayan stared at Hale, stricken. "I thought—I thought we—"

"We what?" Hale's face could have been carved from stone. "We'd get a happily ever after? End up playing house together somewhere?"

Crimson shame flooded Karayan's cheeks, but she tried to shrug it off. "Please. I'm not some vapid teenager with her eyes full of stars."

Hale's voice dropped to a low growl. "You betrayed our friendship, Karayan."

Karayan looked stung, but—struggling to gather the last shreds of her pride—she forced herself to shrug. "That seems a little dramatic, even for a Guardsman. As I remember it, you had a good time in those dreams, too."

"Don't provoke me, Karayan." Something in Hale's glare made the hair stand up on the back of my neck.

"Ah yes. And now we come to the threatening portion of the morning's chat." Karayan crossed her arms, but she couldn't completely sell her feigned indifference. "Let me guess, you're kicking me out of the Guard."

"No. You're too useful to our cause. I'm not going to tell the others what you've done; that would generate unnecessary friction."

I saw Karayan's shoulders ease slightly.

Hale wasn't finished. "You and I will never work together again. Stay away from me, Karayan. I mean it." Without taking his eyes off of Karayan, Hale barked at me, "Braedyn. Grab your things. You're on duty."

"But—I'm supposed to search more caves with Dad today—"

Hale's eyes shifted to my face, silencing my objections instantly. Two minutes later, I was following him out the door to his car, a hastily packed lunch shoved into my backpack.

I risked one quick glance back. Karayan watched us go, frozen at the door. Her eyes looked hollow. A dull ache spread through my chest, but there was nothing I could do to help her. That was the curse of a broken heart; the suffering Karayan faced, she had to face alone.

Hale drove in silence. I wasn't about to intrude on his thoughts.

I sat still as a statue, hands clutched tightly in my lap, through the long drive out to the mission. When he finally pulled to a stop outside the old stone building, he killed the engine and sat, silent, for a long moment, still gripping the wheel.

"Did you know?" Hale spoke quietly, but the pain in his voice was quite audible. "Did she tell you what she was up to?"

I took a deep breath, then let it out. "She never meant to hurt you."

Hale glanced at me. "Why didn't you warn me?"

"I thought—" I shook my head, miserable. "She loves you, Hale. I think she thought you loved her, too."

He winced.

"Look, I'm not making excuses for her. What she did was totally wrong." I couldn't keep my voice from trembling—this was suddenly way too close to home. "But visiting your dreams? It was the only way you two could be together without you getting hurt."

"You don't think I got hurt?" Hale's eyes smoldered.

"You know what I mean." I swallowed, then caught his eye. "I know how it feels to love someone you can barely touch for fear of hurting them. You think it's easy? It's not. If Karayan didn't care for you, do you think she would be fighting her attraction to you so hard? Do you think she'd limit her pursuit of you to dreams?"

"She has no right to *pursue* me," Hale snapped.

"You don't see how you led her on?" My voice came out sharper than I'd intended. Hale looked up, gauging me closely. "All those long post-shift conversations on our front porch? All that talk of how two adults shouldn't have to explain themselves to anyone else?"

Hale had the good grace to lower his gaze then.

"Come on, you got drunk with her, alone, and ended up wrestling all over my living room floor. I hate to be the one to break this to you, but where I come from that's pretty obviously flirting. Are you honestly going to tell me you don't have feelings for her?"

Hale didn't respond.

"Hale." I wasn't willing to let it go. "Do you have feelings for Karayan or not?"

Hale was silent for an aching moment. When he finally spoke, his voice was hoarse with conflicting emotions. "It doesn't matter. A relationship between a human and a Lilitu will never work." In one swift motion, he opened his door. "That's something I shouldn't have to explain to you." He climbed out of the car and slammed the door behind him.

I stared after him, stricken. His words trickled icy fingers of despair down the back of my neck. Lost in my own thoughts, I didn't hear the other car pull into the dirt lot behind me. I opened my door and stood, coming face to face with Amber.

But it was another voice that sent a new tension shooting through my body.

"What the hell are you doing here?" Rhea straightened, having just pulled two bags of supplies out of the back of her car.

"Excuse me?" I felt myself bristling. This was getting old, and fast. "I'm doing my job, same as you, Rhea."

Rhea shook her head. She tossed a bag to Amber. "Here." Rhea eyed me as she closed and locked her car. "Listen, demon. You stay out of our way."

Rhea shouldered me aside. Amber's eyebrow quirked up, but she followed Rhea into the mission wordlessly. Perfect. The last thing I needed was for Rhea to take Amber under her wing. If Amber had to train with a spotter, why couldn't it be Gretchen or—well, *anyone* other than that stocky Ice Bitch.

I sighed, closing the truck's door behind me. A brief hope flared in my mind. Maybe now that Amber was here, I'd be excused to return to my previously scheduled cave-day with Dad. Because even that hot, dusty work seemed suddenly pleasant compared to the prospect of spending the day trapped in a stone mission with Amber and Rhea for company.

When I entered the mission, however, that fledgling hope withered and died.

"Braedyn, I need you here." Hale gestured to the front post, facing the Seal straight on.

"Um… what about Amber and Rhea?" I asked quietly. Hale glanced at me, frowning.

"Rhea's training Amber today. I need someone who can devote her full attention to watching for Lilitu movement from the Seal." Hale strode away without another word.

I sighed. Awesome. Not only did I have to share breathing space with Amber and Rhea, I'd managed to alienate the one friend I had within a 20-mile radius. It was going to be a kick-ass day, I could already tell. I let my eyes drift upwards and sucked in a sharp breath. I'd pictured the post-explosion mission with a hole in the roof – but the truth was, most of the structure that had once been the sanctuary's ceiling was completely gone. Somehow—without the ceiling—the stone mission seemed even more beautiful. I could see the faint wispy clouds drifting lazily across an otherwise clear blue sky.

I leaned back against one of the sanctuary's stone columns, fixing my attention on the Seal. It was quiet. The late morning light poured through the two or three stained glass windows that hadn't shattered above. It filled the small sanctuary with splashes of bright color. There was a certain majestic calm to this old mission—if you could forget about the portal-to-a-demon-plane parked right in the middle of the sanctuary.

"Rounds," Hale called. All but two other Guardsmen and Hale left then, to do their quick walk of the mission's perimeter.

Prepared for a long, boring shift, I pulled a bottle of water out of the bag at my feet, not taking my eyes off the Seal for more than a second. Might as well stay hydrated.

But as I unscrewed the cap, I heard Rhea's shrill voice cutting through the quiet sanctuary.

"—made my feelings clear about being in the same place as her!"

I spotted Rhea, nearby in a pool of shade under the sanctuary's balcony. She was confronting Hale as Amber stood awkwardly by. I honed my attention onto them, suddenly alert.

"And I believe I've made it clear that if you wish to continue serving in the Guard, you'll follow the orders given to you."

Rhea shook her head, her lips peeled back in a superior grimace. "You can't see where this is headed? Trusting her is going to end up costing someone their life, and you can be damn sure it won't be mine."

Amber glanced in my direction.

Quickly, I shifted my eyes back to the Seal, caught. I could feel the slow burn of embarrassment coloring my cheeks. I tried to tell myself I didn't care what Rhea thought, that she'd made up her mind about me from the start and there was nothing I could do to change it so why waste the energy? And yet, prickles of shame cascaded over my back and arms anyway.

Hale said something that inflamed Rhea further, but he turned and walked toward the mission's doors without waiting for her response. I glanced back, unable to contain my curiosity. Rhea stared after Hale, rigid with anger. Then she noticed me watching, and her eyes clouded with an even darker rage.

"Amber!" Rhea snapped her fingers, and Amber followed on her heels without argument. In Rhea's hurry to get away from me, she turned her back on the Seal. Amber, following after her, was two steps behind when the Lilitu struck.

It happened so fast I barely had time to scream a warning. "Behind you!"

I leapt forward, drawing my daggers in one smooth motion. The blades snapped apart and I gripped the hilts, ready for the fight. Amber half-turned, sensing too late the demon launching toward her back.

But Rhea's eyes were fixed on me. Her mouth wrenched into a snarl and she drew her own daggers—lunging herself directly at me. I had a fraction of a second to adjust. As Rhea swept her daggers for my throat I dropped, hitting the slick stone floor with my hip and sliding under Rhea's reach.

Amber finished her turn and saw the Lilitu sprinting toward her from the Seal, revealed in her full demon aspect. White skin stretched over a bony frame. Pitch black eyes fixed on Amber's face. The demon grimaced as she charged, baring her weirdly metallic teeth.

Amber let out a blood-curdling scream, frozen in place.

I reached Amber as the Lilitu swiped at her—those long black claws just as fatal as the daggers Rhea had swung at me. Without time for thought, I kicked Amber's feet out from under her. She fell backwards just as the Lilitu's claws shredded the air where her head had been a microsecond earlier. Amber hit the ground hard, but the jolt seemed to snap her back to her senses. The Lilitu's momentum carried her forward—and her legs tangled with Amber, now sprawled on the ground. The Lilitu pitched forward, colliding gracelessly with the stone floor. Wasting no time, Amber rolled to her hands and knees and scrambled to her feet, desperate to get away. The Lilitu's hiss of rage sent a chill spearing through my middle.

"Amber!" I shoved myself to my hands and knees, ready to tackle the Lilitu—

When Rhea's fist closed in my hair. Without a word, Rhea wrenched me back down to the ground and sprinted after the Lilitu. Unprepared, I hit the ground elbow first. A sickening snap just preceded a searing pain that shot through my arm. The pain was so intense it drove the air from my lungs. It wasn't until the next breath that I found the strength to scream.

The Lilitu curled one clawed hand around Amber's shoulder. Rhea attacked her from behind. The Lilitu, prepared for this, whipped around savagely. She backhanded Rhea so hard the spotter dropped senselessly to the floor, her daggers clattering from her hands. Hale was sprinting toward Amber, but he was still halfway to the doors. The other two Guardsmen weren't much closer, and one of them seemed to be heading for the unconscious Rhea.

Ahead of me, Amber crashed into the sanctuary wall, trapped. The Lilitu stood between her and any chance of escape. I grabbed a dagger with my good hand and forced myself to my feet, battling another wave of nausea as my broken arm swung uselessly by my side. Amber turned to face the Lilitu. The demon closed on Amber, reaching for the girl's throat—but Amber made a jerking motion and the Lilitu fell back, with another hiss. Only this time, it was a hiss of *pain.*

Drops of an oily ichor spotted the ground between them. That's when I saw the dagger clutched tight in Amber's fist. She'd managed to slice a thin line across the Lilitu's stomach—not deep enough to cripple her, but it did give her pause.

It was the moment's distraction I needed. I charged forward as the Lilitu recovered. The demon caught Amber's wrist and slammed it into the stone wall, sending her dagger flying into the shadows.

"Spotter," the Lilitu hissed, gripping Amber's neck in one clawed hand. Amber's eyes bulged in panic—

Just as I hit the demon from the side. I drove my dagger into her exposed ribs, up to the hilt. She released Amber reflexively. Momentum did the rest—I'd thrown myself against her hard enough to send us both crashing to the stone floor. We skidded away from Amber, coming to rest at the base of another support column.

I pushed myself up off the Lilitu with my good arm, adrenaline flooding my system.

Only—the Lilitu's eyes were blank, staring. She'd died before we'd finished our slide across the floor.

That's when I started shaking. Bile rose in the back of my throat—a reaction to both the pain in my arm and the bitter after-taste of the adrenaline. I staggered to the column for support, then dropped to my knees, heaving the contents of my breakfast onto the floor.

The Guardsmen reached us then. Hale went to Amber, catching her face in his hands and peering into her eyes. "It's going to be okay, Amber. I just want to make sure you weren't hurt." He ran his hands over her frame, searching her quickly and impersonally for wounds.

"I'm fine." But Amber's eyes were rooted to the dead Lilitu, and her face was pale.

A second Guardsman knelt beside Rhea, trying to revive her. "Who's got the smelling salts?"

"Here." The third Guardsmen reached into his pocket and tossed a small parcel over. Without waiting to see how Rhea responded, he prodded the Lilitu's body with his boot, ensuring the demon wasn't going to rise up again.

I heard Rhea's groan as she was jerked back into consciousness by the powerful odor of the smelling salts.

"Easy," the Guardsman was telling her. "You had a bad fall."

"What happened?" But then Rhea's eyes found me. She pushed the Guardsman out of her line of sight. "You."

Rage flared through my body. "Are you *kidding me?!*"

Hale, who'd finished his examination of Amber, turned. "Stand down, Rhea."

"This marks the *second* time a Lilitu attacked through the Seal. Both on her watch." Rhea rose to her feet, unsteady but driven by fury nonetheless. "Are you going to tell me that's a coincidence? She's a *liability*."

"She saved my life," Amber said. I turned. Amber stood, wrapping her arms around herself as though cold. "If it weren't for Braedyn, that demon would have killed me."

Rhea shook her head.

"It's true, Rhea," Hale said. "None of us could have reached her in time."

"It doesn't prove she's harmless," Rhea said. Her eyes raked over me. "How do we know she didn't put the Lilitu up to this, in an effort to make herself look like the hero?"

"You're insane. I'm on *your* side." I glared at Rhea. But nothing I did would ever be enough to win her trust—that was perfectly obvious now.

"Outside." Hale bent over the Lilitu's body and pulled my dagger free. He cleaned the blade on the Lilitu's clothes. When he looked up, Rhea hadn't moved. "Outside, Rhea. And if you ever raise a hand to Braedyn again, I'll see you court-martialed."

Rhea sneered. "Clay would never discipline someone for attacking a Lilitu."

"Are you willing to bet your life on that?" Hale's voice held a steely note I'd never heard before. "Last I checked, the penalty for mutiny was still death."

Rhea's face grew still. She glanced at the other Guardsmen, looking for backup. They avoided her gaze. She scoffed, smiling faintly. "I could use the fresh air." She turned and walked out of the roof-less mission, where we had fresh air to spare. The doors swung shut behind her before any of the rest of us moved.

Hale moved to my side. "Let me see your arm."

"Don't," I hissed. But Hale was exceedingly gentle. He felt for the fracture, wincing in empathy when I gasped.

"You're lucky the bone didn't break the surface of your skin," he said. He pulled his T-shirt over his head. I glanced quickly away. Hale's chest was a pile of well-defined muscles. They rippled smoothly under his skin as he worked, tearing the shirt into strips. He fashioned a field splint, binding my arm securely to the empty hilt of a set of daggers, then carefully looped a swatch of shirt over my neck to keep my arm secured. "I'll drive you to the hospital. We should get a cast on that before you start to heal."

"What about the Seal?" I glanced at Amber. She looked shell-shocked; she'd be no use for the rest of the shift.

"I'll send Rhea back in here when we've gone." Hale glanced at his watch. "The patrol should be reporting back soon. We'll wait for them."

I nodded, trying to breathe through the pain. Now that the adrenaline was fading from my system, the dull, throbbing ache in my arm seemed to grow more intense with every heartbeat.

Thankfully, the Guardsmen—perhaps alerted by Rhea's appearance at the mission doors—returned sooner than we expected. As Hale was collecting my things, Amber approached me. She shot a look at the Seal, clearly still shaken.

"I guess—I guess Hale was right about you." Amber blushed, staring at her feet. "Look, I'm sorry. I've treated you pretty freakin' horribly, but it's over now, I promise."

I stared at Amber, not bothering to conceal the wash of disbelief moving through me.

Amber read my expression and bit her lip. "Right. I guess it's going to take more than an apology to make up for—"

"No." I cleared my throat. "That's—I mean, it's okay."

Amber met my gaze, troubled. "How can you say that after everything—?"

"Braedyn, we should get a move on." Hale gestured for me to join him at the mission's doors.

"Right." I glanced back at Amber. "See you at practice."

Amber smiled faintly, then nodded. I can't say the moment wasn't awkward. But it was also a welcome relief. After all, we were fighting for the same side. Now—at long last—Amber knew it, too.

Dad joined us at the hospital, freaking out, as expected. After the chaos of the fight at the mission, the long wait in the emergency room felt even more boring than usual. Is it a bad thing that I was starting to get comfortable in hospitals?

By the time we got home—me sporting my swanky new cast—Karayan was waiting for us on the porch. News of the attack must have spread throughout the Guard. I could see the concern etched into Karayan's features.

Dad helped me out of the car and walked me to the door. Hale, carrying my bag, followed.

"Seriously? Tackling a full grown Lilitu with a broken arm?" Karayan caught me by the shoulders, searching my face for any sign of pain.

I shrugged, smiling loopily. "It's cool. Paracetamol. It's definitely doing the trick."

Karayan glanced at Dad.

"Painkillers," he offered by way of translation.

Karayan shook her head, but stepped aside. Dad opened the front door for me. Before I walked through it, I glanced back at Karayan and Hale. I saw Karayan searching Hale's face for any kind of reaction.

He avoided her gaze entirely—seemingly as ignorant of her presence as if she'd been cloaked. When Dad turned back for me, Hale held out my bag.

"Take it easy tonight, Braedyn." Hale put a hand on my good shoulder and gave me a comforting squeeze. "You did good."

"Thanks."

Hale turned and walked away. Not once did he acknowledge Karayan's presence. Her expression fell, the open pain on her face so intense it pierced the comfy haze of my painkillers.

"Braedyn." Dad held his hand out for me. But I saw his eyes shift to Karayan, and his brow crease with concern. "Would you care to join us for dinner, Karayan?"

Karayan looked back at us with a haunted expression. "No. Thanks. I'm not hungry." Across our lawns, I could see Hale ascending the stairs to the Guard's front porch.

"Alright." Dad seemed to sense Karayan needed space. He gestured to me. "Okay, kiddo. This calls for some comfort food." Dad ushered me inside.

Behind us, I heard the sound of Hale slamming his front door and I knew—whether or not he wanted to acknowledge it—Hale was just as miserable as Karayan.

Dad ladled a bowl of steaming chicken tortilla soup out of the stockpot. We'd decided to eat in the kitchen, perched at the island. It felt cozier in here. We'd done this a lot when I was younger. Back when I'd thought I was human.

I'd just taken my first sip when the doorbell rang.

Dad stood, setting his spoon down. "I'll get it. You just rest and eat up."

I was more than willing to take that advice. But when Dad opened the door, I heard a sound that made my heart soar.

"Is she okay?" Lucas's voice was tight with worry.

"Yeah, Lucas. Honey—?"

But I was already crossing the dining room. As soon as he saw me, Lucas's face melted into a smile of relief. I crossed to him, throwing my good arm around him, letting him hold me tightly. For once, I didn't care who might see us hugging.

Dad cleared his throat. "I'll just give you two a minute."

I pulled out of Lucas's embrace and gave Dad a smile.

"Don't let your soup get cold." Dad planted a kiss on the top of my head, then retreated into the kitchen, leaving Lucas and me alone in the foyer.

"I heard." Lucas ran a hand through my hair, sweeping it back from my shoulder.

"Well, it was turning into a crap day even before the demon attack."

Lucas's his face clouded with worry. "What do you mean? What happened?"

I sighed. "Nothing I couldn't have seen coming. Karayan and Hale—" but I stopped, unsure how to explain. "It got—messy."

Lucas's eyebrows drew together as he tried to puzzle out what exactly that could mean.

I cleared my throat, trying for an indifferent tone. "And then Hale said—he said no relationship between a human and a Lilitu could ever work." I may have tried to hide my despair, but Lucas saw through the effort easily.

"Hey." Lucas glanced toward the kitchen. "Come with me." He pulled me into the living room. We sat together on the couch, and Lucas curled an arm around my shoulders. "We're not just any human and Lilitu," he whispered. "You've got an exit strategy. And that means we've got a future."

I sighed, unwilling to contradict him.

"Hale doesn't know us. He's not the one who gets to make that call." Lucas brushed his fingers lightly over my lips. The sensation sent a bolt of sensation zinging through my core. I looked up, meeting his gaze. "Braedyn. I think it's time."

"Time—?" I breathed. My heartbeat kicked up a notch, stirred by his words. But there was so much on the line. "The Guard—"

Lucas lay his finger across my lips once more. He leaned closer, brushing his lips against my ear. "Do you love me?"

"Yes."

"Do you want this?"

"Lucas—"

"Just answer the question. Will you share one perfect night with me, Braedyn Murphy?"

I met his gaze, frozen with indecision. "Yes." I could barely hear my own whisper over the sound of my thudding heart.

"Then what the Guard wants shouldn't matter."

I studied his beautiful face, the line of his jaw, the greenish cast to his hazel eyes. A swell of warmth coursed through my body. I did want this night.

"Okay." With that, it was as though all the walls I'd so carefully constructed against this moment came crumbling down. We were really going to do this. I couldn't fight a giddy grin. "When?"

"You should have a chance to heal," Lucas said, eyeing my cast.

"So—Sunday night?" I knew I'd heal quickly, and now that I was motivated, I'd make every dream from here until the weekend count, gleaning all the energy I could.

Lucas laughed quietly. "Okay. Sunday night."

With those two words, we parted, full of anticipation for what the coming weekend would bring.

14

Once Lucas and I had made our decision, it was hard to think about anything else. This night was something we'd talked about before—but more as an abstract concept than a reality, something beautiful and vague hovering at the edge of perception. Now that we'd chosen our moment, the details were starting to take shape.

I saw Lucas the next morning, as Dad and I were loading another day's worth of water and supplies into our car; I'd been forbidden to lift anything heavier than a book for two weeks by the doctor at the emergency room. Of course, he couldn't know that—thanks to my Lilitu heritage—my arm would be completely healed in another few days. But since the break was still pretty recent, Dad wanted me to take it easy.

"I've got the rest, kiddo." He smiled, then nodded as Lucas headed over. "Make it fast. We've got to hit the road soon."

Lucas joined me on our front drive, waiting for Dad to disappear into our house before he spoke. "I found a place."

He didn't have to say anything else; I knew exactly what he meant. We'd realized early on that we couldn't risk spending our one night together at either of our homes. It would have to be someplace else. My heart flipped over in my chest, and I shot a quick back at my house to make sure Dad was still out of earshot.

"Where?"

"Don't you want to be surprised?" Lucas's eyes twinkled.

"Well, surprises are pretty sweet, but it'll be a lot harder to get there if I don't know where I'm going."

"Yeah. You make an excellent point." Lucas turned and walked back to the Guard's house, smiling mischievously.

"Hey!" I pounced, catching his hand. "That is just mean spirited."

Lucas clasped his other hand over mine. I was acutely aware of the warmth of his skin on my skin. He turned my hand over, tracing a finger across the sensitive surface of my palm. I looked up and our eyes connected. The feeling was so much more intense than anything we'd shared in a dream, and he was just touching my hand. I imagined his hands on my skin, trailing these liquid-fire sensations all over my body. My heart skipped again, and suddenly I was blushing.

"Sorry, you were saying?" Lucas's eyes crinkled; I could see he was holding back a chuckle.

I cleared my throat. "Was I?"

Lucas suddenly dropped my hand, his expression neutral—as though he had no idea he'd just revved up my blood pressure to an all-time high. "Morning, Mr. Murphy."

"You're up bright and early."

I heard Dad emerge from the house behind me, but I was blushing too hotly to turn around. Dad would see my face, and that would raise more questions than I was comfortable answering right now.

"Had trouble sleeping." Lucas's eyes snagged on my face, and I felt another surge of heat light my cheeks. This was getting worse by the second. I dropped my head, letting the waves of my long brown hair shield my complexion.

"Braedyn, honey, I'm almost packed up. Are you ready to go?"

"Yeah, Dad. Ready when you are." I waved a hand over my shoulder, pretending to be distracted by something on my phone.

"Okay. T-minus three minutes to departure."

Behind me, Dad ducked back into the house one last time. I glanced up at Lucas. He was biting his lip, trying hard not to laugh. I smacked the back of my hand across his stomach.

"Clearly you've never heard the part about discretion being the better part of valor."

"Yeah, I have no idea what that means." Lucas grinned openly at me.

"It means if we don't want our business to turn into Guard business, we need to avoid arousing suspicion."

"Roger that." Lucas gave me a faux salute, but he also dialed down the heat in his gaze.

"Thank you."

Dad reemerged behind us. Confident that I wasn't beet red any longer, I joined him at the car, pausing to give Lucas one last look before sliding into the passenger seat. He watched me, his smile full of a smoldering anticipation.

It was going to be a long week.

Long week turned out to be an understatement. I'd never really thought about how many times Lucas and I ran into each other on a given day. Now, each time I saw him, our secret rendezvous leapt to the front of my mind, driving all other thoughts away. I'd be talking to Hale or Dad or Gretchen and Lucas would enter the room, scattering my thoughts as easily as if he'd knocked a jar of marbles out of my hands. More than once, I had to invent an urgent task that needed my immediate attention. After claiming I'd left the water boiling on my stove for the second time, Gretchen scrutinized me closely.

"Are you feeling okay?"

"Huh?" I tried to keep my eyes wide and innocent.

"You just seem a little distracted lately." Gretchen frowned. "Maybe you should see if Hale will give you a day off from Guard stuff. You know, let you hang out like a normal teenager for once."

"Hm." I didn't have to fake interest in this idea.

Gretchen smiled wistfully. "Sometimes I forget that you and Lucas are just kids. We ask a lot of you guys. So—in case you don't hear it enough—thanks. You've really risen to the task at hand."

Her words stuck with me the rest of the day. The creeping guilt I'd tried to keep at bay since Lucas and I decided to claim our night together came swelling back with a vengeance. But now, in addition to the guilt, I also felt—I don't know—wronged. I'd grown up most of my life, thinking I was a human girl. I'd never worried too much about boyfriends, figuring I'd meet the right guy when the time was right. And then I met Lucas—just in time to find out that my embrace could cause him irreparable harm. So here I was, turning 18 in five months, standing on the cusp of adulthood. Only, the future laid out for other girls was something I might never experience. Sansenoy's promise to grant me humanity? There was no telling when—or if—I'd ever be able to redeem it.

Maybe we were rushing into this. Maybe it'd make more sense to wait. But maybe I'd never become human. Maybe the timing for us would never be better. One night. That was all we might ever have.

Lucas and I both wanted this. Yes, our one night together would weaken Lucas, but he'd be able to recover. It was a sacrifice he wanted to make, for something we both wanted to experience. And so I kept my head down, did my work, and lived in anticipation of the weekend.

On Saturday morning, I found Dad in the kitchen drinking his morning coffee.

"I'm ready," I said, hefting my cast in the air. "Let's cut this sucker off."

Dad's eyebrows hiked up. "Are you sure?"

"I'm sure." I brought my cast down on the edge of the counter, hard enough to make the sugar bowl jump. "See? Not even a twinge. Let's do this thing."

Dad shrugged and set his coffee down. "I'll get the saw."

The Guard saw enough broken bones that removing casts wasn't something all that extraordinary. Dad returned with a dremel, and carefully cut through the hard shell of the cast. We worked together to clip away the gauzy interior, and in 15 minutes, my arm was free. I held it up, eyeing the pasty hue in contrast with the light tan on the rest of my arm. One week out of the sun made more of a difference than I'd expected.

Dad examined my arm. "Well, seems you were right, kiddo. Looks good as new, as far as I can tell."

"Thanks, Dad." I planted a kiss on Dad's cheek. "I should go. I told Hale I'd be up for training again this morning."

"Take it easy," Dad cautioned. But I was already running for the front door.

"I will. Love you!" I burst out of my house, taking in a deep lungful of the fresh June air. One day to go. Nothing was going to bring me down.

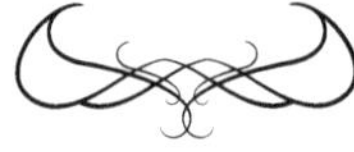

I was the first one in the basement for training, but I had too much energy to sit around and wait. I launched into the form that Lucas had first taught me almost two years ago. Since I'd started training with Hale, I'd learned three more versions, each growing in complexity. Moving through the form, it was easy to visualize the imaginary opponent the motions were designed to fight. I pictured Elyia, falling back before my blades. Having a specific enemy to focus on helped heighten my concentration. It wasn't until I'd finished the form—and Hale started clapping—that I realized I had an audience.

Amber and Hale stood at the bottom of the basement stairs. Hale grinned, but Amber looked startled. No—she looked *impressed.*

"I haven't seen you run through the whole form in months," Hale said. "You've definitely mastered version three. Maybe we should start you on version four. How do you feel about double-bladed axes?"

"Uh—conflicted?" I was still breathing hard from the workout.

Hale laughed and ushered Amber into the room. I sheathed my daggers and left them on the table beside the looming weapons rack. Amber eyed them, curious. Hale noticed her interest.

"Don't worry, you'll get yours soon enough. You've almost made it through our basic hand-to-hand course."

"Ooo," Amber said, her voice clipped with obvious sarcasm. "My very own antique knives. All the other girls will be so jealous."

Hale gave Amber a mild smile, then clapped his hands. "Right. Let's review what we covered last week."

Hale led us through another tough session. We hadn't trained while I'd had my cast on, so we had some catching up to do. And yet, even though it was tough, I was glad of the distraction. I'd take anything that would get my mind off the seconds squeaking by until Lucas and I were alone together.

At the end of the session, I looked up as Lucas stepped off the last stair into the basement, an eager gleam in his eye.

"Okay, ladies. Let's pick this up again tomorrow." Hale glanced at me. "Gretchen suggested I give you a break. What do you say we train tomorrow morning, and then you can have the rest of the day for yourself?"

"That would be awesome!" I glanced at Lucas, and saw the same startled excitement I felt registering on his face.

"Excellent. Shall we start at 9:00 AM sharp?"

Amber made a little groan of protest, but she didn't object.

"Then 9:00 it is." Hale tossed a small towel over his shoulder and headed back up to the main house.

"I don't know how you do it," Amber said, unscrewing the cap from a bottle of water. "I thought cheer practice was tough."

"What do you mean? You're kicking ass." I gave Amber an encouraging smile. She returned it, then downed several long gulps of water.

"A truce between Amberlandia and the great state of Braedyn?" Lucas joined us, hopping up to sit on the table. "Will wonders never cease."

"Careful, mister." I pulled a bottle of water out of my bag, following Amber's example. "You're talking to two trained fighters here."

"Are you trained for this?" Lucas snatched the bottle out of my hands.

I squealed and lunged for it.

"How about this?" Lucas hoisted the bottle even higher over his head, pulling it away just as my hands were about to close around it. I found myself face to face with him, giggling and jumping for the water.

Amber gave a long-suffering sigh. "Seriously, you two. Get a room, already."

My playful mood evaporated. I met Lucas's eyes, feeling somehow exposed. Lucas lowered the bottle of water.

Amber froze, suddenly hearing what she'd said. "Oh. That came out—I didn't mean to say that."

"It's fine." Lucas stood, crossing his arms over his chest self-consciously.

"No, that was—" Amber looked at me, stricken. "I wasn't thinking."

"Really, Amber." I held up my hands, as if to say, *no harm, no foul.* "It's not a big deal."

"Okay." Amber eyed the staircase. "I should probably get going."

"See you tomorrow."

Amber hurried toward the staircase, and in moments we heard her reach the top step.

"Yikes." Lucas reached for me. I let him pull me close. "Little does she know."

"Yeah," I agreed.

"So. Tomorrow."

I looked up, meeting Lucas's golden-hazel eyes. "Tomorrow." Even saying the word lit a small fire in my core.

"I've been waiting so long for this."

"We only get this one night," I murmured. "We have to make it perfect."

"It will be." Lucas traced the line of my jaw with his hand. "We'll be together."

Out of the corner of my eye, I saw movement at the bottom of the stairs. It was Amber. She stared at us. I jerked away from Lucas, feeling heat flooding my cheeks.

"Amber." I couldn't think of anything to say.

"I—" Amber glanced from Lucas to me. "Sorry. I just came back for—I forgot my keys." Amber's voice was tight with tension. Without waiting for a response, she hurried forward to snatch her keys off the table beside us. With the keys clutched firmly in her hand, she raced back to the stairs. In moments, she was gone. An icy wash of alarm spilled over me.

"How much do you think she heard?" Lucas kept his voice low.

"I don't know. By the look on her face? Enough."

"Do you think she's going to tell someone?"

I bit my lip, considering this, then shook my head, no. But when I met Lucas's eyes, I shivered.

Sunday dawned to a perfect, cloudless sky. Drops of dew balanced on the leaves of the climbing rose outside my window, making it look like someone had cast a handful of diamonds across it.

Anticipation bubbled all through me—until I remembered the look on Amber's face. I sat up. I'd need to do some serious damage control today.

By the time Amber parked her car in front of the Guard's house, 45 minutes later, I was sitting on my front porch, waiting for her. She got out of her car, pressing her cell phone to her ear, engaged in a heated conversation. I stood up to go meet her—but something in her voice stopped me in my tracks.

"Seriously? Come on, it's not like I don't know the routines backwards and forwards—" Amber stopped abruptly, stung. "I have to! It's for my job—" Amber winced. "Ally, please. Everything's so screwed up right now, cheer is the only thing I have left that feels like the old me." Amber bowed her head, and I saw her reach up to scrub away a tear angrily. "Fine. Do what you have to do."

Amber ended the call. She crossed her arms and slumped back against the side of her car. She looked totally devastated. And then her thin frame shook with a ragged sob. I stood there, unsure what to do. But I had to try something.

I walked forward. After a few steps, Amber noticed me coming. She straightened, wiping her cheeks with a brusque motion.

"Hey. Sorry if I'm late." Amber reached back into her car and emerged a few seconds later with her workout bag. She'd managed to compose her features; aside from her red eyes, it would have been hard to tell she'd just been crying.

"Amber." I hesitated, then sighed. "Sorry. I couldn't help but overhear. Ally's an idiot if she's trying to kick you off the squad."

Amber eyed me with a hint of her old suspicion. "I didn't think you'd ever seen us perform."

"I've been to some games." I crossed my arms, looking her straight in the eye. "Believe it or not, I actually do have a little school pride."

After a moment, Amber's expression softened. She looked more vulnerable than I'd ever seen her. She glanced down at the phone still clutched tightly in her hand. "She's not wrong. We've got this tradition, three cheer camps during the summer—a week of full day practices each. But now, with our daily training sessions, since the Guard is paying for my tuition—" Amber shrugged. "If I can't make the camps, I can't cheer. It's pretty simple."

I bit my lip, thinking. "Maybe I can talk to Hale," I said. Amber's eyes locked onto my face with a sudden flowering hope. "I'm not making any promises. And we've already lost a week thanks to my arm. But maybe we can double up sessions before and after your camp weeks. We'd still get the same number of hours in. And it's not like you're going to be chilling at home, sitting on your butt." I grinned wryly. "Like I said, I've seen you guys in action. You'll be getting plenty of exercise on those weeks off."

"Thank you," Amber breathed.

"No promises," I said again.

"No, I understand." Amber closed her car door and hefted her workout bag over her shoulder. "Let's get down there. I want Hale in a good mood when you work your magic on him."

Amber bounded toward the Guard's house ahead of me. I let out a long breath of relief. So far, so good.

Both Amber and I put in our best effort that day during training. Even Hale noticed.

"Way to bring the A game, ladies," he said as we gulped down some water at the end of the session.

Amber shot me a questioning glance.

I cleared my throat. "So, Hale, can I talk to you for a second?"

"Sure. What is it?" Hale let me lead him away from Amber.

"Amber's having some trouble fitting our training in around her regularly scheduled life." I glanced back at Amber. She turned quickly away, pretending not to be interested in whatever we were discussing. "The truth is, she's worked really hard at this stuff, and if it's possible, I think maybe we could help her out by altering the training schedule a little bit."

Hale frowned. "Altering how?"

I explained about the cheer camps, and my idea of doubling practice before and after. I also promised to continue my own training while Amber was away. Hale considered this for a moment, then nodded.

"It's a deal. And Braedyn?" He met my gaze, smiling warmly. "I'm really proud of how well you've worked with Amber. I know you two have had some troubling history. But with your help, Amber's turning into a very promising fighter."

It wasn't something I'd expected to hear. I felt myself blushing slightly at the praise. "Uh, sure."

Hale turned back to Amber. "You have a very convincing advocate over here. I don't see any problem adjusting your training this summer."

Amber's face lit up and she clasped her hands together. "Thank you!"

Hale nodded and headed for the stairs. Before he left, he turned back to me. "Enjoy the rest of your day, Braedyn. You've earned it."

And then he was gone. I glanced at Amber.

She squealed her excitement. "I've got to call Ally!"

"Sure." I smiled, packing my training gear up for the day.

Amber called Ally, making a frustrated sound when the phone went to voice mail. "Ally, it's Amber. Listen, I worked something out, so I can make the camps after all. Call me back when you get this. Bye." She ended the call and stuffed her phone into a side pocket of her bag.

"I'll bet Ally's going to be thrilled to have you back," I said.

"I wouldn't be so sure." Amber frowned. "She's been really pissy to me ever since—" Amber flashed me an apologetic smile. "She doesn't like the fact that I'm spending more time with you than I am with her." Amber shrugged. "Besides, with me gone, she's the logical choice for captain. So there's that."

I stared at Amber, surprised. "Seriously?"

Amber gave me a wolfish grin. "What? You don't think cheerleaders have any ambition?"

"I guess I just didn't think it was that big of a—" I stopped, hearing myself a little too late.

Amber gave me a tight smile. "Well, it is a big deal to Ally." Amber packed the last of her things away, growing somber. "It used to be a big deal to me, too. Funny how things change." She shook her head slightly, then gave me a smile a little brighter than necessary. "Enjoy your day off."

If I hadn't been watching her so closely, I might not have seen the sudden flash of concern. She dropped her eyes, trying to conceal the thought. I felt a tightening in my gut.

"Amber."

She looked up, expression neutral once more. "Yeah?"

I cast my mind about for something to say, when my eyes landed on the clock. It was almost 12:00 PM. "Want to grab lunch?"

"Now?"

I shrugged. "Why not? Unless you have somewhere you need to be?"

Amber slowly hoisted her workout bag over one shoulder, thinking this over. "Sure. I could use a bite to eat."

I gave Amber my warmest smile. "I'll drive."

Ten minutes later we were waiting in line at a popular drive-through. Neither Amber nor I wanted to go into a sit-down place looking as sweaty and mussed as we did. Lucky for us, CiCi's Taquería served amazing food to go. While we waited, Amber gave me a considering look.

"Yesterday, you and Lucas—?"

I kept my hands on the wheel, trying not to blush. "Yeah?" I glanced at her, keeping my face neutral.

Amber studied me for a moment, then shrugged. "Nothing. I guess I—" She twirled her finger around her temple. "Let's chalk it up to temporary insanity."

We sat in awkward silence for a moment.

"I love him, you know." My voice trembled, and I cleared my throat, struggling for control. Amber looked at me again, her smile fading. "I would never do anything to hurt him." As soon as I spoke, I heard Karayan in the back of my mind, speaking those exact words.

Amber bit the inside of her lip thoughtfully. "I guess I already knew that. I mean, you guys have been together for almost two years now. And the Guard trusts you." She gave me another sidelong glance. "So whatever I heard yesterday, I'm sure it's not what I thought I heard."

It took all my self-control to force an even smile.

Amber studied me for another long moment, then sighed and sat back in the passenger seat. She glared at the truck ahead of us, which had been parked at the pick-up window for a small eternity. "Jeez, how many tacos did those guys order? My stomach is going to start digesting itself."

My phone buzzed. I pulled it out of my pocket to check the caller ID. It was Cassie. I hit IGNORE; I'd call her back as soon as I dropped Amber off.

When we finally got our food, Amber suggested stopping at a local park to eat. We sat down under a sprawling Catalpa tree. Its branches were full of sprays of gorgeous white blossoms, so intricate they looked almost like orchids.

The little park was nestled up in the foothills with a sprawling view out over Puerto Escondido and into the mountain ranges beyond. As we ate, we talked about training, Hale, the Guard, and the other spotters.

"So what's up with Rhea?" Amber licked the last of the juice from her taco off her fingers. "I mean, she *really* hates you."

"What? No, that can't be. She's always been so warm and fuzzy." I feigned shock, and Amber laughed.

"Right."

I shrugged. "I don't know her story. But most spotters have a pretty fierce hatred for Lilitu."

"Gretchen?"

I snorted. "She scared the living snot out of me when we met."

"But she came around?"

"Well, it helped that I saved Lucas's life." I shrugged. "A lot of spotters—the only reason they can spot a Lilitu is because a Lilitu attacked someone they loved." I glanced at Amber. I didn't have to point out the obvious; she'd seen me for what I was after her boyfriend, Derek, had been attacked by Karayan. Amber had never learned the whole story about Derek's death. Karayan had attacked him, turning him into a Thrall. As Dad had explained to me, once someone became a Thrall, they'd never recover. And so the Guard had been forced to kill Derek. Amber believed a Lilitu was responsible for Derek's death—and in a way, that was true—but she didn't know it was Karayan, or that the Guard had been the ones to officially end Derek's life.

Amber looked down at the remnants of her lunch. "Yeah. I guess that makes sense."

"So—what happened to you guys this year? If you don't mind my asking."

Amber glanced up at me again. "What do you mean?"

"Uh, well, financially." I blushed hotly, suddenly aware this might be a subject Amber wasn't keen to discuss. But the question had been lingering in the back of my mind all semester. "You always seemed pretty—well, loaded, actually."

Amber looked away over the valley. "Yeah. Well. Dad made some mistakes. The kind they seize your assets and send you to prison for."

I stared at Amber, stunned. "Your Dad—are you saying your Dad is in prison?"

"They arrested him just before Christmas." Amber's voice wavered. I saw a tear slide down the side of her face. She lifted her hand and wiped it away almost absently.

"That's why your stepmom wants you home to help with your little brother." It wasn't a question. Suddenly I could see how Amber's life must have changed dramatically in the last few months. "Why didn't you say anything?"

Amber smiled ruefully. "You're asking why I never spilled my guts to *you?*"

"Right. I withdraw the question."

Amber's smile softened. She picked at the grass, lost in unhappy thoughts.

"What about Ally?" I suddenly straightened. "She's been awful to you all semester—"

"Ally doesn't know." Amber sighed. "I haven't told anyone at school." She met my eyes, and I saw an alien vulnerability in her gaze. "You're the first."

I opened my mouth to respond, but I couldn't think of anything to say. Amber gave me an understanding smile and looked away again. We sat in silence for a while then, but it wasn't an uncomfortable silence. It was actually pleasant. The afternoon stretched out in front of us; warm sun, a cool breeze, and nowhere we had to be. It was a perfect summer's day. I startled myself by feeling a little sad when it was finally time to head home.

We pulled up outside my house a little before 3:00 pm. Our afternoon had lasted much longer than either of us anticipated. I parked and said goodbye to Amber in front of the Guard's house. As I turned toward my house, I felt another surge of anticipation. Soon now, I'd be heading off to meet Lucas. Everything we'd been longing for—all our furtive plans—were about to come to fruition.

I pulled my phone out of my pocket to redial Cassie. That's when I noticed all the missed calls from earlier in the morning. They must have come through while I was training with Amber and Hale, and I'd somehow missed them when Cassie had last called.

Uneasy, I hit play on my voicemail as I entered the house.

Two steps into the foyer, I saw the crowd.

Thane, Ian, Gretchen, Matt, Hale, and Dad all turned as I entered, their faces drawn.

"Where have you been?" Thane demanded. Dad put a hand on his arm, warning him with a look.

I lowered my phone, a sudden fear clamping around my heart. "What's going on?"

"Cassie's at a meeting," Gretchen said. "But the Guard we sent to keep an eye on her just called. They're not at the usual clearing."

"So where are they?" A spray of goose bumps shot along my arms.

"Excellent question. Wouldn't it be handy if we had someone who could answer it for us?" Thane's lips pulled back in a snarl.

"Can it, Thane." Dad turned to me, gesturing me forward. "Honey, let's not waste any more time."

I nodded, letting Dad lead me to the couch. I was dimly aware of my hands shaking, but as I sat down, all I could think about was locating the bright bundle of energy that was my best friend. I closed my eyes, and felt her consciousness at the edge of my perception. Honing in on it, Cassie was suddenly with me, and I with her.

She was standing in some kind of cave. I gave an involuntary gasp before I realized it was not the Temple I'd seen in Elyia's dream. I felt Dad squeeze my hand, but shook my head. "False alarm," I murmured, not opening my eyes.

Cassie, already wearing her vestments, stood with Emily and Carrie, while Idris and her attendants, including Elyia, lit candles at the edge of the space.

I'm here, Cass. I urged the thought into her mind, and felt Cassie relax in response. Guilt and fear for Cassie twisted in my stomach, but I pushed them aside. There'd be time for apologies later. Right now we had more pressing concerns. *Where are you?*

We're at the old silver mines on the edge of town, she thought back.

What's going on?

I don't know, she answered. *But Idris seems pretty excited.*

Okay, hang on. I opened my eyes. Everyone watched me intently. "She's at the old silver mines," I said.

Matt was on his phone in an instant. "It's Matt. We've found her." As he relayed the information to the Guardsmen, I turned my attention back to Cassie.

Backup is on the way.

Something's happening, she sent back in response.

I closed my eyes, letting my consciousness slip back into Cassie's mind. Idris stood before the acolytes, arms upraised.

"Be joyful, daughters," she said. "We will see the dawn of a new era tonight."

I felt a shiver travelling through my body at her words.

"Something's wrong," I whispered. "Something's happening tonight."

"Tonight?" Thane's suddenly sharp voice cut across my thoughts. Instead of answering him, I honed in on Cassie, trying to absorb everything she was seeing and feeling.

"Girls, I want to introduce you to someone very special. A miracle, actually. The one who set me on this path many years ago. The living grandson of Lilith. And tonight, he will join us in paving the way for her return." Idris gestured, and the girls turned as one toward the entrance into this massive cavern.

I knew who it would be, even before Cassie laid eyes on him. There was nothing I could do to stop it.

Seth's benign smile slipped as soon as he caught sight of Cassie. I felt her shoulders knot in sudden fear.

"Forgive me, Priestess, but I need a little sidebar with this one." Seth never took his eyes off Cassie's face.

Idris followed his gaze, baffled. "I'm sorry?"

Seth strode forward and caught Cassie by the upper arm. "Come with me, *acolyte*. We need to have a talk."

"No!" My eyes flashed open. I grabbed Dad's arm, desperate. "Where are the Guardsmen?! They have to get there now! Cassie—Dad, it's Seth. *Seth has Cassie!*"

Dad grabbed me by the shoulders. "They're on their way, honey. Stay with Cassie. Hang in there."

My mind was already flying back to her. Seth was propelling Cassie out of the cavern, gripping her arm with cruel force. His fingers dug into her skin and—through Cassie's senses—I could feel his claws emerging. Cassie kept her jaw clamped tightly shut, refusing to give voice to her fear.

"What exactly do you think you're playing at?" His voice was eerily mild.

"I—I can explain." But Cassie's voice trembled.

Seth pulled her out of the cavern and spun her around to face him. "You don't have to." His lips twisted into a snarl of disgust. "And here I thought Braedyn was your friend. She put you up to this, after all my warnings. That's downright cold."

"Seth." I felt Cassie struggling to get a grip on her raging fear.

Seth sighed, looking almost bored. Neither Cassie nor I were prepared when he whipped his fist around, backhanding Cassie so hard she dropped to the dirt at his feet, gasping.

"*No!*" The sound tore itself from my throat.

"Braedyn? Honey? What's happening?!" Dad gripped my shoulders tighter, but I didn't open my eyes.

"Get her out of there," I gasped. "*Get her out of there!*"

Back at the mines, Cassie was painfully pulling herself up to her hands and knees. Seth stepped into view, his shiny black shoes making a sharp contrast to the dust and grit of the earth.

"I'm sorry, Cass. But you've just become an object lesson for Ms. Murphy." Seth reached down and hauled Cassie to her feet. I felt her confusion, heard the ringing in her ears. She blinked tears of pain out of her eyes just in time to see Seth strike out a second time. The blow caught her across the jaw. Cassie let out a strangled cry and tried to pull free. Seth held her tightly.

I heard a moan of pure despair, only recognizing it as mine when Dad pulled me into a tight bear hug.

"Braedyn, I'm so sorry. I'm so sorry, honey." And then, to Matt, "How far away are they?!"

"They're pushing 90, Murphy," Matt said. His voice sounded strained. "They'll get there as fast as humanly possible." Their words hovered at the edge of my consciousness. I couldn't pull myself away from Cassie.

Back at the entrance to the mines, Seth regarded his free hand casually. Long, obsidian claws extended from the tips of his fingers, growing like dark stalagmites before Cassie's eyes. Her breath came out in ragged pants. Seth placed one claw lightly on her cheek. She met his eyes, and I felt a new steel behind her thoughts.

"Ooo, Cassie. If looks could kill." Seth smiled. He sliced his claw down her face in one swift motion. Cassie cried out, struggling uselessly against his grip. "Unfortunately for you, these make far more effective weapons." He waggled his fingers before her face. Bright crimson blood dripped from one obsidian claw down his finger. "We're going to do this slow. I need Braedyn to understand you died a truly hard death."

I felt Cassie's breath catch—and then I saw what she'd seen.

A massive pickup truck peeled off the main road into the dirt lot serving as the parking area for the mines. Seth turned.

Knee him in the junk! I practically screamed it into Cassie's head, visualizing with every ounce of concentration exactly what to do. As her knee came up, it was almost like it was an extension of my own body. Cassie drove her knee squarely into Seth's crotch. An expression of surprise flickered across his face, half a heartbeat before his grip on her loosened reflexively. *Back!* I ordered. Cassie obeyed, jerking herself out of his reach. Seth, doubled over in pain, wasn't fast enough to avoid the truck.

It struck him full-speed, sending him flying into the brush beyond the dirt lot. The truck skidded to a stop and the doors flew open. Marx and Caleb, two of the Guardsmen who'd first arrived to help us face Ais, sprang out of the cab. They made a beeline for Cassie.

"Are you okay?" Marx asked in his gruff voice. Cassie nodded faintly.

"Get her in the truck, Marx." Caleb eyed the landscape uneasily. "We need to get the hell out of here. *Now.*"

Marx helped Cassie up into the cab of his truck, climbing in after her. He shifted the truck out of park as Caleb climbed in on the other side of Cassie. Before Caleb could even close his door, Marx hit the gas and tore away from the mines. As they hit the road, Cassie stared down at her hands. She was clutching at the white, scratchy fabric of her acolyte's vestments. Spots of blood dripped from her chin onto the skirt.

Caleb seemed to sense her distress.

"Hey, it's going to be okay. We've got you now. We're not going to let anything else happen to you. Got it?"

Cassie looked up into Caleb's dark eyes and nodded. He gave her an encouraging smile. She sat back, but her heart was still racing.

I collapsed on the couch, exhausted. "They've got her," I said. The tension in the room broke. Gretchen sat heavily on the edge of the coffee table. Matt gripped her hand tightly, relief plain in his eyes.

Dad let out a long breath. "Thank God."

"And Marx and Caleb," I said. "They got there just in time."

"They would have been ready and waiting if—" But Thane's snarl cut off as Dad turned on him.

"One more word," Dad growled, "and you'll be eating your next meal out of a straw."

Thane sniffed. "I merely state the truth."

"Okay, guys. Enough. Cassie's on her way. We'll get the full details of this meeting when she arrives." Hale looked from Dad to Thane. The men were still glaring at one another. "Are we going to have a problem here?"

Dad looked away first. "No. No problem." He joined me on the couch, curving a protective arm around my back.

"So." Thane turned to face Ian. "Idris wasn't talking about the *winter* solstice."

"No." Ian's jaw tightened. "I suppose she wasn't."

"We thought we had another six months." Dad's face looked suddenly ashen.

I glanced at Dad, feeling clueless. "What's going on?"

"It's today, Braedyn. Today is the summer solstice."

"The *summer*—?" I stared around the room, stunned. "But that doesn't make any sense. The *winter* solstice is their night of power, why would they pick *tonight* for Lilith's return?"

Thane shook his head, grim.

"How did we miss this?" Hale turned to Thane and Ian. "How did we miss something this huge?"

"We have mere hours before the sun sets, do you really want to waste them on a postmortem of our mistakes?" Thane's voice was clipped, but I could see he was deeply disturbed by Hale's question. It wasn't like the Archivist to be caught off guard—and something of this magnitude? Thane's confidence had clearly been shaken badly.

"Right." Hale rubbed at the scar dividing his eyebrow. It was a gesture I hadn't seen from him in a long time; a sure sign of deep concern. "Thane, see what you can dig up about the summer solstice. Anything you can find, pertaining to Lilitu."

Thane nodded and started toward the front door.

"Wait." Ian reached into his satchel and pulled out a pair of old books. "I think I might have something here that could shed some light on this. You search this one, I'll search the other."

Thane took the offered book from Ian. The men crossed through the foyer to settle at the dining room, flipping open the ancient volumes in silence.

In the living room, Hale, Gretchen, Matt, Dad—all of us were lost in our own unhappy thoughts. For my part, I kept replaying Seth's attack on Cassie in my mind, over and over. When Gretchen spoke, nearly 20 minutes later, I was a miserable mess of anxiety and guilt.

"They're here." Gretchen, standing by the window, shot an unreadable look at me. I stood, eager to see Cassie in the flesh, needing to verify with my own eyes that she was okay.

The door opened. Cassie's eyes were swollen from crying. A long, jagged gash travelled from high on her cheek down to her jaw. Her lip was split, and a deep bruise was forming across the other side of her face. Marx and Caleb followed her in, looking grim.

"Oh, Cass!" I darted forward, rushing to my friend.

"I tried to call you." Cassie's words drove through my heart like white-hot needles. "I thought you'd get my message and connect with my thoughts like before."

I shook my head, guilt and helpless rage rising up in the back of my throat.

"Hale, Murphy, we need to talk." Marx stepped past us, into the living room. "Cassie's been filling us in. Tonight's the summer solstice."

"We know." Hale grimaced. "Thane and Ian are looking into some old books. We've never had to research the summer solstice before."

"How long is this going to take? We've only got hours to figure this thing out."

"Wait—" The ramifications of our situation suddenly hit me. "We haven't found the Temple. How are we going to stop—?"

"The mines!" Ian raced out of the dining room, an urgent anxiety spilling across his face. "We'd been focusing on natural caves. What if the Temple was uncovered during a mining expedition?"

"That would explain Idris's field trip," Gretchen said, glancing at Cassie. Thane joined us, listening with a guarded expression.

"We have to get over there. Whatever's happening, it's going to happen soon." Dad's trepidation had vanished; once again, I saw the soldier from his past emerging.

Hale nodded. "I'll call the men."

"Wait, Hale—" Thane grabbed the younger man's arm, holding him back. "We'd be walking in blind. If the incubus is involved—?"

"What choice do we have?" Ian's voice cut through the chaos. "The solstice is here. If we hope to stop whatever ritual Idris has planned, we have to move *now*."

"You're making a very large assumption that this ritual will be held at the mines," Thane growled.

"Yes. I am making an assumption," Ian retorted. "And yes, we can't be sure it's the right location. But I *am* sure that we've checked every likely cave we could find in a 50-mile radius, and we don't have any better leads. Right now, the mines are our best bet. Thane, we have just enough time to try one Hail Mary. And what if this ritual is being held at the mines? It would be stupid of us not to send in the troops." Ian turned to Hale. "That's my advice. Do with it what you will."

Hale gently but firmly removed Thane's hand from his arm. "Ian's right. We've got one shot, and this is our only lead. I'll leave a skeleton crew at the mission, but the rest of us need to make a full-scale assault on the mines."

With that, the group disbanded. Cassie sat still on the couch, struggling to regain control of her breathing. I caught one of her hands, trying to offer what little comfort I could. Cassie's hand tightened around mine.

"Just tell me we're going to get that jerk." She looked up, through her tears. The new strength in her had not diminished.

"One way or another," I whispered. "You have my word."

15

Once they decided to attack, the Guard mobilized quickly. Hale made calls to the heads of each of the nine units stationed around Puerto Escondido. They planned to rendezvous at a turnout half a mile down the road from the old silver mines. It would take everyone an hour to gather weapons and meet up. From there, the assembled Guard would move on the mines as one.

"Braedyn, we need your help." Dad gestured for me to follow him and Gretchen. I eyed Cassie, uncomfortable about leaving her alone.

"I—I need to get out of this thing." She glanced down at the vestments she still wore.

"My room," I said. "Take anything you need."

She nodded gratefully. Dad held the front door open for Gretchen and me. On the porch, Gretchen turned to me. "Have you seen Lucas?"

"Um—he's not around?" I tried to keep my voice level.

"Not that I've seen."

"He's probably taking the afternoon off, like Hale suggested," I said.

Gretchen nodded slowly. "Yeah. Let's hope he's at a movie, and by the time it ends, this is all over."

I gave her a weak smile. Gretchen, clearly absorbed with other thoughts, didn't give me another look.

Dad led the way toward the Guard's house. Amber, standing by her car, looked up. She was talking on her phone, but paused when she saw the sudden flurry of activity. I couldn't stop to update her, though. I followed Dad, Gretchen, and Matt into the Guard's house, down the side hallway, and into the basement.

Gretchen pulled four massive black duffle bags out of a chest by the weapons rack. Dad grabbed one of the bags and handed it to Matt. The second he gave to me.

"Fill it," he said.

"With—?"

But Gretchen and Matt were already pulling weapons down off the rack, packing them carefully into the first two empty duffle bags.

"Ah." I followed their lead, pulling weapons off the rack and packing them into the duffle bag at my feet. We worked in silence for close to 10 minutes, and when we were done, each of the four duffle bags was stuffed full to the brim with wicked-looking knives, swords, axes, and spears.

Dad and Matt each picked up one of the two heaviest duffels, straining to heave them off the floor.

"Careful, guys," Gretchen said.

Dad nodded brusquely. "We've got this."

He headed up the stairs. Gretchen hefted the smallest remaining duffle bag up, struggling to loop the handles over her shoulder.

I eyed the last bag, then bent to pick it up. It was heavier than I'd expected, even after watching the others struggle to lift theirs.

I managed to leverage it up, slinging one strap over each shoulder, wearing it almost like a backpack. It wasn't comfortable, but it made climbing the stairs possible.

When I got outside, Dad was loading Gretchen's bag into the back of Hale's truck. Matt's and his were already packed inside. Dad saw me coming and ran to help while Matt headed back into the Guard's house.

"Easy, honey." Dad helped me ease the straps off my shoulders. The duffle bag clanked as the weapons inside shifted. Dad hefted it into his arms and deposited it beside the other three bags in the back of Hale's truck.

While Dad adjusted supplies in the back of the truck, Hale drew a long, slender blade out of a scabbard. It had a long hilt, wrapped tightly in black leather. The graceful arc of the blade gleamed in the sunlight. I saw the faint rainbow-sheen imbedded in the metal, a side effect of the secret forging process that made Guard weapons so deadly to the Lilitu. He gave it a few practice swings, testing the balance, regaining the feel for the weapon. Hale—and most of the

Guard, actually—usually preferred to work with the Guard's daggers. But he was a master swordsman. He'd given me a few lessons, and what I'd seen of him wielding the sword—let's just say he was quite impressive.

Satisfied with the blade, Hale sheathed the sword and tucked it carefully behind his seat. "How are we doing, Murphy?"

"Packed," said Dad, surveying his handiwork.

Amber watched all of this from the street, still leaning against her car.

Gretchen paused beside the truck, glancing around. She and Dad shared a look of understanding. Dad turned toward me. "I don't want you at this fight," he said quietly.

"But if there are Lilitu—?"

"We've got seven spotters, not including you girls." Dad's eyes cut to Amber. "I think you should stay here. Keep an eye on Cassie. She's tough, but I think she may be in shock. She shouldn't be left alone."

I glanced back at my house, suddenly worried. Dad was right, someone needed to keep an eye on her. Matt hurried out of the Guard's house, holding two sets of daggers. He tossed one to Gretchen. She snatched it out of the air, then turned back to me.

"Look, Braedyn. If Lucas comes back, keep him away from this fight. He's not ready."

I nodded glumly. Making that promise was like promising to hold the ocean at bay at high tide. But it's what she needed to hear. "Okay."

Dad surprised me by grabbing me and pulling me close. "I love you, kiddo." His voice, gruff with emotion, sent a shiver down my spine. This felt like goodbye.

"Dad—?"

"Let's move out!" Hale climbed into the driver's seat of his truck. Gretchen and Matt squeezed in beside him.

Dad met my gaze. It looked like he wanted to say something else. Instead of speaking, he gave me a kiss on the forehead, then turned and strode for his truck.

In moments, the soldiers of the Guard had gone.

Only Thane and Ian stayed back. As soon as the other Guardsmen were out of sight, the two old archivists entered the Guard's house, presumably to consult some of Thane's books for any information they could glean on the importance of the summer solstice in Lilitu lore.

Amber approached me, her face tight with anxiety. "Is everything okay?"

"No," I said, giving voice to some of the panic that had slowly been building in me since Seth confronted Cassie. "No it's not."

I sprinted back to my house, only vaguely aware of Amber following me. Cassie looked up as we entered. She'd changed into some old jeans of mine, and had wrapped a thick sweater over a pale pink T-shirt. My clothes were too big for her by at least two sizes, but she looked more comfortable in them than she had in those horrible vestments. She sat on the couch, feet curled beneath her, blotting at the gash on her cheek with a damp cloth.

"Cassie?!" Amber's face registered horror. "What happened to you?"

"She was attacked by an incubus." I couldn't keep the anger out of my voice.

"Should we take her to a doctor or something?" Amber eyed the long gash on Cassie's face.

"No." Cassie glanced up, eyes hollowed out by exhaustion. "Please. I don't want to leave."

Amber crossed her arms, considering Cassie's wounds. She turned to me. "Neosporin and hydrogen peroxide."

"What?" I stared at her blankly.

"Hydrogen peroxide to clean those wounds, and Neosporin to help reduce scarring. Trust me, I've seen my share of scrapes."

"Um, I—think we have some in the upstairs bathroom." I headed up the staircase to the second floor. I rooted through the bathroom medicine cabinet, coming up with the hydrogen peroxide, Neosporin, and some cotton balls. When I returned downstairs, Amber was sitting next to Cassie on the couch, a roll of paper towels in one hand. I let Amber doctor Cassie's wounds. Cassie winced as the hydrogen peroxide bubbled along the gash, but she gritted her teeth and kept silent through the whole procedure.

Once Amber had slathered the Neosporin over the cut, Cassie sat back on the couch and closed her eyes.

I glanced up at the clock on the mantle. 3:48 PM. Lucas would be expecting me any minute.

"I need to make a call." I turned to Amber. "Do you mind staying with her for a minute?"

"Of course not." Amber twisted the cap back on the Neosporin, studying Cassie with a worried expression on her face.

"I'll be right back." I pulled my phone out of my pocket and headed outside.

I dialed Lucas, not thrilled about having to explain that our rendezvous needed to be postponed. But as I waited for him to pick up, guilt coursed through my body. Cassie had been attacked and the Guard was heading into a battle against unknown forces—how could I feel bitter disappointment that Lucas and I wouldn't have tonight together? Our friends were hurting, they needed our help. Whatever disappointment I might feel, it was time to suck it up and turn my attention to more important things. And so that's what I decided to tell Lucas.

Only, Lucas didn't answer his phone.

I hung up and checked my messages, wondering if he'd left the address for our secret tryst in my voice mail. But Lucas wasn't listed anywhere on my missed calls, and he'd sent me no text messages.

Something was wrong.

I dialed his phone again. And then I heard it. I lowered my phone from my ear. There, in the distance, another phone was ringing. As my call went to voicemail a second time, the other phone stopped ringing.

I dialed Lucas a third time, this time honing in on the other ring. I glanced at the Guard's house. Lucas's bedroom window was open. The ringing phone was inside.

Had he left his phone behind? No. I knew with a growing sense of dread that Lucas wouldn't have left his phone behind, not when our whole day depended on his being able to give me the address to our secret meeting place.

I ran, vaulting the fence between our yards and taking the front porch steps two at a time. The Guard's front door was unlocked. I dashed up the stairs and burst through the door to Lucas's small room.

He was lying on his bed, tangled in his sheets, staring blankly at the ceiling.

I dropped beside his bed, trying to fight the hysterical panic threatening to overwhelm me.

"Lucas!" I cupped his face in my hands, turning his head to face me. His eyes were wide, glazed. A small part of me knew instantly—but I forced the thought out of my head. "No. No!" I grabbed his shoulders, shaking him. "Please, Lucas, get up. Get up!" He didn't respond, other than to turn his eyes back to the ceiling.

I pulled Lucas toward me, lifting his back off the bed. Beneath him, I saw lines of blood staining the sheets. And then I saw his back; his smooth skin crisscrossed with jagged, angry claw marks.

I heard a keening wail fill the room, not recognizing the voice as my own. The pure agony of this scream—a profound, inconsolable pain— rose up through me from the deepest part of my soul.

I gripped Lucas tighter, aware even as I clung to him that he had slipped away from me. We would never have our one perfect night—that one night Lucas would have been able to recover from. That intimate, personal, private connection had been stolen from us by another Lilitu. Were Lucas to spend a night with me now, he would cease to be Lucas; he would become a Thrall.

Dimly, I became aware of a growing pain in my throat. My voice was shredding itself, incapable of expressing the magnitude of emotion trying to manifest itself in sound. I forced myself to choke back the scream. In its place, violent, wracking sobs tore out of my body.

"Braedyn?!" Cassie burst into Lucas's room.

Her eyes landed on Lucas, and she turned abruptly away, recognizing the signs immediately.

Amber, two steps behind her, entered in time to read Cassie's horror. "What?! What's happened?" Amber's eyes settled on Lucas. Her expression went strangely blank, and her eyes moved to my face. "Oh no."

I lowered Lucas back to the bed, burying my face against his chest. Rage—unfiltered, unmitigated rage—rose up in me, burning away all thoughts save one. I would find her. Whoever had done this to Lucas. I would find her and I would end her.

"Braedyn?" Lucas's voice broke through my grief. I lifted my head, suddenly aware of the web of tears sliding down my cheeks. Lucas met my eyes and blinked. He glanced from me to Cassie to Amber. Confusion twisted his beautiful features. "What's wrong?"

I stared at him, stricken. He didn't know. Somehow, he didn't know what had happened. He watched me, hungry for answers. I opened my mouth, but no words came. I stood abruptly, turning away. I couldn't do this. I couldn't be the one to tell him.

I met Cassie's gaze. She watched me, eyes creased with sorrow, gleaming with unshed tears. I had to look away.

"I don't understand," Lucas said behind me. "Cassie? What's going on?"

I faced the window—

And saw something that sobered me instantly. Ian slipped quietly off the Guard's back porch. He had something bundled tightly under one arm, and he cast a nervous look at the back door behind him. Satisfied that he wasn't being followed, Ian moved quickly to the back corner of the yard, to a loose board in the fence. He worked it aside, and in moments, he was through.

"Stay with Lucas," I hissed, not waiting for Cassie to acknowledge me.

With the smallest effort, I cloaked myself and lunged for the doorway. Amber hissed, shrinking back against the wall to get out of the way. I flew down the stairs, my feet connecting with every third step. I barreled through the backdoor, sprinting for the back fence. When I reached the corner Ian had escaped through, I planted my feet, leapt, and cleared the fence as easily as if I'd been stepping over a curb.

I landed hard on the other side, my heart racing but my mind focused on one single task; Ian was up to something. I was going to find out what it was.

16

Despite his head start, I caught up to Ian at the edge of a wide arroyo running behind our cul-de-sac. As soon as he came into view, I slowed my steps. I was cloaked, so he couldn't see me coming, but that didn't mean he couldn't *hear* me. The late afternoon was bright and clear. From this spot near the arroyo, tucked back in a copse of Piñon and fir trees, you couldn't even see the houses of my neighborhood. It felt wild, and strangely isolated. I watched Ian, wondering how often he'd made this trek, and what the hell he was doing out here.

Ian stopped near a large boulder. I froze, hyper-aware of my breath, still ragged from my sprint to catch up with him. The smallest sounds seemed amplified in the quiet of this patch of wilderness. Even the sounds of traffic on the nearby streets was strangely muted. I wrestled my breath under control and waited, watching. But as the minutes stretched on, I got impatient. Was he waiting for someone? After several more minutes' time—without a glimpse of another soul—I was ready to confront him myself. But as I took a step forward, the air seemed to split, like a curtain dividing to let a figure pass through. As soon as I saw the sun gleaming off his pale blond locks, I felt my flesh start to crawl.

Seth.

Ian saw Seth emerge from thin air out of the corner of his eye. He recoiled, startled, then coughed quickly—an obvious attempt to disguise his alarm.

Seth gave him a thin smile. "Do you have it?"

"Yes." Ian pulled the bundle out from under his arm. Carefully, he unwrapped it. I had to bite back a gasp—I recognized the blade instantly. I'd first seen it 6 months ago. It had played a key role on that horrible night at the mission. The memory crashed over me, momentarily blinding me—

A slender form stepped through the rift between our worlds, gaining substance in half a heartbeat. She had long, pale blond hair that fell in undulating waves down her back. She was small, shorter than Seth by a good six inches. Her limbs were delicate, perfectly proportioned. She was achingly beautiful. Of course, *I thought numbly.* She's Lilitu. *She held a weapon loosely in one hand. It was shorter than the stranger's sword, but too long to be considered a knife. The curved blade was tarnished with age, but the edge tapered to a cruel point. Strange glyphs ran the length of the blade. The handle, what I could see of it, was a dark and twisted metal.*

That blade—the same blade Seth had used to kill the angel Senoy—Ian had stolen it from the Guard's armory. And now, *he was returning it to our enemy.*

For a moment, I could only stare.

Seth took the blade and turned it over in his hands, smiling. "I never should have let this fall into the Guard's hands in the first place." He looked up, eyeing Ian with dark anticipation. "I am indebted to you for returning it."

Ian bowed his head, acknowledging the thanks.

"Now." Seth produced an ancient leather sheath and slid the blade inside. It fit perfectly. "What about that other little matter?"

"They left, not 20 minutes ago."

"They took the bait?"

"Just as you anticipated." Ian shrugged with a small smile. "I only needed to give them a small push. Hale and Murphy were chomping at the bit to gather the forces and attack as soon as I gave them a plausible location."

Seth nodded. "Good. We'll be ready for them. And the little trouble maker?"

Ian actually laughed. "She's just discovered her boyfriend. She'll be distracted for a good long while."

My head felt strangely light, but the sensation didn't last. Two seconds later, a rage more powerful than anything I'd ever experienced struck me with the force of a hurricane. My vision swam with red and gold bursts, burning out my peripheral vision, blinding me to everything except for Ian and the smug expression on his face.

I moved, unable to control my body, not even hesitating when I saw the glistening metallic claws protruding from the ends of my fingers—

But someone caught me from behind, clamping a hand over my mouth and hissing quietly into my ear, "don't."

Karayan held me tightly, the both of us cloaked in broad daylight, invisible to anyone but a spotter. As we watched—me struggling in her grip—Seth turned, parted the air, and once more vanished from sight. Ian shuddered, glanced quickly around, and hurried back toward the Guard's house. He passed within three feet of us, but Karayan tightened her grip on me until he was gone. I fought her, trying to shift my weight to throw her off of me. Karayan countered every move I made, keeping me helplessly immobilized.

Once Ian was out of sight, something inside me broke. Hot tears of rage spilled down my cheeks. Karayan felt them on the hand she still held clamped to my mouth.

"Easy, Braedyn. I heard the whole thing," she murmured into my ear. "I know what you must be feeling. But you don't have time to waste on that smarmy bastard. The Guard needs us *now*."

Stricken, I stopped fighting. Seth had said something… *we'll be ready for them.* Ian had sent Dad into a trap.

I ran, feeling strangely disoriented, like the desert around me was merely a background projected on a screen. The center of my world had been attacked; Cassie, Lucas, Dad—my thoughts were trapped in a loop that orbited around them. Everything else was pushed so far to the edge of my thoughts that it no longer seemed real.

I was aware of Karayan running beside me, shouting something. I couldn't hear her. I had one goal; get to my car and drive to the mines. Warn Dad and the Guard.

We approached the fence separating my yard—and the Guard's yard—from the undeveloped land beyond. My eyes snagged on the loose board that Ian had slipped through, but I tore my gaze back to my own fence. With the same ease as before, I vaulted over the fence. I raced through my yard and around to the driveway. My car was still parked in front of the Guard's house. I dug in my pocket for the keys and in moments Karayan and I were climbing inside.

"Wait! Braedyn, wait!" Cassie barreled out of the house. Behind her, Lucas, now dressed, leaned weakly against the front door frame.

I hesitated.

"We don't have time." Karayan turned toward me, her face drawn with tension.

Cassie reached the car. "I think you have a problem." She gasped, breathless from her dash down the stairs to meet me. "Some spotter named Rhea was just here. Ian called her, said you attacked Lucas—?"

"Ian's a traitor." I turned the key in the ignition and the engine roared to life. Cassie stepped back, startled.

"Okay, but Rhea—she was really freaking Amber out. Something about Lilitu messing with people's heads so even bitter enemies start to feel like friends." Cassie looked back at the Guard's house. Lucas stepped out onto the porch, heading toward us with unsteady steps.

"Stay with Lucas," I said. "Dad needs me."

"That's what I'm trying to say." Cassie wrung her hands. "Rhea's going after Murphy right now. She blames him for you being alive."

I stared at Cassie, stricken. Karayan looked from me to my friend, then sighed with impatience. She opened her door and got out, jerking her seat forward. "Get in. You too, kid." She jerked her chin at Lucas. Cassie crawled into the cramped backseat of the Firebird. Lucas slid in a few moments later, falling back into his seat weakly. Karayan repositioned her seat, got in, and slammed her car door shut. "Punch it."

I hit the gas. The Firebird rocketed away from the curb down the street. As I drove, I fished my phone out of my pocket and thrust it at Karayan. "Call Dad. We have to warn him."

Karayan thumbed the phone on and selected Dad's number from the top of my list of favorites. She held the phone to her ear. After several long moments, she shook her head. "He's not picking up."

"Try again."

"If they're in the mine, they might not have reception," Cassie said from the backseat.

I grit my teeth. "Try it again anyway."

Karayan dialed again. As she tried to connect with Dad—then Hale or Gretchen—I sped out of Puerto Escondido proper toward the old silver mines to the east of the city. I had only a vague notion of where we were going, but Cassie—who'd just been there herself—helped navigate.

We pulled up to the old mines about 15 minutes later. The small dirt lot that served as temporary parking was empty. Of course; all the Guard had parked at the turnout half a mile away. I looked around. They'd had a good head start on us. So why couldn't I see any soldiers?

I parked and killed the engine, keeping my eyes fixed on the entrance to the old mine.

"Cassie, stay here with Lucas."

"Okay." Cassie's voice was thin and high, betraying her anxiety.

"You might need me," Lucas said, hoarsely.

"That's sweet," Karayan said, glancing back at Lucas. There was something almost genuine about the way she said it. "But you need to sit this one out. You're not going to be 100% for a long time, kid."

Lucas saw me watching him in the rearview mirror. He dropped his eyes, bright shame flooding his cheeks. Karayan glanced at me and nodded. We needed to move.

Karayan and I got out of the car and walked toward the entrance to the mine. I couldn't hear anything from inside.

A large, welded-steel gate covered the front of the mine, but both heavy barred doors stood open. We slipped inside wordlessly.

I could feel a change in the air almost instantly. The cavern was cool, loaded with a cloying moisture that wasn't present in the high desert air outside; there must be an underground water source somewhere below. It had the sharp, earthy smell of minerals that was both strange and invigorating. A line of bare-bulbs was strung up on one side of the cave. As we moved further away from the entrance—and the natural daylight outside—those bare bulbs became the only illumination. Not that either Karayan or I needed light to see. Our Lilitu vision would have made pitch dark as comfortable for us to navigate as bright daylight.

As we moved further into the cavern, we heard the rustling echo of a large group of people. We hurried down the narrow shaft, and suddenly the path opened up before us. Guardsmen were gathered in the large, central cavern that seemed to be the heart of the planned tourist attraction. Fake mining props lined the space, artfully arranged next to visitor information boards and a ticket booth for a "Wild Mine Ride." In one corner, a wheelbarrow of gleaming fake coal stood next to a pair of plastic pick-axes and some lighted helmets. In another corner, an old mining-elevator stood open.

The Guardsmen were arming themselves from the four black duffle bags I'd helped Dad and Gretchen pack. Hale, slender sword in hand, was calling out instructions for search parties. It sounded like he was preparing to send groups of Guardsmen down each individual path further into the mine, looking for a non-existent Temple of Lilith.

"A fast, thorough search," he was barking. "Down and back. If you find anything, send someone here for reinforcements. Any questions?"

When no one spoke, Hale nodded. "Okay." He pointed out shafts as he called off teams. "First team. Second team—"

"Stop!" I ran forward, entering the cavern as the first team moved toward their assigned shaft. At my command, they froze, glancing uncertainly back at Hale.

Rhea, the spotter assigned to the first team, stepped out of her group. Her fist tightened on the hilt of her daggers. "You've got some nerve coming here."

I ignored Rhea, sliding through the crowd toward Hale. "Listen to me. Ian's betrayed us. This is a trap."

A buzzing murmur spread through the crowd at these words.

"You want to see a traitor, Hale?" Rhea drew her daggers, pointing the blades straight at me. "Look no further than your pet demon." I gaped at Rhea, furious, but she turned to the assembled Guardsmen. "I was going to spare you this until after the fight," she glared at me, "but if you want to force the issue, fine. We can do it now. Do you want to confess your sins, or shall I confess them for you?"

"Rhea," I said, trying to force a patience I didn't feel into my voice. "You don't know what you're saying."

"Don't I?"

"What sins? What is she talking about?" Hale frowned, turning to face me.

"She's been misinformed! We have to get out of here!" I turned to Dad. He watched me, eyes creased with concern. "This is a trap.

They wanted us here. I don't know why, but we have to—"

"Don't listen to her!" Rhea cut me off. "You can't trust anything that little bitch says."

"Excuse me?" Dad turned to face Rhea, unmistakable fury flashing in his eyes.

"Wait," Gretchen said. "We should hear Braedyn out—"

"You say that now," Rhea spat, smirking with dark amusement.

I felt my heart wrench in my chest. Ian had told her I'd attacked Lucas. It didn't matter that it wasn't true; if the Guard heard her accusation before I had a chance to get us out of here, I might lose this chance. Dad seemed to sense my panic.

"Enough, *spotter,*" he growled, taking a step forward. "You've been gunning for Braedyn ever since you arrived."

"With good reason." Rhea glared at Dad.

I stepped in between them. "Listen, Rhea! I don't care what you think of me, but if we don't get these people out of here *now,* they are going to *die.*"

"Trying to distract me, little demon?"

"You are so blind." I strode toward Rhea, my frustrating adding strength to my voice. She gripped her daggers tighter, ready to spring. "I'm done trying to prove myself to you!" I turned my back on Rhea and faced the assembled Guard. "This is a trap! Lilitu are on there way here to—"

"Braedyn!" Dad lurched forward, his face ashen.

I spun around as Rhea's dagger sliced down, angling straight for my heart. Electricity shot through my muscles and my hand whipped up, catching her wrist. We stood there, frozen, for a long moment, eye-to-eye. Behind us, the Guard watched, unmoving. Two soldiers had grabbed Dad's arms, keeping him from intervening. Rhea's muscles quivered as she fought to drive the knife home. I squeezed the pressure point on her wrist and she sucked in a sharp breath of pain. Her hand opened reflexively, and I caught the dagger as it fell. I released Rhea. She took two steps back quickly, as though I were poised to attack.

"I am not your enemy," I said, breathing raggedly. "And we don't have time to do this right now."

Rhea eyed me with deep mistrust. I turned the dagger and offered it to her hilt first. She took it quickly, never letting her eyes leave my face. "Is this supposed to make me trust you?"

"I don't care whether or not you trust me, Rhea. Just stay out of my way." I turned back to the guard, seeking out Hale. "We don't have much time."

Hale nodded slowly. "Okay. Let's pull back."

There was a rustle among the Guard. More than one Guardsman shot a look of disbelief toward Hale. But those who knew me started heading toward the exit. I felt a swell of relief and let my shoulders relax.

"Dad," I said, starting toward him. "It was Ian—"

Rhea grabbed my arm and spun me around to face her. I was so startled I could only stare at her. I sensed rather than saw the assembled Guard turn back toward us.

"I know what you're trying to do," she hissed quietly. "Painting Ian as a traitor so they won't believe you'd harm your beloved Lucas? It's not going to work."

"It's the truth, Rhea," I hissed. "I didn't touch Lucas. Ian's been working with the enemy this whole time!"

"Liar. I'm outing you. Right now." She turned toward the crowd. "Hale! Listen up! You should know what your little pet's done—" Rhea's head snapped back, her mouth opening in a voiceless "O" of surprise. Her back arched, and her feet wrenched up a foot off the ground—lifted by some unseen force. She released me. I staggered backwards, stunned.

"Lilitu!" someone shouted. Guardsmen drew their weapons in a resounding scrape of metal, listening intently for an enemy they couldn't see.

I stared—but I could see no cloaked demon attacking Rhea. The stocky spotter spasmed, coughing out a spray of blood. And then she fell forward—no, she was *thrown* forward—to sprawl face-first on the ground at my feet. I lurched back away from her body. Karayan rushed to my side. A gaping wound tore through the center of Rhea's back, leaving little question; she was dead.

"Spotters!" Hale roared his command into the cavern. The Guard responded, each unit snapping into formation, waiting for their spotters to call out directions.

Only—

"I can't see anything," the spotter I only knew as Taryn said. She scanned the space around her, eyes wide with panic. "Where did she go?! Does anyone else see—?"

Taryn jerked back, staring down as three vicious wounds opened across her chest. Then her eyes rolled back into her head and she dropped to her knees before pitching forward onto the floor.

Chaos erupted throughout the cavern. Whatever had killed Taryn? She'd been facing it directly as it attacked, and she hadn't seen a thing.

"Oh no," I whispered, clutching Karayan's hand. "It's Seth. Seth is here."

17

Karayan shot me a terrified glance, then spun back to face the Guardsmen. "Incubus!" Her voice cut through the chaos. "Protect your spotters!"

Instantly the formations changed. Spotters were thrust into the center of their units. Hale, Matt, and Dad ringed Gretchen, but the three of them together were woefully inadequate protection. Looking around, I could tell—Gretchen was the next easiest target.

"Karayan!" I darted forward to help protect Gretchen. Karayan followed, half a heartbeat behind.

"Take this." Dad pulled a spare set of daggers from a sheath on his belt and handed them to me. I separated the daggers and gave one to Karayan. It wasn't a lot, but it was better than facing an incubus unarmed.

"Somebody tag him!" Dad's voice cut across the growing panic. "It's the only way to reveal him!"

I tightened my grip on the dagger, then swung out blindly. Dad was right; if Seth came close enough to a blade—and the wielder was lucky enough to swing at the right moment—even a small scratch from a Guard weapon would shred Seth's cloak, leaving him visible for all to see.

I clutched the dagger, feeling naked and vulnerable. The graceful blade suddenly seemed much smaller than it ever had before. Seth could be standing right in front of me—right in front of Dad, or Gretchen, or Matt, or Hale—and none of us could see him.

Across the cavern massive, we heard another short scream. It cut off in a gurgle, followed by a frenzy as Guardsmen tried to slash at the invisible enemy who'd just murdered another of our spotters. I did the math in my head. Rhea, Taryn, now a third. That meant we had only three spotters left.

And then the number dropped to two. I saw Jane fall. The petite redheaded spotter was in the group closest to us, clutching her daggers, while her unit ringed her closely. But someone heard a sound and shouted, drawing the others' attention. It was the opening Seth needed—he must have slipped between two distracted guardsmen. Jane's head snapped back and she dropped. It was sudden and silent. I stared, feeling hot bile rising in the back of my throat. A few of the soldiers in Jane's unit dropped to her side, but there was nothing to be done for her.

We were sitting ducks—blind, unable to predict where Seth would next strike.

"We have to do something," I said, my voice hoarse with panic.

"Hold your position." Hale, next to me, swung out with his sword, clearing the air before him with fast, competent slices. He, like me, believed Seth would come for Gretchen next.

But the incubus wasn't following any logical pattern.

Minutes later, although I was sure Seth was practically breathing down my neck, we heard another scream from the far end of the cavern.

One spotter left. I turned and glanced behind me. Gretchen's eyes were wide with terror. She clutched her daggers, but her muscles were rigid with tension.

"To me!" Hale's voice cut through the chaos and grief. Some of the Guardsmen heard and started to move, but the scene was one of disorganized paranoia. The normally disciplined Guardsmen were falling apart. I cast my eyes around, desperate for anything that could help us locate Seth.

And then I saw the wheelbarrow of fake coal. I raced toward it.

"Braedyn?!" Hale called after me, alarm ringing in his voice.

I grabbed the handles of the wheelbarrow and pushed. It moved easily—the fake coal was little more than Styrofoam painted black. But it would do.

I raced the wheelbarrow back toward Hale and Gretchen, trying to anticipate the route Seth would take from the last murdered spotter to Gretchen, knowing I was running out of time.

I reached my target and upended the wheelbarrow in front of Hale.

Styrofoam poured out across the floor—

"What the hell are you—?" But then Hale's voice caught.

Scattering Styrofoam parted in thin air, rolling away from some invisible obstacle. Hale slashed out with his sword, and even though Seth had already started to retreat, Hale managed to make contact.

The blade caught on something—and an instant later, Seth was revealed, a line of dark Lilitu blood spreading from a wound on his shoulder. It was a mild cut—if he'd taken the same wound with a regular blade it wouldn't have slowed him one second. But the strange quality of Hale's sword, forged by the Guard centuries ago, was more than enough to banish Seth's Lilitu cloak.

"Here!" Hale's roar of triumph reinvigorated the men.

But Seth's trap had just begun to spring. He darted back from Hale's next lunge, screaming, "Attack!"

"Braedyn?!" Karayan's voice trilled, straining with tension. I turned. The massive cavern was dotted with openings leading to other parts of the mines; there must have been a dozen entrances. Cloaked Lilitu sprang from the shafts—they'd been hiding, waiting for this opportunity since we'd arrived.

"Guardsmen, behind you!" Gretchen had also seen the fresh wave of Lilitu pouring in to join the fight.

Her warning came too late for several of the soldiers. The Lilitu moved fast, their attacks brutal and merciless. But where each Guardsman fell, others joined up in formations and turned to face their invisible attackers. I was overwhelmed by a sudden understanding of the bravery it took for these men to fight against an enemy they could not see. They wouldn't make it easy for the Lilitu, but—blind as they were—they were achingly vulnerable.

Hale saw this, too. "Spotters!" He gestured to Gretchen, Karayan, and me. "Help them!"

Gretchen raced to the far end of the cavern, joining up with a group of Guardsmen facing three Lilitu. Matt followed her with a hoarse curse.

"Wait for me, Gretchen!"

Before they reached the far unit, the Lilitu had taken down four more soldiers—

I pulled my eyes off that fight, searching the crowd for Dad. He'd joined up with a group of a dozen others, all moving in unison through the form, driving back another four Lilitu. I raced to Dad's side as one of the Lilitu timed her attack for a pause in the form—

"Ahead!" I screamed.

The Guardsmen acted without hesitation, each spearing forward with both daggers. The Lilitu, already darting toward one of the soldiers in line, was moving too fast to change direction. She took two blades to the torso, both from the Guardsman she'd been targeting. Her cloak fell away instantly, but it made little difference, she was dead by the time she hit the floor.

I pulled my eyes off the fallen demon. The three other Lilitu had pulled back, eyes fixed on me with burning hatred. They split, meaning to slip around the line and attack from behind.

"Cover the flank!" I moved into the center of the group, and they reformed seamlessly around me, blades flashing out. As one, the three Lilitu attacked, all from different directions. "Incoming!"

Two of the Lilitu took glancing blows from daggers, stepping back as their cloaks slipped away. The last dodged through the line and impacted with a young Guardsman, spearing her claws into his throat and ripping clean through. The Guardsmen nearest to him reacted, stabbing blindly into the air, but she dodged them and danced back, out of range.

"You!" Dad tapped two Guardsmen and pointed at the first revealed Lilitu. "And you!" He gestured to another pair of Guardsmen. The teams split, racing after the visible demons while the rest of the men reformed to battle the cloaked Lilitu.

Only, she had slipped away into the fray. I looked around, trying to spot the next attack. What I saw filled my stomach with a sinking dread.

Of the eight units of Guardsmen, only three had a spotter to aid them. Gretchen and Karayan were guiding their units well; under their direction, soldiers managed to fight off attack after attack with minimal casualties. The other five units were not faring so well. While the soldiers relied on their forms to drive Lilitu back, there were simply too many demons. Each time one Guardsman fell, the others would spring, desperate to reveal the demon who'd attacked him. That left them open to attack from behind, and more and more Guardsmen were lost as the minutes dragged on.

And yet, there was nothing I could do for them. Lilitu continued to attack my unit. Leaving one group of soldiers to help another simply meant these men would become the next targets. *And that's not going to happen,* I acknowledged to myself grimly. *I'm not leaving Dad.*

Lilitu launched a fresh assault against us. I kept the soldiers focused, directing their efforts as each Lilitu struck. But as the minutes passed, I realized the demons were playing with us. They'd dart forward, always pulling back just as the soldiers struck. They danced out of our reach again and again. In each lull between attacks I'd look up and see more fallen soldiers.

As the units without spotters fell, one by one, more Lilitu turned their attention toward us. We might be outnumbered very soon. I glanced back at Hale; we had to join the remaining guard into one line.

But just as I'd opened my mouth to call to Hale, two Lilitu broke through the ranks surrounding him. They must have identified him as the leader; each of them bypassed easier targets and set their sights on Hale.

"Hale!" It was the only warning I had time for. Karayan heard my voice and spun.

She saw the breach and launched herself at the first Lilitu, knocking her off her collision course with Hale. Karayan nicked the Lilitu with her blade, revealing the demon for the Guardsmen—

But the second Lilitu connected with Hale, swinging for his throat with her claws. Hale, alerted by my scream, was already in motion. He dropped to one knee, spearing his sword up into the air before him. The movement saved his life; the demon's claws raked through empty air, missing his throat by half a second. Unfortunately, Hale's aim was off; he missed the demon. She knocked his sword aside, dropping on top of him. Hale fell back, his head impacting the ground with a sickening crack. Dazed, Hale wasn't immediately able to defend himself. The Lilitu clasped her hands around his throat—

But Karayan dropped onto her back, driving two daggers straight through the demon's ribs, both angled for the heart.

The Lilitu arched back in agony. Karayan twisted the daggers and plunged them further into the demon's torso. The Lilitu went slack, her head tilted up, eyes strangely blank. Karayan retracted the blades and shoved the Lilitu to one side. Without the demon between them, Karayan and Hale's eyes connected.

Karayan offered him a hand. Hale took it, sitting up. The move brought him face to face with Karayan.

I stared, breathless.

The look in Hale's eyes was one of naked love—this was beyond gratitude, beyond friendship, beyond desire. He reached up to touch Karayan's cheek. Karayan smiled, but the battle still raged around them. Together they stood, weapons in hand, and faced the next enemy.

"We need to combine our forces!" But my voice, shaken as I was, couldn't reach Hale over the clamor of battle.

Dad heard me. "Guardsmen! Draw in!" The remaining Guardsmen pulled toward the center of the room. In a few minutes, we had linked our disparate units into one last, cohesive group. Soldiers formed a ring around Karayan, Gretchen, and me. Gretchen had grabbed a few prop crates on the way back. We each stood on one of them, and the crates gave us the added height we'd need to see over the soldiers to the enemy beyond. The extra height also gave me a clearer picture of the battlefield. The bodies of the fallen lay all around us; the dead greatly outnumbered the living. There were maybe 25 of us left, including Gretchen, Karayan, Matt, and me. Just 25, and only an hour ago we'd numbered over 80.

The remaining Lilitu surrounded us. I saw that we, too, had taken our toll on them. There were a dozen Lilitu left, perhaps a little less than half the original number. Of those, only five had maintained their cloaks.

Behind me, Gretchen rifled through one of the black duffle bags. I spared a moment to watch her, curious. She pulled a thick leather pouch out of the bag. Out of this pouch, she drew a wicked looking knife.

Gretchen climbed back onto the crate wordlessly. She fixed her sights on one of the cloaked Lilitu, hefted a knife, and launched it. The knife flew end over end, flashing in the theatrical lighting of the cavern. The Lilitu spotted it at the last second—she had time to throw herself to one side, but the blade nicked her arm in passing. One less cloaked demon.

Fascinated as I was by Gretchen's skill with the throwing knives, I ripped my eyes off of her and forced myself to concentrate on the soldiers before me. Three uncloaked Lilitu edged toward us, putting the soldiers on edge. Behind them, two cloaked Lilitu examined the line for weaknesses.

But then—I noticed movement at the main entrance to the cavern. Lucas staggered in, clutching his daggers. He stared at the carnage, face drawn. I saw him grip his daggers tighter. He clenched his jaw, summoning the strength to race forward and help his fellow soldiers.

Every other thought was driven from my head. I zeroed in on Lucas, reflexively sending my consciousness out to his mind.

Stay, I ordered. *Hide. You can't help us, you'll only get yourself killed.*

Lucas's eyes lifted from the fighting and found me. So he'd heard. The pain, shame, and agony moving across his features tore at my heart—but he nodded. I saw him withdraw, edging behind an outcropping near the entrance to the cavern. Relief so strong rushed through me that I felt my shoulders sag forward.

Lucas was safe for the moment; the same couldn't be said for the rest of us. And a question started gnawing at my mind with increasing urgency; where was Seth?

Nightmares are pale comparisons of what we went through in that cavern. Gretchen loosed knife after knife, but after that first hit, none of the other cloaked Lilitu stood still long enough for her to accurately target.

The visible Lilitu kept trying to draw Guardsmen away from the line, where they'd be easier targets for the cloaked to attack. But the soldiers refused to take the bait. As Gretchen threw knives at the enemy from her perch, Karayan and I called out directions to the soldiers any time a cloaked Lilitu came close enough to warrant it.

It was a grueling fight, but bit-by-bit we started to turn the tide. Gretchen hit two of the visible Lilitu, wounding one badly enough to eliminate her from the fight, and killing the other instantly. Guard soldiers tagged another invisible demon, leaving us facing just three cloaked Lilitu.

Around the time I started to feel a surge of hope, we made a critical mistake.

Karayan and I saw an attack coming and shouted our directions at the same instant—but where she directed the soldiers to close ranks, I ordered an attack.

Some men planted their feet, anticipating the others to form a solid line on either side of them. But others charged, confident their fellow soldiers were by their sides.

The resulting chaos left the line vulnerable. Two cloaked Lilitu slipped through while four visible Lilitu engaged the scattered forces. Dad, seeing the carnage, ran toward the fray, unable to see the two cloaked Lilitu barreling toward him.

"Dad, stop!" I leapt off the rickety wooden box and raced forward, intercepting the first of the cloaked Lilitu.

We went down in a tangle of limbs. She pushed away from me, rolling to her feet—but my dagger had pierced her skin, just below her ribs. Her cloak unraveled, leaving her visible for all the Guardsmen to see.

One of them shouted and turned on her. I didn't wait to see what happened.

Across the circle of Guardsmen, Dad dropped to his knees, clutching at his side. The cloaked Lilitu's claws glistened in the darkness, slick with blood.

"Dad—?" My feet moved of their own accord. As the Lilitu reached for Dad's throat, I gripped two fistfuls of her hair and wrenched her away from him. The Lilitu screamed her rage, but I didn't let go.

She swiped for me, those razor-sharp claws coming within inches of my face. I moved as she thrashed in my grip, trying to stay behind her, limiting her ability to reach me. Dad stood shakily, drawing a sword out of the black canvas bag. He saw me struggling with the invisible enemy. He watched the fight with the intensity of a hunting hawk, then struck, lunging forward and spearing the demon sideways through the chest.

Her cloak fell away as the scream died on her lips. She went heavy in my hands and I released her, letting her fall.

"That's it!" Karayan shouted. "Only one cloaked demon left!"

Hale glanced around grimly. Final tally: 15 Guardsmen, 7 Lilitu. "Teams of two! Go!"

The Guardsmen moved. It was like watching the inner workings of a well-maintained clock. The soldiers paired up wordlessly. Each team tracked one demon, focused on their prey, no longer worried about a sudden attack out of thin air.

Karayan, Gretchen, Matt, and Hale took on the last of the cloaked demons.

I ran to Dad. He still gripped his side, and when I pulled his hand free it came away bright with crimson blood.

"Dad!"

"I'm okay." He pulled up the side of his shirt. "Just a flesh wound. Help Hale finish this."

I turned. Several of the visible Lilitu were fleeing for the dark paths out of the central cavern. If they could get the soldiers away from light, they'd have the advantage.

"They're leading you into darkness," I shouted. If they heard me, the Guardsmen pursuing these Lilitu gave no sign. I pulled my attention back to the last cloaked Lilitu. Gretchen and Karayan had hemmed her back against one wall of the cavern. Hale was closing in on her. It would be over soon.

But then, the lights failed—plunging us into darkness.

My Lilitu eyes needed no time to adjust. If anything, the lack of artificial light casting all those deep shadows made it easier for me to see.

"Strike now, Hale!" Karayan's voice cut through the sudden silence. I turned in time to see Hale lunge forward. His body blocked the Lilitu, but I heard the sword hit its mark.

"Braedyn?" Dad reached toward me, groping blindly in the perfect darkness.

"Here, Dad."

"We need light," he said, his voice hoarse with tension.

"I'm on it." I glanced around, conscious of the fact I hadn't heard a pop or any sound to indicate mechanical failure. I glanced at the string of bulbs, now hanging dark against the wall. A strand across the room was swaying slightly. I zeroed in on it and saw the problem; someone had unplugged it from its power source.

I raced forward, catching the free plug and reinserting it into the industrial outlet that powered this cavern. Light flooded the space once more. I had to clamp my eyes shut against the sudden brightness. When I blinked my eyes open once more, the clarity of the darkness had been replaced once more by the jarring light and shadow.

But, for the Guardsmen, light meant life.

I watched as the last Lilitu in the cavern were surrounded by soldiers. The men made quick work of the job, and when they withdrew, the demons joined the other lifeless bodies on the ground.

I felt something inside me give way. It was over. It was finally over.

Someone let out a ragged sob, but cut it short. The sound echoed hollowly in the chamber before falling away, leaving an oppressive silence behind. Matt embraced Gretchen fiercely; both had survived.

Behind them, Lucas emerged from his hiding place at the entrance to the cavern. His eyes scanned the space. A desolate shock washed over his face. I turned and saw what he saw. Of our forces, less than a dozen living Guardsmen remained. Bodies covered the cavern floor, soldier and demon alike.

Hale took the devastation in, then bowed his head. The others joined him, paying silent respect to the fallen. When he looked up, his expression was grim.

"We need to move. Idris is still out there. It might be a slim chance, but we have to try and stop her."

"Weapons." Dad barked the word crisply. As Hale wiped the ichor off his blade, other soldiers moved over the battlefield. They collected the irreplaceable swords and daggers of the Guard—weapons that the dead could no longer use. I turned back to Lucas, offering him my hand. He stepped forward gingerly, but he didn't reach for me.

"I can't believe it." His voice rasped hollowly; it sent a shiver down my spine. "The Guard—the Guard is basically gone. What are we going to do now?"

"The only thing we can do. Rebuild." I lowered my hand, feeling awkward. "They've done it before. We can do it again." Glancing back at the group, I let out a long breath. "I'd better help. The faster we get out of here the better."

I moved forward, joining the others, gathering weapons. I tried not to look at the faces of the dead, but my eyes continued to pick out men I'd come to know.

Jeremy, the artist who'd drawn a picture of Senoy before we'd known he was an angel.

Marx, who'd just saved Cassie's life—and not five feet away from him, Caleb.

Chris, whom I'd practiced sparring with, who'd tried to preserve the last vestiges of Lucas's innocence regardless of the fact that Lucas didn't want him to.

All these people had given their lives to protect a humanity unaware of the peril it was facing. I bit my lip, fighting against the surge of grief threatening to overwhelm me.

With my hands full of weapons, I headed back to the nearest duffle bag.

"No—Hale!" The force of Lucas's panic pierced my thoughts. I looked up. Lucas raced forward. I followed his gaze—

Seth tapped Hale on the shoulder. As Hale turned, Seth head-butted him, sending Hale staggering back, grasping for the hilt of his sheathed sword blindly. Seth slipped behind him, lips peeled back in a grimace of rage. Just as Hale drew his sword, Seth reached across Hale's face with one hand and gripped the back of his head with the other—

With one brutal motion, Seth twisted Hale's head to the side. I heard a crack like a gunshot. Seth stepped back, releasing Hale.

"*Hale!*" Weapons clattered from her hands as Karayan sprinted forward—

Hale dropped like a ragdoll, dead the instant his neck had snapped. His sword clattered to the ground beside him.

"God—oh, God!" I raced forward, but Dad caught my arm.

"Braedyn, no!" he hissed.

Lucas skidded to a stop, frozen with horror. Karayan dropped beside Hale. A guttural scream unlike anything I'd ever heard before tore itself out of her throat—a pure grief of unimaginable intensity. Her hands hovered over his face, as though she were afraid to touch him.

"*Hale?!*" The desperate, hollow quality of her voice stabbed a fresh jolt of pain through my heart. She laid one hand to his cheek. His body was still under her touch. Karayan's shoulders shook, but when she looked up at Seth I could see it was rage—not grief—that made her tremble.

Seth ran. He grabbed Lucas, catching him round the neck and poising his free hand, claws extended, against Lucas's carotid artery.

Karayan stood slowly.

"Easy!" Seth pressed his claws tighter to Lucas's neck. Lucas took a sharp breath, his nostrils flaring. Seth glanced at Gretchen. "Keep her back, or your little brother dies."

Karayan took a step forward.

"Karayan, no!" I ripped my arm out of Dad's grasp and barreled for Karayan. Gretchen, seeing the same intention in Karayan's eyes as I had, reached her first, gripping one arm tightly. Matt was two steps behind, her. He caught Karayan's other arm.

"Get your hands off of me." Karayan never took her eyes off of Seth.

"He has Lucas," Gretchen hissed.

I reached them two seconds later, skidding to a stop in front of Karayan, planting my hands against her shoulders. "Don't, Karayan, please."

Karayan's eyes shifted from Seth to my face.

"It's Lucas, Karayan."

Karayan's gaze swiveled back to Seth. But she didn't make a move to attack him. I turned to face Seth.

"Let him go."

"Braedyn. Did you get my little present? I meant to finish wrapping her for you, but—well, we were interrupted." Seth gave me an icy smile.

"Please," I whispered. "You've already won."

"I'm glad someone noticed." His voice was rich with amusement. He edged toward the cavern's entrance, dragging Lucas with him step by step. When he reached the edge of the cavern, he stopped. Then his eyes settled on my face. "I vaguely remember warning you to stay out of my way. What happens next is on you."

Before I had time to worry about what that might mean, Seth crashed his shoulder into the prop elevator car. The heavy metal cage swung to one side, revealing a dark shaft beneath it. Seth wheeled Lucas around, sending him careening into the pit.

"Lucas!" I sprinted forward, not caring that Seth was escaping. I dropped to my knees at the edge of the shaft, peering over the side, trying to see past the still-swinging elevator car. The drop was a good 20 feet down. Lucas lay at the bottom, struggling to push himself to his hands and knees. He groaned and turned himself over, looking up.

Relief flooded through me. He was alive.

Gretchen and Matt dropped beside me a few moments later.

"Lucas?!" Gretchen peered into the darkness of the shaft. Matt caught the swinging elevator shaft, bracing it with his hands, slowing it to a stop.

"He's okay," I said.

"I wouldn't go that far," Lucas groaned. But he was able to haul himself into a sitting position, even as he winced at the pain.

"Seth," Karayan growled.

"We'll get him." Dad glanced at me, worried, then turned back to Karayan. "You stay here with Gretchen and Braedyn while they help Lucas. Keep an eye out for more Lilitu."

Karayan nodded slightly. I saw a muscle jump along her jaw line. But as Dad led the remaining Guardsmen after Seth, her eyes fell back to the ground. She sank down beside Hale, gripping his hand in silence.

Dad paused beside us on his way out. "Braedyn, get Lucas and get home." He shot a quick look around. "I don't want you in here any longer than necessary."

"Seconded." I caught Dad's hand and gave it a brief squeeze.

Matt stood beside Dad, turning back to Gretchen. "Gretch—?"

"Go. Get that little bastard." She gave him a tight smile. "Just be careful."

Matt nodded. Then he and Dad were gone, pounding up the entrance tunnel after Seth.

My eye snagged on movement at the entrance to the tunnel. Cassie emerged, starring at the carnage beyond us.

"Cassie, you shouldn't be here." I stood, worried. Cassie pulled her eyes off the bodies. She looked shaken to the core.

"I heard a scream."

At that moment, we heard a loud, metallic clanking from the mouth of the mines. Everyone turned, creeped out.

"Maybe we should get out of here," Cassie whispered.

"Uh, a little help here?" Lucas called from the bottom of the shaft.

Cassie glanced at the shaft, alarmed. "Is that Lucas?"

"Yeah." I looked around. "We need rope. I think I saw some—there." I pointed at another faux mining supplies display, which included a coil of thick rope. Cassie picked her way around several bodies to retrieve the rope. I turned my attention back to the shaft. "Hang on, Lucas," I said. "We're getting some rope."

"I don't think I'm going to be able to climb up with this leg."

"No kidding." Gretchen eyed the prop elevator car. It was suspended over the hole on a metal I-beam. "I've got an idea." When Cassie returned with the rope, Gretchen loosed a long length from the coil and tossed the edge up and over the metal beam. I caught the other end and fed it into the hole. We had just enough rope for Lucas to tie a loop around his chest. Together, Gretchen, Cassie, and I hauled on the free end of the rope. We pulled Lucas up to the edge of the shaft, but the elevator made the opening too narrow for Lucas to fit through. I had to brace my shoulder on the edge of the car and push in order to buy Lucas enough room to crawl through.

Lucas collapsed on the ground, rolling over onto his back. "I don't ever want to come here again."

"How's your leg?" I bent beside Lucas, examining his left leg gingerly. "Is it broken?"

"Um, I don't know." He hoisted himself up to a sitting position, bending his injured leg slowly. He winced, letting out a low hiss of pain. "Could be just a bad sprain."

I closed my eyes, letting some of my tension release. If Seth had meant to kill Lucas, he'd failed. For one brief moment, I felt lucky. The feeling didn't last.

Seth had destroyed the Guard.

18

"We need to get the weapons out of here." Gretchen stood, rubbing her hands where the rope had chaffed her skin raw.

"Right." I started to rise to my feet.

"Wait." Lucas caught my hand, stopping me. I glanced back at Gretchen.

Gretchen studied Lucas, then gave me a curt nod. She turned to Cassie. "Think you can give me a hand?"

"Yeah. Yes, of course." Cassie followed Gretchen onto the battlefield. Where Cassie couldn't help but stare, transfixed, at the bodies, Gretchen seemed focused only on the duffle bags. Together, they each grabbed one strap of the first duffle and hefted it up off the ground, dragging the heavy load back to the mouth of the tunnel leading to the entrance.

I eased back to the ground. Alone with Lucas, I found it harder than I expected to look at him. When I finally met his eyes, I saw him wince.

"I know," he whispered. "I know. But, Braedyn—" He shook his head, helpless with grief and frustration. "I thought she was you."

An ocean of complicated emotions roiled through my stomach. I couldn't think of anything to say to this. All I could do was stare at him.

"She was waiting in my room. She—I thought you'd changed your mind about the hotel—"

"You thought some other Lilitu was *me?*" My voice grated in my ears. I pulled my hand out of his grip.

Lucas closed his mouth, watching me with an agonized look on his face. "Okay. Okay, I get it. This isn't the time."

"No." I shook my hand, trying to clear my head enough to process what he was saying. "I want to know. How exactly did you mistake some strange demon for me? How could you let some other girl—?" I squeezed my eyes shut, fighting nausea.

Lucas licked his lips, but he held my gaze, unflinching. "She came up behind me, put her hands over my mouth and whispered 'shh' in my ear. I thought it was you, warning me to be quiet so we weren't overheard but—Braedyn, I never heard her voice. She never spoke, or I would have known—"

"You couldn't *see?*" I heard the fury in my voice, but couldn't dial it down.

"She'd pulled the blinds closed. The room was so dark. She could have been your twin, Braedyn. All I could make out was long brown hair—" The instant he said those words, realization struck. Lucas must have seen something in my expression. His brow furrowed. "What? What is it?"

"Long brown hair—?" As I said the words, her face swam to the front of my mind. Elyia. The Lilitu who'd seemed to have something personal against me long before I gave her a reason to hate me.

"Braedyn?" Lucas searched my face.

I could only shake my head, unable to form the words I'd need to explain. She'd warned me she'd make me regret taking the memories out of her mind. I forced myself to meet Lucas's gaze. Even now, the aftermath of his encounter was obvious. He looked sick and tired, like Royal had looked after Seth's attack. But more than that, he was punishing himself for the mistake, swimming in a guilt only sharpened by my anger. But the truth was, if it weren't for me, he'd never have made Elyia's radar. I'd painted a target on Lucas when I'd broken into her dream.

Lucas hesitated, afraid to touch me but unable to stop himself from reaching a hand toward me. I turned into his embrace, pulling him close, burying my face into the warmth of his chest. After one startled moment, Lucas's arms closed around me, holding me. A thousand questions must be swimming through his mind, but he held his tongue.

This—Lucas's misery, the loss of our one night together, the torment of guilt and anger she'd subjected us to—this was Elyia's revenge.

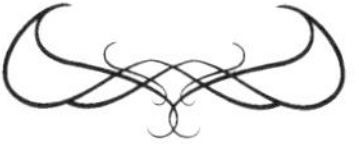

Gretchen and Cassie worked together dragging the repacked duffels to the mouth of the tunnel leading to the world outside. I scanned the ground for any weapons we might have missed. I only saw one.

I joined Karayan as she knelt beside Hale. Gingerly, I picked up his fallen sword. It felt heavier than I'd expected. Hale had wielded it so adeptly, it had seemed an extension of his arm, almost as though it weighed nothing. I rested it, point down, against the ground. Hale lay before me, unmoving. His head was now cradled in Karayan's lap, his eyes closed. There was no blood to mar his face. He looked peaceful, but his lips had already started to take on the bluish tinge of death.

"We should move." Gretchen glanced back at Karayan and me, then seemed to really see the carnage for the first time. She shook her head slowly. "I don't understand." Her voice sounded older than I'd ever heard it. Tired. Defeated. "How did this happen?"

"It was Ian," I murmured.

Gretchen turned toward me, stricken. "Ian? Our archivist, Ian?"

"He was working with Seth." I stopped, suddenly remembering the short sword Ian had delivered to Seth earlier today. I hadn't seen it in the battle.

"That can't be—are you sure?"

"She's sure." Karayan wrenched her eyes away from Hale's body. "Ian betrayed us. This—" She eyed the carnage surrounding her, "can all be laid at his feet." Then she dropped her eyes back to Hale. "Ian has much to answer for." Her voice crackled with dark intention.

Gretchen's jaw tightened. For once, she and Karayan shared exactly the same look on their faces—rage melding with determination. Ian better hope he never came face to face with either of them again; the reckoning would be brutal, and it would be final.

"So that's it?" Cassie wrung her hands, her anxiety ratcheting up. "How are we going to stop the human sacrifice? I mean, we're still going to try to stop it, right?"

All of a sudden, I had to plant my hand on the ground to keep from falling down, dizzy. An idea was trying to force its way from my subconscious to my conscious mind. I was dimly aware of the others, staring at me, surprised. Lucas made a move toward me. I saw his lips moving, but couldn't make out any of the words he was speaking.

All I could hear was Seth's voice, as my mind replayed his last words to me--

I vaguely remember warning you to stay out of my way. What happens next is on you.

Warning me. The pieces of a puzzle started to click into place in my mind. He had warned me. He'd been very specific.

I'll have to destroy your boy, Royal. As I'm killing him—and, trust me, the process will take some time—I'll tell him all about this little conversation, and how easy it would have been for you to spare him an agonizing death, simply by doing nothing.

"It's Royal." I shot Cassie a look of pure terror. "He's going to sacrifice Royal."

For a moment, no one made a sound.

"Braedyn?" Cassie's voice wavered. She lifted her hands to her mouth, her eyes wide and pleading for answers I couldn't give her.

"You can't know that," Gretchen managed.

But I was sure. I had to get out of here. I rose shakily to my feet and sprinted back through the main tunnel, Hale's sword still clutched tightly in my hand. I was conscious, as I ran, of the changes in the air. The crisp desert afternoon smelled harsh after the earthy moisture of the cavern. Up ahead, I could see daylight. The summer sun was dropping in the west, but it wouldn't set for hours yet. I pushed myself to run even harder. My feet impacted with the ground, springing me forward with such intensity that I had no time to stop when I saw that the way ahead was barred.

Someone had closed the gate.

I struck the metal bars hard, setting the gate clanging as I recoiled off of it. Hale's sword clattered to the ground, skittering off to the side. I shook off the pain of the impact, searching the gate for a handle or knob.

I found the latch and froze.

Someone had padlocked a heavy steel chain over the gate's lock.

"You've got to be kidding me." I pulled on the chain, straining as hard as I could.

I heard the others approaching, breathing hard from the sprint.

"Help me!" I turned back to the gate, pushing on the welded steel of the bars themselves.

Without a word, Lucas joined me, lending his strength—what little he had—to the task at hand. Cassie and Gretchen joined us half a second later.

The gate did not budge, even under our combined strength.

"What about some kind of lever?" Cassie cast her eyes around, looking for something useful. "We might be able to pry the padlock open."

"There are tools on display in the cavern." I gripped Cassie's hand. "What do you need?"

Cassie turned to the padlock. She pulled it through the bars so we could get a better look at it. "Something thin enough to fit between the body and the arm of the lock," she said. "The longer the better. And it needs to be strong."

Lucas studied the space between the body and the arm of the lock. "It looks like a piece of rebar might do the trick."

Gretchen shot me an urgent glance. "I'll help you look." We raced back to the cavern to begin our search. Only, there was no rebar to be found. The prop mining tools were all too thick to fit in the space we needed them to.

"What about those throwing knives?" I glanced at Gretchen.

"Worth a shot." She ran to the pile of duffle bags and started rooting through the first bag, coming up empty. The knives were in the second bag she searched. She picked out three and we raced back to the gate.

Cassie fed the first blade through the padlock, then pushed. The blade strained as Cassie tried to pry the arm free from the body. Cassie's arms started shaking, but the lock didn't budge.

"Let me try," Gretchen said, taking over for Cassie. She put her full strength into the effort. The blade started to bend as Gretchen increased her force—then it snapped. Gretchen fell forward, struggling to catch herself before she hit the ground.

"Try another," I growled.

"It's no use." Lucas's voice was soft. "The knives are too small. We need something that will give us more leverage for this to work."

"We have to warn Royal." Cassie turned to me. "Seth took my phone earlier—you'll have to call him."

I reached into my pocket—but I'd given it to Karayan. I turned to Lucas. "Let me borrow yours."

Lucas reached for his pockets, then blanched. "It must have fallen out when I took off my—" He stopped, dropping his eyes.

Gretchen glanced around at all of us. "No one has a phone?"

"What about yours?" Lucas stared at Gretchen. "You don't have one on you?"

Gretchen's face twisted in a miserable grimace. "Didn't you know, it's *déclassé* to take a purse to a knife fight."

Cassie spun on me. "Braedyn, do that thing you do. Contact his mind."

"Right." I closed my eyes, trying to summon Royal's image into my head. But something was wrong. The flickers of my friends' consciousnesses seemed weak and hazy. I concentrated on them, but couldn't seem to bring them into clear focus. It was like the whole dream world was slipping out of my reach. *Oh no…* I opened my eyes, breathless.

"Braedyn?" Lucas saw the rising panic in my eyes. "Can't you make the connection with—?"

"Braedyn—" Gretchen interrupted, grabbing my arm. "If you're right about Seth going after Royal, he could be taking him to the Temple. You have to find Royal and jump to his location."

"Jump?" I stared at Gretchen. Pinpricks of fear dotted the skin along my arms.

"You've got to stop this thing." Gretchen's hand tightened on my arm. "If Seth goes through with the sacrifice, he'll reawaken Lilith. You're the only one who can keep that from happening."

I shook my head. "I—I don't have the energy."

Gretchen released my arm, a little of the fire dying in her eyes.

"What do you mean? What energy?" Cassie glanced between Lucas and me.

"All Lilitu powers use a kind of spiritual energy," Lucas said numbly.

"I cloaked myself earlier." As I spoke, I turned to Lucas. "Then the fight, and calling to you—I'm completely drained."

Gretchen bit her lip. "So—so take what you need from Lucas."

I shook my head. "Gretchen, I can't."

"No." Gretchen took a step closer to me, hope springing alight in her eyes once more. "Braedyn, it's okay. Look, even if you take a third of his energy, he'll be able to recover. Yes, it'll take time, but—"

I stared at her, speechless. She still didn't know—she couldn't know—what Lucas had been through today. Gretchen misunderstood my horror.

"I know this is hard for you, but the situation is desperate, Braedyn—"

"Gretchen." I took Gretchen's hands in mine. She fell silent, reading my sorrow. "Lucas was attacked by a Lilitu this afternoon. If I so much as kissed him now—" But I couldn't finish the thought.

It took a moment for this news to sink in.

Gretchen pulled her hands free and turned abruptly away from me, but not before I saw the grief washing across her face. "I—I didn't know."

Cassie glanced from Gretchen back to me. "So take it from one of us."

"I can't." I blushed, unable to look Cassie in the eye.

"Why not? Lucas is too weak. I might not be in the best condition ever but I'm doing better than he is—"

"It won't work," Gretchen said heavily. "We don't *desire* Braedyn."

"Desire—?" Cassie's eyes widened slightly. "Like, you mean—?"

"Romantically," I answered. "Without that connection, it doesn't work."

Cassie stared at Lucas, finally understanding the full weight of our circumstances. "But, if Braedyn takes the energy she needs from you—?"

"She'll turn him into a Thrall," Gretchen answered dully. "She could save Royal, but only by destroying Lucas."

"It would destroy both of us," Lucas said, his voice hard.

"How?" Cassie's voice was edged with sick curiosity.

I caught Lucas's hand, but I couldn't bring myself to look at him.

"It'd wreck her only shot at a normal life. She'd never be able to become human." Lucas squeezed my hand. I felt another wave of hot tears threatening. It was true, but compared to what Lucas would sacrifice, my dreams of becoming human seemed insignificant.

"But if you don't?" Cassie turned and looked directly into my eyes. "Doesn't that mean Royal dies?

Gretchen leaned back against the gate. When she spoke, her voice sounded hollow. "No. It means Royal dies, and the end of the world begins."

19

T*here has to be another way.*

I turned away from Lucas, staring numbly at the gate. Sturdy steel. Thick chain. Formidable lock.

There has to be another way.

And then I had an idea. I sprinted back toward the cavern.

"Braedyn!"

Their voices rang behind me in a chorus of protest. I kept running. As I reached the main cavern, Karayan looked up. She was still sitting on the ground, holding Hale's hand. I could see a fine web of tears glistening on her cheeks. When she saw me, she swiped the back of her hand across her face.

"Weren't you and the gang off to save your snarky bud—?"

I sprinted past her, darting into the recent battlefield. Somewhere in here, there had to be an alternative. I reached the center of the cavern and stopped, trying to calm my mind, trying to heighten my senses. Revulsion shivered across my skin but I pushed the feeling to the back of my mind. If any of these men were alive, I could borrow just a little energy—it might be enough to contact Royal, at the very least. I tried to hone in on any flicker of life. But, aside from Karayan and myself, this cavern was devoid of living energy.

My eyes lifted to the walls surrounding us. There were many tunnels leading out of the main cavern—a dozen at least. The tourist board had posted quaint little signs over each tunnel, giving them all useless titles like "The Chimney Cavern" and "Dead Man's Drop." But on each sign beneath the title, neat little letters spelled out "NO EXIT." There was only one way out of these mines. And it was locked.

There has to be another way.

"There *has* to be," I moaned.

Behind me, I heard Karayan stand. "What's wrong?"

I spun on her, desperation lending a keening edge to my voice. "I need a way out of here." Karayan glanced toward the tunnel leading to the entrance. Her cheeks were dry, even if her eyes were still red. Before she could open her mouth to ask, I growled out the answer. "The gate is chained shut."

Karayan's mouth drew down into a considering frown. "Seth?"

"I don't know," I moaned, "but if he's given the Guard the slip, then Royal is in danger right now and I can't get to him without—" I choked off the last of the sentence.

Karayan's eyes zeroed in on my face. "Without what?"

I shook my head.

"You know of a way you can get out of here? Why are you hesitating? This is about more than saving your playmate's life. You talked me into joining your side of this little war. Well, here I am—but if we don't keep that little shit from opening the door for his Grams, this war's going to be over before it begins, and not in a good way. In a now-the-Lilitu-run-the-show, hope-you-like-being-cattle kind of way."

"No." My voice was a haggard whisper.

"No?" Karayan stared at me, her eyes burning with anger. "You do realize this is the capital 'M' moment, right here, don't you? Whatever it is you have to do—"

"I have to drain Lucas."

Karayan's mouth hung open for a moment, but no words came out. Her fury melted into an agonized understanding. She took a step toward me. "Oh, sweetie—"

"Don't. Please." I jerked back, even though she was still yards away. "I—I can't." My eyes fell to the floor. A heavy despair settled over me. All these soldiers, dead—and for what? If we let Seth win, their deaths would mean nothing.

Karayan regarded me, letting her hands drop to her sides. "Okay." She glanced around the cavern. "These tunnels all lead down," she murmured. "You can tell from the heady bouquet of dust and wet rock. None of them leads to fresh air. Your best bet is still the gate. Let's go. I'll help you find a way through." As she passed me, she paused to grip my shoulder. "It's not over yet."

In an instant, deep gratitude flooded through me. I followed Karayan back to the main entrance. Gretchen and Cassie were examining the hinges closely. My heart soared with hope.

"What did you find?" I asked.

They turned at the sound of my voice. My hope died as I saw the expressions on their faces. Gretchen shook her head. She didn't have to say it; I could see as they moved aside that the hinges were bolted together. Presumably to discourage people from breaking in. Of course, that meant it would be equally impossible for us to break out.

Cassie slumped against the wall of the cavern, sliding to a seat on the ground. Half a heartbeat after she made contact with the cold stone ground, she burst into tears.

I felt my own eyes welling at the sound. Royal was running out of time, and we were trapped here. Deep in the back of my mind, a little voice chastised me. *You're not trapped here…* But I shut it down.

Gretchen regarded Cassie, then turned. She gripped the steel bars hard and looked out over the late afternoon. We were running out of time.

Karayan strode up to the gate and took hold of it with her hands. She strained, trying to pry extra space for someone to slip through the gate, but the chain fastening the gate closed was tight. Even if she'd managed to win us another six inches, it still wouldn't be enough room for me to squeeze through the opening. She didn't give up, though. She climbed the gate to the top, searching for a weak bolt or anything we might use to our advantage. After a few minutes, she made a little noise of frustration.

"Okay, not over. Maybe we can go under." Karayan slid back down and tried digging her Lilitu-strengthened claws into the stone floor at our feet. Her nails shredded against the ground and she gave a low hiss of frustration—we wouldn't be digging our way out of here without some heavy construction equipment or dynamite—

I felt a hand on my shoulder.

"This time, there isn't another way." Lucas's voice travelled across the opening of the cave.

Karayan froze. Gretchen turned from the bars. Her eyes shone with tears of frustration. Even Cassie looked up, her sobs dying down with a few ragged breaths.

I couldn't face him. "Lucas. Don't."

"I know this has to happen." He turned me toward him, holding my shoulders in his hands. I met his eyes, expecting to see fear or grief. Instead, I saw determination and hope. "You can stop Lilith from returning."

"I can't—"

"*Yes you can.*" Lucas smiled, that beautiful lopsided grin of his. His dark hair fell forward, framing those hazel eyes—the same way that had so captivated me the first time I saw him.

"Lucas is right, Braedyn." Gretchen's voice broke. This was costing her almost as much as it was costing Lucas and me. "You can do this."

Lucas never took his eyes off my face. He just waited, trusting that I would come to the same conclusion. I bit my lip, but they were right. A tear slid free and snaked a trail down my cheek.

Karayan saw the change in my demeanor. "Ladies." She turned to Cassie and Gretchen. "We should give them some privacy."

I made the mistake of looking at Gretchen. Her face was a study in pain. Was she reliving the night she'd found the Lilitu killing her young husband Eric, Lucas's older brother? Is that how she would see me, after tonight? Gretchen realized I was watching her. She did her best to control her features. She turned to help Cassie to her feet, and together, she, Cassie, and Karayan retreated down the entrance tunnel until they were out of sight.

Lucas took my hand, then lifted it to his face. He bent and kissed my fingers. Then, in a voice too soft to carry, he said, "turns out this is our night after all."

Lucas was standing so close that the warmth of his skin radiated out to me. I took a deep breath, picking up the scent of him, both clean and musky.

Lucas took a step closer, bringing our bodies just inches apart. He reached up, catching me under the chin and tilting my face toward his. I met his eyes, and saw his naked desire. Something within me responded. The deep, powerful Lilitu storm rose up, as if it could sense willing prey.

I panicked, stepping back, but Lucas caught my hands.

"Not like this," I whispered. "Lucas, I love you."

"I know." Lucas pulled me close, wrapping his arms around me in a fierce hug. For a moment, we just stood there, clinging to one another. "I love you, too. I'm not afraid."

I took a shaky breath, almost unable to articulate my fear. "What if I go too far?"

Lucas cupped his hands on either side of my face and drew back, laying his forehead against mine. His eyes were closed. "This is our moment, Braedyn. Don't think about what comes next." He opened his eyes, regarding me with a calm intensity. "Just be here with me, now."

I nodded.

Lucas kissed me. I felt my eyes flutter closed, lost in the sensation of the moment. His lips were warm and firm. He slid a hand through my hair, cradling the back of my neck. The gesture sent little fireworks cascading over my shoulders.

As our kiss grew more heated, I forced the Lilitu storm into the back corner of my mind. I ran my fingertips down Lucas's chest. I felt him react, shuddering with longing. I curled my fingers under the edge of his T-shirt. Reading my mind, Lucas stepped back and slipped the shirt up and over his head. He let it drop to the floor beside him.

My eyes raked over Lucas's chest—I felt my heart stutter. Lean muscles bunched and strained under his smooth skin with each breath he took. I could see the throbbing pulse of his heartbeat at the side of his neck. I reached toward him, hesitant. Lucas caught my hand and pressed it to his chest, over his heart. The heat of him, the sudden contact of my palm on his skin, added fuel to the Lilitu storm within me.

It raged, battering against the walls I'd thrown up around it—but still, I kept it contained. I looked up into Lucas's eyes. He waited, a question unspoken between us. Nervously, I pulled my own T-shirt up and over my head. As it slid free, I shook my hair out. The glossy brown waves fell down over my bare shoulders. I'd worn a simple, blue-lace bra in anticipation of our evening together. Lucas swallowed, letting his eyes drop.

Gingerly, I caught his hand and guided him closer.

I kissed him again, but when his hands made contact with the skin of my back I gasped. His touch shot through me like a spray of gasoline, igniting the Lilitu storm in an explosion of power. It thrashed inside me, desperate to break free, focused on connecting with Lucas. I gritted my teeth, battling against it, unwilling to give it what it wanted—Lucas's life energy.

Lucas's brows knit together. "Don't fight it."

I looked up, unable to spare the concentration it would take to answer him. It took all my focus to cling to the Lilitu storm, to keep it from attacking him.

"Don't fight it," he said again. And then he caught my jaw in one hand and pulled me into another kiss. Our torsos connected, skin-to-skin, the only thing left between us my lacy bra. Lucas's kiss was hungry, insistent. I couldn't help but respond.

The Lilitu storm broke free.

Something wild and feral moved through me. I gripped Lucas's arms, pushed him back into the bars of the gate with more force than I'd intended. My lips fastening to his, urgent, hungry. I heard Lucas moan with desire. His arms curled around me, pulling me closer. One of my hands slid down his chest while the other gripped a bar behind him, locking him in this embrace. As my free hand slid around his chest to his back, I felt the marks *she'd* left behind.

A swell of irrational rage tore through me. *How dare she touch him?! He was mine.* The thought coursed through me—followed by the urgent need to claim him. I felt the tips of my fingers tingling. I drew my nails across Lucas's back. He arched into me, this time his gasp was a mixture of pleasure and pain.

I surged closer to him, pressing him against the bars of the gate—my every thought fixed on *joining* with him. The storm within me surged toward him, forcing a connection our bodies were too slow to make—

Like a catastrophic dam failure, I *felt* something crack within Lucas—and then a glorious, brilliant wash of energy was flowing into me. I pressed myself closer to him, our kiss growing in intensity until I had to break free to breathe—

Once the connection was broken, the wild tempest within me started to recede. Not because I was pushing it out. Because it was *sated.*

Before me, Lucas's eyes were heavily lidded. His head lolled back against the bars of the gate. He managed to meet my gaze.

"Did you get what you need?"

Before I could answer him, he collapsed in my arms.

I caught Lucas, easing him to the cold stone floor. His eyes fluttered closed. His breath sounded shallow, raspy. I moved to pick up his shirt, only noticing as I reached for it that my fingers were covered with blood. A sick horror took root in my stomach.

"Lucas?" I leaned over him, suddenly afraid to touch him. "Lucas?!"

Lucas did not respond.

"Braedyn! Easy. He's just unconscious." Karayan pulled me off of Lucas. I fought her, but she hauled me away, pushing me against the bars of the metal gate. "Give him a minute."

I tore my gaze off of Lucas. Karayan was studying me, concern etched into every contour of her beautiful face. Dimly, I realized I'd been clinging to Lucas, screaming his name over and over, trying to get a response.

Gretchen dropped to her knees beside Lucas. She covered his bare chest with the shirt he'd tossed aside just minutes ago. Her head was bowed. Her shoulders shook with grief. But then she looked up, her gaze spearing directly into me.

"I tried," I said numbly. "I tried to hold back—"

Gretchen shook her head, cutting my apology short. But it wasn't rage I was reading in her eyes. It was something else. "I know," she said, her voice coming out harsh and low. "You're stronger than anyone I've ever met."

I stared at Gretchen, unsure I'd heard her correctly. She bent to look at Lucas, stroking the side of his face with maternal care. Then she sat back, turning to me once more.

"Go. Stop Seth. You're our last line of defense, Braedyn."

Numb, I felt my eyes shift to Karayan, who still held me, pinned against the gate. She growled softly, "Damn right you can do this. Go get that son of a bitch."

Cassie edged into the cavern, her eyes picking me out against the golden sunset beyond the mouth of the cavern. I saw a desperate belief in her eyes. She had to believe; I was the only hope Royal had of surviving the night.

I nodded, putting a hand over Karayan's. Karayan released me. I stepped away from the gate, aware of the blood still coating my hand, the ache in my back from the gate, the cold air on my bare stomach. Karayan bent and retrieved my shirt off the floor. I took it from her wordlessly and pulled it over my head. When I straightened, Gretchen stood before me, offering up Hale's sword. I took it from her wordlessly.

Then I turned away from my friends, closed my eyes, and sought out Royal. I could feel the energy I'd taken from Lucas snapping just under the surface of my skin.

It was the fastest connection I'd ever made.

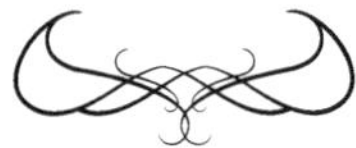

Terror. Pain. An awful understanding of what lay ahead—

Royal writhed under Seth's hand.

The Incubus had him pinned down on some kind of table. Almost casually, Seth laid the edge of the ancient sword against Royal's side and sliced, adding one more thin wound to the dozen or so he'd already cut into Royal's vulnerable flesh. Royal choked back a growl of agony.

"Such a waste," Seth muttered. "I like you, Royal. You were a lot of fun. If things had been different, you would have made a very nice pet."

"That's funny. I kind of hate you." Despite the fear roaring in his ears, Royal managed to summon up an anger that made Seth smile.

"See? This is exactly what I mean. The spirit of a fighter. Infinitely more interesting than most of your brethren." Seth sighed with faux-regret. He drew the sword lightly across Royal's arm, leaving another crimson line behind, and earning another hoarse scream of pain from Royal. "Unfortunately for us, the time has come for me to bring this little party to a close. I promised your friend I'd make you suffer before killing you. I think we've succeeded on that first front, wouldn't you agree?"

I reeled, stunned by his off-handed cruelty.

Royal twisted in Seth's grip. Beneath him, I spotted the distinctive carvings of the altar. I felt the hairs raise on the back of my neck. I had to move. *Now.*

Royal. I sent the thought into his mind. *Hang on. I'm coming.*

Everything faded to a dull hum, everything but the need to reach Royal. I felt little waves of static electricity traveling along my arms. I raised my hands, keeping my eyes closed and my thoughts focused.

In the back of my mind—that part of me still connected to Royal—I felt him smile.

The gesture caught Seth by surprise. "Something's funny?" he asked.

"I wouldn't want to ruin the surprise." Royal's voice was tight with grim satisfaction.

Seth's eyebrows knitted together briefly, but then he shook the concern off. He hefted the ancient sword high in the air. The point gleamed wickedly in the flickering light of candles. "Goodbye, lover. I'm afraid you're out of time."

Seth plunged the dagger down, straight for Royal's heart.

20

It's a strange feeling, using the dream world to travel from one place to another.

The cave before me seemed to shimmer, then *change.* Like a bubble popping, or a wine glass shattering into a thousand bits—each shard not merely glass, but a piece of reality, separating one from the other. I pushed forward, an effort of will more than body. Part of me was conscious of the dream world. I was moving *through it,* after all, even if it seemed like I was simply walking through a door from one room to another. The dream world was that liminal space between; it took almost no effort to simply step over the threshold—and yet it took every ounce of will-power I had to force open that breach in our world and hold it open as I moved across the city in one step. And then, in less time than it takes to blink, I was through.

I had no time to marvel at my success.

My fist shot out, catching Seth's wrist a microsecond before the blade pierced Royal's chest. The Incubus gave a startled growl, releasing Royal reflexively.

The last time I'd travelled this way, I'd been disoriented, weakened to the point of uselessness. But I was stronger now. I twisted Seth's wrist cruelly. He fought to keep control of the knife. I didn't have room to wield the sword properly, so I smashed the hilt into Seth's throat hard and fast.

Seth choked, dropping the weapon. I grabbed Royal and hauled him off the altar.

"Excellent timing," Royal wheezed, clinging to me with shaking hands.

I scanned the cramped cave looking for a way out. Intricate carvings, like the ones covering the altar, lined the floor. Grooves—

the perfect width and depth for a glass marble to traverse—twisted across the cave in strange patterns.

But then I caught sight of something that made my blood freeze in my veins. A shimmering curtain of shadow, swirling in and out of view. Just like—

I glanced up. Overhead, I saw a large, round stone, braced in place by massive, ancient wooden beams. It was all the confirmation I needed. I'd never seen this side of it, but I knew instantly what it was.

The Seal.

Which means, all this time we'd been searching for it, the ancient Temple devoted to Lilith had literally been right under our noses at the mission.

I heard someone chuckle and turned. Ian strode into the cave from the tunnel. "Ironic, isn't it?"

"Get behind me!" I pushed Royal back, then spun around to face Seth and Ian, holding Hale's sword up before me like a shield.

Seth glanced at Ian, irritated. "You were supposed to keep her occupied, Archivist. She nearly ruined my ambush."

"She's more resourceful than I anticipated." Ian glanced at me, sizing me up.

"I could have told you that." Seth rubbed carefully at his throat.

"You." I glared at Ian, pouring every ounce of rage and hatred into the word.

"You should be thanking me, Lilitu. I'm giving you the keys to this world." Ian spread his hands, as if making a peace offering.

"You're a Guardsman." My eyes slid to Seth, then back to Ian. "How did he recruit you, Ian?"

"You've got it backwards, little girl." Seth crossed his arms, grinning at my confusion.

"You used him. You had him send the Guardsmen into your trap, you made him steal that sword from our armory—"

"You think I need the help of a Son of Adam?" Seth's sneer of disgust was so genuine I felt my conviction falter.

"But—the sword—? The sacrifice—?"

"Sure. I'll admit, he was useful. But joining forces? Not my idea."

I turned to Ian. "What is he saying? This was all your idea?"

Ian opened his mouth to answer, but before he could speak, Royal gripped my shoulder.

"Braedyn." He was staring across the cavern at the tunnel's narrow entrance. Idris entered the temple, emerging from the shadows. Her long white hair flowed behind her like a veil.

"No, child," she said. "The idea was mine."

"Mother." Ian turned to Idris, opening his arms. She walked into his embrace, then planted a dry kiss on his cheek.

"*Mother?!*" My voice rang through the cave. I gawked at the two of them, suddenly picking out the tiny features they shared in common.

Seth gave Idris an arch smile. "Welcome to the party. I was starting to worry that you'd miss the big night."

"A night I've been preparing for my entire adult life? No." Idris beamed serenely at Seth. "Your Priestess is honored to be here, Grandson of Lilith."

Seth shrugged, amused. "If we're standing on formalities, it's Seth, Son of Eadryth, Daughter of Lilith."

Idris glanced at me, then turned to Ian. "Is this the young Lilitu you told me about?"

"Yes." Ian gave me a considering look, then sighed. "She still believes she's protecting this world from her own kind."

Idris shook her head, giving me a sad smile. "Oh, dear. How I wish we could spare the time to show you the truth. But we cannot allow you to interfere with our great work. Please stand aside, child. I truly do not want to harm you."

My eyes cut to Seth, and I saw dark amusement brewing in his eyes. "Ian," I turned to the archivist in desperation. "Why are you doing this? You've seen what the Lilitu are capable of!"

Ian met my desperate gaze. He was unapologetic. "They have been cast out of their home, made to watch from afar as the Sons of Adam have plundered their world—"

"But *you're* a Son of Adam."

Ian ignored my interruption. "How can we blame them for attacking us? It is a war we began."

"You don't honestly believe that?" I stared at Ian, stricken.

"It is the truth," Idris said simply. "I have devoted my life to researching the history of Lilith and her children. For years, I published books and articles on my findings, assuming her story was simply a myth—a subversive, feminist, alternate history that the women who came before us developed as a way of coping with the crimes against our gender. But then I was contacted by a Lilitu, and everything changed." Idris beamed at me, her face alight with inner peace. "You cannot imagine the feelings that swept through me, discovering that this myth was based in real power. Suddenly, I realized *why* I was put on this earth."

I felt my mouth go dry. "To reawaken Lilith."

"Yes." Idris smiled. "Lilith, the bringer of storms, the first mother nature, she is the fierce protector this world needs. She will save what remains from the ravaging hands of humanity." Idris spread her hands wide, as though suggesting the conclusion was obvious. "The era of the Sons of Adam is coming to an end. It is time for Lilith and her Daughters to begin their work."

I shook my head, too numb to speak.

"I know, it's a lot to take in." Seth bent, retrieving the ancient blade from where he'd dropped it just minutes ago. "Now, if you don't mind, we're on a tight schedule." His eyes shifted to Royal.

Adrenaline surged into my system. I dropped into a fighting stance, holding the sword before me tightly. "Forget it, Seth. You can't have Royal."

Seth sighed, giving voice to his frustration. "You really are becoming the bane of my existence," he muttered, half under his breath. "It'd be so much easier if I could just kill you."

I stared at him, unsure if I'd heard him correctly.

But at that moment, a finger of sunlight speared through the center of the Seal—a finger of light so thin and precise, suddenly I knew it could only penetrate this darkness once a year, when the sun was in perfect alignment with the stone overhead. That was why they'd destroyed the mission's roof. They needed the sun to pierce this darkness for the ritual. And that's why it had to happen on the summer solstice.

Seth's eyes fastened onto the spear of light, then shifted to Ian. "It's too bad. I would have liked you to see Lilith's return." Seth grabbed Ian by the scruff of his shirt and threw him down onto the altar. The blade flashed as he swung it around, catching the beam of light. With as little remorse as a butcher slaughtering a pig, Seth slit Ian's throat. Ian thrashed, a bubbling gurgle spilling out of his throat along with a wash of bright red blood.

"No—!" Idris's breathless cry echoed through the chamber.

"God—!" Royal recoiled. I turned to him, ripping my eyes away from the gruesome sight.

"Ian!" The sounds of Idris's grief filled the cave. Even after all she'd done—and all Ian had done—Idris's raw agony wrenched at my heart. In response, my nose stung with a hot prickle of grief. I forced myself to turn back and look, afraid of keeping my back to Seth.

Idris rushed forward toward her dying son, but Seth planted a hand on her chest stopping her. For a moment, Idris could only stare at Ian, now lying still on the altar. Then she turned wide eyes to Seth. She looked shaken to the core. "Why?! We have done nothing but help you—"

"Indeed." Seth gestured to the altar. Ian's blood, still flowing freely from the wound on his neck, seeped into the carvings. Bright red lines flowed down from the altar and across the floor, tracing out those ancient patterns with more speed than I would have thought possible. Seth regarded the spreading pattern with satisfaction. "You have both served very well."

I watched with sick fascination as fingers of blood—flooding different paths in the pattern—began meeting up. One after another, the carved ruts of the pattern filled with Ian's blood, until only one last stretch remained empty. My eyes followed two lines of blood, edging toward one another until they connected.

The pattern was complete.

The ground beneath our feet *surged.*

"Holy crap, is that an earthquake?" Royal grabbed my arm, panicking. "We have to get out of here! Braedyn? Braedyn?!"

He tugged on my arm, but I couldn't respond.

The quake wasn't limited to our physical reality. A violent upheaval shot across the dream world, buffeting against my mind with the force of a category five hurricane. I flung out my free hand, trying to brace myself against the cavern wall. But—struggling against the storm in my mind—I couldn't see clearly. I felt Royal's arms fastening around me.

"Braedyn? Are you okay?"

"I—I don't know." My voice sounded tinny in my ears, distant and small. It sent a wave of goose bumps prickling over the skin of my arms.

I felt Royal's hands tighten around me. "Okay. I've got you."

After what seemed like an eternity, the storm in my mind died down. I blinked to clear my vision.

Seth had a hand braced against the far wall. I saw him straighten, presumably recovering from the same spiritual upheaval I'd just experienced. Then he looked up and met my eyes. The air around Seth shimmered, folding back like some kind of trans-dimensional origami.

"Done and done," he whispered. "It's starting."

And then Seth stepped through the dream world. In less than a second, he was gone.

21

Idris knelt beside the altar, laying her hands across Ian's lifeless body. She bowed her head. Her tears glimmered in the last thin thread of sunlight. And then the sun continued its journey overhead, plunging the Temple back into a murky dimness lit only by candlelight.

"I—I don't understand." Idris's voice was so low I almost couldn't make out what she'd said.

"He played you." I glared at Idris, but she didn't lift her eyes from Ian's face. "They all played you. Lilitu are not the victims. They're the predators, and you just woke up their queen."

"But—" Idris finally looked up, pain and confusion twisting her features into a mask of agony. "Lilith was created from the same earth as Adam. She is as much entitled to this world as he is."

"Did a Lilitu tell you that?" I shook my head at Idris's look of dim comprehension. "All the research you've done, and you glossed right over the part about how God kicked Lilith out?"

"Because she refused to submit to Adam." Idris straightened, regaining some of her confidence.

"No. Because she refused to be a part of *building* this world," I snapped. "Together, she and Adam were supposed to begin the human race. She shirked her one great responsibility; what makes you think she deserves any part of this world?"

Idris shook her head, but I could see defiance settling behind her eyes. "If not for Adam's arrogance, she would have—"

"We have *no way* of knowing what she would have done. All we know is what she did." I shook my head. "Why are we even arguing about this? Seth just killed your son! Doesn't that make you angry?!"

I saw the raw emotions playing across Idris's face. But then she turned back to Ian, stroking his cheek tenderly. "He has made the ultimate sacrifice," she whispered. "Because of him, we have ushered in a new era of peace."

"Peace?" I stared at Idris, truly dumbfounded. "You've just experienced firsthand the kind of peace the Lilitu will bring to this world!"

Idris's shoulders tensed, but she did not answer.

I took a step toward her, then swayed on my feet, still unsteady. "You can't honestly still believe you were right about all of this?"

Idris looked up, her eyes clear and calm once more. "I stand by my life's work."

"But—?"

Royal squeezed my arm gently. "She just watched her son die because of her own deluded mistakes; she'll believe whatever she needs to believe," he whispered. "You're not going to change her mind. Come on, let's get out of here."

"Yeah, fine." I let Royal help me across the Temple. He stopped along the way to pick up one of the lanterns harboring a flickering candle inside. But as we reached the tunnel, I froze. "Wait." I spun back to face Idris. "The acolytes."

Idris's eyes flicked to my face, suddenly alert.

"Three girls, with 'courage, conviction, and a lightness of spirit akin to that of a child.'" I saw once more the selection in my head. Idris had been looking for specific qualities among the eager volunteers. She chose the girls she chose for a reason. "What did you need the acolytes for?"

It was as if a veil came down behind Idris's eyes, obscuring her emotions. "I'm sorry, child, but until you are willing to open your mind to the truth, you are an enemy of Lilith." She shrugged her shoulders sadly. "Unless that changes, I cannot—I *will not* answer your questions."

"You initiated them—"

The ground lurched under our feet. Royal and I braced ourselves against the walls of the cave. I clung to the rough wall, once again rocked from within by the spiritual upheaval in the dream world.

"It's not over." Royal reached for my hand, his voice strained with urgency. "We need to *move*."

"The ritual," I hissed, glaring back at Idris. "Their blood—what was it for?"

Idris met my gaze evenly. "You ask all the right questions, Daughter of Lilith. But again, I will not provide answers to an enemy."

"One of those acolytes is my friend. You'd better believe you're going to answer my questions." I took a step toward her, meaning to cross the distance between us and grip her forehead; if she was unwilling to give me the truth, I would take it directly from her thoughts.

The ground heaved once more, and a few chunks of rock broke off from the walls surrounding us. While I stood there, still dazed from the tremors shooting through the dream world, Royal grabbed me around the middle with one arm.

"That's it." Royal hauled me into the tunnel. "We are leaving *now.*" In his free hand, he held the candle aloft, lighting our way.

I was too weak to offer much of a fight. "Wait. She knows something. We have to find out what she's done to Cassie—"

Royal didn't answer. He dragged me up the tunnel with more strength than I could have anticipated. The ground jolted beneath us once more, sending us crashing into the tunnel wall. As I struggled against the riptide in my mind, I forced myself to look back.

I could just barely see into the Temple. Idris lay her head down across Ian's chest, unmoving. Around her, larger chunks of rock were breaking free from the walls, and a small shower of dirt rained down on her.

"She's not leaving." I heard my voice, but it sounded like someone else was speaking. "Royal, she's not leaving."

"Right now, I'm more concerned about us." Royal grabbed me, looping my arm over his shoulders. "You have to run, Braedyn. Can you do that?"

I heard a great crack, like the earth splitting open. I glanced back. The Temple was caving in on itself.

"Run!" Royal didn't have to ask twice.

We tore down the passage. It took all my concentration to force one foot in front of the other, all the while clinging to Hale's sword. It was much longer than I'd expected—we ran for nearly ten minutes before the tunnel reached an apex, then slanted sharply down.

"No!" Royal stopped, breathing hard. "How the hell do we get out of here?"

"It has to be this way." I darted down the passage, scouting my way through the darkness ahead with ease. I knew Royal was close on my heels; I could see the flickering of the lantern casting its meager light against the tunnel walls around me.

Soon, I could hear the sound of water. The muted roar lent me another burst of energy.

"Up ahead." I pressed on, and in another minute or so, the tunnel dropped sharply, letting out into a deep stream. "Through here." There wasn't much to it; the level of the water was low enough that we could see a sliver of daylight above the surface of the river.

That being said, we still had to take a deep breath and submerge ourselves underwater to clear the front edge of the tunnel.

We came up in the stream, gasping. The sun had dipped behind the mountain. Overhead, the sky glowed with the last light of day.

"Now what?" Royal looked at me, his wet hair plastered to his head.

"We have to warn the Guard—" But I stopped myself, remembering the battlefield, strewn with most of our forces. "What's left of the Guard," I amended, my voice shaking. "They should be at the mission."

We paddled our way toward the closest shore until our feet found the sandy bottom of the stream. Water cascaded off our bodies as we hauled ourselves out. The temperature was already dropping, and I shivered in my wet clothes. I scanned the area, trying to get my bearings. Thanks to Dad and my cave-hunting excursions, I managed to figure out roughly where we were. And even though the mission was out of sight, I was fairly confident I knew which direction to go.

"This way." I took off, trusting Royal to follow. It wasn't easy running with the sword—in sopping clothes—through the high desert prairie. Our path took us up the side of a low foothill, winding around cacti and Piñon trees. When I crested the hill, I could see the mission ahead of us, nestled on the next ridge. Royal joined me a moment later, breathing hard.

"Oh good." He eyed the mission miserably. "I was hoping we'd get to do more running."

"We're almost there," I said.

Royal squinted, catching sight of something. "Isn't that your dad's truck?"

I turned in time to see Dad's truck pulling into the parking lot. It was followed a moment later by another car. The vehicles squealed to a stop, their tires kicking up plumes of dust. The Guard soldiers poured out and raced into the mission. I counted just six men.

"How did they know where to go?" I glanced at Royal, mystified.

He shook his head, but then we had our answer; the ground shuddered beneath our feet once more, and I saw one of the mission's elegant stained glass windows shatter into a cascading spray of rainbow glass.

"It's collapsing," I hissed. I sprinted forward, pumping my arms and legs as hard as I could. The desert flew past as I raced toward the mission—toward Dad.

As I rounded the front of the mission, I saw the main doors standing wide open. I charged through and skidded to a stop. Dad and a dozen or so Guardsmen stood—weapons drawn—around a deep pit in the center of the mission. The Seal was *gone.*

"Dad?!"

He turned at the sound of my voice. Half a second later, he sheathed his daggers and moved quickly toward me. Matt moved to join us wordlessly.

"Not so fast, Murphy!" One of the other Guardsmen stepped forward, eyeing me with naked hostility. I recognized him from the fight at the mines, though I couldn't recall seeing him before then.

"She's not your enemy," Dad growled. He reached me and grabbed my arm, propelling me toward the mission's doors. "Quickly, Braedyn." His voice was low and tight with anxiety.

Another Guardsmen stepped into our path, blocking our route to freedom.

"No? It was her little friend who sent us to the mines to die."

"What?!" I turned to the Guardsmen, incensed. "That's insane! It was *Ian* who sent you to the mines. Ian who insisted we commit all our forces. He's the one who betrayed us!"

"It's true," Matt said. "I was there. Murphy was there."

"Aren't you the one she kissed?" one of the Guardsmen muttered, glaring at Matt. "How do we know she hasn't messed with your head?"

Matt's face flushed with anger. Dad put a hand on his arm, warning him to cool off.

Other Guardsmen were drawing closer. Among them, only my father's and Matt's were friendly faces. Of my other allies, Gretchen, Lucas, and Karayan were still locked in the mines and Hale, Marx, Caleb, the others who knew and trusted me—they were gone forever.

"She tried to warn us," Dad said, his voice unnaturally calm. "It was only because of her and Karayan that the rest of us made it out of there alive."

And then I spotted Amber. She was standing beside a column, clutching her arms tightly around herself.

"Amber, tell them! You saw Ian running off, he's the one who betrayed us." I stared at Amber eagerly. Her eyes swept across the gathered men. "Amber? Tell them they can trust me."

"I—I don't know."

"What?" For a moment, I thought I'd misheard her.

"You were going to sleep with Lucas. You had it all planned for tonight." Amber's eyes landed on my face. "Even though you knew what it would do to him."

Matt's eyes sought mine out, a startled expression washing over his face.

I shook my head. "It's not that simple—we—we had a plan—"

"Braedyn." Dad's hand tightened on my arm. But the damage was done. Guardsmen edged closer, gripping their blades.

I stared at Amber, empty, numb. I'd saved her life. *Twice.* I'd pushed aside my own feelings about her for the good of the Guard who so desperately needed spotters. And still, after all of that, she refused to trust me.

"Rhea warned me," Amber whispered. "She said that's what Lilitu do. They get you to trust them, to believe they're your friends. Suddenly you find yourself doing all sorts of things you wouldn't usually do. You drift away from old friends. You give up secrets you'd never tell another living soul." Her eyes hardened, and I felt a chill. "It's just like she said. They worm their way into your heart, and then they betray you."

"I didn't betray you," I snapped. The Guardsmen around me started to mutter to one another, shooting dark looks at me. "I didn't betray the Guard!"

"Rhea's dead now." Amber clutched her arms tighter around herself.

"Rhea was an idiot!" My voice cut through the noise of the crowd. Shock registered across more than one face, but I was too pissed off to care. "If she'd listened to me right when we got there, we might have had time to escape the mines before the Lilitu attack." I turned on the Guardsman I recognized from the mines. "You were there. Tell me I'm wrong."

The Guardsman hesitated, glancing back at his peers.

"He can't," I growled. "Because it's the truth." I took a step forward. "I've made mistakes, but today wasn't one of them."

"No?" Another Guardsman stepped up, his eyes glinting, hard. "Today the Guard was nearly wiped out."

"Nearly," Dad said quietly. "Without Braedyn, we might have lost everyone in that mine. We have eleven lives to thank her for, including Gretchen's and Lucas's."

"Make that twelve." Royal entered the mission, breathing hard. "Braedyn stopped Seth pretty much immediately before he sacrificed me on a way-too-creepy-to-be-believed stone altar."

Dad turned to me, eyes lighting with hope. "Does that mean you stopped the ritual before—?"

"No." I met Dad's eyes. "Seth sacrificed Ian instead. He completed the ritual."

The Guardsmen shifted their feet as this news sunk in. Silence settled around us, heavy and pregnant with a new fear. Amber's eyes cut to the hole in the center of the mission, where the Seal once stood. I walked forward. Guardsmen parted, letting me pass.

As I reached the edge of the hole, I felt my heart flip over in my chest. I'd expected to see the Seal below, having fallen through the floor, maybe cracked, but still recognizable.

What I saw, instead...

I shivered. It was as though the Seal had burned out from the center. What remained looked more like ash than stone. Whatever power the Seal had once contained, it was gone now. There would be no closing this door, not ever again. The twining ropes of shadow danced freely around the edges of the hole, tracing out the boundaries of the fully open portal between our worlds.

The Temple below—if it even still existed—was completely obscured by the rubble. Idris's body, Ian's body, there was no sign of either of them, or of the altar, or of the strange carved patterns traced out in Ian's blood.

I turned back to the Guardsmen. More than a dozen pairs of eyes watched me. No one made a sound. Dad's eyes shone with anxiety as he studied me. Amber's expression was cold, distant. Whatever flicker of friendship we might have kindled, this afternoon it had guttered out.

How had this happened? I'd played by the rules—done everything the Guard requested of me—and still we found ourselves staring into a nightmare-come-true. The crushing weight of this failure threatened to squeeze the breath out of my lungs. My vision narrowed. My head felt strangely light. Panic settled into every nook and cranny of my being.

I felt someone take my hand. I turned. Royal nodded his head with the barest movement. His eyes held such faith, such conviction.

"We're going to survive this," he whispered. "It's not over yet."

Moisture welled in my eyes, and I had to bite my lip. Royal squeezed my hand. In that moment, it seemed like the only real thing in the world. I held onto him, drawing strength from his conviction. After a moment, I let out a long breath. He believed in me. Nothing, not even the events of this awful day, had shaken his faith. I felt the knots ease in my shoulders.

One thing. This was one thing to be thankful for. In the midst of everything, at least I had managed to save Royal's life.

EPILOGUE

The drive home was silent and somber. Matt was on his way to the mines to free Lucas, Gretchen, Cassie, and Karayan. Royal and I rode back with Dad in his truck. As we turned up the quiet streets of my neighborhood, I felt like a stranger in a strange land; unaccustomed to tranquility after our battle. We may have left the fight behind, but it haunted everything around me, the violence of it jarring against the backdrop of spreading aspen trees and the soft dusting of evening stars across the sky.

Walking into the Guard's house felt worse. The silence, which I had so longed for these last several months, was ominous now. I carried Hale's sword to the fireplace and laid it on the mantle.

Memories haunted me from every corner. Hale—who had always seemed so invincible, so in control—was gone. The banter of off-duty Guardsmen was forever silenced. Even Rhea and her clique of spotters—hard as they'd been for me to stand—would never again fight alongside the people I loved, protecting them from the unseen as only spotters can.

Dad followed me into the living room. Royal stayed in the foyer, sinking onto the staircase cradling his lacerated stomach gingerly. We needed to get him to the doctor.

"Thane. Where are you?" Dad headed to the back study, searching for the old archivist. I heard him hiss in surprise. "Thane?!"

I turned. Through the door to the study I could see Dad drop to the floor. Behind him, a still figure lay sprawled across the floor. My heart sank—had we lost yet another soldier tonight?

I was halfway to the study when I saw Thane's legs move. Relief poured through me, and I had a moment to marvel at the sensation. Thane had never been anything but cold or cruel to me; why would I feel such gratitude that he had survived? Because, I realized dimly, he'd become a part of my family. Sure, he was like the misanthropic, crotchety old uncle no one wanted to get stuck sitting next to at Thanksgiving. But he was one of us, and that meant something. Thane, Gretchen, Hale, Matt, Lucas—even Karayan—they had all become my family over these last two years.

"Easy," Dad said. "You're bleeding."

I watched from the door as Thane struggled into a sitting position. An ugly gash ran the length of his temple to his cheekbone. Dried blood streaked across his face from the wound. He waved Dad away.

"I don't need a nursemaid, Murphy." Thane reached a hand up to the wound, wincing as his hand made contact. The movement cracked open the fragile scab, sending a fresh trickle of blood down the side of Thane's face.

"Let me get you a towel." Dad stood, frowning. "And I think we need to take you to the ER."

"Don't be ridiculous. I've no need of a visit to the ER." Thane rose shakily to his knees, leveraging himself slowly into one of the study's chairs. "Though I will take that towel."

"I'll get it." I stopped Dad at the doorway, gesturing at Thane. "You should stay with him."

"You might want to wrap it around some ice," Dad muttered. "That looks like a nasty bump."

I nodded and made my way to the Guard's kitchen. Two minutes later I'd returned, holding a towel already moist with melting ice. Thane took it from me and nodded, meeting my eyes.

"Thank you."

"Sure." I gave him a thin smile, trying to cover my surprise. It was the first decent exchange I could remember having with Thane.

"What happened?" Dad sat in a chair across from Thane, watching as the older man gingerly laid the icy towel over his wound.

"I'm not exactly clear," Thane said. "Ian and I were looking for any mention of Lilitu in conjunction with the summer solstice—" Thane's eyes took on a far away look. "Someone must have struck me from behind."

"Ian," I whispered.

Thane looked up at me sharply, then glanced at Murphy for confirmation.

"He betrayed us," Dad said simply.

"But, the search for the Temple—?"

"A wild goose chase." Dad rubbed at his own temples miserably. "It was beneath the Seal, Thane. This whole time. The mine was a trap."

"That scraggy bastard," Thane growled. "Where is he?"

Dad dropped his eyes. A fresh knot worked its way into my stomach.

Thane glanced briefly at me before leaning forward in his seat, turning his attention back to Dad. "What aren't you telling me, Murphy? What's happened?"

"Seth completed the ritual. Ian was his sacrifice." Dad couldn't pull his eyes away from his hands.

Thane sat still for a long moment. "I see." He adjusted the ice pack on his head and gestured at a book on the floor. "Hale will want to see this. I think I've identified—"

"Hale is gone, Thane." Dad looked up then, his eyes radiating a deep pain.

Thane's mouth hung open for a moment. "Gone?" He lowered himself back into the chair. "You said—the mine was a trap?" His eyes focused on Dad's face. "How many did we lose?"

Dad nodded, unable to answer the question for a long moment. When he did speak, his voice was scratchy with emotion. "Most. All the spotters but Gretchen."

"Karayan?" Thane's voice was strangely devoid of emotion, but something about the way he said her name sent a shiver across my back.

"She survived."

Thane barely moved, processing this stoically—but I saw a muscle in his jaw ease. It was a tiny change, but it seemed to speak volumes. I caught myself staring and forced myself to look away. After all his vitriol against Karayan, Thane was *relieved* she'd survived.

The front door opened and I spun around. Matt and Gretchen ushered Lucas into the house. His head lolled forward, but he was conscious enough to walk with assistance.

Cassie hovered behind them, clasping her hands tightly before her.

"Cassie?!" Royal surged to his feet in the foyer.

Cassie gave a shout of relief and ran to him. They embraced, holding each other fiercely. Gretchen and Matt led Lucas into the living room and helped him onto the couch. As they lowered him down, I saw the back of his T-shirt. Blood had seeped through it; blood from wounds dug into his skin by two sets of claws.

I turned away, unable to face what I'd done. Unable to bear seeing the vacant look in Lucas's eyes—the look of a Thrall. I caught Thane studying my face.

"What else aren't you telling me?"

"What do you mean?" Dad looked up, surprised. He didn't know. He glanced at Gretchen, then at Lucas. I heard him let out a harsh breath. "Lucas?!" Dad darted to Lucas's side. Thane followed, after giving me one last glance.

I stayed frozen in the office as the first wave of grief washed over me. I hadn't had time to think about Lucas since fleeing the mines. But now, in the aftermath, it spread through me like a sinkhole, swallowing my heart, my joy, my future. Lucas was gone. No. Worse than gone, Lucas was a Thrall. Numbly, I wondered whether the Guard would kill him, or wait for him to fade away to nothing and simply die, an empty shell of the boy I loved.

I could hear voices in the living room.

"What? What do you mean?" Gretchen's voice broke. So she knew I'd failed to stop Seth. We'd lost Lucas for nothing.

I forced myself to take a step into the living room. Gretchen clung to Matt. He caught my eyes, then looked away.

Dad sat on the edge of the coffee table, staring out the front windows, face hidden from me. Thane leaned against a wall. He looked older than I'd ever seen him look.

And then my eyes caught on Lucas. He was sitting on the couch, his glossy black hair as rich as ever. I moved, walking through the grief as quietly as I could. When I sat beside Lucas, he turned toward me, blinking as if he were having trouble focusing his eyes. "Braedyn?"

"Hey." I gave him an encouraging smile. "How are you feeling?"

Lucas screwed up his features, thinking. "I must have fallen asleep." His skin looked thin and leathery, hanging off his frame as if he hadn't eaten for a month. Deep bags weighed down his eyes. But most disturbing of all, that customary gleam was gone from his gaze.

"Well," I forced my voice to remain light. "The important thing is you're home." I looked up, catching sight of Cassie and Royal. They had hung back in the foyer, concern and curiosity warring with their desire to give us space.

I reached for Lucas's hand. He let me take it, then squeezed mine back in response.

"We might as well get this over with," Thane said, approaching from the wall.

"Thane, wait." Gretchen turned, suddenly afraid.

"We need to know what kind of danger he poses," Thane murmured.

"Danger?" Lucas glanced at Gretchen, mystified.

Thane took Lucas's free hand and turned it palm-up. He placed two fingers on Lucas's wrist, feeling for his pulse.

"What do you remember from this afternoon, son?"

"What do you mean?"

Thane gave Lucas a shrew look. "I think you know what I'm referring to, Lucas. Answer the question."

"I—uh, a Lilitu came to my room." Lucas licked his lips. He blinked again, his brows drawing tighter together. He lowered his eyes to his hands. "I'm guessing you already know what happened."

Thane frowned. "Look at me, please."

Lucas looked up. It seemed like it took a lot of effort for him to raise his head.

"But you had a *second* encounter." Thane watched Lucas's face closely.

Lucas started to turn toward me, but Thane caught his jaw, stopping him. "Keep your eyes on me, boy."

Lucas's whole body seemed to go stiff. "Why? What's this all about?"

Thane sat back. "Tell me about your second encounter. Your encounter with Braedyn."

Lucas looked up at his sister-in-law, stricken.

Gretchen looked like she could break at any second, but she swallowed down her grief. "Do what he says, Lucas."

"No." Lucas jerked back from Thane, suddenly angry. "It's none of your business." He glared up at Gretchen. "It's none of your business, either."

Gretchen's hands tightened around Matt. Thane gave Dad a knowing look. Dad's eyes dropped to his hands, as if a question had been answered. Thane leaned back, his eyes flicking to me.

"He protects you," Thane said quietly.

"Lucas." I put a hand on his arm. "Don't. Just tell them what happened."

"No." Lucas stared at his hands.

"*Tell them, Lucas,*" I pleaded.

"*No.*" Lucas spun on me, his eye flashing hurt. "I know it wasn't what we'd planned, but it meant something to me. Didn't it mean anything to you?"

I stared. My heart skipped a beat. If he was refusing me—?

Thane's eyes sharpened on us. "What did you say, Lucas?"

"I said no," Lucas snapped, rounding on Thane. "This is personal, between me and Braedyn. It has nothing to do with you." Lucas turned back to me, the anger clear in his eyes. "I thought you felt the same."

I looked up. Gretchen took a step toward us, her face awash with shock.

"Did you hear that?" I whispered.

"I don't believe it," Gretchen breathed.

Thane sat back, giving us a long, considering look.

"What?" Lucas looked around, unsettled. "What the hell is going on here?"

"I don't know how," Thane started, turning toward Gretchen, "but he's not a Thrall."

I don't know who *whooped* louder, me, Gretchen, or Cassie and Royal. All I know is that one moment I was sitting there, drenched in sorrow, and the next moment I was embracing Lucas—my Lucas. Some miracle had saved him from me. He might be weak, but he was still whole. Gretchen launched herself at Matt. He caught her and swung her around, beaming his relief.

I even caught a glimpse of *Thane* smiling.

After a long moment, I pulled back, shaking with relief and the release of tension.

"Well, now that you've got that out of your system, you should take Lucas up to bed." Thane glanced at Gretchen. "Perhaps he should sleep in your room for the time being."

"Right." Gretchen offered her hand to Lucas.

I moved to help, but Thane cleared his throat, catching my eye. "If you don't mind," he said, "I have a few questions for you."

Lucas met my gaze. I caught his hand, still too full of emotion to speak. Lucas understood. He gave me a small smile, then let Gretchen lead him toward the foyer. After they'd made their way upstairs, I turned on Thane.

"How?" The question burned in my mind. "I *know* I drained him. There was nothing left to take."

Thane frowned, thinking. "My best guess? Both you and the other Lilitu attacked him on the same day. We've never understood why repeated Lilitu attacks are always separated by a full 24 hours, but perhaps this gives us a clue." He shrugged. "It could be that our souls are like a well, once drained it takes time for the groundwater to seep back in before it can be drained again." Thane sighed. "Regardless of the reason, Lucas is a very lucky young man. But that luck will end if he ever spends another night with a Lilitu."

His eyes sharpened, but he didn't verbalize the warning; *hands off of Lucas from now on.*

The human body is a strange machine. Our brief celebration died down quickly, and a somber silence took hold of the group. It had been a grueling day, yet none of us felt the pangs of hunger, or the need to sleep. A gaping hole had been torn through the center of our lives. Those we had lost were still fresh in our minds. The dead would not leave us alone.

I slipped outside when the silence of the once boisterous living room became too difficult to bear.

Royal and Cassie saw me leave, but they didn't follow, perhaps sensing that I needed a moment alone.

As I stepped into the cool summer night, I found I was finally able to cry. Grief, fear, relief, guilt, frustration—the emotions boiled within me until I was hollowed out and exhausted.

I stumbled onto the grass, dropping to my hands and knees.

One question remained. After what I'd taken from Lucas, after my failure at the Temple, was I still redeemable?

I closed my eyes, trying my hardest to reach Sansenoy with my thoughts.

Please hear me. Have I crossed the line? Can I still become human?

"Please, Sansenoy," I murmured. "I need to know."

"I wouldn't hold my breath, if I were you."

I turned, startled. Karayan sat on the back porch, shrouded in darkness. I must have walked right past her.

"Praying to angels—it's never done much good as far as I can tell." She rose from the old garden chair she'd settled onto.

"Karayan?" I scrambled awkwardly to my feet as Karayan made her way down the porch steps. She joined me in the grass, turning her face upwards. Overhead, a beautiful crescent moon shone in the clear night sky.

"Think you can still become human?" She didn't look at me, just kept her gaze fixed on the moon.

I shrugged, suddenly conscious of how little my own desire mattered, compared to how much we had lost today. How much Karayan had lost. "It doesn't matter," I said.

Karayan turned to look at me. "Don't. Don't give up. You're the only thing keeping me together right now."

"Me?" I stared at Karayan, mystified.

"Hale believed in you," Karayan whispered. I saw fresh tears glistening in the corners of her eyes.

I nodded. Maybe I would one day become human. Maybe I would not. Regardless, it was time to focus on the larger task at hand.

There was one battle left to fight in this war. And if we didn't win it, we'd lose everything.

Lilith was coming.

A NOTE FROM THE AUTHOR

Thank you so much for taking the time to read this book. If you were entertained or moved by the story, I'd be grateful if you would please leave a review on the site where you purchased this book.

Even a few sentences would be so appreciated—they let me know when I've connected with readers, and when I've fallen short.

Reviews are also the best way to help other readers discover new authors and make more informed choices when purchasing books in a crowded space.

Thanks again for reading,
Jenn

ABOUT THE AUTHOR

Originally from New Mexico (and still suffering from Hatch green chile withdrawal), Jenn includes Twentieth Television's *Wicked, Wicked Games* and *American Heiress* among her produced television credits.

Outside of TV, she created *The Bond Of Saint Marcel* (a vampire comic book mini-series published by Archaia Studios Press), and co-wrote *The Red Star: Sword Of Lies* graphic novel with creator Christian Gossett.

She's also the author of the award-winning *Daughters of Lilith* paranormal thriller YA novels, and is currently realizing a life-long dream of growing actual real live avocados in her backyard. No guacamole yet—but she lives in hope.

Follow her on Twitter: @jennq
Visit her blog: JenniferQuintenz.com

You can also sign up for her newsletter at JenniferQuintenz.com to be among the first to hear about new books, deals, and appearances.